Praise for Jory Sherman

"[A] master storyteller."

—Richard S. Wheeler,
Spur Award–winning author of the Skye's West series

"To read the poetry of his prose is to be
transported bodily to the wind-lashed plains and
blue-iced peaks of Sherman country."

—Loren D. Estleman,
award-winning author of *The Long High Noon*

"A highly skilled, always dependable storyteller."
—*El Paso Herald-Post*

Praise for *The Medicine Horn* and *Trapper's Moon*

"Among . . . novelists of the Old American West,
Jory Sherman has no peer for powerful, poetic
storytelling. Read *The Medicine Horn* and see a gifted
writer at the top of his craft."

—Dale L. Walker, *Rocky Mountain News*

"Lush prose and minutely detailed action."
—*Library Journal* on *The Medicine Horn*

"A vigorous look at the world of the mountain men
of the Old West."

—*Publishers Weekly* on *Trapper's Moon*

By JORY SHERMAN
from TOM DOHERTY ASSOCIATES

The Barons of Texas

The Baron Range

The Baron Brand

The Baron War

The Baron Honor

The Ballad of Pinewood Lake

Grass Kingdom

Horne's Law

The Medicine Horn

Song of the Cheyenne

Trapper's Moon

Winter of the Wolf

The
Medicine
Horn

and

Trapper's
Moon

Jory Sherman

A TOM DOHERTY ASSOCIATES BOOK · NEW YORK

This is a work of fiction. All of the characters, organizations, and events portrayed in these novels are either products of the author's imagination or are used fictitiously.

THE MEDICINE HORN AND TRAPPER'S MOON

The Medicine Horn copyright © 1991 by Jory Sherman

Trapper's Moon copyright © 1994 by Jory Sherman

A Forge Book
Published by Tom Doherty Associates, LLC
175 Fifth Avenue
New York, NY 10010

www.tor-forge.com

Forge® is a registered trademark of Tom Doherty Associates, LLC.

ISBN 978-0-7653-8360-0

Our books may be purchased in bulk for promotional, educational, or business use. Please contact your local bookseller or the Macmillan Corporate and Premium Sales Department at 1-800-221-7945, extension 5442, or by e-mail at MacmillanSpecialMarkets@macmillan.com.

First Edition: March 2016

Printed in the United States of America

0 9 8 7 6 5 4 3 2 1

CONTENTS

The
Medicine
Horn

For Terry C. Johnston

Middle Mississippi Valley and Adjacent Areas, 1793—1843

1

Lemuel Hawke slipped the harness reins from his shoulder, wiped his broad, sweat-beaded forehead. The last of his boyhood freckles had faded during the winter; he was growing through them so fast since his marriage that the few that were left seemed like they would wash off in the next rain. His muslin shirt, streaked with soil, clung to his lean hard frame. He watched the rider leave the freshly plowed field, his horse switching its tail like a metronome. There was a taste in young Hawke's mouth like brackish water, a tightness in his chest. He felt closed in, caught like a rabbit in a box trap, choking on his own breath.

"Damn you, Dan'l Brown," Hawke muttered. "Damn tax collector." He crumpled the scrap of paper in his hand, shoved it in the pocket of his trousers. Sometimes he wished he'd never learned how to read and write.

Daniel Brown stopped at the road, turned his mottled gray mare with a light touch of the reins. The mare swung sideways, jerked to a halt, stood there hipshot.

"I'll be back, Lem. You have that money for me."

Hawke compressed his still boyish lips into a tight frown. A drop of sweat dripped from his brow, struck his eye with a crisp saline sting. He blinked involuntarily, rubbed his eye and brow. Beyond a low hill, a lark stammered a lyrical trill, the notes bright and saucy as dandelion wine. The late afternoon sun beat down on him, a distant seething flame shimmering like an orange mirage rising out of mist. The air steamed, heavy with humidity, but the sky was cloudless, a vast blue void that stretched from horizon to horizon.

"Go on, Dan'l," said Hawke, too low for the tax collector to hear, "less'n you aim to take your dole in sweat."

Brown touched blunt spurs to the mare's flanks, drifted down the road through watery waves that distorted the animal's image into a quivering gray blur. The earth, fecund with moisture, gave off the dank aroma of decay and compost in air as cloying and vaporous as steam. The hard rains of March had come, bringing with them the tax collector, as inevitable as the first robin in the piedmont. The assessor, Lemuel knew, rode all the trails connecting the scattered farms that lay along the courses of the Hazel and Thornton rivers west of the Rappahannock. This was Brown's district, the northern half of Culpeper County, extending from the tidewater over the red loam hills through the stands of thick hardwood and evergreen timber to the precipice of the Blue Ridge.

Lem gathered up the harness, unhitched it from the single moldboard plow. The plow tilted to one side, leaned at an angle over the worm-threaded furrow, and the jenny brayed softly. He took the harness off the mule, left only a tattered rope halter. He pulled a short rope from his pocket, attached the narrow-gapped hook to one of the D rings.

"Come on, Goldie," he said. "You done plowed your last Virginny pasture." The jenny's hide, glazed sleek with sweat, twitched with ropy tremors, the ripples striped with blood where the horseflies had gotten to her with needled teeth. Hawke slung the tangled harness over his shoulder, pulled Goldie across the field toward the house and barn. The sun stood just above the horizon, framed by the gentle, forested hills adance with the bobbing heads of spring flowers. After weeks of rain, the land had dried out enough to plow, but he knew he was in the fields early. He had to squeeze time from a year's growing like water from a stone.

"The worst thing, Goldie," he said to the mule as he came up to the ramshackle barn, "was Dan didn't even put your sad spavined carcass on the tax rolls. Just the horse and two mules." One of the mules, grazing in the short pasture behind the house, lifted its head from a thatch of emerald grass as if it had overheard. The other mule switched its tail at the interminable swarm of flies and continued to graze, its shaggy chestnut hide burnished by the sunglint until it shone like oiled rosewood.

He hung up the harness in the tack room, grained the jenny in a stall, forked some hay into the trough, saw to it that Goldie had water in the wooden bucket hanging from a pitchfork tine he'd driven into the wood like a nail. Lemuel slopped the hogs before he washed up at the wooden pump and went into the house. The sun furred the fresh-turned earth with the liquid gild of wild honey and he turned to look at the field for a moment. He could smell the soil, fresh and loamy, exuding a musky nourishment for crops he would probably never plant.

When he slammed the door, his wife Roberta called out to him as if she knew for sure the noise was his doing, no other's.

"Lem, you take them boots off before you come traipsin' through the house." Her voice still chirped with adolescence, tiny, lyrical as feathered dulcimer music.

Lem shucked the dirt-encrusted boots, left them sagging forlornly on the small porch. He padded barefoot into the kitchen, the boards groaning under his weight. The house was under a spring siege by carpenter ants and termites. He had seen the little white devils marching under the porch logs only yesterday. Given time, they would eat the cabin to dust and there would be no trace of man's intrusion.

"Feet're dirtier'n the boots," he said. He smelled the aroma of last year's turnips boiling on the woodstove, waded through a thin cirrus of steam that misted into his sinuses.

"I'm in the front room," called Roberta.

"I hear you," he said. He hated turnips, but they were down to grubbing for their vegetables now. They'd eaten the last of the dried beans last week. Turnips. The thought of them made his stomach tauten like a drumhead.

"I'm going to fry squirrel for your supper," she said.

"It won't brighten me none." He had shot three squirrels that morning. They were small, thin from the winter's den, but he dearly loved fried squirrel, the lean gravy Roberta made with pork fat, buckwheat flour, and goat's milk.

Roberta sat in the one halfway comfortable chair they owned. He had whipsawed the frame from oak, stuffed the dyed burlap upholstery with hog bristles. The bristles had worked through the fabric like small black wires that stung like the needles of mosquitoes. When he sat in it, he felt like a pincushion. The chair wouldn't last another winter. It no longer rocked, but sat crooked on its broken arches, a hopeless cripple. She looked up from the dress she was sewing, a piece of dark thread dangling from her mouth. Roberta seemed always to be making new clothes for herself, while his were in tatters. Even now, he thought, she was dressed almost as if she were going to church. She kept the house well, he gave her that. Never mind that she always looked as if she was going to a ball. This was hard country, and they had few visitors. None put on special clothes for visiting. Roberta, he mused, had ideas about life and such as if she were in the center of a grand painting hanging on a museum wall for everyone to ogle. She always told him that he should dress as if he was going to die and be seen by strangers. Lem thought such talk was nonsense. If you are dead, you are dead, he always told her, and your shame is only in the shroud they wrap about your rotting corpse.

He loved her; he loved her deeply. It was just that she always pretended that they were gentry, when in truth, they were churchmice, scurrying in the aisles for crumbs. He looked at her delicate hands, cringed at their redness. Lye soap did things to a girl's hands, burned them harder than the sun on the plow-crimped hands of a farmer.

"You got a sour look on your face. I saw Dan'l Brown snoopin' around."

Lem sank wearily into another chair he had cut and hammered to shape, braced with elk sinew, latticed with cowhide. The resin that held it all together had long since lost its gleam. The chair creaked with his weight. He tapped his shirt pocket. He hadn't had any tobacco for a month, but the habit was still with him, like skin. He had been smoking since he turned thirteen, trying so hard to be a man he got the habit quicker than he grew.

"Yair, Dan says he's goin' to take them two hosses for taxes. Says they be the only things we got what's worth a tupenny." His voice was soft, low, laden with the slow vibrato of his Virginia accent, an accent filtered down from the singing voices of his coal-mining ancestors in Wales and Scotland, blended with the English lowborn, altered only slightly in the last hundred years of living in the New World, cultivating Virginia-grown latakia tobacco.

Roberta plunged the needle into a pincushion that had once resembled a cloth tomato. She leaned down over the dress and cut the thread with her teeth.

"Dan'l's goin' to tax you? He didn't last year."

"Probably felt sorry for us." He paused, wishing he had some tobacco left. "I work, damn it all, from sunup to sundown and got nary a thing to show for it."

"Ain't no call to curse, Lemuel Hawke. You've got grain and tobacco, cattle and hogs. More'n some folks."

"Hah! Dan Brown wants more shillings than I have. Pay up, he says, or he'll take the mules. We got to leave here, Roberta, or I'll be in the poorhouse. I owe ever'body and his brother as it is. Dan'l takes my mules, that'd put me afoot and nothin' to work with 'ceptin' Goldie. She's plumb tuckered."

"Leave here?" Roberta asked, as if the notion had stuck there in her mind like a flame in a storm lamp.

"Yes. Get out from under these damned bone-crushing debts." When he got angry, his voice rose in pitch, squeaked like a choirboy's going through the puberty.

"Where would we go? What would we do?"

He sensed the growing panic in her tone, as if she was teetering on the edge of that craziness that made a female wail and screech and rip at her hair like someone hanging onto the edge of a cliff in a high wind. He didn't understand such caterwauling behavings. Scared him halfmost to sobriety, into turning Christian witness.

"Kentucky." The moment he said it, he knew it had been on his mind all along. All winter, leastways. Something in him wanting to move on, to get away from people and laws and government. Get out from under the yoke. He knew what it was, but he had never voiced it aloud before. It was a yearning, a yearning to leave the yoke of civilization and venture into the frontier of a new land. It was more than a yearning. He knew that now. It was a hunger, the hunger of a man to go westward, a burning to see and touch and feel what was beyond the boundaries of this rented Virginia land. It was a lust in the heart to push beyond the isolation of a plot of ground, the walls of another man's house, the frontiers of an earthbound soul.

"Kentucky," he said again. "Rent some good bottom land. I hear tell Lexington's got some fine folks there. Kind of folks you like, fancy and such. Place to wear your pretty dresses. Lots of folks already gone there, folks in predicaments same as us. Good green land, good as any, better'n Virginny."

"I don't know, Lem. I'm plumb leery of just movin' with no place to go. No sure place to go. You been talkin' to that Silas again?"

"No'm," he said, puzzled by her question.

"He come by today. Again. Gives me the chilblains.

Looks in the winders. You didn't see him? No, I speck not. He come up to the back porch and like to scared me out of my wits. Old man like that."

"Silas ain't old. He can't be more'n twenty-five or thirty."

"Old, and scaresome. I don't like him."

"He don't mean no harm. Fact is, he was the one tolt me about Kentucky. He talks about other places too. Good places for a man to go."

"A woman needs roots, Lem. Kids. I want to raise my kids in a good home, a fine home, on land we own. This Kentucky, it's wild, full of Indians and renegades. We ought to raise us some kids here, in Virginia."

"We're gonna raise us kids, you say. Hell, we ain't nothin' more'n kids ourselves. You want 'em to grow up like us, poor and dumb as bumpkins? Kentucky's a new state. A promised land. Good weather, they say, good land, plenty of it. Woods full of game to feed a man and his family until he can bring in a good crop. We can drive what cattle we got, butcher the hogs and smoke 'em, or sell 'em on the hoof. Start over fresh. No debts. No tax collector a-houndin' me, no money-grubbin' creditors breathin' down my neck."

Roberta set her dress on the arm of the chair, rose and walked to the hand-wrought maple cabinet set along the wall. She stooped, opened the door and pulled out a tin box, its paint worn off from use, battered from travel.

She opened the box. Lem heard the paper rustle, the clink of coins.

"We have only a few pounds," she said, her voice dropping into a lower register. He could almost measure the deepness of her despondency. She was pretty low, he thought. They had been into court at least four times, dragged there by creditors. He had given the bloodsuckers almost everything he had. His crops were promised out to them for at least two more seasons. What was the sense of it? Earning money you would never see. Working for people who didn't give a damn if you broke your back pushing a plow. As long as they got paid. All wanting their shylock-ian pound of flesh. It didn't matter to the creditors if he starved, as long as he paid on time. That was all that mattered to them, the bloodsuckers, the leeching sonsofbitches.

"Money don't mean much, if you're free," he said stubbornly.

"I want a family," she said, just as stubbornly.

He leaned forward in the chair, his intensity burning into her, scorching the very room.

"But not here, Roberta. Not here. In the promised land. Kentucky."

"Promised land, indeed. Why, there is no such thing except in the Bible, Lemuel Hawke. One must pay for what one obtains."

"There you go, actin' like your mother, talkin' uppity as if you were gentry."

"I pride myself on my education," she said stiffly.

"Haw, you ain't got much more'n me. My pa read me Shakespeare and lots of books and I don't try and talk like none of 'em. Neither does anyone I know. You're always tryin' to be something you ain't, like you had more brains than anyone else. It's pure common sense to go on to Kentucky. That's somethin' you might try and get more of, 'stead of puttin' on airs like you was a fine lady."

"It's that damned Silas," she said. "He's the one turned your mind."

"No," he said, "it's seein' us breaking our backs on the land here, and it's knowin' there's somethin' better a-waitin' for us."

He rose, moved to her, opened his arms.

"Yes," she said, and he kissed her softly on the mouth. He held her to him as the only dear thing he possessed, as the only thing nobody could take away from him. Roberta was beautiful, and he thanked the stars a hundred times a day that he had such a woman for his wife.

Lem loved her, had known her since he was twelve. They

had married when he was fifteen, a year ago. She was but thirteen, yet she was comely, with fine brown hair, brown eyes, like his, soft skin, a pretty chin, and sweet soft lips, and those sweet tender hands that were scorched raw from washing his clothes, the pots and pans and dishes, the woodwork. But her lips were what he cherished most. They were rubied now, from the force of his kiss. Her cheeks flared with pale crimson, flamed like a pair of autumn sumac leaves. She was not shy like him, but bold in her lovemaking, and this always startled him. He was still scrawny, lean as a whip, with dark hair, eyes brown as coffee beans, lighter than hers, perhaps. Dreamer's eyes, she called them, set in a face chiseled angular. She loved his face, she told him. Loved to touch the wide high cheekbones, stroke the narrow chin, rub the wide forehead. She laughed at him sometimes when he talked. He knew why; his Adam's apple bobbed up and down in his throat every time he spoke. It seemed sharp enough to cut through the skin of his neck.

"Lem, don't," she said, and there was a dry husk in her voice, like a cat purring in season.

He touched one of her breasts, drew her to him again.

"You really don't want me to?" he asked.

"It's full daylight."

"That's what it means to be free," he said. "Loving day or night."

"Oh, you; you're wicked, Lemuel Hawke."

"With a wicked woman to love me."

When he kissed her again, she fed on his lips eagerly and they spoke no more as he lifted her in his arms, carried her easily to the bedroom.

She giggled brightly as he lay her on the bed. He threw up her skirts and her complexion flared with a rose flame.

"My," she said.

He turned away from her, heard the rustle of cloth as she slid out of her clothes. Sometimes he couldn't understand her cockeyed modesty. She did not want him to see her shuck out of her dress, but in a moment they would both be as naked as Adam and Eve. It didn't make any sense to him, but it was part of her mystery. When he turned back to her, her eyes opened wide.

"You can see how it is, woman."

He slid onto the bed, took her in his arms. It would be slow. She liked it slow, the beginning part, the loving part. The kissing, the hide-and-seek, the exploring.

"Yes, yes," she said, when he entered her and the sunlight streaming through the window made her hair shine, made the light in her eyes dance like flames in the winter hearth.

2

The rifle was a Virginia-made flintlock, wrought by a German smith living in the Shenandoah Valley. The low-combed butt-stock had a pronounced drop to it; the four-piece brass patchbox in a golden flourish rendered a touch of elegance to the rifle's clean, graceful lines. The rifle was 57 inches long, rifled, in .53 caliber. Its heavy octagonal barrel was browned to a smooth rust, adorned with an open V for the rear sight, a dovetailed blade for the front. Like the patchbox, the buttplate, heelplate, keyplate, trigger guard, and ramrod were all of brass. The lockplate was flat-faced with a detachable, iron-faceted pan, flat-faced gooseneck cock, and roller on frizzen. There were no maker's markings on the barrel, but Lem knew that a man named Samuel Steinbach had built it for his son, who had taken sick and died before the rifle was proof-shot. Hawke had traded three hogs for it two years ago and thought he had gotten the better of the bargain.

He stood behind a sturdy hickory, the pan primed, frizzen pitched upward at an angle. Inside the barrel, a patched ball, .526 in diameter, sat atop 90 grains of double fine black powder. Lem wore buckskins, carried a powder horn and a possibles sack filled with patches and balls he had molded himself. A wide-bladed skinning knife, sheathed in cowhide, with a buckhorn handle, graced his belt.

The doe had been moving up the gully between two ridges, feeding on mast, nibbling on shoots of grass along the seasonal stream that arrowed the hollow. Lem felt the slight breeze against his face, knew that if it did not shift, the deer would not scent him. He had listened to her for fifteen minutes, knew she was very close. Now, he saw the tips of her ears, knew she would come under his sights in a few moments. He held the trigger down, pulled the hammer back, snugged the frizzen down tight. The lock made only a small sound as the sear engaged, but he completed the action while the deer moved past a clump of noisy brush.

He held his breath as the doe ambled behind a stand of sassafrass. He brought the rifle slowly up to his shoulder, braced it against the bark of the hickory tree. He sighted along a path just to the right of the sassafrass cluster. The doe was moving higher, would be in full view when she emerged from the brush. He did not want his ball to deflect when he fired. Carefully, he looked down the barrel, sighting along the invisible path the ball would travel. There were no obstructions.

It seemed to take forever before the doe stepped out from behind the slender shoots of the sassafrass. The step was only tentative. She raised her head, frozen for a moment in midstride. Her ears twisted to pick up any sound. Her eyes, like giant magnifying glasses, scanned the slope of the ridge where Lem stood. He had the feeling that she was looking straight into his own eyes. He did not flick an eyelash, stood breathless as a statue for an eternity.

Only her forequarters, front legs, chest and head, showed.

The air in Lem's chest turned hot, yet he dared not expel it. Not yet. Finally, the doe finished her stride, stepped into the open. She dropped her head to the ground, wrenched at a clump of grass.

Lem picked a spot behind her right foreleg. He expelled his breath, drew in another, held it. When the doe raised her head again, her ears flirting at the slight shift of breeze, Lem squeezed the trigger, caressing it in a steady pull. The hammer popped forward, the flint striking the plate, showering the fine powder in the pan with sizzling sparks. The rifle bucked against his shoulder. A cloud of white smoke billowed out from the muzzle, followed by a burst of orange flame. The ball hissed through the air, struck the doe just behind her shoulder. She hunched down, but was too late. The ball kicked up a puff of dust from her russet hide and she staggered sideways, blown into the opposing slope by the force of ninety grains of powder pushing the lead ball through her flesh. The ball flattened on impact, slammed into her heart, hammering it into bloody pulp.

It was a clean hit, Lem knew. When the smoke cleared, he saw her lying against the hillside, struggling to regain her feet. He dropped the rifle from his shoulder, grasped it just in front of the trigger guard and raced down the slope at a dead run. He hurdled the ditch, drew his knife. The doe bleated softly, but its eyes were glazed, its tongue lolling from its gaping mouth. He slashed the throat quickly, stepped back as the blood spurted onto his moccasins. The doe quivered and her eyes frosted over with the mist of death.

Hawke panted for breath. Time stood still as he looked down on his kill. The doe would dress out to better than a hundred pounds. Out of habit, Lem measured out ninety grains of powder, poured it down the barrel of his flintlock. He wet a precut patch of pillow ticking, placed a ball in the center. He pushed the patch and ball down the barrel with the short wooden starter, then took his ramrod and seated the ball on the powder. He did not prime the pan, but he could do this quickly by pouring very fine powder out of a small horn hanging from his neck by a leather thong.

He propped the rifle in the fork of a sturdy sassafrass and drew his skinning knife, took a length of rope from his possibles pouch. He turned the doe over on its back, tied one leg to the trunk of an uphill beech, spread the other one. He drew his knife, made the cut, began to dress out the doe as deftly as a surgeon. In less than ten minutes he was finished. He roped a tree limb, hoisted the deer up in the air. He began to skin it out from the neck down.

Lem almost missed the movement. A leaf jangled silently twenty yards from where he knelt. He froze, peered intently into the brush. He gripped the knife more tightly. The handle and his fingers were slippery with blood.

The bushes moved again and this time they made noise. A buckskinned man stepped through them, shunting branches aside with the barrel of his long rifle.

"Silas," said Lem, breathing a sigh of relief. His hand loosened its grip on the skinning knife. He sank to his haunches, waited for Silas to come up.

"Fair shot, Lemuel," said Silas Morgan, coming to a halt. He stabbed the butt of his rifle into the hillside, leaned on it for support. A lean wiry man, Silas stood five foot seven, wore a coonskin cap over his shock of curly dark hair, hair that was slashed with streaks of steeldust. His friendly smile showed that he had teeth missing. His hooked nose bent over a brushy moustache that dripped over his upper lip like shaggy moss. His blue eyes crackled with the cool blue fires of cut diamonds. He spat a stream of tobacco juice onto the ground. Viscous droplets clung to his moustache, glittered like gobs of amber resin.

"Old Smokey shoots true," said Lem, glancing at his rifle.

"That she does."

Silas set his rifle down, squatted next to Lem. He pulled a bundle from his bulging possibles pouch, lay it on the ground. Lem stopped his skinning, looked up at Silas.

"What you got there?"

"Made yer some mokersons."

"What for?"

"Might be yer gonna wear out them you got."

"Might. Silas, what you got in your craw, 'sides ter-baccy?"

"Haw! Son, I seen you sellin' off your stock to ever' Tom, Dick and Benedict Arnold. Smokehouse burnin' hick'ry shavin's night 'n day, hog bristles stenchin' up the air. You ain't hauled that plow in a week. Grass is high enough 'long the trails for you to be settin' out. Kentucky, I reckon."

"We're fixin' to leave, all right. Didn't think nobody knew but us."

"Tax collector knows. He's been makin' noise, gettin' him together some cronies to come out and grab what you got left."

"Dan Brown? He'd do that?"

"You got maybe a week."

Lem put the skinning knife to work again. He used the blade deftly, separating the hide from the flesh, sliding the point along the fat layer with smooth strokes. He would have hung the deer up by the hind legs, but that would have taken too much time. He made an incision around the deer's throat, just below the head, and started peeling the hide downward.

Then, he switched to the deer's hindquarters, skinned the hind legs, cut the tail at the base and stripped the hide down to the place where he had stopped. He severed the rest of the hide, laid it out and began to quarter the deer. It was hard work.

"Reckon I'll leave tomorrow," Lem said, puffing at the end of the sentence.

"Might not be too soon." Silas opened the oilcloth, shook out the moccasins. He held them up for Lem to see. There was nothing fancy about them. He had stitched two sturdy chunks of leather for the soles, fringed the tops. "You take these along."

"Thanks," said Lem. "I'm mighty obliged."

"Wish I was goin' with you."

"It's you what told me about Kentucky, how it was."

"I been there. Goin' on meself, way out yonder." Silas waved an arm in a westward arc. "Heard tell of good huntin' beyond the line." The "line" was something Lem had heard about for years. The British had set a boundary line, but many settlers had pushed beyond it, and the "line" had kept changing for years. No one really knew where the "line" was anymore. It was imaginary; it was where restless men like Silas went to get away from civilization. It was always a place to cross; a frontier meant to be conquered.

"Wherebouts you goin'?" asked Lem. He cracked a hind leg, sliced the tendon. "Didn't you get your tailfeathers singed enough?"

Silas showed no visible sign of emotion. Lem stared at his impassive face and wanted to bite his own tongue for bringing up Morgan's past like that. Everyone knew the story; everyone talked about the Morgans and their troubles during the Indian wars, when Silas and some of his kin were ranging. Fifteen years before, in 1778, when Silas was in his late teens, he was hunting with his older brother, Virgil, in the Clinch River valley. Virgil was a ranger, had been fighting against the British in the east, the Indians in the west.

Their father was plowing that morning, accompanied by their little brother, Lucas, who was only ten years old. Silas and Virgil waved to them, entered the woods. They heard shooting coming from the field. Virgil broke into a dead run, Silas at his heels. Some Delawares had slipped through the outlying ranger patrols and had surprised their father, Benjamin, as he turned the plow horse at the end of a row. Silas watched in horror as his father was cut down, scalped in the field. Little Lucas never made it to the stockade in the settlement. He was shot as he tried to climb over the split-rail fence surrounding the field.

Virgil shot two Delawares before they charged him as he was stuffing a ball down the barrel of his rifle. They broke one of his legs with tomahawks and Virgil went down, screaming in pain. Silas's rifle misfired and he was swarmed over by a half-dozen Indians. They dragged him to where Virgil lay stricken. Virgil was still alive, but they broke his other leg. He did not scream this time, but glared at the chief, cursed him.

The chief of the Delaware band, Iron Lance, reached down, picked up a handful of dirt. He stuffed the dirt into Virgil's mouth.

"You want our land, I give it to you."

Then, as Silas watched, Iron Lance drove his tomahawk into Virgil's skull, splitting it in two.

The Delawares kept Silas as their prisoner. They also captured his mother, raped her repeatedly as he watched. They sold her to some Wyandottes. Silas finally escaped from the Delawares and ransomed his mother from the Wyandottes, but she was never the same after that. She had died the year before, in 1792, and was buried someplace in the woods that only Silas knew about.

"There's a big river out west, bigger'n any in the whole world," said Silas, as Lem finished dressing out the deer. "I aim to go on beyond it. They say they's mountains out yonder make the Smokies look like anthills."

"How do you know about this river?" He broke the doe's backbone just below the ribs, put pressure on the knife to work through a pair of vertebrae.

"I heered talk, seed a map."

"Somebody's pullin' your leg, Silas."

"Maybeso. I aim to find out. Might be I'll see you out there someday."

"Roberta won't go. Kentucky's far enough for her."

"Welp," said Silas, rising to his feet, "luck to you."

"Take the heart and liver, Silas," said Lem. "You want a haunch?"

"I'll take the vittles and gladly. You keep the rest."

Silas wrapped the liver and heart in fresh leaves, stuck the organs in his possibles pouch. Lem had seen the man eat such meats raw more than once.

The frontiersman picked up his rifle. In a few moments he was gone, a stillness of green leaves in his wake, like a curtain hanging in an airless room.

Roberta fought the smoke, retrieved a ham from the little wooden shed out back of the house. The wood smoke spooled a tangy fragrance into the air. She plopped the ham into a wicker basket at her feet. She picked up two chunks of hickory soaking in the wooden vat outside, placed them on the smouldering fire. Picking up the basket, Roberta started for the house. Something caught the corner of her eye and she stopped. She saw Lem emerge from the woods, wave to her. She set the basket down, rescued a vagrant wisp of hair from under her nose, brushed it back. She waved back.

Lem grinned when he came up to her, cocked a thumb to show her the deerhide on his back, all bundled up with the meat inside.

"I'll bone her out and smoke her tonight," he said.

"I've a ham here."

"Yes. I saw Silas Morgan. He's headin' out too."

Roberta frowned. A shadow seemed to cross her face and her eyes dulled as the gaps between the lids narrowed. Her long, carefully tended eyelashes veiled the dark look in her eyes. She looked at her husband's blood-smeared hands, at his blood-streaked face, turned away in disgust.

"You better wash up," she said. She lifted the basket, trudged away, as if to carry her feelings with her, hide them in a closet where her husband could not see them.

"Silas ain't goin' with us," Lem said. "He's goin' far away, to the west."

Roberta stopped, turned around. Her eyes now were thin inscrutable slits, but the sun glinted off her hair, turning it auburn. The fine strands shimmered like fine copper wire spun from a magic loom.

"What do I care?"

"I thought you might be mad if you thought—"

"If I thought Silas Morgan was a-goin' with us to Kentucky," she said coldly, "I would not go at all."

"Why? Why don't you like him? What's he ever done to you?"

"I don't know. I just don't like him," she said, a quaver in her voice mirroring the fear she could not define, could not quell. Something inside her rebelled against such men as Silas Morgan. They were rootless, ungentlemanly, wanderers without substance. Deep down, she knew she was afraid that Silas would infect her husband with his wanderlust. Indeed, he already had. In Lemuel, she sensed the same wild, free spirit. Lem cared nothing for fine clothes, grooming, the elegance of a fine home in a prosperous community, the comradeship of well-to-do gentry. She yearned desperately for such things. She thought of herself as a bright graceful flower, an orchid, perhaps, blooming in a dank and neglected cellar, hidden from the sun and every admiring eye. She dreaded becoming an ugly toadstool pushing up through mud, destined to live and die in a drab darkness of the soul, unknown and unsung. This was more than fear, she realized. This was terror, stark and raging, frightening as an unexpected eclipse at noon. She could not express this fear to Lemuel, nor to anyone. This was the secret she carried in her bosom, in her heart, and sometimes it emerged and engulfed her, smothered her until she could not breathe, could not speak.

"You done something to your hair," he said.

Her heart froze and the panic made her heart pump hard until she could hear its pounding in her temples.

She turned and tramped away from him.

"I washed it," she said, blurting it out so that he would not question her, would not know that she had spent some of their money on henna and vermilion, yardage for a new dress to wear someday when they lived in a town manor, gentry at last. She had bought these things that morning from a passing drummer, paying the exorbitant prices not only in shillings, but in guilt and shame.

These were some of her secrets, locked away, like the dress material, the beads, the henna, vermilion, rouge and lace, all of the other things she had been hoarding, from the prying eyes of her husband.

"Looks nice," said Lemuel and she almost stopped again so that she could turn slowly in the sun and let him see how beautiful she was. For a moment she did feel beautiful and she wanted to bask in his praise, tell him how she felt, tell him everything. The moment passed, and she knew that the beauty was only superficial and temporary. Inside, she felt the drabness of their existence pulling on her, pulling her back down into the cellar, into the mud of anonymity and neglect. She went on, toward the house, without saying more, the secret of her yearning safe once again, safe only in her silent terrifying prison.

3

In the dark before dawn, Roberta packed the wagon with foodstuffs, cooking and kitchen utensils, clothing, Lem's farming tools. Lem hitched up the team of mules, saddled his horse, a six-year-old sorrel gelding he called Hammerhead for its blunt nose, short ears. There was a moment when he felt his stomach turn queasy. The scent of fresh-plowed fields, the heady musk of dewy soil assailed his nostrils, tugged at him with a longing for the home he was leaving. A lump clogged his throat and he had to swallow hard to wrench it loose. He wondered if Roberta felt as he did, homeless and lost, edgy over the coming journey. He fought off the feelings by dreaming of the new land, steeling himself to walk away from their first home. The lump in his throat returned, nevertheless, as he poked Hammerhead's belly, drew the cinch up tight. The gelding had a way of swelling out so that he could carry the saddle with a loose cinch.

A sniffing wind rose out of the highlands, prowled the piedmont, crept through the valley like some dark Arabian rider swathed in dark linens. A curious sound, the wind in the darkness; it made the dead things seem alive: a shutter creaked on the empty house, the leaves of a maple rustled in conspiratorial whispers, a skeletal leaf from the previous fall crabbed across the stony road. From far off, he heard the lonesome sound of a cowbell, a disembodied clanking from a neighboring farm that he continued to hear long after the sound had ceased. The gelding shook its head, snorted. One of the mules rattled its traces. Even the animals were impatient to be on the trail, Lem thought.

"You ready, Bobbie?" Lem said to Roberta. It was a name he called her in private.

"Lem, it's dark as pitch."

He caught the impatience in her voice, the frustration of being uprooted.

"We got to get going," he said. "Dan Brown catches us, he'll take it all. Maybe us too. We'll take turns driving the wagon. I'll spell you whenever you want."

She sighed heavily and he made out her form by the wagon. He walked over to her, helped her up on the seat. Her skirt got tangled on the brake and she kicked at it. He heard the sound of cloth ripping.

"Damn! My petticoat," she exclaimed. "You ruined it, you clod."

"Bobbie, hey. I didn't do anything."

She sagged onto the seat, muttering something under her breath. He wondered at the things she kept inside her. She was not a talkative person. When she did say anything it was usually a complaint or telling him something to do. Still, he loved her. That was just her way. The German in her, maybe, from her parents. Folks said Germans were hardheaded, stingy with talk. Just like Roberta was most times.

"We'll start out slow," he said, to mollify her. "It'll be light right soon."

She turned to him, then.

"I feel like a criminal," she said. "Why couldn't we leave in daylight, hold our heads up proud? We could have gone with the Pilchers, or the Stamps, had some company. 'Stead, you steal away in the dead of night like a thief. I don't see the sense of going all that far and taking our poorness with us. You don't have to quit."

It was true. Others had left Culpeper and Stafford counties, days before. Roberta had wanted to go with them, have company on the journey. Well, there were hundreds of others leaving Virginia. It was likely they'd run into other families along the way.

"Bobbie, Bobbie," he said, soothingly, "don't you see? Here, we're nothing. We're dirt. Less than dirt. If we don't own land, we can't vote and the guv'mint can just run right over us, plow us under. We got to go. We got to find a life for ourselves."

"Oh, Lemuel, don't whine."

"I ain't whinin', Roberta, dammit. I'm just tellin' you whichaway the wind blows. Give me a chance, will you?"

"Or what? You'd run off and just leave me, wouldn't you?"

That surprised him. He stepped back, filled his lungs with a staunch breath. The air tasted like wet tree bark, like hickory.

"Why, I don't rightly know. I always thought you would go along with me, wherever I went. You're my wife and—"

"And I got to obey you," she said, her tone razor-edged, slicing.

"You put it hard," he said.

"I'm only saying what's so," she replied, sulking, and he saw her as shadow, dark and brooding, pulling away from him into that private world of hers where he could not venture. Just a shadow, he thought, and not the laughing shy girl he had watched curiously at Arbor School, helped pick berries in the green spring of yesteryear when the sun played in her hair and pebbled her face with freckles. He felt that same ache again, recalling those first days of seeing her, watching her, wondering about her as he wondered about the sky and the clouds, the growing trees, the vast migrations of wildfowl blacking out the sun for days on end.

"We'd best get on," he said lamely, because there were no words to argue with her, to tell her how sad he was inside, how he felt the sadness growing like the shadows that hid her face, blurred her eyes to hollow sockets. He shambled away, crushed by something hard in her silence, shattered by something in her eyes he could not see, could only feel knifing at his heart like a surgeon's cold blade.

He mounted Hammerhead, heard the cowhide saddle

creak under his weight. He clucked to the horse, laid the right rein against his neck. The horse turned, moved ahead of the wagon.

"Don't forget to take the brake off," Lem said as he passed the blackened hulk on the seat. She released it with a snap and the wagon lurched forward on freshly oiled wheels, the thorough braces groaning under the strain of the load. Everything they owned, he thought, and food enough to feed them for a time.

In the cool of morning, when the light brought everything to life again, they headed for Swift Run Gap in the Blue Ridge Mountains. The lilting chromatic trill of a lark floated over a hill greening up like a raw emerald. Roberta sat on a shabby pillow she had brought along, seemed to take no notice of their surroundings. But Lem Hawke felt the morning in his bones, felt the heat of the sun warm him, brighten his spirits as if he had taken whiskey into his belly.

Long slow dreamy miles of riding through magical country, the dew turning to steam each morning, pockets of mist clinging to the hollows of the earth like fairy gauze and the earth giving up its scents as the larks tweedled in the hedgerows, crows cawed raucous from the forest fringe. Down into the Shenandoah Valley to the settlement at Rocktown they went, wending their way wide-eyed with the wonder and beauty of a land hemmed in by graceful hushed hills. They turned southwest, taking the Great Valley Road, felt it rise steadily under them as the Shenandoah Valley rose gradually out of the bottoms, preening in the sun.

They met other families going their way, heading for Kentucky and Tennessee, bundles piled high in their wagons, driving hogs and cattle ahead of them, making but a few miles a day. People waved and greeted them with fervor, asked questions: "Where do you hail from?" and "Where are you bound?" Lem and Roberta rode through the parted waves of people, but sometimes grazed the horse and mules with others who had stopped by the wayside.

The trough through the mountains was long and fertile, and they lingered one long afternoon in a meadow. Lemuel pitched their tent, set stones in a circle for a cookfire. At sunset, another wagon pulled up, set up camp near theirs. There was good water in the brook, and the people settling in for the evening waved to the Hawkes. One of them walked over to Lem's campfire shortly after dusk. He was short, lean, with curly red hair, a thin, bony wedge of a nose, a soft, fleshy jaw, cheekbones round and smooth as knee sockets, flashing blue eyes. His buckskins showed him to be a man of the woods as well as the trail. He carried in his hands a pouch of tobacco, his pipe.

"Smoke?" he said to Lem. His small crooked slit of a mouth looked as if it was carved out of his skull with a knife. The ragged, reddish moustache plastered his upper lip like a makeshift bandage.

"Set," said Hawke. "I'd be much obliged." He fished out his empty pipe, held the bowl upside down and laughed.

The stranger sat on a downed log that Lem had dragged over from the stream. It was dry and shimmering in the light from the fire. Roberta looked at him closely, but he seemed not to notice.

Lem dipped his bowl into the tobacco pouch, tamped it down. He handed the pouch back to the stranger.

The road was empty and they heard only the clatter of pots and pans from the other camp across the greensward. A light breeze rippled through the grasses, ruffling them like feathers on a chick.

"Name's Lemuel Hawke, what's your'n?"

"Barry O'Neil. Where you headed?" He stuck a twig into the fire.

"Kentucky."

"I be going back to Lexington, myself."

"You been there, then?" Lemuel leaned forward, the pipe

in his mouth as O'Neil held out the flaming twig. He sucked on the pipe, drew the flame through the tobacco. His cheeks collapsed into two large dimples.

"Been there a year. Come back for my brother and his family."

Roberta cleared her throat with a discernible rasp.

"Barry, this here's my wife, Roberta. You married?"

O'Neil turned his head. He fixed his gaze on Lem's wife. His mouth crinkled in a warped smile.

"Glad to meet you ma'am," he said.

"You married?" asked Hawke again.

"Nope." O'Neil's gaze didn't waver. He lit his pipe, drew on it as he continued to stare at Roberta. She did not turn away, but regarded him boldly, an almost wistful look in her eyes.

"We been married a year," said Lemuel, filling his lungs with the smoke from Virginia-grown tobacco. The faint aroma of apples wafted to his nostrils. "Mighty fine ter-baccy," he added.

"My brother growed it," said Barry. "Landlord took most of it for hisself. James won't have to do that no more in Kentucky. He aims to grow barley and wheat, corn, make his own whiskey."

"Tell me about Lexington," said Roberta, moving close to the fire. The water for the dishes had not yet boiled. The fire-blackened pot hung on the irons, flames licking its bottom. "Is it nice there?"

"Mighty nice, ma'am. It is like a pretty flower blossoming at the end of a long stem. That stem's got its roots in Virginia, mostly. There's maybe three or four hundred homes there, all clustered around the courthouse. It stands in the middle of a wide plain like Philadelphia."

"How about the land thereabouts?" asked Lem. "Can it be bought cheap?"

"Land aplenty," said O'Neil. "Sells for about seven shillings the acre."

"Oh," said Lem, crestfallen. He brooded behind the smoke from his pipe.

"What about the town?" asked Roberta. "What industry have they there?"

"Oh, there's much dealing to do in Lexington, ma'am. We got smiths and shoemakers, brewers and wagon-makers, hatters and clothiers. It is the center of Kentucky, the anvil on which all commerce is forged."

"You sure do talk pretty," said Roberta, and Lem detected a new tone in her voice, a softness that had not been there in a long while. He looked at her across the fire, but could not see her eyes. They were filled with shadows and only her face stood out, daubed with soft orange flames. She looked mysterious and exciting, as if the bloom of love-making had rouged her face.

"Thank you, ma'am," said O'Neil and he smiled wide, showing his teeth for the first time. He was in his twenties, Lem figured, certainly older than they were.

Roberta asked Barry a lot of questions about Kentucky and he answered her politely and noncommittally as far as Lem could tell. He let the talk wash over him, drift in and out of his mind like the vagrant smoke from the campfire and his pipe. He thought about the land in Kentucky, wondered how he would ever be able to buy any. No matter, he would lease some good bottom land and that would be almost the same as owning it.

The sound of Roberta's laughter jarred Lemuel out of his reverie. He had missed whatever it was that the redheaded man had said to make his wife laugh.

". . . you make it sound so romantic," said Roberta. "That's the trouble with most men. They have their nose to the grindstone and can't smell the flowers."

"Well, I don't know about that," said O'Neil, laughing with her. "A man has to pay his own way."

"All work and no play . . ." said Roberta, her voice trailing off as she angled a glance at her husband.

Barry's low chuckle rattled in his throat, the sound of a stick rapping a rolling wagon's spokes.

"Welp," said Lem, "I'm ready to turn in." He knocked the dottle from his pipe against the heel of his boot. "Bobbie?"

"I want to set by the fire a spell, Lem. You go on."

"Long one tomorrow."

"I'll be there by and by," she replied.

"O'Neil. 'Night. Thanks for the tobacco."

"I'll leave a few pinches with the missus," said O'Neil.

"Much obliged."

Lemuel walked to the tent, dropped to his knees and crawled inside. He pulled off his boots, kicked them to one side of the tent. He crawled atop the blankets, lay down on his back. He felt the tiredness seep through him. A feeling of drowsiness shut down his senses. He closed his eyes, listened to the distorted garble of voices out by the fire. He couldn't make out the words. They were soft-toned, so low he couldn't do more than separate Roberta's from Barry's. He heard a low laugh which turned into a girlish giggle.

The lassitude set in like mortar hardening and Lem rolled over on his side, sank into the soundless sea of sleep, the drone of voices fading away in the dark of his mind.

He didn't know how long he slept. Some sound outside startled him, jarred him awake. For several moments he lay there in the tent, disoriented, confused. At first he thought he was back home in Virginia, in his own bed. He shook out the tangled threads of dream and sleep, sat up. He felt beside him.

Roberta was not in the blankets. He groped around the pitch tent.

"Bobbie?" he whispered, but he knew there would be no answer.

He heard the faint tinkle of laughter, then. It was the sound he had heard in his dream, the same sound that had awakened him.

Lem strained to hear the laugh again, but his ears only buzzed with the small whispers of silence like the faint vacant roar in a conch shell.

A moment later he heard the padding of feet across the greensward. He reached for his rifle, but did not pick it up. The sounds were not furtive. The tent flap rustled and he saw a shadow as it opened.

"Bobbie?"

"Lem," she gasped. "You awake?"

"I just woke up. What are you doing out there?"

She crawled onto the blankets, shook out her hair. He touched her dress, felt the reassuring contour of her thigh. It seemed to him that she flinched, drew away from him, but it was only an impression. Perhaps his touch had startled her. She sighed deeply, shook out her hair.

"I—I was heeding a call to nature," she said, her voice weak, breathless.

"You went out there in the dark? You should have used that old oak bucket I brought along."

"I—I couldn't, Lem. It wasn't just one thing I had to do."

"I didn't hear you come to bed, Bobbie."

"You were dead to the world."

"Hmm. Maybe so."

"Go back to sleep. I'll get into my night clothes."

But he couldn't go back to sleep. He listened to her in the dark, felt her moving around, riffling through the carpetbag, slipping out of her clothes, pulling her nightgown over her head, settling in under the blankets. When he drew close to her, she curled up.

"I want you," he whispered, close to her ear.

"Lem. Not now. I'm awful tired."

"Christ."

"Don't curse," she said.

"Hell, I don't know what you're doin', wanderin' around in the night. You always used to be scairt of your own shadder."

"Mmmph. Let me sleep, Lem."

"Oh, all right. Go to sleep, Bobbie."

He turned over, away from her. He lay there for a long time, unable to go under, until he heard her breathing slow down and grow even. His thoughts crowded in on him, but he pushed them away with other thoughts. He didn't want to think that Bobbie might be a bad woman. He had to trust her, didn't he? She probably had to go real bad, like she said, and wanted privacy.

He shut down his thoughts, thought only of sleep. The faint burble of the creek worked a soporific spell on him and he drifted back down into sleep and, later, into dream. The dream was complex and he could make no sense of it, then or when he awakened in the morning.

4

The barred owl woke Lemuel early the next morning. Mucus that had dried and turned gritty sealed his eyes shut. He rubbed the "sand" free as the owl's throaty baritone sounded again.

He shivered in the chill, tried to pull the blanket around him. But Roberta, her back to him and still asleep, jerked it back. She lay curled into a ball, her hair a-tangle on the pillow. Lem sat up, pulled on his boots, groped around for his coat, a light sheepskin-lined buckskin he had made himself. The buttons were made of deer antlers, with hand-drilled holes, sewn to the garment with sinew.

He crawled outside the tent, blinked in the pale, mist-gauzed light. He looked across the creek toward the other side of the meadow, steaming wisps of ground fog. The other wagon was gone. He hadn't heard them leave. Usually folks made some noise when they packed up. Strange. They left mighty quiet. But why?

Lem stood up, rubbed his eyes. A light mist hung over the valley. The fire was out. He poked it with a stick, found some small coals. He drew his hunting knife, made from an old leaf spring, a staghorn handle that was rough enough to give him a good grip. He kept it sharp, used it now to shave a stick. He placed the dry shavings on a cluster of coals, made a cone with larger trims from the same stick. He leaned close, blew on the coals. The shavings bristled as they caught fire. The larger pieces caught and Lem added kindling to the blaze until it was large enough for bigger chunks of wood.

When he had the fire going well, he made a circle of the camp. He prowled the fringes of woods, looking for sign. He wouldn't put it to words in his mind. Just sign. Hated himself for doing such a thing behind Roberta's back. But, a man had to know, he told himself. Why? He just had to know. Had to know what? Things. Dammit, just things.

Lem knew how to read tracks, how to tell if a foot had mashed grass down and if that foot was human or animal. Since he was a boy he had felt a profound kinship with nature. His curiosity had compelled him to study all sorts of tracks in all kinds of weather conditions. He had watched animal footprints over long periods of time, watched how they aged from fresh to cold, watched what the wind did, and the rain.

He found a place on the other side of the meadow that wrestled his attention. A large swatch of grass was mashed down. Blanket marks in the soft earth between the blades where they poked out of the ground. It might not mean much, he reasoned. It wasn't far from where the other wagon had been moored overnight. Mashed grass between the wagon and the flat spot.

He took another look at the woods near his own tent. He could find no place where Roberta had heeded a call to nature during the night. He might have missed it, though.

His sense of smell was good, but he could have missed it. Something tightened in his stomach and his jaw line hardened without conscious thought.

He sat by the fire, looked into the flames for a long time as the sun came up, a swirling ball of fire hanging in the risen mist like a disk hammered in bronze, fired in a kiln and plunged into cloud. It didn't hurt his eyes to look at it for a few seconds. The rising sun, a dark steamy red, made him feel good, and when the birds started singing he felt even better. There was a fresh green smell to the morning and his stomach growled with hunger. He drank from the creek, lying flat, holding his head sideways. His buckskins were slick with dew when he got up and the sun had cleared the ground fog, shimmered yellow as goldenrod now, fatally blinding to any man's stare.

He called to Roberta as he approached the tent, two woolen blankets he had sewn together in a rectangle. Half a blanket for the backside, the other half slit and buttonholed for the front. String tied to wooden stakes kept the sides apart; longer stakes held up the inverted V of the roof.

"Mornin' Bobbie," he said when he drew near. "Time to get crackin'."

"Let me sleep," she argued, her voice muffled in the blankets.

It took him twenty minutes to bring her out of her stupor, and she took her time dressing. Lem tended to the stock, watering the horses, putting them in harness. He folded up the tent while she stood by the fire, embracing herself as if she was still cold.

"One morning, couldn't we just sleep late?" she asked.

"Some morning, maybe. Not this 'un."

"Lem, there's never going to be any grass grow under your feet."

"In Kentucky, there will."

She made a face, crinkled her nose at him.

Lem laughed.

"You going to cook anything or do you want to eat on the trace."

"We've got broth and yesterday's flour biscuits. Let's just go."

He soaked the fire with water while Roberta sat on the wagon seat tying on her bonnet. He shouldered his rifle and climbed into the saddle, tapped his heels to the horse's flanks. They left the meadow behind, gained the road. Roberta fought the ruts all morning until Lemuel spelled her and she rode his horse until they nooned at the road junction market town of Staunton.

Lemuel looked for O'Neil's wagon, but saw no sign of it, or him.

Roberta came out of her grumps after they ate roasted ears of corn they bought from a farmer for a few pence, sliced ham wedged between the hardened biscuits, washed it down with dandelion tea. After eating their humble meal, Roberta ladled honey onto a spoon for Lem.

"To sweeten your tongue," she said.

He gave her a peck on the cheek and she looked around, blushing. She spoke to some of the other women while Lem helped a man fix a loose spoke on his wagon wheel.

In the days that followed, the Hawkes followed the other migrants in a slow stream southwestward, going through the small Virginia settlement of Lexington, a few days later through Hans Meadow. They gazed raptly at the natural bridge over Cedar Creek. At Radford, they crossed the natural divide between the waters flowing to the Atlantic and those spilling into the Ohio. At Ingles' Ferry, they forded the New River, too poor to afford the float.

Lemuel's spirits perked up, there was a spring in his step, a boil of wings in his belly when they got beyond New River. There, the road turned almost due west and the country was less populated between old Fort Chiswell and the new settlement at Evensham. He had sought campsites well off the trail in days past, but now it was not so difficult to avoid the company of people. Roberta was sick most every morning and he knew it embarrassed her. He didn't know what was wrong with her and she never told him.

"Why can't we travel with other folks?" Roberta asked him, after they got gone nearly 275 miles from home. "You always stay away from their camps when we stop for the night."

"Maybe I like to keep you for myself in private."

"What's that supposed to mean?"

His lips creased in a lewd smile.

"You know."

"Oh, Lem," she said, "is that all you think of?"

"Mostly," he grinned. They had made love almost every night, and sometimes at dawn when he was most hungry for her. It seemed better, somehow, with no people about. He still had not seen Barry O'Neil, but he knew the man was somewhere along the road, either ahead or behind them. He didn't care if he never saw him again. He was sure, though, that Roberta wouldn't do more than flirt with the man. He had been wrong to doubt her. In the dark of their tent, she was willing enough, passionate as ever. He wasn't so sure how she'd be with other folks as camping neighbors.

Five miles later, some thirty miles west of Abingdon, they came up on the blockhouse near the Holston River.

"Yonder it lies," said Lem, stopping to spell the horses before taking them down to the river to drink.

Roberta looked in the direction where Lem's extended hand pointed.

"All I see is a passel of trees and a bridle path," she said.

Lem laughed.

"That path is the Wilderness Road, darlin'. Hell on a wagon, they say, and thick with painted redskins, b'ars and such."

"You oughten not to scare me, Lemuel Hawke."

"Aw, I didn't mean nuthin', Bert. It'll be mighty slow

goin', but I reckon we ain't in no big dither to get to Kentucky."

"You had red ants in your britches back home," she snapped. "That way looks real bad, Lem. Why the trail's nary wide enough for a horse, much less this wagon."

"You foller. I'll find us a way."

There was no real road through the wilderness. Sometimes, they were able to follow the rough path, but when it narrowed, Lem left the trail and blazed trees so Roberta could follow. The small branches lashed at her face, raised rude welts on her face. The going was slow and tortuous and often she thought they might be lost. Sometimes she got sick and they had to stop until she finished throwing up her breakfast. But Lemuel Hawke forged on, keeping his bearings by the sun, finding his way by dead reckoning. Always, he used the narrow trail as his guide, crossing and crisscrossing it several times in the course of that first day in wild, untamed country that made his heart sing with its savage rhythms. They made camp by a small melodic stream that night. The tiredness seeped through them on silent runners when they finally stopped long enough to catch their breaths. They ate a cold supper of roast ham, corncakes, washed down with cool water, and retired early, closed in by centuries of growing things, things green and timeless, like the eternal stars floating above the dark treetops in a dark and endless sea.

They came upon the frightened families late the next afternoon. In a clearing just off the main trail, men and women huddled around a ring of wagons and carts. Snuffle-nosed children herded hogs and goats and cattle away from the grown folks, their eyes wide with wonder and shadow-laced with fear. One man was fixing a wheel broken on the dry, rocky streambed that crossed the path at right angles.

Two men on guard at the edge of the clearing leveled rifles in Lem's direction, until they saw he was a traveler like themselves.

"Sorry," said one as Lemuel waved his hand at Roberta, ordering her to hold back. "We thought you might be a Injun."

Lem saw a man lying in the shade of another wagon, his face bloody, a sleeve torn from his muslin shirt. A woman dabbed at his face with a wet cloth, trying to clean away the blood. The man winced every time she touched him.

Three men were wrestling with another man, trying to prop him up against the wheel of a two-wheeled cart. A woman sobbed as she watched them. They placed him upright, but the man toppled over and Lem saw the fist-sized hole in the back of his head, the gore on the back of his shirt like flung barn paint. Roberta gasped.

"Stay here," he said softly. "I'll see what they're about here."

Lem walked over to one of the guards, whispered to him.

"What happened?" he asked.

The lean, bony man, his face charred with three days of beard stubble, squinted, shoved a chaw of tobacco to one side of his mouth, nudging it up from between his lower teeth in the front.

"We heered some hollerin', women a-screamin', wagons a-rumblin' like a slide o' rock and come up on this clearin' where they was a couple of buck savages terrorizin' these folk. I reckon the men come up on the Injuns fust and got into a tangle with 'em. The redskins run off when we struck 'em some flint sparks."

"You reckon there's more out there?" Lem asked, looking beyond the clearing.

"Can't rightly say. Me'n Orm here told the folks to calm down and we'd set with 'em a while. That's our wagon over yonder under that water oak. We got women too and we don't want to see 'em get to Kentucky in widderhood."

The man speaking said his name was Dick Hauser. His traveling partner was Ormly Shield. Six of the pasty-faced children were theirs, but Dick didn't say which. There were a dozen kids, their eyes big and black like prunes sunk in the pudding of their faces, keeping the stock bunched up.

Lem told them his name.

"You goin' after 'em?" asked Lem.

"After who?" asked Ormly, speaking for the first time. He stood a half-dozen inches over six feet, as unshaven as Hauser, with a razor-sharp Adam's apple puncturing the tight skin of his throat. He was lean as a slat, carried a rifle that must have had a barrel length of 65 inches or so. Both men wore dirty linsey-woolsey shirts with the sleeves cut off above the elbows. Their arms were the color of tanned leather from the sun.

"The Injuns."

"I reckon not," said Hauser. "We'll just set her out, wait for more folks to come up. You got a fusil?"

"I do."

"Best check yore powder," said Dick. He glanced over at the dead man. They had him laid out now. The woman put a blanket over him, crumpled up when she covered his face, fell on his body, sobbing so hard it hurt Lem to watch her. He saw Roberta set the brake and climb down from the wagon. She walked over to the woman, squatted down next to her. She put a hand on the woman's shoulder, just to give her comfort.

"We could be here for days, waitin' for folks," said Lem.

"At least our hair wouldn't be danglin' from no buck's sash," said Ormly. "They's red niggers all through these woods."

"You been here before?" asked Lem.

Orm nodded.

"What kind of Indians was they?"

"I make 'em to be Tuscarory," replied Hauser.

"Weren't Cherokee, ner Shawnee, neither," affirmed Shield.

Some of the men broke shovels out of their wagons. They walked around, testing the ground. Some distance from the stream, one of them started digging. He tried to be quiet, but Lem could hear the shovel strike stone. The other man started digging about six feet away.

"Sounds godawful, don't it?" said Hauser.

"Which way did them Injuns go?" asked Lem.

Orm pointed a long arm to the west of the clearing. Lem turned on his heel, went back to his horse. He slipped the rifle from the blanket sheath tied to his saddle's D rings. He poured fine powder into the pan, blew it thin. The rifle was loaded with powder and ball. He checked his possibles pouch, weighed the powder horn in his hand. It was almost full. Satisfied, he walked back over to where Hauser and Shield were standing.

"I reckon I'll do some tracking, see what I run across."

"Lemuel, is that your name? You're either plumb crazy or you got a set of nuts big as cannonballs. They was at least two of them sneaks, and by gum, I'd bet more's jest a-waitin' out there for fresh white meat. You'd best take your woman into the shade and set a spell."

"I can't set," said Lem.

He walked over to Roberta. She was sitting down on the grass, holding one of the grieving woman's hands.

"I'm goin' huntin'," Lem said. "Likely we'll spend the night here."

"Lem, is that all you think about?"

"I got to go," he said awkwardly. "Ma'am, I'm real sorry you lost your man."

The sobbing woman looked up at him with red-rimmed eyes. He turned away.

"I'll be back directly," he said to Roberta. She speared him with a look that made a lump form in his throat. He padded away, his head down, already reading sign in the flattened grasses, the barely visible furrows made by footsteps only moments before.

Lem melted into the forest. The sounds of the digging faded away. He stepped carefully, looking harder than he ever had for sign. His pulse throbbed in his ears and he drew deep slow breaths to calm his heart. He saw the crushed grass, the blades just starting to creep back upright.

Something came over him when he entered woodlands. A change that he recognized, a change in him, in his senses. It was as if he became a different person, entered a different world. All of the references changed for him. He shifted his senses to the stimulus of the forest. He became part of it, blending into its lush growth, its furtive sounds, letting it all penetrate deep into him, letting himself soak it all in until he was part of it, part of its pulse, its faint heartbeat. It was a thrilling experience and it worked faster and better if he was alone. He felt at home in the woods, felt part of a larger world, a secret world that was shared by animals and trees and birds, even the fish in the streams. It was a powerful feeling. It made his muscles feel sleek and tireless, it made his step light, his hearing and sight acute. The forest changed him and he exulted in the magical world of his own senses, the opening of secrets that always followed once he left civilization and its trappings behind.

His stomach fluttered, but he was on the trail.

It was better than sitting back there with strangers, waiting for something else to happen. He marked the sun's position. He followed bent twigs, ground broken so slightly it strained his eyes to see the tracks, but they were there. He moved slow, stopping often to listen behind a tree. He put a kerchief to the ground and put his ear to it. He heard no sounds, but he had often heard deer moving around by doing just that. It was something he had learned from old Silas Morgan back in Virginia. He wished Silas was with him now. Lem had never hunted Indians before. He didn't know what he'd do if he found one. Would he shoot him? It was something to study, all right. Shooting a man, that was something he hadn't figured on. But, he knew Silas would, after what had happened to his kinfolk.

He thought about the dead man back there at the camp. That was reason enough to kill an Indian. Maybe he would think about that man if he ran across any redskins. Maybe that would help him pull the trigger when it came time to take a man's life.

The birds stopped singing suddenly. It grew quiet as a graveyard. Lem's senses perked up as if he'd been stung in the eye.

The stillness seeped through him, but he resisted its sleeping-powder allure. He listened, as always when it was so quiet in the woods, for the sounds beneath sounds, the faint stirrings of leaves, the quiver of a sapling's branch, the muffled tread of a footfall. Lem held his breath, strained his ears to pick up the undertones that would warn him of another human's presence in the forest.

He heard it then, a low wheezing sound, the whispery prattle of a sapling brushed in passing—by an animal, a deer, maybe, or a man. He put his ear to the ground and listened as a surgeon would listen to a man's chest for a heartbeat.

Lem crept forward, careful to step softly and avoid brushing his buckskins against a leaf or bare branch. He moved when he heard sound, froze when the forest steeped itself in stillness once again. His ears tracked the direction of the sounds. As near as he could figure, there were two men, or two deer, stepping carefully through the woods. He guessed he had found his Indians because he would have expected even a wary deer to make more noise, to crack a dry twig or overturn a stone. He heard none of these sounds. Instead, they were as furtive as any noises he'd ever heard.

The two sounds drifted apart and he knew the Indians, if that was who was making the sneak, had split up. This made his tracking more dangerous. Lem hunched low, held his rifle slanted in front of him, frizzen closed down tight, thumb on the hammer.

He moved closer, towards the last sound he had heard. He crept as silently as a panther, his eyes narrowed to shut out the sunlight. He heard a grunt and froze.

That's when he saw the feathers, dangling from a man's scalp lock. He saw only part of the back of a head, and the feathers.

And a single bronze arm glistening sleek in the sun.

5

Lem felt his blood surge out of his brain fast as rain down a waterspout. He felt lightheaded, giddy as a kid sipping fermented cider. His temples drummed with a rapid thunder.

His heart turned wild as a flushed timberdoodle, seemed as if it would jump from his chest cage. The Indian, standing next to a scaly bark hickory, was so gaudy with feathers and orange roach, Lem had the almost uncontrollable urge to rub the bright pigments from his eyes.

The tip of his nose began to itch from an unseen irritation. A gnat discovered the glassy water of his eye, flew at it like a miller against a lighted windowpane.

The Indian seemed part of the tree, part of the forest. Lem stretched his neck and more of the savage came into view. Still, he could see only the bare bronze of the Indian's back, the bright plumage dangling like a gutted ring-necked pheasant from his stiff roach, the long rifle in his hand studded with brass tacks along its stock, a single goose feather twirling on a thong attached to the frontplate. The Indian wore a breechclout over his deerskin leggings, a knife in a beaded leather sheath. An iron tomahawk jutted from a wide, colorful cloth sash that girded his midsection.

A bird called. Lem didn't move. Another bird answered with a short melodic trill. This call was closer, and Lem saw the Indian's head move slightly. That's when Hawke saw the other Indian, forty-some yards beyond, crouched behind a grassy mound, ferns and saplings sprouting profusely in emerald fountains over its surface.

In the distance, Lem heard a heavy pounding, a clang of metal against wood. He realized that he had been tracking in a wide arc, returning to his starting point along a ragged half-circle. The settlers' camp could not be far away. The Indians, he was sure, meant to double back and do them harm. The prickle in his nostril increased to a maddening degree.

Lem wriggled the tip of his nose, willing the itch away. The gnat stung the corner of his eye, stuck in the viscous fluid. Finally, it freed itself and Lem's eye swam as his tear ducts flowed to soothe the irritation.

Two of them, his mind whispered.

Both Indians carried long rifles. They had a pair of shots to his single. If he shot one, the other could shoot him. Fear strangled Hawke's thoughts, twisted his innards into knots. It was one thing to track them; another to see them so close, alive and breathing and armed. His lungs ached until he realized he was holding his breath. He let the dead air out slow and batted his eyelids. Slowly, his normal vision returned, but the one eye itched worse than his nose.

Maybe there were more than two, he thought. Maybe there was a whole band of them sneaking up on the travelers, ready to pounce on them. His nose started to run. He dared not sniff nor blow to clear it. Sweat trickled down his chest underneath his buckskins. A thousand little annoyances plagued his flesh and he was powerless to attend to the least of them.

The Indian farthest away moved into the underbrush, disappeared. A few moments later, Lem heard the *toowit tweet tweedle* of another artificial bird call. The Indian closest to Hawke replied with a replica of the same call.

It was then that Lem heard the singing.

The hackles rose on the back of his neck. The Indian, too, seemed startled. He slid around in back of the tree, exposing more of his body to Lem.

The settlers' voices were lifted in song. Lem could just make out the words.

"We shall gather at the river," they sang, and Lem could picture them in his mind, all standing around the fresh grave, with their Bibles and their hymnals, oblivious to the danger in the forest, just singing away as if they was in church back in Virginia or at a Sunday arbor meeting down by the creek.

Lem wondered if he should shoot the Indian. He could see all of him now. That would bring the other one a-runnin', and by God, he'd have to load and prime real fast, faster than he ever had before. Someone, maybe his pa, had once told him that during the Revolutionary War, the British soldiers could load a musket in twelve seconds. That was powerful fast. He had tried it a time or two, counting seconds, and the closest he could come was nearly twice that. And that was by himself, with nobody a-runnin' at him fixin' to kill him dead. If one of those Indians came after him, he didn't think he could reload inside of twenty-five seconds or so. He would probably be so scared he'd shake to death before the other buck could come up on him. But, at least the settlers would hear the shot and maybe a couple of the men would have sense enough to pick up their rifles and get the kids and womenfolk hid out.

What if he missed? He was so scared now, he didn't know if he could hold his barrel steady. That redskin was so close he could smell him and he looked oversized and fierce with all that paint and feathers, those glistening muscles rippling under his ruddy skin.

Lem held still, knowing that if he fired his rifle, it might be the last thing he ever did. He wasn't afraid of missing, not at this range. He figured he might not have time to reload before that other Indian came up out of the brush and shot him or brained him with his iron tomahawk. It was a decision he made suddenly, not out of fear so much as from practicality. Maybe this Indian would join the other one and he could sneak up behind them both. Knowing there were at least two Indians and one of them out of sight tilted the odds in the redskins' favor.

The Indian took the decision out of Lemuel's hands.

The buck turned, looked straight at Hawke. Lem felt the redskin's eyes boring into him like a pair of fire-tipped skewers.

The Indian raised his rifle before Lem could recover from the shock of being discovered. The motion was so smooth and flawless, Hawke just stood there as if he was mired in wet clay. It seemed to take the Indian no time at all. One minute he was looking the other way, the next he had a long rifle pointed straight at Lem. Hawke felt his stomach sink four feet past his belt line, clear down to the tips of his boot moccasins. His head floated a foot above his shoulders.

Lem heard the click of the cocking hammer. It seemed as if he could hear the sear engage inside the massive lock on the rifle. He heard the report, saw an orange flame spew from the barrel, blossom into a bright, hideous flower. He heard the thunk of the ball as it smacked into the bark of the tree next to him, heard it rip wood like a crosscut saw. Chunks of bark spanked the side of Lem's head; slivers and splinters sliced into his face and forehead. He closed his eyes involuntarily, flinched at the sharp suddenness of the pain.

The Indian was obscured by a cloud of white smoke when Lem opened his eyes. Then, he heard the underbrush crash with the flail of the buck's body as he charged straight toward Hawke.

Lem lifted his rifle, knowing there was no time to get off a shot. The Indian dropped his spent rifle, drew his tomahawk. He leaped over bushes, smashed through tough young saplings like a man splashing across a shallow creek. As Hawke brought his rifle up to his shoulder, thumb poised to hammer back, the Indian loomed less than five yards away, his lips flayed back from his carious wolf teeth, his face a painted, scarifying mask, more animal than human.

In that single terrifying moment, time fractured into chunks like mud flying off a wagon wheel. Lem saw everything happen in pieces, isolated fragments that seemed separate yet were all part of the same thing. It seemed as if he had no power over himself, that his movements came from outside himself. He did not think of what he must do. His body worked like something magical. His hands and feet moved of their own accord. There was no thinking at all. His mind was frozen in time, locked on that horrible face. Only his body was free and it performed as if it had been trained for just one single task: to kill a man.

Lem brought his rifle up, but it seemed to weigh more than a hundred pounds. It was so heavy and moved so slowly, some part of his mind knew he would never make it. There was no time to cock the hammer back. The Indian bounded over that last five or six feet like a bolting deer with its tail afire.

Hawke felt the rifle sting his palms as the Indian swung his tomahawk like a flailing scythe. The rifle spun out of his hands, the lock rattling with the dry metallic sound of shot in a tin cup. Lem's right hand shot downward in a spearing dive for the knife in its sheath. He crouched as he jerked the blade free, turned the sharp tip toward the charging savage.

Lem lunged, shoving the knife forward. The Indian tried

to bring the tomahawk back to a striking position, but his right flank was exposed. Hawke shoved the blade of his knife into the soft flesh beneath the buck's ribs. He brought up his left hand and grasped the Indian's throat, throttled him.

The redskin grunted and twisted free of the knife. Lem felt blood spurt over his knuckles, warm and slick as oil. He squeezed the Indian's neck, his fingers tightening in a vise-grip as both fell to the ground, mashing the brush down with the weight of their bodies. The Indian rolled, trying to break free of the white man's grip. Lem drove the knife into the small of the brave's back, hammering it home to the hilt with a powerful thrust. The Indian kicked out, tried to capture Lem's legs in a scissor-lock. Lem twisted the knife, pushed hard to cut across the gristle of the buck's back muscles. He felt the red man thrash as he tried to escape the skewering blade, free Lem's grip on his throat.

The knife would not move. Lem jerked it from the Indian's back, swung it back over the man's belly. He slammed it hard into the buck's diaphragm, drew it toward him. He sliced through to the warrior's intestines, felt the coils pour over his hand like a clutch of water snakes. A terrible stench, mindful of a disemboweled hog, assailed Lem's nostrils. He felt the Indian shudder, his body go slack. He squeezed the throat again, but felt no response. He kicked away from the dead Indian, pushing him away as he rose unsteadily to his feet.

Panting, Hawke looked down at the limp body of the Indian. Excitement thrummed his veins, a giddy exhilaration smothered him until he managed to draw a deep breath into his lungs. He wiped the bloody blade of his knife on the right legging of his buckskins, sheathed it without thinking. He retrieved his rifle, flipped open the frizzen, checked the coating of powder in the pan. He clamped the frizzen back down and crouched there in the brush, listening, trying to hear above the booming throb of his heart.

He squeezed the trigger slightly, thumbed back the hammer. The lock made the faintest tink as the sear engaged at full cock. Hawke waited, strangling on the fear clotting his throat. He looked at the dead brave again in disbelief. The Indian lay there with his innards covering his groin in shiny gray coils. Flies peppered the intestines like miniature vultures. He heard their annoying buzzes as they fed on the offal from a knife-torn section of gut.

Lem crawled slowly to a position behind a tree, some ten or twelve yards from the slain Indian. He looked at his bloody hands, swiped his forehead with his sleeve as sweat stung his eyes. There was a bloodstain on the front of his buckskins, bright as a new swatch of cloth.

Lem dug a round ball from his possibles pouch, fished out a round patch pre-cut from a small bolt of mattress cloth. He centered the ball on the patch, tucked both in his mouth like a wad of tobacco.

Then, he heard the bird sound.

Toowit tweet tweedle.

Hell, thought Lemuel. *I can do that.*

He pursed his lips, gave the whistle.

It sounded just like the other Indian's call, he thought.

A strange calm came over him. He knew, somehow, that the other Indian would come. He knew, also, that there were only two. Only one now. Lem readied his rifle, peered in the direction of camp, where he had heard the last fake bird call.

But the other Indian didn't come in from that direction. He had circled to Hawke's right, and if he hadn't made a noise, Lem would never have heard him.

The Indian called out in a low, gutteral voice. A moment later, he whistled another bird call. Lem swung around silently, brought his rifle up halfway to his shoulder. He waited, alert to any sound.

The Indian crept forward, hunched over. He struck an unerring path to the place where the dead Indian had been.

He seemed intent on finding his companion. This Indian was some younger than the one Lem had killed. He was no less fearsome.

Lem brought his rifle up, seated the butt in the hollow between his shoulder and chest. Then, he puckered his lips and gave a similar low whistle.

The Indian stood up full-length, his orange roach bristling like a Hampshire red hog's hackles.

Lem dropped the sights on the Indian's chest, cradled the trigger with his finger. When the front and rear sights lined up, Hawke took a shallow breath, held it, then caressed the trigger, drawing it gently toward him. The hammer struck the frizzen plate, showering the pan with golden sparks. There was a puff of smoke, a sound like someone blowing on a dandelion. The fire exploded through the touchhole, igniting the main powder charge in the chamber. The rifle bucked in Lem's hands as 90 grains of coarse black powder exploded. A cloud of white smoke rushed out behind the rocketing flash of orange sparks.

Hawke heard a low grunt, jerked himself up to his feet, clawing for his powder horn. Frantically, he poured powder down the rifle barrel, just guessing at the measure. He spat out the ball and patch, thumbed them into the muzzle. He pulled the short starter from his belt, started the ball down the barrel with the long end, pounded it with the heel of his palm. He jerked the ramrod from its mooring, rammed it down the barrel. He jerked it downward with both hands, then pushed it against the tree to seat the ball. He pulled the ramrod free, let it drop to the ground. Quickly, he primed the pan with a small horn, blew away the excess grains, slammed the frizzen shut.

When the smoke cleared, Lem stood behind the tree, ready for another shot.

There was no sound.

Lem whistled.

No answer.

He whistled again, louder this time.

Still no answering toodle. He stepped out from behind the tree. Wisps of smoke drifted skyward like torn shreds of gossamer, like the conical shrouds of webworms.

A crashing of brush drew his guarded attention. He stepped toward the spot where he had drawn bead on the younger Indian. He heard white men's voices. *Christ,* he thought, *they make a lot of noise.*

The Indian was not dead, but blood and foam bubbled out of a hole in his chest. The warrior lay flat on his back, staring up at Lem with a venemous look of rage in his black eyes. The ball had entered just to the right of the Indian's thorax. Splinters of a rib bone jutted through the blue-black hole.

As Lem looked down at him, the mortally wounded Indian shuddered as if gripped by a sudden pain. His mouth opened wide and he seemed to be trying to breathe in more air. A fleeting shadow passed across the Indian's face. His eyes closed for a moment, opened again, glazed with that same wet patina Lem had seen in the eyes of wounded animals. The dying man was in pain, he knew. Pink foam, blood saturated with air bubbles, oozed from the chest wound.

The Indian couldn't have been much older than Lem himself. Perhaps, he thought, the other warrior was this one's father. There was a resemblance, beyond their costumes, their painted markings. Their noses were built out of the same mold, their faces shaped the same. Brothers, maybe. One much older than the other, anyways.

The brush crashed and Lem turned toward the sound for a moment.

"Hawke!"

Someone was calling his name.

"Over here," yelled Lem. He turned back to the wounded Indian.

The redskin's eyes flared and he lifted both his arms.

He struggled to rise. Halfway up to a sitting position, he fell back and a low sigh escaped from his lips. His eyes bulged with one last look, then the glow in them faded like dead coals turning to ash. His body went slack and the blood stopped leaking from the hole in his chest.

"Jesus Gawdamighty!" hollered Ormly Shields as he bounded gangly as a wobbly-legged colt through the leafy undergrowth toward Hawke. He carried his rifle at the ready. "You get 'em, boy?"

Behind him, Dick Hauser scrambled to keep up with his long-legged partner, rifle held across his chest at a slant, possibles pouch and powder horns slapping against his buckskins.

Ormly stopped where the first Indian lay dead. He wet his lips, looked long and hard at the knife wounds. Then, he looked at Lem with something like raw wonder in his eyes. His gaze lingered over the bloodstains on Hawke's 'skins. He chewed at a nonexistent cud in his mouth.

"That the other'n?" he husked.

Lem nodded, eased the hammer of his rifle back down off of cock. He leaned against a water oak, swabbed sweat off his forehead with a swipe of a bloody finger.

Hauser halted in his tracks, stared down at the dead Indian Lem had knifed.

"You gut him like that?" he asked Hawke, that same distant rasp in his voice.

"He come at me," said Lem. "No time to shoot him."

Ormly walked over, inspected the other Indian. He leaned down, turned him over. There was a hole in the young buck's back the size of a sugar beet. A pool of blood lay beneath the body, already growing a skin as it dried.

"Hoo de haw," breathed Ormly. "You got him good. Both'n of 'em. Judas, I never seed such doin's."

Dick looked at the younger Indian as Ormly stepped back, drew his knife. He let out a low whistle.

"Them is prime bucks," he said.

"Those the ones you saw?" asked Hawke.

"I reckon," said Hauser. "They all look pretty much the same to me."

"You want their rifles, Hawke?" asked Shield.

"What for?"

"Why, you can brag on 'em, or sell 'em."

Hawke's stomach turned over like a griddle cake. It didn't seem right robbing the dead. He wanted nothing to do with the Indians. He'd see them enough in his dreams, day or night. The young one, the way he had looked at him, well, he wouldn't forget the glare in his eyes for a long time. He felt a queasy swirl in his stomach.

"Naw, you keep 'em."

"What about their hair?" asked Hauser.

"Huh?" asked Lem.

"Why, looky them orange bristles, proud as peacocks. Braggin' fodder what to carry on yore belt."

Ormly grinned, drew his knife. He knelt down and started cutting through the young buck's scalp. Lem knew he was going to be sick if he stayed there.

"You cut them nut bags off, Dick," said Ormly. "Hoo de haw, we done got us some prime souvenirs."

"One of them scalps is mine," said Hauser.

Lem walked away, the sounds of the scavengers' grisly banter fading as he made his way back to the wagons.

He couldn't make sense out of it. Which of them, the Indians or the white men, were the savages?

6

Emma Hauser, Dick's wife, gasped when she saw Lem enter the clearing, the front of his buckskins covered with blood, rifle over his shoulder. The others peeked from hiding places behind their wagons. Snouts of rifles dropped from view, or tilted toward the sky as Lem walked across the sward.

"Look at the blood. He's been shot!"

Lem saw a woman standing behind a wagon wheel, pointing at him. He looked around for Roberta. There was no sign of her. His wagon was gone.

"Poor man."

"Where's my Dick?" screeched Emma Hauser.

"And Ormly. Where's Ormly?" Lucasta Shield came running toward Hawke, awkward as a goose, her skirt billowing about her short stocky legs, her bonnet and its sash flapping like wounded swans. She looked like a washerwoman's clothesline in the swirling zephyrs of a dust devil. "Have they kilt my man?"

"Them two's out in the woods yet," said Lem. "They ain't been kilt."

"We heard a shot," said a boy crawling out from under one of the wagons, his rifle pointed carelessly at Lem.

"Son, you better p'int that fusil in another direction," said Lem. The boy, his face sanguine with embarrassment, pulled the rifle toward him, laid it under the wagon.

"Did you see any Indians?" asked another boy, peering from behind a flour barrel.

"A couple," said Lem. He saw his horse, Hammerhead, tied to a tree just inside the fringe of woods. He turned to the woman who had rushed out to question him about Ormly Shield. "Where'd my woman go?" he asked.

"Why, her brother come and got her," said Lucasta Shield. "She went on ahead with him."

"Her brother?"

"Why, yes. I believe his name was Barry. He come riding up on a mule just after you went a-huntin'. They seemed in an all-fired hurry. Didn't even stay to help us bury poor Mr. Dowell. He said somethin' about their sister-in-law bein' ill."

Lem looked at the fresh grave.

"I'm right sorry, Ma'am. Was he kin to you?"

"No. Ormly Shield's my man. You say he—he's in no fix?"

"I reckon not."

He heard the brush crackle, turned to see Ormly and Dick emerge from the woods. Their arms were full with booty taken from the Indians: rifles, knives, moccasins, sashes, beaded pouches—and a pair of bloody scalps. The kids rushed forward, passing the women and men who had emerged from hiding. Hogs grunted; sheep bleated. Hammerhead whickered, switched his tail.

Lem felt the ground quiver and fall out from under him. A fleeting giddiness temporarily addled his thoughts. What was Barry O'Neil doing back here? And why did Roberta tell these people he was her brother? Why had he taken her away? None of it made sense to him. He regained his balance, staggered toward Hammerhead. The horse eyed him with a baleful look of suspicion.

Roberta hadn't left him much. He searched through the saddlebags. At least she hadn't taken anything. His canteen hung from the saddle horn. He had powder and ball, plenty of flints. Not a scrap of food.

The murmur of voices seemed distant to him as he sagged against a tree, rested his rifle on its butt. The dizziness left him, but his gut swirled with fear. He couldn't imagine Roberta riding off like that, not even saying goodbye. She must have had a pretty good reason. Maybe Barry O'Neil's sister-in-law was ailing and that's why she had left. Lem remembered Barry saying something about traveling with his brother and his family. But why did she tell it that Barry was her brother? That didn't make no sense at all. Seems like she would have told someone where she'd gone so he wouldn't worry none.

He thought of Barry O'Neil. He had never expected to see the man again. He was just someone they had come across along the trail, like a lot of others. Except there was something different about this one. He pestered a man like a fruit fly. Persistent as dust in a spinster's parlor.

Lem heard his name mentioned, turned to look at the people milling around Ormly and Dick. Dick pointed his way and everyone looked at him. Ormly beckoned to him.

"Hawke," said Shield, "we got something to put to you."

Lem walked over, leaving his rifle leaning against the tree. The people's faces swam like tethered buoys. He was beginning to feel sick over Roberta leaving like that, just up and following O'Neil like a puppy after a stranger with grub in his pocket.

"Yeah?" Lem said.

"We want you to lead us on to Kentucky," said Hauser. "Everybody's agreed. The way you took care of those two redskins."

"We'd be much obliged," said Mrs. Hauser, her face shaded by the brim of her bonnet.

"I reckon I got to go on by myself," said Lem. "My wife . . ."

"Surely, she'll wait for you up ahead," said Emma.

"Uh, well, she may need me," Lem said awkwardly.

"We're ready to go," said Ormly. "You lead the way."

Lem saw the anticipation in their faces. Even the children looked at him oddly, their faces scrooched up quizzically, eyes squinted against the sun. He felt very uncomfortable, itchy uncomfortable, like a man facing a jury, awaiting their verdict. The man who had been hurt now seemed to be all right. He, too, was standing there with his mouth open, his wife hanging on to him as if she were afraid he'd up and leave her. The other men seemed to be standing in their wives' shadows, taller than their children, but still little boys.

"I want to see the dead Indians," said a small boy, breaking into the silence.

"Yes, Pa, I want to see 'em too," said another, looking up at Dick Hauser.

Other children picked up the refrain and their voices rose in chorus. Hauser and Shield began to retreat as the children surged toward them, all clamoring at once. Their mothers raced after them, but they slipped out of each woman's grasp like tadpoles.

"We want to see the dead Indians!" the children screamed, over and over, and finally their mothers threw up their hands and gave in. Boys tugged at their fathers' buckskins and dragged them toward the woods. Ormly escaped the clutches of three children and ran to a wagon, depositing his booty inside. Dick Hauser gave his Indian rifle to his wife, and Emma scurried away toward her wagon.

Lem watched as the travelers bunched up and headed across the sward, determined to see the two butchered Indians. Hawke shook his head and turned away from them.

"Look, Hawke, we got to let the kids see them two redskins or they won't give us no peace. You come too. Take your mind off your troubles."

Lem looked at Ormly in total bewilderment. He heard the words, but he could not digest them. Hawke shook his head.

"Suit yourself, Hawke. We'll likely catch up to you by the by."

Lem strode to Hammerhead, grabbed up his rifle. He heard the voices fading as he swung up into the saddle. He laid the rifle across his legs, turned the horse into the clearing. He saw Ormly running to catch up to the crowd disappearing into the woods. In a moment, he was gone. He heard the children gabbling like a flock of gray geese long after he rode away from the wagon stop, and then there was only the susurrus of the afternoon humming in his ears above the steady clop of Hammerhead's hooves on the rutted trail to Kentucky.

* * *

His kisses flared on her bare neck like a heat rash. She writhed in his torrid embrace, her breasts swelling in his sweaty palms, the nipples hardening at his touch, heating up like walnuts in a roasting pan.

"Stop it, Barry. No! Get your hands off me!"

"Too late for that, woman. You got me in a rut."

Roberta slapped at him, struggled to crawl out from under his crushing weight.

"My dress is going to be smeared with grass stains," she said incongruously.

Barry laughed and tugged at the bodice of her dress, exposing more of the flesh of her breasts. She tried to roll away from him. His fingernails clawed the soft skin of her breast. Roberta shrieked, began to kick wildly.

"What's the matter with you, Roberta? You wanted it bad enough the other night."

"No, no I didn't," she sobbed breathlessly. "I—I was just . . ."

How could she tell him? It sounded so silly, so stupid in the light of day. She had entertained his attention, his affections, but she never thought it would lead to this—this attack in broad daylight. She had let him kiss her and caress her, but she never dreamed she'd ever see him again. He said he and his brother and their family were leaving in the morning. There was no need to give any more of herself to him than she had. It was nice to be held and hugged and kissed, but she had not wanted to violate her marriage vows. It was wicked enough just letting Barry go as far as he had. Now, she realized that he expected more. And, he had lied to her. There was nothing wrong with his sister-in-law. They were probably way ahead and once Barry had his way with her, he would leave.

"You teased me," he husked, his mouth breathing hot in her ear.

"No, I didn't mean to. Barry, let me go. If Lemuel catches you . . ."

"He'll what? He'll laugh, Roberta. He knows what I know. You want it. You want it from every man you meet. I saw it the other night. I saw it today. I knew you wanted me and your husband couldn't satisfy you."

Anger boiled inside her, tore at her heart with razor-sharp talons. Barry O'Neil had no right to say those things about Lemuel. Yes, she had been infatuated with the stranger, but she didn't think a little harmless flirtation would turn him into a savage. He had brought her to this glade off the trail under false pretenses. He had lied to her, and now he was attacking her husband.

She jerked away from him. She felt her bodice rip, but she broke his clutch on her breasts, at least.

"I'm having his baby!" she cried hysterically. "He's my husband." She broke into sobs. She knew that what she said made no sense. But anything, anything to get Barry to leave her alone. "Liar, liar, liar!" she screamed.

She kicked him away from her, tugged at her torn blouse. Tears glazed her cheeks, soaked through her closed eyelids.

"Look what you've done to my dress," she sobbed. "What will my husband say?"

She stared at Barry, at the squinch of his face, the little powder-duster moustache, the greedy eyes, the slash of his mouth, and wondered at herself. She wondered at her brazen behavior, the submerged lust inside her that he had drawn out, first in the darkness of a firelit meadow and now in the harsh, glaring light of day.

It seemed to her that this was happening not to her, but to someone else. This was not she squatting soiled in a great forest, her dress smeared with grass stains, her bodice torn open, her breasts exposed to Barry's hungry eyes. Yet, she could feel his hand burning on each of her breasts, feel the burn of his kisses on her neck, the scratch of his moustache on her face.

"Go away," she pleaded. "Leave me alone. I—I hate you. I never want to see you again."

"Yes, you do," he gruffed. "You want it, Roberta. You want me to do it to you."

"No," she said, and buried her face in her hands, buried her face in shame. "Just go away."

She heard him, then. Heard him chuckle to himself, heard the rustle of leaves as he rose to his feet. She knew she could not face him again. She clutched her shorn bodice to her breasts and heard her heart thump hollow in her ears as if it was going to tear through her chest and punish her for being a fool. She deserved to die, she thought at that moment. She deserved to have her heart break open like a melon and gush its blood like a fountain.

She heard his footsteps as he walked away; heard him mount his mule. She heard the rustle of leather as he slapped the reins against the animal's neck. She heard the soft pad of the mule's hoofbeats on grass.

"You come see me in Lexington," Barry called to her. "You come see me when you grow up, Roberta."

And then his laughter, soft and disembodied, shredding the empty ocean sounds in her ears, kneading the thump sound of her heart until it quieted.

She pulled her legs up close to her, wrapped her arms around them for steadiness. She held her eyes tightly closed until she no longer heard the mule's plodding footpads, no longer heard the echoes of her heart's pounding.

Lemuel rode up on her. She heard him coming, raised her head. She looked to see him guide Hammerhead over to her. She saw the bloody stains on his buckskins and looked for the deer across the saddle. She saw no game, even when he dismounted, tied his reins to a sapling, laid his rifle down as he knelt beside her.

"You been cryin'," he said.

She sniffed, avoided his gaze. She just couldn't look at

him. Not now, with the shame inside her. He could probably see it blooming on her face like some wicked flower, like a huge red flower with bright red petals. She heaved with a sudden, involuntary breath and it caught in her throat like a bone, choked her for a moment.

"Well, I come after you," he said after a moment and he sat down beside her as if it was the most natural thing in the world and she stole a glance at him to see if he was angry, to see if he was going to slap her. "They said you went off with that Barry feller and I come after you, Bobbie."

"Yes, Lem. I—I'm glad you did."

"Did he run off?"

"I told him to go. I hate him."

She looked at him, then, let her eyes meet his just to see if he was angered, just to see if he meant to beat her with his fists.

"I hate him, too," Lem said softly.

She felt something dark inside of her brighten. It seemed, then, as if Lemuel was the sweetest, most understanding husband in the world. She reached out, touched his arm. She needed that steadiness just now. She needed to weld the sudden bond between them.

Her fingers clasped his wrist, tightened. He laid his other hand atop hers and patted her reassuringly.

"You tore your dress," he said.

She looked down at her breast, expecting to see Barry's finger marks all over it. But the skin of her breast was white and smooth and the nipple had lost its tumescence, had flattened into its round nest like a nightjar setting on eggs, all brown and sleepy in the sun.

"Oh, Lem. He—he was so mean. I—I kicked him. I hit him."

"You want me to fetch your sewing things?"

"No. I'll put on something else." She pulled the dress up with her free hand, covered her breast. She didn't want Lem to look at it. She didn't want him to think about Barry seeing her like that.

"We can set here long as you want," he told her, and it seemed to her that he was saying he wouldn't accuse her of being bad, that he was not going to punish her for running off from him like that. "There ain't no hurry, really."

"Lem," she said, something breaking down in her, breaking apart without her being able to stop it, "I'm scared. Scared of myself, scared of you, scared of everyone and everything. Do you—do you know what I mean?"

"Sometimes we all get scared of things. Mostly things we can't see, don't know nothin' about. Mostly things we can't put a name to."

"Yes, that's what it's like. You do understand. I'm scared of something I can't see, something deep inside me that I can't find."

"And no name to it," he said, looking off beyond her, beyond the sunlight in her hair, the look of terror in her red-rimmed eyes.

"I don't know what it is," she said, squeezing his arm, pulling on him as if to draw herself inside him where it was safe.

"Be better if you could call it out in the open. Take a look at it, maybe. Put a name to it."

"Your ma tell you that?"

"My grandma. When I was a kid, afraid of the dark and all kinds of boogers. My grandma was real sick and I guess that's what I was afeard of. Afeard she was goin' to die and I couldn't tell anyone about that because I was scared if I did she really would die. My grandma told me it didn't make any difference what I said or didn't say. She was going to die anyways, and she did. But I got so I wasn't afeard of the dark no more."

"I'm still afraid of the dark," she said. "It's easier when you're there with me, but I always had to see a candle burning or have the lamp lighted before I could close my eyes and sleep."

"You got to get over that, Bobbie. Ain't nothin' can hurt you, 'less you let it."

"Grandma?"

He laughed.

"No, my grandpa told me that, after my ma run off. We was poor and he worked for a rich man. This rich man had a kid what made fun of me and called me a beggar boy and it hurt so much I used to bawl my eyes out ever' night until my grandpa got on me about it."

"Then your grandpa died," she said.

"He died. Mule kicked him in the head and he died and I went and beat up that rich kid, knocked the ticking out of him."

"Why?"

"I wanted him to know I wasn't no beggar boy. I buried my grandpa next to my grandma and run off. I kilt that mule, too. The one what kilt my grandpa."

"I remember," she said, and laughed. "That's when I saw you. Hiding out from the sheriff."

"Well, we ain't hidin' out no more," he said, heaving a sigh. "We ain't got nothing to be afeard of, Bobbie. Not when we get to Kentucky. Not never again."

She felt her stomach swirl as a feeling of hope surged through her heart. Maybe, she thought, Lemuel was right. Perhaps there was no longer anything to fear. It might be that they could make a new life for themselves in Kentucky.

"Could we live in a city?" she asked. "In a clean and elegant house like decent folks? Could we ride in carriages and wear fine clothes? Maybe we could settle in Lexington and you could learn a trade, become a gentleman, and buy me French lace and china and take me to dine in places where they have linen tablecloths and silver knives and forks, candlelight and wine. We could buy a big house and there would be servants in livery where merchants could call

and show us their wares, where I could invite my friends
for tea in the afternoons, with a parlor and a sitting room.
I would wear jewelry and gowns and bright ribbons in my
hair . . ."

"Bobbie," he interrupted. "I'm a farmer. I got to find land
to lease and work. We got to buy stock and raise it for market. Where did you get these fool notions?"

She jerked her hand away from Lem's arm and covered
her mouth. She saw the look in his eyes and knew that she
had gone too far. She had said things to him that were
secret, that were so private she had never expressed them
to another human being.

"I know," she said, tightly, her lips pressed together so
hard they were bloodless. "I know what you got to do. But,
we don't always have to live poor, do we?"

"No. We can make a life for ourselves. We got a new
chance now. Just let us get to Kentucky with no more
trouble."

The space between them filled up with silence. Lem tore
off a sprig of grass, stuck it in his teeth. Roberta fiddled
with her torn bodice as if trying to bond it back together
with pressure from her fingers. Lem sucked on the grass
stem, looked at the light playing in his wife's hair.

"Yes," she said, after a moment, but the tightness was
still in her voice. She looked again at his buckskins, then
at his hands with blood caked on them like rust. "Did you
kill something when you went huntin'?" she asked.

"Almost the other way around," he replied. "Saw me two
real Indians out in the woods. They was fixin' to jump them
people again."

"What happened?"

"Oh, I got into some fur-pullin' with 'em. One come at
me with a knife. The other'n I shot."

"You killed two Indians?"

"Well, I didn't dance with 'em, Bobbie."

She looked again at the dried blood on his buckskins, at

the flakes on his hands. She looked at his knife in its sheath and tried to imagine what Lem had done. A sense of horror filled her, struck her mute.

There he sat, she thought, sucking on a blade of grass and he had just killed two men. He no longer looked like a boy who was still wet behind the ears. There was something hard and distant about him, something terrible and unexplainable inside him. She knew Lem wasn't a braggart. If he said he'd killed two Indians, then she believed him. Two Indians lay dead in the woods and he had killed them with his own hands. He had broken one of the commandments. He had taken a human life and it didn't seem to bother him at all. He showed no signs of remorse or repentance.

Roberta shuddered inwardly, quelled the feeling of panic that rose up in her. Her stomach twisted as if had been wrenched from its moorings. She felt it swimming around inside her abdomen. She knew she was going to be sick.

She stood up, ran to the wagon. She fell against one of the wheels and held onto the side. Her stomach turned over, then, and she began to retch. Nothing would come up, and yet her stomach kept contracting.

Lem came to her side, grabbed her shoulders.

"You sick?" he asked.

She squeezed a spoke of the wagon wheel, draining her knuckles of blood.

"Yes," she gasped. "I'm sick. I'm sick of men, sick of you, sick of everything. God, I'm sick."

"Is there somethin' I can do?"

"Take a bath," she spat. "Wash your filthy skins. Leave me alone."

"Christ, Bobbie . . ."

"And quit swearing like a dock walloper," she said, pulling herself to a standing position. She held her stomach, staggered to the front of the wagon. She climbed up, began to rummage through the bags. In a moment she pulled out a dress, began to stretch out the wrinkles.

"Well, what are you waiting for?" she asked. "Get your-self cleaned up. I can drive the wagon after I get changed. I'll meet you up ahead somewheres."

"I reckon I'll have to scout me up a creek."

"What's wrong with the one back there? Can't be more'n an hour's ride."

Lem shrugged. He started for his horse, stopped dead in his tracks.

"What's that?" Roberta asked, looking back up the road.

"Shh!" he said, holding up his hand.

The popping sounds seemed to come from just around the bend in the trail. They sounded like Chinese fire-crackers.

Then, they heard the sound of human voices. Men yell-ing, kids and women screaming. The hideous screeches of Indians.

The firing lasted for several seconds then stopped as abruptly as it had started.

The last thing they heard was the most terrible of all. A man screamed and screamed until they thought he would never stop.

He kept yelling: "No, Jesus God, no! Please, God!"

The stillness hardened over them like a pane of coffin glass.

7

Lem turned around, looked at Roberta. She stood in the wagon, clutching the wrinkled dress to her breast. She was shivering as if she had taken chill. Her teeth chattered and her eyes stared up the road, fixed on nothingness, fixed on the echoes of that last scream.

"I'm really scared now, Lem," said Roberta.

"I got to go back yonder, Bobbie."

"It's them people, ain't it?"

"Couldn't be nothin' else," he said.

"It's none of our business, Lem. We ought to go on. Get away from this place."

"Might some of 'em need help. You go on if you want. Or wait here."

"Don't leave me alone," she said, and sank down on a carpetbag in the wagon.

"You better get to changin' or sewin', Bobbie. I got to find out what all the ruckus was about back there."

"Wait—I—I'll go with you."

"Well, don't be dawdlin' none."

He listened to the stillness, the murmuring saw of insects, the empty-headed twitter of birds. He didn't look at Roberta as she changed her dress. He heard her, though, heard the restless shuffle of the mules in harness, the faint tap of leather against hide, the tink of metal bits and D rings.

He wondered what he'd find when he rode back up the trail. Those people hadn't ought to have lingered, he thought. They oughtn't to have gone into the woods to look at those dead bucks. Their curiosity might have cost 'em. Might have cost 'em dear.

"Lem, do we have to go back there? Can't we just go on about our own business? Please."

Hawke twisted at the waist, looked at Roberta. She had changed into the wrinkled dress, but stood in the wagon like a child afraid to climb down from a barn loft. Her face was shadowed by leaves, but he could feel her fear.

"I'll hobble them mules," he said, and walked over to the wagon. He reached into the bed, got the rope hobbles from a box of spare harness. Roberta climbed down as he tied the last knot, stood nearby all pouted up as if to begin whimpering.

"What do you think happened?" she asked, her voice quaky.

"I think them folks got into some bad trouble," he told her.

"Indians?"

"Likely. I won't know till I look, Bobbie."

"I don't want—I can't—look at them if—if'n they're dead."

"Me neither. But, we can't just ride off as if none of this ever happened. We got to find out."

He stood up and she heaved a deep, quavering sigh. He wondered if she was going to make up her mind on her own. He could see that she was wrestling with it. People didn't scream like that less'n they was bein' got after. Kids didn't cry out for no reason. If he rode on, though, he'd always wonder what had happened to those folks. He'd always hate himself for not helping them what needed help. If any of them was still alive.

"We wait much longer, we might end up in misery worse'n them," he said, and if that didn't convince her, he was going on back by himself.

"All right. But, I don't want to look. Don't make me look at nobody dead, Lem. I seen one die already and that was just horrible. Just to see him die like that. One minute alive, the next they was puttin' him in the ground."

Lem wanted to slap her, but said nothing. He took Roberta's hand and led her over to Hammerhead. He helped her up into the saddle, grateful that she had stopped yammering like an idiot child. He climbed up behind her, snugging his crotch up under the bony cantle. He rode over to the tree, leaned over to snatch up his rifle.

They rode back up the leaf-shadowed trail, neither of them speaking. He felt Roberta's shoulders tremble against his arms. Hammerhead balked just before they rounded the second bend in the trail. Lem thumped the horse's flanks with the heels of his moccasins.

The horse almost stepped on the goat. The dead carcass lay alongside the trail, its head nearly severed from its body.

Hammerhead sidestepped the carcass, began to bristle as a shiver coursed its spine.

At first, the Hawkes saw only the scattered garments. The clothing looked as if it had been blown from a drying line, or hurled against the brush, tossed into the branches of the trees. A woman's bonnet flapped silently from a quivering bush. A child's pale blue shirt hung from a sapling's thin limb; a man's hat, the crown crushed, lay in the center of the trail surrounded by kerchiefs and undergarments in disarray. Boxes and trunks and crude wooden toys littered the grass for fifty yards like flotsam in a ship's wake.

Lem reined in Hammerhead when he saw the first human body.

"You better wait here," he said, swinging a leg down.

"What is it?"

"I just saw something."

He helped Roberta dismount. He held on to her for a moment when her knees buckled and gave way. He felt her trembling. He wrapped the reins around a low limb, checked the rifle's pan for primer. An eerie stillness clung to the spot, spooky, like the silence of a graveyard.

Lem didn't recognize the woman at first. Her face was caved in, her brains leaking from a massive hole in the top of her skull. His stomach lurched and he fought to keep the bile from gushing up into his throat. The woman was lying face up, her dress rumpled up around her waist exposing her naked privates. There was a hole the size of a man's fist in her chest. Part of a breast had been blown away by the exiting rifle ball. Shreds of cloth from her dress clung to the wound. He recognized her as Dick Hauser's wife by her dress. They had driven part of a tree limb up into her womb and it stuck out of her obscenely.

He turned away from the woman and began to see them all, parts of them, in the grasses, hanging from the wagons, lying among the dead horses and cattle. The Indians seemed to have slaughtered everything that was alive. Sheep and hogs, cows and horses, chickens and goats, all lay within a radius of a hundred yards from where Lem stood in stunned disbelief.

He saw a man, what was left of him, sitting under a bloody tree, his teeth knocked out, his eyes gouged from their sockets. They had sliced away all signs of his manhood and stuffed his bag and penis in his mouth. There was a large patch of hair missing from his scalp. Flies ragged the torn spot like ants at the grease pail.

Lem stalked the killing ground, finding children and dogs, pigs, goats, along a line of flight that resembled an abattoir. He had never seen so much blood. It streaked the grass, spattered the leaves in the brush like barn paint. The attacking Indians had spared no one, it seemed, although Lem didn't count or try to identify every corpse. Some of the horses were gone, perhaps some of the stock. What they hadn't taken with them as booty, they had slaughtered.

One faceless man's body recked of urine. Both of his hands had been cut off. His genitals, too, had been carved away, and his heart had been cut from his chest. Lem could no longer hold down the sickness. He caved in against a tree and heaved up the hot bile.

"Lem, are you there?" He heard Roberta calling him and he knew he had to get her away from this place. He couldn't even bury these poor people. There were arms and legs strewn through the brush, ears and heads all around him like garbage in a pigsty.

His stomach contracted as he staggered away from a young man's mutilated body. He could no longer look at the women. So far as he could tell, they were all dead. The Indians had probably not taken any captives. Maybe that was the only mercy they had showed, finally. He shuddered to think of a woman alive with such men. He looked at an eye lying in the open and his mind shrieked with outrage.

It might have been a child's eye, it was so small and hideous, strangely bloodless in the impassive flicker of sunlight through the leaves.

"Christ," he swore, and stumbled back toward Roberta, who stood by the horse, her eyes covered with her hands. He wondered how much she had seen.

"Lem?"

"Don't look," he said. "I'll help you get back on the horse."

"Wha—what are you goin' to do?"

"We got to get out of here, Bobbie. Ain't nothin' we can do for these folks no more. Jesus, they're all dead. Every goddamned one of them."

For once, Roberta said nothing about his swearing. When he helped her aboard the horse, she began to whimper. She had held it in long enough, God knows, Lem thought. He pulled himself up behind her and swung Hammerhead in a tight circle. The last thing he saw when he left the place of ambush was a man's head sitting on a broken keg, mouth propped open with a chunk of striking steel jammed in so that he appeared to be grinning.

L em and Roberta drove the wagon along the trail until well after dark. Roberta didn't ask him about what he had seen back there and he was grateful. He could get none of it out of his mind. Every time he tried to think of something else, a hideous image would bob up in his mind unbidden. He recalled things he didn't remember seeing. Little things, like a split-open sack of coffee beans piled on the ground like buck droppings, a woman's broken parasol, a child's wooden play-toy, a hobby horse broken in two, a crushed milk pail lying next to a dead horse, a man's glove with the hand still inside it. He hadn't seen a rifle or a knife, nor the scalps Hauser and Shields had taken from the two braves he had killed.

That must have been what angered them, Lem thought.

Finding those scalps on the white men. The savages had swept through the travelers like a storm, killing everything in a blind rage.

The trail was no longer easy to follow in the darkness. It seemed to Lem that they had topped a ridge and that was the place to stop. He directed Roberta to pull the wagon off the dim trail. He helped her from the seat and put a finger on her lips. They stood there listening for a long time. Finally, satisfied, he whispered to her.

"Make as little noise as possible. I'm going to hobble the stock. Be real quiet."

Roberta made a bed for them beneath the wagon. She shivered in the chill of the mountain air. Lem returned but she did not hear him come up, so quiet he was. He crawled under the wagon and she felt the stock of his rifle brush against her leg. His powderhorn rattled his knife until he grabbed it.

"I ain't hungry," he said. "You get what you want to eat and don't worry none about me."

"What are you going to do?" she whispered.

"Stand guard as long as I can."

"You think they'll come after us?"

"No. You get some sleep, Bobbie. I'll wear the worry cap."

"Wake me when you get tired. I can listen well as you."

He started to laugh, but he knew the sound would travel. It was quiet. Not even an owl made a sound. Hammerhead sniffled in the grasses and he heard the mules munching. He had run a rope through their hobbles, trailed it back to the wagon, looped it around the left front wheel.

He crawled out from under the wagon. Roberta squeezed his hand. He walked some distance from the wagon, keeping its boxy dark shape in view. He stopped, listening for the slightest sound. After a while, he heard Roberta crawl into her bedclothes. She tossed and turned for several minutes and then was still. Lem listened to the sound of his breathing and then forced himself not to listen to it. He was not sleepy, but his senses seemed drawn up tight like fiddle strings, ready to pop if he turned the tuning keys one more twist.

He kept seeing the distorted features of the dead people, the severed limbs, the vacant eyes. He thought about the two men he had killed and he wondered if his actions had caused all of the others to die. What if he had not hunted the two braves? Would they have gone on, content to leave the travelers alone? Or were they waiting there for others of their tribe to show up so they could slaughter all of the whites? If he and Roberta had joined up with that bunch, they might be lying dead out there tonight just like them. What if he had agreed to lead them? He might be dead, too, and Roberta left all alone, never knowing what had happened to him.

A great emptiness filled Lemuel when he thought about these things. There were no hard and fast answers. The more he thought about it, he was sure he had done the right thing. Those red savages had meant to kill some white people and were sneaking up on the travelers when he had tracked them down. Maybe the two redskins he had killed were scouts sent out to the wilderness trail in advance of the main bunch. Maybe the Indians had planned all along to kill every white that came through their lands.

He tried not to think of the dead people lying along the trail, in the woods. He tried not to think of their last tragic moments. He tried not to hear the screams of the women and children.

But there was no solace in the bleak night, in the far cold stars that blinked so impassively and silent across the dark sky. In the ageless heavens, what did these lives matter? What did his own life matter?

His thoughts stunned him, left him with an immense sadness. There was no reason behind the deaths of the other travelers, yet he had seen reason when he had killed the two braves. Or had he? If he had not hunted them down . . .

Lem shook his head, struggling to dislodge the ifs that surged through his scrambled thoughts.

He tore off a stalk of grass, chewed it to the bitter root. He stopped looking up at the sky. The stars made him feel so small, so insignificant. The sky itself made him feel even emptier than before.

He waited for morning, praying that the light would wash away the images of the mutilated dead.

R oberta was sick again the next morning. Her vomiting jarred Lem awake. He had not meant to doze, but just before dawn, the exhaustion caught up with him. He jumped to his feet, ashamed. He walked over to the wagon. Roberta was doubled up, holding onto a tree. The sounds of her retching tore at him.

"What's the matter, Bobbie?" he asked.

"I'm sick."

"You been sick most ever' mornin'."

"And I missed my time of the month twice," she said.

"What's that mean?" he asked dumbly.

She stood up, wiped her mouth with a sun-browned arm. Her eyes were wet from exertion.

"It means I've got a baby growin' inside me. Don't you know anything?"

"A baby?"

"Yes. Your baby. My baby. Our baby. That's why I get sick. You are really a dunce, Lemuel. Didn't your ma ever tell you about babies?"

"I reckon not," he said, self-consciously. "Christ, what are we gonna do?"

"There you go, swearing blasphemous again. We're not going to do anything until the baby comes."

"When's that?"

"Oh, Lemuel," she cried, sweeping past him toward the wagon. "Can't you count?"

He finally figured it out after he got the mules hitched, Hammerhead saddled. By then, Roberta was in a pout and didn't want to talk about it anymore. He led off down the sloping trail, leaving the ridge where they had camped behind them. They forded the Clinch River, descended Walden's Ridge to Martin's Station in Powell Valley. The worst part of the Appalachians seemed to be behind them and they both breathed easier when they saw the settlement.

"That'd be Martin's Station," said Lem, holding up Hammerhead until Roberta could stop the wagon. "My, ain't it a sight?"

"I never saw anything so blessed to look at," said Roberta, the tension draining out of her at the sight of man-made structures. The settlement was dominated by a fort, or stockade, surrounded by stumps left when men had cleared the forest. It was small, by any standards, but it was the first human habitation they had seen in many days. There were a few log dwellings scattered over the clearing, and they saw travelers' tents and lean-tos pitched near the stockade's walls. They saw people walking about, peaceful as farmers at Sunday go-to-meeting.

"Let's go there, Lem. I can't hardly bear to sit here and look at it."

The trail widened into a road and they drove up to the stockade, eyes wide and bright as brass buttons. A half-dozen dogs, sure signs of civilization, bounded out to greet them. The pack followed them right up to the gates of the fort.

"Where you folks bound?" asked a man they encountered outside the stockade.

"Kentucky," said Lem.

"Well, you're most there already," he said. "Spit'n a holler away. Folks've been goin' through the gap yonder like bees to a honeycomb. Just got back from Lexington meself and Lord, it's a-growin' faster'n Philadelphy. Sam Parsons's the name. Got any goods to sell? Needin' any supplies? This be the last civilized settlement for a good long hunnert and twenny miles."

"Nope," said Lem. "We ain't got nothin' to sell. Nothin' we need."

"Lem, you goin' to tell him about those folks. . . ."

"Eh, what's that?" Parsons cocked his head. He was a short, scrawny man dressed in simple, homespun clothes. His wagon stood next to the gates of the stockade, its slat sides painted with the legend in red: PARSONS TRADE GOODS. Underneath, in smaller letters, the words BOUGHT & SOLD were scrawled in black paint.

Lem dismounted, slackened the cinch on Hammerhead's saddle. The horse heaved a deep sigh.

"We heard screamin' and hollerin' back up on the trail," said Lem. "A whole passel of folks was kilt, cut up by Indians. Warn't nothin' we could do."

"See 'em?"

"Who?"

"Them redskins. Did you get a gander at 'em?"

"No. They was gone." Lem didn't like Parsons's question. He didn't want to tell him about the two bucks he killed.

"Been a bunch of renegade Tuscaroras roamin' them woods. Ain't the fust time they caused a commotion. Thought they was all driv out. How many white folks they kill?"

Lem made an estimate. He sheepishly told Parsons that he did not try to bury any of the dead. Parsons seemed to understand.

"Likely as not, their bones will serve as warning to others comin' through the wilderness," said Parsons. "I'll speak some prayers fer 'em. Now, you got anything to sell or trade, son?"

"Nary," said Lem, anxious to get away from the settlement. He avoided making eye contact with Roberta. He
knew she'd probably want to stay the night, where it was
safe. "How's the trail ahead? Any Indians?"

"Well, now," said Parsons, stroking his chin, "they is and
they ain't. Injuns don't know no better. They comes and
they goes as they please."

"Any other folks goin' our way?" asked Roberta.

"I don't rightly know," said Parsons. "Just come in from
the settlements myself. I kin ask. Passed a bunch what come
through yestiddy. Musta been nigh onto twenny souls or so,
not countin' niggers."

"Makes no never mind; we're going on," said Lem.

"Lemuel. Can't we stay the night, leastways?" Her voice
held just the trace of a whine. "Rest up some."

Hawke squinted when he looked at her.

"I'd like to get on," he said firmly. "Mr. Parsons, can you
point us the way?"

"Why, son, you jest go on toward Pinnacle Mountain
yonder. Foller the trail up through the Cumberland Gap.
You got some mountains beyond, but you'll go down and
strike a ford at the Cumberland River. Easy goin' from
there on, maybe, less'n you get rain."

"Thank you kindly," said Lem. He tightened Hammerhead's cinch, climbed back in the saddle. He beckoned
for Roberta to follow. People emerged from the stockade
and stared at them. Lem ignored their looks. The people
behind the fort hardly gave them a second glance.

They camped that night at the base of Pinnacle Mountain.

"Beautiful, ain't it?" said Lem, after he finished pitching
their lean-to. "That there's Cumberland Gap up yonder."

The dying sun rimmed the gap with gold, painted the
clouds a salmon hue.

"I'll fix us some supper," said Roberta, still in her sulk.
Lem listened to the clatter of pots and pans for the next

several moments, finally shrugged and walked away and rubbed down the mules with grass just so he wouldn't have to think about her anger.

The next morning, before the sun was up and after Roberta finished with her toilet and being sick, they started the short ascent through a steep ravine leading to the summit of the pass. At the top, they gazed out over a Kentucky shrouded in morning mist. As the sun rose, they followed a tortuous mountain trail that strained every spoke on the wagon wheels, slowed them to a turtle's pace. The rough trail dropped them to a ford, well rutted with wagon tracks, at the Cumberland River. A dead pig lay on the far bank, crows picking at its carcass. That didn't stop Roberta from stopping on the eastern side to wash Lem's buckskins. He swam in the shallows downstream while she squatted at the bank, scrubbing the blood from his 'skins with lye soap. When they crossed the ford, the buckskins flapped from the wagon. Lem wore only a pair of homespun trousers until the flies got at him.

They followed the trail on a northwest course, meandering through gently rolling foothills rising on either side of them, reminding them of Virginia in the late afternoon. Beyond Flat Lick, they saw deer and turkey, heard the hens clucking on the ridges in the evening. Early one evening, Lem loaded his rifle with birdshot and brought down a gobbler that he had tracked atop one of the hills.

Two days later, the sky scudded over with black clouds at dawn. By noon, the Hawkes were in the midst of a blinding rainstorm, the trail awash, impassable. Streams flooded, became dangerous. Lem couldn't see twenty yards ahead, but when they came between two low hills, they were confronted with a raging stream that spooked the mules, made Hammerhead balk with fear.

"We got to turn back, find high ground," yelled Lem above the howl of wind, the slash of rain.

"Turn back where? Where are we?"

"God, I don't know, Bobbie. Just let's back up the wagon. That flood's rising fast."

It took Lem three hours to find a hill they could pull up with the wagon in a series of switchbacks on muddy terrain. Once, the wagon almost tipped over and Roberta screamed into the teeth of the wind, her hysteria full-blown. Lem drove the mules hard, made them stay on a safe line until the danger was past. When they reached a level, high above the roaring flood, Lem fell from his horse, exhausted. Roberta had to block the wheels and tie up the stock before she dared crawl under the wagon for shelter against the storm.

Lem dragged himself under the wagon. Roberta was shivering, chilled to the bone. Her teeth chattered so much he thought she was going to rattle apart.

Below them, the flood boiled between the hills, twisting and writhing like a huge serpent as it sought a path to the raging Cumberland River.

Lem put his arm around Roberta. She was soaked to the skin, shaking out of control.

"Damn, Bobbie, I'm sorry," he said.

"Make me w-w-warm, Lem," she pleaded. "God I'm so cold."

But he sat there, helpless, knowing there was nothing he could do.

8

The rain churned the open places on the hill to mud. Lightning razored the sky, speared the earth with jagged lancets of electricity. Thunder boomed in their ears, made them jump inside their skins. The wagon sagged under the weight of soaked clothing, foodstuffs. The sun went down and the wind never stopped for a breath. Lem finally climbed up into the wagon and began to throw things down to keep the bed from collapsing and crushing them. Water, he knew, was heavy; his pa had told him once that a gallon weighed eight pounds. He grabbed blankets and hung them over the sides to give them some shelter. But, there was no dry clothing. When he had finished all that he could do, he was shivering as bad as Roberta.

He clutched Roberta to him, holding her tightly, hoping he had some warmth to give her. He worried about Hammerhead and the mules, Goldie, the jenny, and Gideon, the jack, knew they were being battered by the storm without any safe place to go. The thunder had stopped, but there was no peace for them in the ranting bluster of the wind and, although lightning no longer ripped electric scars in the sky, the rain speared the earth with silver lances sharp enough, it seemed, to break the skin.

The blankets helped to keep out the wind and most of the needling rain. But Lem and Roberta were sodden and trickles of water ran beneath the wagon. Their butts itched from the dampness and they could not lie down to sleep. In their discomfort, they clung to each other like half-drowned shipwreck victims washed up on a barren shore. Lem scooted toward one of the wheels on the high side of the hill and dragged Roberta with him. He leaned back against it and drew her to him. Her head fell on his shoulder and he closed his eyes, listening to the drum of rain on the wagon and the whip of wind against the blankets.

They dozed, despite their discomfort, occasionally sinking into fitful sleep only to awaken, startled, to find a new stiffness in a joint, a numbness in a foot or a toe, a cramp in a leg muscle. Lem dreamed of a warm fire and dry clothing. Roberta dreamed of a soft, dry bed, herself buried under thick warm comforters in a quiet breezeless room.

By morning, the storm relented, swept on past them with

only an occasional rattle of rain in a wind gust, a tattoo on the wagon boards, a spatter against the soggy blankets like fine sand thrown against a windowpane.

Roberta whimpered in sleep, drawn under finally, by fatigue and some part of her mind that found shelter in dream. Lem lay awake, blind in the darkness, listening to the storm's tail lash feebly as its lumbering dragon cloud-breath passed to the south, losing strength as its thunderheads emptied and scattered, stripped of their plumpness and watery weight by the sheer force of its assault on the earth.

Rivulets of water still ran under the wagon, but they seemed harmless in the relative silence, feeble little streams that would peter out at the first furnace blast of sun. Lem heard only distant grumblings from the thunder, and the rain that fell now was so light he had to listen hard to hear it. The drip from the trees was stronger. A spoke from the wagon wheel had left a furrow of pain in his shoulder, but he didn't move. He knew that Roberta was asleep and she seemed so small and helpless in his arms he had not the heart to awaken her.

He dozed off again, shifted in his sleep. Sometime before dawn, he awoke again when he heard the scream of a woman. Jarred out of dream, it took Lem several seconds to remember where he was. Roberta scooted closer to him. He felt her breath on his neck. Her fingers dug into his arms. They both heard the terrified cries of children.

"What's that?" she whispered in the feeble half-light of dawn.

"Down on the flat," he said.

"I'm scared, Lem. Could be Indians."

"Sounds like just kids."

"I heard a woman."

"Me, too," he said. "But I don't hear it no more."

They listened, heard only the roaring of a distant stream. The silence stretched out from them, made them grow apprehensive. The rain had stopped, but the trees still dripped and water spattered on the ground in intermittent taps, off-kcy and without meter.

The dawn widened its crack and Lem tugged one of the blankets aside. Roberta slid away from him and he saw her sodden hair plastered against her face, the dark sockets of her eyes. She looked pathetic in her wet clothes, so child-like. He smiled, despite the ache in his shoulder, the cramps in his legs.

"You look like a drownded rat," he said. The blanket, weighted with water, slipped from the wagon, sogged to the ground.

"So do you," she retorted. "I have never in my life spent such a miserable night. I swear I thought the rain would never stop. Can you build a fire, Lem? I'm so cold my bones hurt. I fear I'll catch my death."

"I might find us some dry wood, cut us some tinder," he said, crawling out into the open. The sky was still overcast, but he no longer heard the rumble of thunder. He looked at his surroundings. They were on the slope of a round-topped, gently rolling hill, stippled with birch and maple, hazelwood, and other trees, grasses that had been flatted by the storm. The slope was not as steep as he had thought the night before and the grass had helped to keep the ground from turning to mud. They could make it back down if they were careful. He looked for fallen trees, something that might be dry inside. He made a circle around the perimeter of the summit. At a bare patch, he looked down and across to the other hills. He saw no sign of the trail, but he heard the faint roar of rushing water somewhere beyond his sight. He made a mental note to seek the stream out, see if the trail did not cross it at some point. He took his bearings, knew the general direction they must head.

Lem found some downed trees and dragged dead wood back to the wagon. Roberta was combing out her hair. She had clothes hanging from every conceivable low-hanging tree limb, and the wagon looked like a ragman's cart.

"I'll have to drive the wagon down this hill when we leave," he told her. "Be some brakin' to do."

"I'll walk," she said. "Bones are stiff."

He found the ax inside the wagon, began to tear at the wood with the blade, splintering off the driest chunks from the heart of the biggest log.

Lem started a fire with dry shavings, fashioned a drying rack from saplings that he stripped of leaves. The sun still lay behind banked clouds, but the morning brightened by the time some of their clothes were dry. Roberta was too sick to eat, but Lem ate dried turkey and a stale biscuit, washed it down with water. When he was through, he packed everything up in the wagon, left his buckskins and one of Roberta's dresses laid out to dry in the air. He rubbed Hammerhead down, tightened the saddle cinch. Roberta led him down the hill while Lem took another course, careful to point the mules straight and ride the brake. As they traveled down the slope, he and Roberta both heard the sound of a hammer thunking nails into wood.

On the flat, Lem halted the wagon. Roberta climbed up, handed him the reins to Hammerhead.

"Do you know where we are?" she asked.

"No, but I got my bearings. We'll find the trail directly."

"What's that noise?"

"Somebody a-hammerin', I reckon. You just foller me, Bobbie. Maybe we'll find out what's a-goin' on."

"We should have stayed back there at Martin's Station," she said.

Lem said nothing, but mounted Hammerhead and rode out toward the sound of the carpenter's hammer.

After rounding a pair of low hills, Lem found the trail. It had been all but washed out by the storm, and he saw where the flash flood had unleashed its brief torrent during the night. Tree limbs, leaves, chunks of lumber marked its ravaging path. Along this floodline, he and Roberta came upon a couple working on a cart that looked as if it had been hammered together more than once. Broken pieces of lumber lay strewn nearby, and Lem saw drag marks in the mud that indicated the couple had lugged salvaged lumber for some distance. The odor of skunk hung in their nostrils, faintly pungent, faded, perhaps, in the scrub of rain and morning breeze.

"Mornin'," said Lem. "Looks like you had some trouble. Come far?"

"All the way from Winchester, Virginia," said the man.

"We're alluz breakin' down," said the woman. She had a high-pitched, squeaky, almost childlike voice. It was incongruous in a woman so broad of bosom and stout of frame. Her face was beautiful, despite her chubbiness. Roberta thought it cherubic and sweet.

"We're down to two wheels and a considerably shortened bed, having started out with four wheels and a good ten foot of wagon from Winchester," said Elmer Fancher. His corpulent wife, Belinda, her face streaked with dirt, her dress soiled, put her shoulder to the wheel as Fancher drove a wedge into a new, makeshift spoke. Two children napped under a tree, rag dolls clutched to their bosoms.

Lem dismounted to help, glad for the stretch. Roberta set the brake and climbed down from the wagon, carrying a jar of sun tea. She seemed relieved to see other human beings. She gave Lem a begrudging look of gratitude.

"Give you a hand?" asked Lem.

"We pert near got it licked," said Elmer as he hammered the shim tight against the spoke and wheel. "Lordy, I don't know if this buggy will make it to Lexington. We've left so much in sutler's gulches, the missus has her a list a yard long. Most of what's gone, I built, so I reckon I can build 'em again for her. Say, you'ns didn't see a little boy 'bout eight or nine wanderin' about yester evenin' or earlier of a mornin' anywheres?"

"Sorry," said Roberta, puzzled.

Elmer stood up, extended a delicate, lean hand. He was slender, in contrast to his wife's stout frame, billowing flab.

"I'm Elmer Fancher and this is the missus, Belinda."

"Would you like some tea?" asked Roberta, glancing over to the tree. "My, you have a couple of nice children, I see. They look all tuckered out."

Belinda grunted and glanced over at the children.

Roberta crinkled her nose. The skunk smell seemed to emanate from beneath the tree where the children slept.

"Land, where's Martin?" Belinda screeched. "Elmer, you seen Marty anywheres?"

Roberta wondered if that was the missing boy Fancher had asked her about.

Elmer tapped the wheel's spoke with the butt of the hammer. It seemed solid.

"He was with the young 'uns last I looked," he said. He spoke quietly in a thin, featureless voice. Although he couldn't have been more than twenty-five, he was losing his hair on top. Beneath the thinning dark locks, his bald pate glistened with sweat. He had a square, beard-shadowed jaw, fleshy lips, a slightly hooked nose, eyebrows that bristled like caterpillars over close-set, intense hazel eyes. He stood no more than five foot five, weighed no more than a hundred pounds. He turned to the Hawkes. "We done lost one young 'un somewhere back down at Flat Lick. Them two under the tree found 'em a pet skunk last night just before that flash flood struck us. We was right on your tracks until you turned off. A wonder you didn't hear us rattle-trappin' ahind you'ns."

"You *lost* one of your children?" Roberta asked incredulously.

Belinda, oblivious to the conversation, waddled over to the tree, holding her nose with tweaking stubs of fingers. Her dress dragged on the ground and she stepped on it more than once with mud-caked boots. Her curls bounced in dark ringlets with every chunky step.

"Little Danny," said Elmer, without a trace of sadness. "He wandered off one day when we was all catching forty winks after comin' through the Gap. We looked for him high and low, stayed three days, hoping he'd come back to where we was. The missus cried her eyes out."

"You couldn't find him?" Roberta asked, in a daze. "And you just left him out there?"

"Well, we had to get on," said Fancher. "Danny, he was always confused about things. We found him ever' damned time until we got to Flat Lick. Danny took a fancy to salt, I reckon. We saw him a-settin' at a salt lick, pickin' at it and a-puttin' it on his tongue. We hollered at him to catch up, but he never come. No tellin' where he went. The dog went with him and he never come back neither."

Lem stood there, transfixed, uncomfortable as a man standing on a gallows' creaking trapdoor.

"You mean that little boy is still back there all alone? Hell, it can't be more'n a day's ride back to Flat Lick."

"Well, he's got Skipper with him. Skipper's the beagle pup what tagged along with us. Boy might be dead for all we know. We knew we wasn't going to find him. I mean we looked all over them hills and woods and hollered till we was hoarse. He just never come back. We didn't figger he'd turn up anytime soon and what was we goin' to do? Couldn't wait on him forever."

"Jesus Christ," said Lem.

"Lemuel," said Roberta, her eyes in full flare with disbelief.

Belinda woke up the two children.

"Where's Marty?" she squeaked.

"Aw, I don't know," cranked Earnest.

"Harriet, did you see your big brother?"

"No, Ma, I ain't seen him," said the little girl, rubbing her eyes.

"Marty! Martin Fancher! You come on back here!"

There was no answer. Lem and Roberta stood there,

struck dumb by what appeared to be another tragedy in the making. Belinda Fancher began to climb a low hill, calling out her son's name every few feet. Elmer looked at her once, then began to gather up his tools.

"Want to make yourself some cash money?" he asked Lem.

"Huh?"

"I notice you'ns got a big wagon there. We got goods scattered from hell to scrapple and I got no room in this shrunk-up cart. My horses are tied about a half mile from here where I gathered up all our trunks and goods. Flood caught us during the storm and tumbled the wagon a good quarter mile or so before it struck a tree. Coulda lost the whole shebang. One thing. I got plenty of spare parts. We ought to make it to Lexington with this outfit." He tapped the single-axled cart and picked up a saw, threw it in the box with the hammer and other tools.

"How much you got to carry?" asked Lem.

"Oh, not much. I'll pay you five pounds when we get to Lexington."

"What about your son?" asked Roberta. The look she gave Lemuel was dark, with more than a trace of latent ferocity.

"Well, we ain't goin' back for him. He's either lost or dead or maybe he found his way somewheres. We rode back clear to Martin's Station. Saw you folks when you passed. We come along right after you'ns and passed you last night by no more'n a hair's thickness."

"I don't mean Danny," said Roberta. "The other one. Martin?"

They all heard Belinda calling Marty's name. She stood on the side of the hill, shading her eyes from the bleak sun, squealing in ever higher pitches.

"Oh, Marty's twelve years old. Danny was only eight or nine. I reckon Marty'll do some better."

"My God," said Roberta, not quite under her breath. Elmer picked up a wood chisel and a mallet, tossed them into the box. Harriet and Earnest began to tease each other. Earnest pulled on her single braid of hair and Harriet slapped him. Neither of them paid any attention to their mother.

"Ernie, stop it," whined Harriet. She jerked the braid out of her brother's hand.

"Don't you hit me no more," said Ernie.

Belinda disappeared from view. Her piercing voice carried, however. She was still screeching for Marty.

"Want to bring that wagon on down?" asked Elmer. "We just as well get to loading. We can pick up these tools when I bring back my horses and hook them up to the cart."

"What about your wife?" asked Lem. "Shouldn't we help her look for Martin?"

"Well, if your missus wants to help. We got to load my goods, bring them horses back here."

Lem looked at Roberta for help. She speared him with a look of pure puzzlement.

"I—I'll help Mrs. Fancher look for her boy," she said, after a moment. "You go on, Lem. We can do with the five pounds."

Lem tied Hammerhead to the cart, climbed up in the wagon. Elmer Fancher pulled himself up, sat next to Hawke.

"Giddap," said Lem, easing off the brake.

"Just foller that wash," said Fancher.

Salt from the licks had washed down the path of the flood, leaving traces white as lime. The mules kept stopping to lick at it. Lem and Elmer said nothing during these pauses, for Belinda's voice penetrated their thoughts. Elmer reached into his pocket, pulled out a twist of tobacco. He cut a piece off, handed it to Lem. Lem wedged it into his mouth, glad for something to take his mind off the skunk smell and that intolerable screechy voice of Belinda's.

"What's your business, Mr. Fancher?"

"Call me Elmer, Lemuel. Well, I do a lot of things, carpentry, hide tanning, tailoring, blacksmithing, a little tinkering."

"What you aim to do in Lexington?"

"Maybe a little of everything, Lem. Jack of all trades."

"I aim to lease me some farmland."

"A man of the soil. I wish you luck. They say Kentucky's got good land for farming."

"I just hope it's cheap," mused Hawke.

"Well, everything has its price, of course."

They no longer heard Belinda's screeching. Instead, they heard the croak of frogs along the wash. Soon, they heard the whicker of the horses. Gideon and Goldie perked up their ears, picked up their pace a little.

Lem heard the sound of rushing water, wondered about it.

"Well, there they be," said Fancher, as they rounded the base of a hill. "And there's Rockcastle River. Roarin' full, I'd say."

Two hundred yards from where the horses were tied, the wash ended up at the bank of a swollen river. Now Lem knew where the flash flood had gone. The choppy waters bobbed up tree limbs, logs, every kind of debris, carried the detritus along in its muddy race.

"You took a chance, leavin' your horses here," said Lem.

"Couldn't see anything in the dark. Looks like we got off the trail some. There's my goods, too. The Lord was watchin' over us, I reckon."

They loaded the trunks and wooden cartons into Lem's wagon, hitched the skittish horses to the back of the wagon. They kept eyeing the river, fighting their bits.

"They must have had quite a night," chuckled Fancher, as he climbed back into the wagon. "Glad to get my tools back. A man don't want to lose his tools."

"What about your boys?" asked Lem before he thought to hold his tongue.

"Sad, very sad," said Fancher, spitting out the dry husk of mangled tobacco. "God works in mysterious ways."

Lem snorted and cracked the reins. The mules pulled out in a wide turn. The wagon was considerably heavier now. He wondered what was in the trunks and boxes. No farming tools, he was sure. The trunk must have weighed two hundred pounds. He wondered if Belinda and Elmer had loaded it onto their wagon without using a block and tackle.

Fancher's horses whickered again as the mules began to trot back the way they had come. The river purred in their wake, then the sound faded away as the sun climbed high enough to make the men pull their hat brims down to shade their eyes.

The two children stood next to the cart, naked as the day they were born. There was no sign of Belinda or Roberta. Hammerhead stood hipshot, shading them from the sun.

"Where's your ma?" asked Elmer as the wagon lurched to a stop. The children's faces were streaked with dark lines. They had been crying.

"That lady took her away," said Earnest, pointing.

The smell from the children was unmistakable.

"What did you kids do?" asked Fancher.

"Nothin'," said Harriet, a sullen scowl fixed on her face as if it had been painted there.

"Ma found our pet skunk," gloated Earnest, a mischievous gleam in his eye.

"What?" Fancher bolted down from the wagon. The children cringed as he came close, but he went right past them, began to search through the cart. "You kids stink to high heaven. What'd she do with your clothes?"

"That lady took them," said Earnest.

"She stole them," said Harriet, crinkling up her face.

"Where's that skunk?" asked Fancher, rummaging through a valise full of loose clothing.

"That lady run it off," said Earnest. "It chased Ma all the way here. You should have heard her scream."

Lem sat there, his nostrils full of skunk smell. It seemed he was watching some kind of strange dream unfolding in broad daylight. He looked around, wondered where Roberta had taken Belinda Fancher.

"Earnest, you take your sister over by that hickory tree and put some clothes on her. You get some pants on. I'll fetch your ma."

"Yonder she comes," said Earnest.

Belinda was wrapped in a blanket, her hair dripping water. Roberta led her through the brush, an arm around her shoulder. Elmer tossed some clothes to Earnest. Neither of the children made a move to leave. They stared at the two women in wide-eyed fascination.

"I washed her off in a little creek back there," said Roberta. "I don't think she can ever wear that dress again."

Lem climbed down from the wagon, but he kept his distance from the Fancher woman and her children. There was so much skunk smell in the air, his nostrils were burning.

"You get squirted?" Elmer asked his wife, as if he didn't know.

"Oh, I could skin those kids alive," said Belinda, fixing them with a murderous gaze.

"When you get finished, help me load up the cart. We got to get on, woman."

"I wish I knew where Marty had gone to," said Belinda. But she began gathering up the bedding and clothing. She dragged more trunks from a grove of trees. Soon, the cart was full. The children helped some, but only after their mother took a willow switch to them. Lem tried to help, but Fancher had his own ideas about loading and lashing down, so he finally retreated to Roberta's side.

Fancher hooked up his two horses to the little cart. It seemed a sound carrier. He had even built a little seat on the back for the children. The seat in front rode high on sturdy iron braces that were curved to take the shock from the road.

"You get to Lexington, ask for us," said Fancher. "I'll give you five pounds when you unload my goods."

"Good-by to you'ns," said Belinda. "If you run into that scalawag Marty, you tell him he'd better run and catch up." Belinda choked back a sob as the cart lurched forward. The Hawkes stood there watching the Fanchers as they wheeled back up the main trail. The two children waved for a long time, then Earnest began pulling on Harriet's hair again just before the cart disappeared from sight.

"Well, Lemuel, I just don't know what to make of those people," said Roberta, heaving a sigh.

"Me neither," he said. "Reckon we ought to look for them two boys?"

"Where? Little Danny probably got washed away in the flood last night. If he was still alive. They haven't seen him in at least four days, maybe longer. That strange woman screamed for Marty. If he was anywhere around he would surely hear her."

"I reckon so," he said. He thought about calling out Marty's name himself, but it was so quiet now he felt awkward about it.

"It's so sad," said Roberta wistfully. "I feel sorry for that woman."

"Looks like they got used to losin' kids," said Lem.

Roberta gave him a funny look. He cleared his throat, caught up Hammerhead. By the time he was mounted, Roberta had the mule team turned and heading back to the trail.

Lem looked back over his shoulder several times as he rode behind the wagon.

He saw no sign of a young boy wandering lost in the wilderness of Kentucky.

9

The trail meandered, took a wide cut to the northeast, and then the Hawkes reached Hazel Patch, a flat, grassy plain at the foothills of the Cumberland Mountains. It had taken them almost five days to go that far, even though the trail was not that difficult. All along the way, they saw signs of others' passing, the detritus of other families left behind to blow in the wind, rot in the sun and rain. They saw the skeletons of furniture broken in transit and tossed beside the trail, articles of clothing that had worn out or had been torn beyond repair or caring, worn-out pots and pans, empty sacks, the remains of campfires, a crumpled boot, slats from a keg, parts of wagons. The junk littered the deeply rutted trail, the castoff parts from faceless nomads. It was depressing to Roberta, who felt as if she had been cast out of Eden, shamefully driven from home into the terrifying wilderness. She said nothing to her husband, but he felt the vibrations of her suppressed hostility at the end of each long day. As they drew farther away from their abandoned home, she kept looking back over her shoulder like Lot's wife, and every time she did, she stiffened on the seat of the wagon and she tugged hopelessly on the reins as if to halt their journey before it was too late.

But it was more than homesickness that tugged at her, she knew. A growing fear for her unborn child began to grow in her. And this, she knew, came from thinking about the two lost Fancher boys. She could not help her thoughts, could not keep the images of the children from turning hideous in her troubled mind.

Lem called a halt when the sun lay just above the western horizon, a disc of hammered gold, frozen there for a long moment.

"Bobbie," he said, "we ain't ever gonna get up to Lexington you keep jerkin' on them reins. You've plumb wore out them mules' mouths a-tuggin' on them bits."

"Lemuel Hawke, you just shut your flappin' mouth," she snapped. Her shoulder blades felt like wooden stakes jabbing into her back. Her legs quivered from fatigue. She had dawdled, she knew, because she couldn't bear to think of those two lost boys. Something in her heart told her that one or the other one might still be alive, crying his eyes out, looking for his parents. As for the Fanchers, she was sorry she had made Lem take their goods on the wagon. She thought they were cruel to just go on about their business knowing their sons were all alone, lost out in the wilds. She couldn't imagine anyone going off like that and leaving their flesh and blood behind.

Roberta set the brake, looked at the hills they had crossed. They shimmered golden in the sun, blazed with a green fire bright as emeralds. She was sweaty under her loose dress, her hands clammy from perspiration.

Lem stripped Hammerhead, hobbled him in grass, tended to the mules. Roberta laid out the camp, gathered stones for a fire ring. There were signs that others had camped there, but she liked to make her own place. Lem dug her a pit and searched for firewood as the sun crawled down the sky, stretched their shadows long and thin across the sward.

"What do you want for supper?" she asked, when Lem finished chopping kindling for the fire.

"You ain't goin' to keep lookin' under every damned bush and behind every damned tree for them boys, are you?"

A pair of red squirrels scampered past the wagon, quill-like hairs twitching on their nervous tails. High in a scaly-bark hickory tree, another squirrel barked a throaty invective.

"Lem, I got bad feelings about leavin' that place without lookin' for the Fancher boy. He could be lookin' for his folks."

"Well, you've wasted enough time," he said, setting the kindling in the center of the hole he had dug in the fire ring. "We'd a been to Lexington already if you hadn't dawdled every damned mile."

"Must you always curse?"

"When it's called for, hell yes."

"What are you really mad at, Lemuel?"

He stared at the crates that belonged to Fancher.

"I'd just like to carry my own baggage," he said.

"We need the five pounds," she said.

"Well, I need my freedom a whole danged lot more."

"You won't have to look at them much longer," she said.

"I done looked at 'em too much now. I see 'em in my sleep. Goddamn it."

"There you go again, Lemuel. Blaspheming the good Lord. He'll strike you down one day."

Hawke didn't say the next curse out loud. He picked up a chunk of dirt, bounced it off one of Fancher's crates.

Roberta went to the wagon, banged pots together in a deliberate attempt to vent her anger. She looked long and wistfully back down the trail as she slammed the pots down next to the fire ring. Lem flinched involuntarily as she tossed a ladle into the bigger iron pot. It rang like a horseshoe.

"Ham and beans," she said defiantly, as she whisked back to the wagon. "Fetch me some water."

"Ham and beans," echoed Lem. "You got any cornmeal left?"

"Maybe," she said, digging into the wooden box that held her condiments, flour, and meal. "You want corn cakes?"

"Naw, I was just exercisin' my gums, Bobbie."

"You don't have to be a smarty britches."

"Corn cakes would be fine. Keep them beans from swimmin' around in my belly."

"You ought to be grateful we have beans," she said.

"I am. I just don't like 'em swimmin' around in my stomach like water bugs."

"Lem, just stop flap-mouthin' about ever' little thing. You fray a body's nerves."

Lem set a piece of charred cloth on the ground, covered it with fine shavings. He took a small brass case from his possibles pouch, opened it. He struck flint against the curved face of the steel, showered sparks into the fine tinder. When the shavings caught, he leaned down, blew into them. They glowed a flickering orange. The edge of the cloth caught fire and he lifted the little bundle off the ground, set it against the cone of kindling. He blew on the tinder until it flared. When the kindling began to burn, he leaned back, grabbed some larger sticks and waited until the blaze was high before laying them on. Roberta shook beans into the big pot. They clattered like pebbles in a tin funnel.

The two squirrels scampered up a tree. Soon, all three of them were barking.

Lem looked up.

"That old bull sounds like he's got the croup," he said, but he knew that something was bothering the squirrel on the hickory branch.

"Probably doesn't like the fire," said Roberta.

"No, it ain't that."

Lem stood up, walked slowly over to where he had leaned his rifle against the wagon tongue. It wasn't the fire, he knew. It was more than that. Nor was it that they were interlopers into the fox squirrel's territory. The pair of scamperers had sensed what the old boy had been trying to warn them about. That's why they had treed.

Roberta lay out an oilcloth, retrieved her knives and a two-tined fork from one of the boxes in the wagon.

"Lem, what's the matter?" she asked.

"I don't know. Them squirrels are sure skittery."

Roberta looked around. Everything looked peaceful. There was no sign of danger.

"Bring that half a ham over when you get shut of lookin'," she said.

Lem gazed at the countryside. Far off, he heard other squirrels barking, but he didn't know if they were just responding to the ones nearby or whether they were spooked by something in the trees.

He waited several moments, then climbed up into the wagon. He found the half butt of ham in a cedar box, lugged it over to Roberta's oilcloth.

"Might be nothin'," he said aloud.

"What?" She unwrapped the cheesecloth from around the ham, sniffed at the meat. It was not spoiled.

"Them squirrels. Somethin's got 'em riled."

"Oh, Lem, you worry about nothin'. I still need you to fetch me some water. The keg in the back is nigh to full."

"I'll get it."

"Then, leave me be. You make me nervous with all your twitchin'."

"Yes ma'am," he said sarcastically.

Lem sat on a low hill, his rifle across his lap, surveying the surrounding country. Bees worked the patches of spring flowers in the wide meadow, birds flitted in the trees. The squirrels had gone silent. Wafted aromas of the beans and ham simmering in the pot floated to his nostrils. He smelled the heady scent of cornbread baking in the covered skillet. His stomach knotted into kinks of hunger, made low grumbling noises. The sun was setting over his back when he saw the slight movement, across the flat. It was such a slight ripple in the serene fabric of afternoon that he almost missed it.

But something had moved.

He forgot his hunger, leaned forward, his eyes narrowed

to shut out the back light, focus on the movement he had seen. A squirrel barked in rapid staccato just above the place where he had seen a shadowy glimpse of an animal. He saw it again, and puzzled, grimaced. A fox? No, and not a rabbit, either.

Then, he saw its tail, saw the animal move along an invisible path at the edge of the meadow. The tail switched back and forth, almost making round circles in the air. The animal reversed its course, then reversed it again. A few yards closer, a cottontail broke from cover.

The beagle took up the chase, yelping in the high register of the tonic scale. The rabbit veered and the beagle's yelps grew higher in pitch. Lem stood up, thrilled to see the pup, hear its voice.

Roberta stood up, looked toward the sound of the beagle's cry.

"What's that?" she said.

"Might be that beagle pup Fancher told us about."

Lem called out.

"Skipper! Come here, Skipper. Here, Skipper!"

The beagle stopped in its tracks. Lem called to the dog again. Skipper began wagging its tail. The tail went round and round, scribing erratic circles with its black tip. The dog forgot about the rabbit, came waddling across the meadow. It seemed to smell the food cooking. Its tail wagged more furiously.

"Come on, Skipper," Lem said in a soothing voice as he arose from his seat. He walked toward the fire, talking low to the dog.

Roberta blew a vagrant hair away from her face, put her hands on her hips, turning them inside out.

"Seems to know his name," she said.

"Skippoo," said Lem, reverting to baby talk. "Skippoozers. Come on, boy. 'At's a boy."

The dog came right up to him as Lem stopped at Roberta's side. He reached down to pet it.

"Got a chunk of ham for this little feller?" he asked.

Roberta took a fork, raised the lid on the kettle, gouged out a chunk of ham. She blew on it, handed it to Lem when it was cool.

"Here you go boy," said Lem, kneeling down. He put the morsel in Skipper's mouth. The dog wolfed it down in a fraction of a second.

Lem rubbed the dog's back, kneaded him behind the ears. Skipper's tail continued to whirl in a circular motion. His brown eyes pleaded for more meat.

"Cut him another chunk," said Lem.

"Would you give him all of our food?" she asked.

"I want to keep him here. Might be that boy is close by."

"Boy? What boy?"

"The Fancher boy. Danny."

"Oh," she said, and forked a thick finger of ham from the butt, blew it cool before handing it to Lem.

Lem walked a little distance away from the fire and the dog followed him. He made the dog jump for the piece of ham. Skipper plopped down and swallowed twice. It didn't seem to Lem that he had chewed the meat at all.

"Where's Danny, Skipper?"

Skipper wagged his tail. He was brown and white and black, with soft floppy ears, a dust smudge on his nose, burrs in his dirty coat. Lem looked across the meadow.

"Danny!" he called. "Danny, come on. Have some supper."

There was no answer. Roberta looked all around, then at Lem.

"You're crazy," she said.

"This dog's been somewhere," he told her. "He's going somewhere. You think he followed our wagon tracks by himself?"

"I suppose he might have," she said, a trace of annoyance in her voice. "Maybe he smelled the Fanchers' wagon wheels."

"He's not no bloodhound," said Lem. He patted Skipper gently on the head. The dog wagged his whole body.

"Come on here, Danny!" Lem called. "You hungry?"

Lem saw movement again. The hackles on the back of his neck bristled. He strained to see into the long tree shadows that striped the far reaches of the meadow's tall grasses. At first he saw only a boy's head, then as the boy approached, he saw the upper part of his body. Then, he saw another head, and part of another boy. Lem held his breath, but his mind roared like a wind before a storm.

"Roberta, just don't make no quick moves to scare 'em off," Lem whispered.

"Whatever are you talking about?" she asked, but her eyes tracked the path of Lem's gaze. She stood there, rigid as her husband, as the two boys, one taller than the other, walked slowly toward them.

"It's them," said Lem, his voice low. "It's both of them Fancher boys."

Roberta gasped involuntarily.

The smaller boy was limping. The older boy helped him along, an arm around the younger one's shoulders.

"Martin Fancher," called Lem. "That you?"

"Who are you?" The boy's voice sounded thin and high-pitched, almost like a girl's.

"Why, I'm a friend of your ma's and pa's, son. I knowed you was lost. Come on, get yourself some vittles. Hungry?"

"I sure am," said the older boy.

The younger boy started to run toward them, but he stumbled and fell down. Martin helped his brother up. He had to carry him the last fifty yards.

Roberta dropped her utensils and rushed to take the smaller boy from his brother's arms.

Skipper cavorted like a double-jointed dog with a case of the fits.

"I'm Marty Fancher," said the older boy. "This here's my

little brother, Danny. He's plumb tuckered. We ain't had no food in three days."

Roberta snatched Danny away from Martin. The boy's shoes were worn through the soles. The bottoms of his feet were blistered, black from dirt. His clothes were in tatters. His dark shock of hair was matted with dust and sand. His face was burned to a deep burgundy by the sun. Martin did not look much better. He, too, was dirty, and his shoes were rattling on his feet, the bottoms flayed to ribbons. He stepped gingerly over to Lem, looked up at him.

"Where you been, boy?"

"I—I went lookin' for Danny. He was plumb lost and scared. I took a bait of food with me, but he et it all up."

"You didn't save none for yourself?"

"No, suh, I give it all to little Danny there."

Lem smiled.

"Well, you done good, boy." He patted Martin on the top of the head. His hair was as hard as a saddle. "You set down and we'll put some pork and beans in you. Nice dog you got."

"Yes suh, Skipper he's a mighty good dog. He's a beagle pup with a good nose."

Lem laughed.

Marty was bright-eyed, dark-haired, chubby as a turnip, like his mother. He, too, had been sunned brown, but he seemed in much better shape than Danny.

Roberta washed the bottoms of Danny's feet, took off his shredded shoes. His legs were a mass of sores, insect bites, and red streaks. They looked as if they had been lashed with switches.

"Poor boy," she said. "He must be scared pure to death. Leavin' him alone out there like that."

"Bobbie, don't you say nothin' now. Just clean him up and put some vittles in him."

"But I—yes, poor thing. We'll take good care of you, Danny. Lem, he's thin as a rail."

Danny looked at her with dull brown eyes. He smiled weakly.

"That feels good," he said, in a soft voice. "My feet's pow'rful sore, I reckon."

"Why of course they are," soothed Roberta. "We'll get you all cleaned up after you've taken some food into your little stomach."

"Where'd you find your brother?" Lem asked Martin.

"Way yonder. He was a-follerin' the wagon tracks and Skipper, he barked when he saw me. Danny was scared, all right. He cried like a little baby when he seed me."

"I expect he did," said Lem. "Come on, that ham's got to be cooked. Beans might be a little hard yet."

"I don't much care how hard they are," said Martin, with a slow grin. "I'd as soon eat 'em raw."

Roberta fed Danny. Martin wolfed down his food, would have eaten more but Lem restrained him.

"Let your stomach swell back," he told the boy. "Then you can eat all you want."

Roberta made a bed for the two boys under the wagon. Lem pitched their lean-to on one side. Skipper crawled in with the boys, snuggled up to Danny. The youngsters were asleep in five minutes.

"It's a miracle," said Roberta, when she lay down next to Lem.

"That Martin's a mighty fine boy, all right. Takin' care of his brother like that."

"I'm going to give that Fancher woman a piece of my mind."

"Give her the whole thing," said Lem wearily. "And some of mine to boot."

A week later the Hawkes pulled into the town of Lexington, five hundred miles from their former home in Culpeper County, Virginia. For half a day, right after they passed Boiling Spring Station on Dick's River, they had followed a caravan of wagons bearing fresh-cut timber from the highlands. Lem had fretted at the slowness, but had been unable to pull out and pass the wagons because recent rains had made the ground soft. Through Harrodsburg and McAfee's Station, they followed the slow-moving wagons as if bound to them by gravity.

"Damn," he said. "A man can't go where he wants."

"Lem, it'll only be for a little ways. Can't you have some patience?"

"Oh, I got all the patience in the world when it's mine to spend. Not when it's forced on me like them damned crates of Fancher's."

"You're still frettin' about that."

"Hell, we got some of his kids now. Next thing you know, they'll be wantin' us to take them other two in, too."

He felt strapped in, trapped. The wagons lumbered along like turtles and he might as well have been tethered to them. The only times he'd enjoyed on the trail were when he was making his own way, looking at the country without seeing a whole lot of people cluttering it up. The boys seemed to pay no attention to the land they passed and it galled him. If he ever had a son, he'd by God teach him to use his eyes and ears and not be so damned caught up in foolishness. Roberta fawned over them like a mother hen and he didn't like that much either. At night they couldn't do anything and she seemed to thrive on continence. Didn't bother her none at all. Well, when he got his own place, all that was going to change. She'd not have Fancher kids underfoot nor neighbors wearing out their welcome. Her and them boys. He stared at the back of the timber wagon and grated his teeth on the grit in his mouth.

Roberta had taken possession of the boys, had mended their clothes, sewed harness leather to their shoes to make soles. After two days they were calling her "Aunt Berta."

"Aunt Berta, look, look," cried Danny as they glimpsed the town sprawled across the middle of the plain.

"Why there must be hundreds of homes here," said Roberta, "and it's so flat you can nigh see 'em all."

A multilayered pall of smoke hung over the plain, streaks of gray, and black wisps like dusty cobwebs. Plowed fields, some of them greening up, bordered small cabins well away from the town, and people had planted young trees near their homes that would bring shade to porches they would someday build. The scents of country and town mingled in a clash of zephyrs that scattered the lingering dust from the wagons. Lem smelled the change in the air. They'd be among people again and he bristled at the thought of it. Necessary, he knew, but he wished he could get him a place and just tend to farming, do some private hunting and fishing.

They drove for the center of town, asking directions as they went. They passed shops of every kind, heard cries of "welcome, pilgrim," and people waved to them, laughed at Skipper who barked at every dog, cat, chicken, hog and goat he saw.

Buggies and wagons, carts and sulkies streamed between the crowded courthouse square and the myriad shops on every street. People stood at open stalls, bartering, selling their wares. There were shoemakers and farriers, barrel smiths and whiskey drummers, tinsmiths and brewers, taverns and dry goods stores, greengrocers and butchers all plying their trades amid the mingled smells and sounds of a teeming, growing city.

Lem halted his wagon in front of the courthouse, for he and the boys had been riding with Roberta, pulling Hammerhead behind, as she sewed and fussed over their clothes.

"I'll see can I find the boys' folks," he said, setting the brake, wrapping the reins around it.

"It might take a year with all these people," said Roberta. "Lord, I've never seen so much bustle."

She looked longingly at the women in their poke bonnets, their crinoline dresses with high bodices and small frilled collars. The men dressed in a variety of clothing, from buckskins to frock coats; most of them wore hats, of every style and description.

"You boys stay right close to the wagon. I'll see can I fetch your pa."

"We want to go with you, Uncle Lemuel."

"Stay with Aunt Berta; mind her well. And, I ain't your damned uncle."

"Lem, there's no call to be mean to these poor children. They ain't done you no harm."

"I'll be glad to be shut of them," he said, and stalked off. He knew he was nervous. People made him so. And he'd never seen so many people, all strangers, at one place. He almost wished he had his rifle in hand so that he could make him a wide path through them.

Lem left the three in the wagon, wandered across the open spaces, dodging small barrows and handcarts pushed by industrious lads wearing linsey-woolsey shirts and little billed caps, knickers and long stockings. Chickens squawked as they were hauled to market in open slat-boarded crates; hogs grunted and squealed, goats bleated. The air smelled of fresh-cut lumber, cooked tripe and animal dung, of boiled turnip greens and corned beef, summer sweat and rain-soaked straw. The busy world of commerce teemed about him, so many people doing so many things, he felt as alien in their midst as they might have felt in his deep woods back in Virginia.

He saw the cart before he saw Fancher. It stood in the shade of a large stall with a striped canvas top near one of the side streets. The cart was empty when Lem looked inside and no sign of Fancher. The people manning the stall were selling cooking utensils, linens, bedding, even crudely fashioned wooden furniture. The women wore bonnets that hid their faces and the men were all young, mere boys, who stacked and arranged the goods at instructions from the almost faceless women. One old woman poured coins into a box and he saw her pull a bundle of pound notes from a pocket and deposit them with the metal shillings and pence. She slammed the box shut and hovered over it like a hen guarding eggs.

Lem's chest got tight when he looked at the people walking everywhere with no seeming purpose. None seemed to pay him any mind and he felt lost, all alone, even with all the people about. A sense of inane and inexplicable loneliness assailed him.

He looked around in panic for Fancher. He thought of calling out for him or asking after his whereabouts, but he was stricken with a kind of nameless fear that he had never experienced before. The ground seemed to quaver under him and he felt as if he must run as fast and as far as he could to catch his breath. He felt a suffocation that was strange to him. He felt that if he was not careful, the people would all move toward him and shut him off from light and air.

"Ah, there you be, Lemuel Hawke," said a voice. Lem jumped, literally, and was ashamed of his sudden fright.

"Fancher," said Lem as he caught sight of the man approaching him from a shadowed road between a pair of log buildings. "Been lookin' for you."

"You brung my crates?"

"Yonder. Brung you som'pin else, too."

"Eh? What's that?"

"Foller me," said Hawke.

"Hold on, Hawke. I got some news for you."

Lem stopped in his tracks. He looked at Fancher.

"What you got?"

"Why you wanted some farm land, didn't you?"

"So I do."

"You see a man named Horatio Bickham. South of Lexington. You'll see a road going to Frankfort. About two mile west, is where you'll find Bickham. He'll sell you good land, seven shillings the acre. Just tell him you're the man

what Elmer Fancher told him about. My woman's working for him already, here in town, and his daughter's
mindin' the childrens. Horatio Bickham. Fine man, Hawke.
Fine man."

"Why, much obliged, Mr. Fancher."

"Call me Elmer, Hawke. We're going to be jolly friends,
you and me. Now, let's get to that wagon of your'n. I'll fetch
my cart."

Fancher bobbed back to his cart, bounced up onto the
seat. He freed up the reins, clucked to the pair of horses.
Lem's heart soared with the news of farm land. But the
price was much too high for Lem's purse. Perhaps he could
talk Horatio Bickham into leasing him a few acres until he
made his crop.

The cart rattled along behind Lemuel. When he got to
his own wagon, neither Roberta nor the boys were there.
His heart felt clogged with heaviness.

Fancher pulled up alongside, hauled back on the wheel
brake. He clambered onto the cart, stood ready.

"Now, if you'll help me with my goods, I'll pay you the
five pounds I promised, Hawke. A goodly sum, mind you,
but my tools be worth many times that."

"I wonder where my wife's gone to," said Lem.

"Be quick about it, son. I've much to do."

Lem nodded dumbly, climbed up into his wagon. He
looked around for Roberta, finally saw her at the entrance
to one of the shops. She carried a new dress over her arm.
There was no sign of the boys.

"Bobbie!" he called.

Roberta looked up at him. She was beaming. She scurried towards him, radiant. She held the dress close to her.
It was dyed with pink stripes and had a white collar. He
saw that she had a matching bonnet dangling from one
hand.

"Oh, Lem," she exclaimed, "look at this. Isn't it pretty. I

just couldn't help myself. It was only two shillings. A bargain."

"Two shillings!" he exclaimed.

Her face darkened.

"Why, I knew you'd find Mr. Fancher and be paid for your hauling."

"Where are the boys?" he asked tightly.

"I'll discuss that with Mr. Fancher," she said.

Fancher swayed to keep his balance in the shaky cart. He looked at Roberta in abject bewilderment, his face a blank bowl of paste.

"Boys? What boys?" he asked.

"Why your boys, Mr. Fancher," she said sweetly. "We found 'em. But first I want to discuss the price you must pay for their return."

Fancher scowled.

Lem went to his knees, gripped the side of his wagon. His eyes squinched to dark slits and his stomach swirled with a sudden sickness.

10

Elmer Fancher's eyes bulged from their sockets. A band of color rose from his neck and suffused his face with a pink stain. His shirt swelled under an apoplectic strain.

"Are you holding my boys for ransom, Mrs. Hawke?" he asked, his voice a phlegmatic rasp.

"You offered to pay my husband five pounds for carrying those crates," she said. "I thought you might be willing to pay for hauling your sons all that way practically from Hazel Patch. I'd think the boys would be worth a lot more than your personal goods."

"Mrs. Hawke, this ain't hardly toler'ble," spluttered

Fancher. "This is . . . why, you're some such, no better'n a damned brigand. You fetch my sons to me right quick, hear?"

"What are they worth to you, Mr. Fancher?" she asked, her tone hard and flat as a sterling coin and just as cold. "If you're a-payin' Lemuel five pounds for those crates, why I would think Martin would be worth fifteen and little Daniel at least ten pounds."

"Bobbie," interjected Lemuel, "what are you doin'? Those boys ain't for barter. We found 'em, we brung 'em here. Now, fetch 'em for Mr. Fancher here."

"When he's made me an offer," she said, her gaze fixed on Fancher the way a snake watches a cornered mouse. "We did you a service, Mr. Fancher. We expect payment in kind."

"If this don't beat all," said Fancher.

"I'll talk to her, Mr. Fancher," said Lem, bounding down from the wagon.

Roberta backed away when Lem approached her. He grabbed her upper arms, held her tight in his grip.

"Don't touch me," she muttered under her breath.

"Have you gone daft, woman? You fetch them boys to their pa right quick or I'll lay a leather strop to your behind."

"You wouldn't dare!"

"Bobbie, do what I say," he said through gritted teeth, "or I'll put you over my knees right here and now."

His grip tightened on her shoulders. He shook her once, hard enough to jar her.

"Damn you," she said and her eyes narrowed. She stiffened as if in shock.

"I mean it," he said. "You get them boys now, woman."

Roberta paled. Lemuel had never talked to her in this way nor had she ever felt his strength used against her. His fingers dug into the soft flesh of her upper arms, burned furrows of pain clear to the bone.

"Let loose of me. I—I'll get the boys." People had begun to gather around. Roberta looked at them, panic flaring in her eyes.

An old woman glared at her accusingly. A man in a leather apron frowned at her. Children crowded forward and stared at her so hard that she cringed.

"You better," said Lem, releasing his wife. Roberta dashed away, disappeared between two buildings.

"Maybe you better go after her," said Fancher.

"She'll be back," Lem said defiantly, but he wasn't so sure. "I'll load them crates for you."

He climbed back up into his wagon, wrestled the heavy crates into Fancher's cart. Fancher reached into his pocket, pulled out a crumpled five-pound note.

"You'll get this soon's I get my boys back," said Fancher.

"Fair enough," said Lem. "I'm real sorry about this, Mr. Fancher. I don't know what got into Roberta."

"I wouldn't let no woman shame me like that," said Fancher, sitting atop one of his boxes. He folded the five-pound note, unfolded it, folded it again.

Lem's mouth went dry. He turned away from Fancher, sick to his stomach. He needed the money, but Fancher was right about Roberta. She had shamed him. She had done it deliberate and open. Lord, no wonder she had fussed over them boys. She had a scheme all set up to get her some money for bringing them to Fancher. It made him sick inside. It made him too sick to look at what she was doing to him.

A few moments later, Skipper ran from between the buildings. Fancher saw the dog, stood up in his cart. The crowd had dispersed, but there were still a few shop people looking their way. When Roberta and the boys appeared, Fancher waved his arms.

"Pa, Pa!" squawked little Danny.

Marty broke away from Roberta, who had his hand in hers. He lifted Danny up in his arms and ran to the cart. The beagle danced on his hind legs when Fancher lifted

Danny up into the cart with him. Marty threw the dog inside the cart and scrambled up over the side.

"Danny, God, your ma will faint when she sees you.
Marty, ah Marty, where did you go?"

The boys hugged their father. Fancher set Danny down
and reached across the space between the cart and Lem's
wagon. He handed Hawke the five-pound note.

"I'm mighty obliged you found my boys," said Fancher.
"I thank you kindly."

"Twarn't nothin'," said Lem, taking the note. "Good-by,
boys."

"Good-by, Uncle Lem," said Danny.

"Good-by," said Marty.

"Come on boys, let's be gettin' to our new home," said
Fancher. He looked at Roberta coldly as he climbed onto
the seat of his cart. Danny sat beside his father. Marty
stayed in back. He did not wave to Roberta as the cart rumbled away.

Lem watched them go, sighed deeply, and climbed down
from his wagon. Roberta stood a few yards away, biting her
lip as she watched the wagon thread its way past the Clark
Courthouse, turn onto a road leading south.

"You take that dress to where you got it," Lem said to
Roberta. "See can you get our money back."

"I won't," she said.

"You better, or I will," he said. "We can't spare a shilling on such foolishness."

"Foolishness? I buy myself a dress to wear so that I'll
look nice for you. You been tellin' me about a new life in
Kentucky and now we're here and still poor. You got five
pounds from Mr. Fancher and begrudge me a few shillings.
Here, take the dress back yourself. I won't never ask another
thing from you, Lemuel Hawke. You're stingy, mean, cruel,
and I don't know what all. I hate you. I hate you for drag-
gin' me all this way so's we can live poor as churchmice
and get in debt all over again. Where will it end? Where

will we run to next? You got no gumption. We could have got somethin' with that money I asked Mr. Fancher to pay us. We did him a favor and he owed us. Oh, you blind, dumb no-account. Foolishness? You're the fool, Lemuel. You're the stupid fool."

She threw the new dress and bonnet at Lem. She opened her small cloth satchel and took the money purse out, threw that at him too. The purse struck him in the chest, then fell to the ground. People stared at him as if suddenly discovering he had leprosy.

"There," she said, "you might as well have it all. All of our miserable savings."

Roberta stormed past him, climbed up onto the wagon seat. She sat there, stiff as a post, then crumpled over as the tears boiled up in her eyes.

"You beast," said a woman, scowling at him a long moment before she jerked her child away.

He picked the purse out of the dirt, stuck it in his waistband. Ignoring the woman, he entered the store with the dress and bonnet. A woman glared at him from behind the counter.

"I've a shilling for you," she said. "That's all I'll pay for used goods. It's more than fair for the likes of you."

"Ma'am, this dress ain't been wore."

"One shilling. Take it or leave it."

Lem slammed the clothes down on the board counter, picked up the single shilling, made a fist over it.

He stalked from the store without a word. Whispers rose up behind him like mosquitoes from a stagnant bog.

Lem mounted the wagon, sat next to Roberta. He sighed heavily as he unwrapped the reins, released the brake.

"Well, did you get your money back?" she snapped.

"One shilling is all."

"Ha. Cost you a shilling, did it? You miser."

"Bobbie, if you say another word, I'll take you across my knee like the brat you are."

"Right here? In front of everybody?"

"Right here, in front of God and everybody," he said.

He flapped the reins, made them ripple across the mules' backs. They moved. Hammerhead snorted behind them as they pulled across the commons. Lem found the road leading to Frankfort on the west, stopped at a roadside inn. He noticed an unplowed field beyond the inn, grass for grazing, plenty of open sky. The inn was a ramshackle affair, unpainted, slapped together with crooked boards, logs, scrap lumber. The sign out front read: ROOMS AND MEALS. There was a stable, a stock pen that bordered a grazing pasture, pigsty full of fat Hampshire reds, a corncrib. A row of haymows bordered one edge of a fallow field. A boy out back was chopping kindling. Four cows grazed in a far pasture that was fenced with split rails.

"Why are we stopping here?" asked Roberta. "I thought we'd stay in town where I could bathe and see some of the sights."

"I aim to see can we camp in that field yonder."

Roberta slumped, shook her head wearily.

"I want to sleep in a real bed," she said.

"We got to watch every farthing for a time."

Lem sprang from the wagon, strode to the inn. Mud clung to his moccasins. He knocked on the door. A stooped-over man stepped outside. He was bald except for thatches of tangled white hair that clung to the sides like snow-covered moss. He looked at Lem, beyond to the wagon.

"Reckon you got the Kentucky fever, son. You want bed and board?"

"Wondered could we camp in that field back there. For the night. I'll be looking for land I can rent from a man named Bickham."

"Horatio Bickham? Lives about seven miles down yonder road. He might sell you some land. Don't know if he rents. You want to stay here? Two shillings the night. Either in the bed or in the field."

"I could chop wood. Do some chores for you."

"I got a boy what does all that."

Lem thought of the shilling he had gotten back on the dress and bonnet. He looked back at Roberta. She was watching him intently.

"Anyplace we might camp?"

"Son, I'm in business. This is all private land hereabouts. Cost money to clear it. We all got taxes to pay."

"Two shillings you say?"

"That's the cheapest you'll get anywheres."

"All right."

"Pull your wagon out back. They's a door back there. First room on your right. Pay in advance."

Lem pulled out the two shillings in his pocket, placed them in the man's hand.

"Supper's at dark, breakfast at sunup. Put your stock up in that pen out there. Feed's a shilling extra."

"They can graze," said Lem. "I'll hobble 'em for the night."

"Still a shilling."

Lem pulled the purse from his waistband, fished in it for the right coin. He put another shilling in the man's open palm.

"A pleasure to do business with you," said the man. "Well's out back, too."

"It's a damn wonder you don't charge for that too."

"Thinkin' on it."

Lem held his tongue. He was raised to show respect for his elders, but the old man tried his patience. So far all he'd found in Kentucky was a hole in his money pouch. Not even a full day in Lexington and he was already short four shillings. At this rate, they wouldn't be able to rent enough land to support them, much less buy seed and food to put on the table.

The door slammed shut. Lem walked back to the wagon.

"You got yourself a bed," he told Roberta.

She glared at him in tight-lipped silence.

The Hawkes spoke little during supper. The innkeeper introduced his wife, Katrina, and their son, Wolfgang. He said his name was Adolph Werner, but he pronounced his last name with a V sound.

Katrina was a dour woman, round as a beer keg. Wolfgang seemed a quiet, brooding youth, respectful of his parents. He had flaxen blond hair, a small, thin mouth like his father's. All of the family had blue eyes, but Adolph's were dark, his wife's lighter and Wolfgang's lightest of all.

They spoke with a thick Germanic accent, shoveled the pork and potatoes into their mouths as if they were eating at gunpoint. Lem watched them furtively, but Roberta stared at her plate, picked at her food.

"You not hungry?" Katrina asked Roberta.

"Huh? Oh, I don't feel well."

"But you must eat, child. The baby. You must think of your baby."

"Oh, I didn't know you could tell," said Roberta.

"I can tell. We don't have no more babies. Little Wolfgang, he tore me all up."

Roberta blushed. Wolfgang stared at Roberta with his cold, pale eyes.

"Eat," said Adolph to his wife and son, as he took another helping of boiled turnips.

Lem got up from the table.

"Thank you for the food," he said. "I'll see to our stock, Bobbie."

Roberta didn't answer. She picked up a small piece of roast pork, chewed it daintily. There was no more talk at the table. The back door slammed shut and there was only the clank of eating utensils on metal plates. She excused herself and walked to their rented room without saying good night to the Werners.

The room was dreary even after she lit the small lantern hanging from an overhead beam. The wick smoked and blackened the glass chimney until she turned it down. She looked at the homely bed with its lumpy mattress, its simple gray coverlet. There was a small chest of drawers with a pitcher atop it. A chamber pot stuck out from under the iron bed. She shoved it back under with the toe of her boot. The sound, like a knife scraping bone, grated in her ears.

She opened the trunk Lem had brought inside. She rifled through her clothes until she got to bottom, to the new things she had made for herself. She touched the material and felt the bitter ache in her throat as her eyes stung with unbidden tears.

She thought of the pretty dress she had bought that was now back on the display rack. She looked at the dreary room and sank into a rising sea of self-pity. She patted the clothes back down and closed the trunk. She took a kerchief from her valise and dabbed at her eyes. Lem would never know what he had done to her today. She would never tell him how much it had hurt to have him take the dress back.

Roberta removed her nightgown from the valise. She had been saving it for Kentucky. It was made of soft spun cotton and had been dyed a pale pink. She had sewed little satin ribbons into the collar and onto the sleeves. The ribbons were blue and she liked the feel of them between her fingers. She undressed, put on the gown and brushed her hair.

Lem came in after a while and she pretended to be asleep.

"Bobbie," he said. "You awake?"

She didn't answer.

She listened to him undress, heard him blow out the lamp. The bed creaked under his weight. He moved close to her, found her hand. She stiffened.

He kissed her on the cheek. His hand sought her breast. She turned away from him.

"Bobbie," he whispered. "I want you."

"No," she said.

"What's the matter?"

"You're cruel," she said. "I hate you."

"Don't say that," he said. She pulled the covers up over her head and thrust his hand away from her breast. She heard him grumble for a moment, then turn over on his side, his back to hers.

She lay there for a long time, gloating in the dark.

"I guess I hate you too, Roberta," he said, and his voice surprised her. She had thought he was asleep. "I guess I started hating you when you tried to ransom them kids to Fancher. And now you're using your body like it was a weapon. I won't have no woman treat me like this."

Roberta fought for words to say, but her heart was pounding and the fear in her heart rose up so big it smothered her. She lay there, fighting down the trembling, hoping Lem wouldn't notice that she was shaking.

Soon, she heard him snoring and she stopped quivering for a moment. She felt a sudden impulse to reach over and touch him, draw him close to her, but the gulf between them was too great. Their first big battle was over. She had fought him and won. She had kept him from entering her body. That was a victory. Surely, it was. When he came to her and apologized, maybe then she would allow him to exercise his husband's rights. When he someday brought her the dress she wanted, then and only then, would she allow him to share her body as well as her bed. The quivering began again and she didn't know why. It was as if something small had broken loose inside her and was slithering around like a worm. As if something inside had broken open and was bleeding very slowly.

She couldn't sleep for the rest of the night. Her decision, the decision to deny Lemuel his marital rights, was like a scratchy woolen coat against her soft, delicate skin.

That something that was loose inside her, that little worm that was making her bleed, began to grow in her mind until she thought she knew what it was. She hated Lemuel, hated him for reasons she couldn't even say out loud because they were so little and hard and darted around so fast, making her bleed in secret because she couldn't see any wound, couldn't feel any real pain. A tapeworm devouring her innards. A parasite so small it could not be seen nor felt except in her mind. But it was hate, she was sure of that. And the wormy hate began to fester inside her like a cancer.

She touched her swollen belly and sighed. The baby would be still another weapon she could use against Lemuel Hawke.

11

Lem struck a deal with Horatio Bickham, the ambitious and miserly owner of considerable property in Woodford County. Hawke moved Roberta into a wood and stone shack built by Bickham's slaves on 80 acres of land, penned up his stock, bought seed and rolled up his shirt-sleeves. For a few shillings and a portion of each crop, the land belonged to Lem. The contract had to be renewed every year. Lem was required to clear so many acres of woodland on other property owned by Bickham. He had to provide the landowner with three cords of firewood each fall.

The work was backbreaking. Lem had to turn the fields with a crude, homemade wooden plow, harrow it with brush, harvest the crops by hand. Roberta was unable to help since she was growing heavy with child and had her hands full just doing the chores morning and night, tending to their little garden where they grew beans, corn, squash, melons, cabbage, lettuce, tomatoes and cucumbers for their own table. The distance between them had grown since that night at the inn, but they were civil to one another.

Lem finished plowing, planted small crops of corn, hemp and tobacco, knowing he'd have to tend and harvest the crops himself that first year. He planted ten acres in alfalfa, wondering how he'd ever get it mowed and stacked without help. But, the hay would feed his horses through the winter, and he hoped to have a milk cow following the sale of his tobacco crop.

Lem put his energy into his work. Roberta spoke to him when he came in from the fields at night, but when he tried to touch her, she took his hand and pushed it away.

"A man has needs," he told her, more than once.

"It hurts with the baby," she said.

So Lemuel lived with his rage and quelled his desire. Roberta continued to swell until she walked with a backward tilt and let out her thin dresses so that she could breathe. Some of the dresses rode high on her belly so that the hems were above her knees.

She did not glow like most pregnant women he had seen. Her face grew ruddy from the sun, but when Lem looked at her she seemed to be in perpetual shadow. She combed and brushed her hair at night, endlessly stroking her locks until they shone. She patched his clothes and darned his socks, cooked his meals, but she gave him none of herself. Her body was locked away from him, like her mind.

In October, he heard Roberta scream. He raced across the field to find her in agony.

"Get Mrs. Bickham," she said tightly. "Quick."

"What's the matter? What's wrong?"

"It's the baby. Hurry." She clenched her teeth and he saw that her face was drenched in sweat, her hands balled up tightly into fists as she leaned against the doorjamb, propping herself up to keep from falling.

"I'll be right back," he said. "Hold on."

He rode Hammerhead bareback at a gallop the five miles to the Bickham place.

Nancy Bickham heard him yelling for a quarter mile. She stood up from the butter churn, went to the window. She was a thin, hawk-faced woman with sunny copper hair and hazel eyes, piercing as needles.

"Mrs. Bickham, you got to come quick. My wife's having the labor pains."

"Lands," said Nancy Bickham through the window, "you get back there and put some water to boiling. I'll be there directly."

"God, hurry," said Lem, wheeling Hammerhead in a tight circle.

"I'll be there within the hour. You put that poor woman to bed and tell her to hold on."

An hour later, Horatio Bickham drove his sulky into the shadow of an oak tree bright with autumn leaves. Nancy Bickham, wearing a loose shift of striped calico, carried a satchel and an armful of towels as she trotted up to the shack on long, lean legs.

Roberta lay on the bed, drenched in sweat, her body flexing in agonizing spasms. Lem stood like a stick at the foot of the bed, his face blank as clay.

A pot of water boiled on the wood stove. Clouds of steam floated toward the sod ceiling.

Nancy took one look at Roberta and gasped.

"Land, the baby's coming now. Mr. Hawke, you go on outside. Now."

Confused, Lem seemed rooted to the floor. Nancy had to give him a shove to get him started. Before he was out the door, Mrs. Bickham had begun to strip Roberta's clothes from her. Before he reached the oak tree, where Horatio waited in the sulky, Roberta screamed. Lem hesitated, started to go back to the shack.

"Son, you come on over here. You'll just be in the way

in there. Mrs. Bickham knows what to do. We've got three daughters and three sons of our own."

Bickham climbed down from the sulky, took a pipe from his pocket, filled it from a leather tobacco pouch. He wore a shirt of fustian, trousers of gray wool, a felt slouch hat, boots made of ox-hide. He was a broad-shouldered man, at five foot six two inches shorter than his wife. His brushy face was florid from good living, bronzed lightly by the sun. His slightly bulbous nose was spider-tracked with blue veins and mottled with small red splotches. His belly hung a quarter inch over his wide belt. He stuck the pipe between pudgy lips and held a magnifying glass above the bowl to catch the rays of the sun.

"Got your pipe with you, Hawke?"

"Nope." Lem kept looking over at the shack. "I reckon I'd be too nervous to smoke right now."

Bickham directed a shaft of sunlight into the midst of the tobacco. In seconds, a thin tendril of smoke curled up out of the bowl. Bickham sucked air through the pipe until the tobacco caught. He inhaled deeply.

"It's women's business now, Hawke. Nancy will tend to your wife and newborn."

"Yes sir."

"You'll have to work harder now, Hawke. Children are a responsibility. I have six of them. Fine children. You should think about your wife, too. She'll need some help. You might want to think about buying a slave, maybe a man and wife. A Nigra woman can help with the household chores. A strong Nigra man could help you with the field-work. You'll have to plant bigger crops next year."

"I don't rightly think I could afford to keep slaves just now," said Lem.

"Well, you think about it, son. This is good land, but until you have grown children to work it with you, it'll sap you. Nigras are cheaper to keep than children, in the long run."

"Yes sir," said Lem, respectfully.

Fifteen minutes later, the two men heard a squawl. Lem started to bolt toward the shack, but Bickham restrained him. Then, it was quiet for a long time before Nancy appeared at the door of the cabin. She beckoned toward the two men.

"It's a boy," she told Lem, who burst past her into the shack.

Roberta's eyes fluttered. The baby lay next to her, swaddled in a tiny blanket. His face was squinched up, flushed a dark red. A shock of black hair adorned his pate. He waggled tiny fists in the air, moved his mouth as he drew air into his lungs.

Bickham slapped Lem on the back.

"By God, a son!" he exclaimed.

"Thank you, Mrs. Bickham," said Lem. "I'm going to call him Morgan after a friend of mine back in Virginia."

"That's a fine name," said Nancy.

Roberta opened her eyes for a moment, glared at Lem. The baby squawled again. Roberta turned over, her back to little Morgan Hawke.

"She'll be all right," said Nancy Bickham nervously. She picked up the baby, held it to her breast. "It's the shock."

Lem looked at the child, then at his wife.

"I reckon so," he said.

Horatio coughed.

"You need anything, you come by," he told Lem. "Come on, Nancy. It's time we let these folks to themselves."

Nancy put the baby back down on the bed, next to Roberta.

"Here, Mrs. Hawke. Your new son. You'll need to nurse him soon."

"Go away," said Roberta. Lem's face reddened and he hung his head in shame. The Bickhams left and it was quiet in the cabin for a long time.

"You ought to have been more polite," Lem said to Roberta.

"What a terrible name for a child," she said.

"It's a good strong name, Bobbie."

"It's a poor name, Lem. As poor as you're bound to be all your life."

Her words stung him. They bored so deep he knew he would never forget them.

Morgan Hawke was a bright, playful baby. He had dark brown hair, brown eyes, rubbery features that soon became shaped into composites of Roberta and Lemuel. If anything, he favored Lem the most, which pleased the boy's father. Roberta nursed the tyke through the winter, but she refused to call him Morgan. Instead, she gave him a middle name, Llewellyn, after her father's name, and she called him Lew, which irritated Lem.

"You'll confuse the boy," he told her.

"Lew is a prettier name than Morgan. Why would you name your son after a dirty, filthy, ne'er-do-well like Silas?"

"Silas was a good man. He taught me a lot. Like I aim to teach young Morgan."

"Well, if you have your way, Lew will never amount to much. Look at you."

"We're doing just fine. I'll be able to pay my taxes next year."

"Pshaw. Look at this hovel we live in. Our place in Virginia was nicer than this."

"I'll build another room on in the spring, put a porch out front."

"It'll still be a shack," she said.

Her milk dried up when baby Morgan was five months old. Roberta seemed to lose interest in her son when he stopped suckling at her breast. The winter seemed long to Lem, but he hunted the canebrakes and roamed the forests of maple, walnut, sycamore and oak, brought home deer and turkey for the larder. He sold venison in town, added a

few shillings to his meager savings. He had sold the tobacco and hemp, some of the corn following the harvest,
put the money aside.

The hunting did not take away his desire for a wife, nor
the fishing on cold winter streams. One evening, early in
March, when there had been sun for days and little snow
on the ground, he came home and hung his rifle over the
door, his possibles pouch and powder horns on the wall
underneath where he had set hard deer antler tips in knife-
carved holes and glued them there for hooks. Supper sim-
mered on the stove; Morgan played on the floor with a ball
made of buckskin sewed around scraps of cloth. Roberta
was lacing grosgrain to the front of a bodice she had made of
coarse linen. She sat by the fire in a rocker he had made
from a lightning-struck walnut that had aged for three years
in the sun at the edge of cleared land.

"Put the boy in his crib," Lem told Roberta.

"Let him play," she said. "He ain't botherin' me none."

"Do what I done told you," he said sternly.

She looked at him, her face splashed with firelight.

"You better set down and put some of those vittles I fixed
in your belly," she said.

"You can have it hard or easy," he said, grabbing Morgan
up and carrying him to the dark corner of the room where
his crib stood in the shadow. The boy made sounds in his
throat. Lem put him in the crib.

"Don't you start up," said Roberta.

"I aim to take my pleasure of you," he said.

She set the bodice aside, stiffened in the chair. Morgan
cooed in his crib, filling up the silence between them. Lem
strode over to her, stood above her. He had filled out; his
muscles had hardened at the plow and the stump.

"You leave me be," she said.

Lem slipped a hand under her armpit, lifted her from the
chair. He looked deep into her nut-brown eyes, stroked the

fine brown hair that took on sheen from the dancing fire and remembered other times when she wanted him as much as he wanted her.

She jerked away from him, but he grabbed her, drew her close.

"I'll say please, first," he said. "Let it be like it was."

"It can't never be like it was," she said and her nostrils flared with anger.

"Then, by God, it'll be like it's got to be."

He lifted her up in his arms and started to carry her to their bed in the corner of the room opposite the place where Morgan slept. Roberta began to kick and pummel his head and shoulders with her fists.

"Put me down," she said.

He threw her onto the bed. The wooden slats took up the shock of her sudden weight and the sound they made was like groaning. Lem blew out the lamps until there was only the firelight throwing shadows around the room. He slipped his galluses from his shoulders and the ribands hung from his waist like military gun-slings.

Roberta tried to get up from the bed, but he blocked her way, pushed her back down.

"You're cruel," she said.

"You don't know what cruel is," he said, thinking of how he had wanted her all these months and how coldly she had treated him.

"You're no better than a savage."

"If you don't get out of them clothes, Bobbie, you're going to be sewin' well into summer."

"Damn you," she said.

Lem stripped to his skin and went after her. She struggled, trying to fight him off. Little Morgan saw the shadowy figures from his crib, heard his mother scream. He began to cry. The noise of the shaking bed scared him. He whimpered for a long time before he dropped off to sleep, alone and untended.

Lem added a room onto the shack in the spring, as he had promised. Late in the summer, he built a porch onto the front of the shack. He hired one of Horatio's sons to help him during the harvest and still earned enough to pay his taxes, set money aside. For Morgan's first birthday, on October 7, 1794, he gave the boy a beagle puppy that he had gotten from Bickham in trade. Lem named the puppy Friar Tuck. Morgan called him Tut. At Christmas, he gave Roberta enough money to buy herself a dress. He made a wooden rifle for Morgan, sewed him his first pair of moccasins.

As Kentucky grew, so did little Morgan. Roberta began to spend more and more time in Lexington, since she had begun working in a print shop during the winters. Although she didn't tell Lem, she ran into Barry O'Neil in town one day when Morgan was five years old.

Barry was dressed like a gentleman in a striped waistcoat, top hat, shiny boots. Roberta, wearing an inexpensive summer frock, tried to avoid him.

"Roberta," he called. "I've been looking all over for you." He tipped his fine beaver hat and the sun flared in his red hair for a moment.

"Me?"

"Why, yes. I knew you had come to Lexington. I've hoped to see you every day."

"Barry, I—I must get to work."

He stood close to her, blocking her way. He smiled at her. His eyes scoured her, brought a rosy blush to her cheeks.

"Where do you work?"

"Kroger's printing."

"Why, that's right on my way. I'll walk with you. I'm a hatter. My office and plant is just over on Fourth and Main. Kroger's is in the next block."

"I know." She had passed B & J Hatters almost every day since they had opened a year before. She saw it on her noon walks to the dress shops on Broadway. She had never

associated it with Barry O'Neil. "Do you own the establishment?" she asked, trying to appear sophisticated.

"With my uncle John. Oh, it's a fine business. There are
only five or six hatters here, but we're the biggest. We make
beautiful and fashionable hats of wool and fine felt hats of
raccoon, beaver and muskrat. We buy only the highest
quality furs."

"I've seen your hats," she said. "They are truly most
fashionable. The one you're wearing now is most attractive. It looks elegant." She looked at his moustache. It was
neatly trimmed, made his lips more sensual than she remembered.

He laughed, and took her arm as they crossed the bridge
over the little spring-fed stream that coursed through the
city. The dreary tanyards bordered both sides and beyond
them, Lexington's industries thrived, the powder mills, print
shops, potteries, ropewalks, breweries, ironworks. People
bustled past them, smiled at them both. Some nodded
to Barry and spoke his name, calling him "Mr. O'Neil."
Roberta was impressed.

"What do you do for Bill Kroger?" he asked.

"Everything. I file the type and the furniture, help set
type in the chases. I'm learning to do the books."

"Ah, then you might be interested in a proposition I have
for you."

"For me?"

"Yes. I need someone to help with our accounts. You
would be perfect."

"Oh, I'm not very good at figures yet. Really I'm not."

"Well, I have a lady who will teach you. Think about it.
I'll pay you more than Kroger does. Besides, it will give
us a chance to see more of each other. Lexington is growing. Kentucky is an important state. You should be a part
of it. I think you would look wonderful wearing some of
our hats when buyers come to call."

"Me? A model? It could only be for the winter. I must work on the farm in spring and summer."

"We'll see. Kroger is a slaver at heart. I'll bet he doesn't invite you to tea in the afternoons."

"Well, no."

"There, you see. We always have tea in the afternoons, talk about new fashions, look at hat designs, talk to artists. Important people stop by to chat. Dressmakers show us their latest goods. Some of our ladies even try them on and they can buy them at a discount."

"It sounds wonderful," she said, thinking of the few dresses she owned. She had made them herself and they were all a step or two behind what she saw in the shops.

Barry squeezed her arm and she felt a tingling shock ripple through her flesh.

"Why don't you come by tomorrow 'bout noon? I'll buy you lunch and show you around."

"Why, that would be fine," she said, surprised at her own boldness.

They reached the offices and plant of B & J Hatters. The name stood out in large letters on the outside of the brick building, one of the few in Lexington.

"I've missed you," said Barry, as he stood at the entrance. "Did you think about me?"

"A little," she admitted. But, it was more than a little. She had often wondered what would have happened had she let Barry partake of her favors that last time they saw each other. It was wicked of her to think such things, but she couldn't help herself.

He doffed his hat.

"See you tomorrow," he said.

"Yes," she said. "Tomorrow."

She skipped lightly down the street. She hesitated before entering the shop that bore the legend: KROGER'S PRINTING. Her heart thrummed with excitement. She clutched her purse to her breast, took a deep breath to clear her mind, compose herself.

Suddenly, she didn't want to enter the print shop. Not now, not ever again.

She looked down the block toward the hattery. She wondered if she could wait until tomorrow.

Roberta had already made up her mind what she was going to do. She was going to live the life she wanted.

Before the farm life crushed her; before Lem stripped away her last shred of dignity and hope. Lem didn't care about her suffering, about living poor. He didn't long for better things as she did. He offered her no hope for a better life. That's what she needed. Hope.

Barry O'Neil could give it to her.

12

During those winter days, when Roberta was working in town, Lem took care of the raising of their boy, Morgan. Sometimes Bickham's slave, Calvin Moon, would come by, bringing some of the slave children to play with young Morgan. Sometimes Lem would take him over to the Bickhams' where he could play with the older children. The boy was always ready to come home, but he said he liked Mrs. Bickham. Horatio, he told his father, scared him.

In Morgan's seventh year, Lem made a little rifle for him. Roberta was working for Barry O'Neil at the hattery, had been there for two years. Lem thought she was still working for Kroger because she hadn't told him about Barry. She kept the extra money for herself, bought dresses which she kept at a friend's, another woman who worked in the hattery, Ernestine Gerson. Ernestine was the head bookkeeper and had taught Roberta how to keep the ledgers, where to file receipts, bills of lading, orders, employee records.

Lem found an old .36 caliber rifle barrel in a heap of scrap at the edge of Bickham's land one day. The stock had rotted away, but the lock was still intact, a small German mechanism that could be cleaned up, oiled, made to work. Both the rifle and lock were rusted, but he soaked them in hot grease, bear oil, to make them shine. He carved a new stock from walnut, sawed off part of the long barrel and set it in the rough hollow of the stock for measure. Morgan watched the whole process, compared it to his father's long rifle.

"Papa's goin' to make you a rifle just like his'n," Lem told him.

"Can I shoot it?"

"For certain."

"I'll make you a possibles pouch, too, and powder horns. We'll find us some good flints."

"I want to go huntin' with you, Pa."

"We'll do it," said Lem. "You'll be a reg'lar Kings Mountain boy when we get finished."

The boy doted on his father. Morgan followed Lem everywhere, especially during the winter when Roberta spent long hours in town. There were times when she said she had to work late and would not come home for supper. At such times, Lem fed Morgan and they worked on the rifle until their eyes drooped with tiredness. Often, Roberta would return home to find Lem and their son asleep on the floor in front of the fire, the cabin smelling of bear oil, sweat and burned meat.

"I don't want to be a King's Mountain boy," said Morgan. "I want to be your boy."

"Them was fightin' men, son. Happened about the time I was born. My pa, he was there."

"What happened to him?"

"Your grandpap? Why, nothin' son, I don't reckon." Lem frowned, pulled in a deep breath. "You ask too many questions for a little feller."

The truth was that Lem didn't know what had happened to his father. One day he just disappeared. But it was after his ma had been seeing a man Lem knew only as one of his uncles. After his pa left, the uncle, a man named Cletus McEllerby, moved in and slept in his ma's bed. Now, he knew that Cletus was no kin, but he never had figured out why his pa had run off like that without saying good-by.

In Lem's hands, the file and the rasp were sculptor's tools, capable of great artistry. The rifle he fashioned for Morgan was not fancy, but he took off all the metal burrs, burnished the iron down past the rust, worked the stock delicately with emory cloth he had made himself of grit and linen. At a table set in the center of the room, in front of the hearth, he polished and carved, hammered in a tenon that made the short barrel fit snug in the stock. He made a new front blade sight, a fancy buckhorn for the rear. He oiled the lock until it worked smooth and quietly. The spring was tight enough to set sparks off quartz.

One morning, before noon, Lem sat again at the table, wiped the rifle down, held it to his shoulder, sighted down its 19-inch barrel.

Morgan, who had been going through his father's possibles pouch, one of his favorite pastimes, looked up. Lem held the finished rifle out to him.

"Pa! Is it really finished?"

"It's your'n, Morgan. We'll load her up with maybe twenty grains of powder, see can you shoot true enough to pop the eye out of a squirrel."

Morgan took the rifle in his hands. He held it with a kind of reverence, looking at the polished walnut stock that gleamed from butt to an inch below the muzzle.

"It's even got a ramrod," said the boy, grinning.

"Be careful, it ain't the best. Mighty small caliber, so the rod's thin as any I ever saw."

Morgan held the rifle to his shoulder. It felt light in his hands. He sighed with pleasure as he swung the barrel toward the door, then back to the stove, squinching his left eye shut.

"It's real beautiful," said Morgan. "But you ain't put no flint on it yet."

"Give me back the rifle and we'll set you in a flint. I got me some of Brandon's best from England I been saving."

Lem walked over to the bed, slid out a small box. He took it over to the table where he had been working. Morgan's eyes grew wide as Lem opened the box. It contained more than two dozen flints, all chipped square, but of different sizes.

"My own flint," breathed Morgan.

"See you set it right in the cock," said his father. "You put the flat side either up'ards or down'ards. Depends on how big it is and what its shape is. You want to set it just so."

Lem twisted the screw on the cock, the arm that held the flint, opening the jaws.

"Fetch me a small piece of leather. Might be a piece in my possibles bag, son."

Morgan gathered up his father's tools and such, put them back in the pouch. He brought the pouch over to the table. Morgan felt around inside, retrieved a small patch of leather. Lem took his knife and cut a square piece just big enough to cushion the flint. He folded the leather over the flint, leaving the striking edge exposed.

"There," he said to Morgan. "We just push this outfit in the jaws of the cock, screw her down a bit and check to see it hits the frizzen just so."

Lem let the cock down gently and hunched over. He and Morgan peered at the place where the flint touched the frizzen.

"Every part of that flint's got to scare sparks off that frizzen plate," said Lem.

"Whole thing's got to touch," said Morgan seriously.

Lem smiled.

"You pay partic'lar attention after each shot to see it stays square and strikes true."

"I will, sir," said Morgan, an obedient tone in his voice.

Lem jiggled the flint until it was perfectly set, then screwed the jaws down tight on the leather.

"There," he said to himself. "Morg, get Tut and let's go see can he scare us up a rabbit."

"Yes, Pa," said Morgan, taking the proffered rifle.

Lem stood up, wiped oily hands on his woolen trousers. He grabbed his wool-lined buckskin jacket off a peg, picked up his rifle, horns, the possibles pouch off the table.

"Come along, son," he said. "Let's make that rifle talk."

Morgan beamed. He grabbed his little coat from his bed, wrestled into it. He set a coonskin cap on his head, stuffed mittens in his pocket. He shouldered the new rifle like a soldier, marched outside behind his father.

There was snow on the ground; the sky was overcast. Their breaths made steam in the frosty air. Lem looked at the sky, the tendrils of smoke rising from the sugar camps in the hills. Bickham had the only sugar house around and he forbade Lem from tapping the maples in the gaunt forests that surrounded his rented land. But, he could buy a white loaf from his landlord at low cost and Lem supposed that was good of the man. Roberta and Morgan could not live without sugar.

"More snow comin'. Your ma may not get back from town tonight, less'n she leaves pretty quick." Sometimes Roberta stayed over when it snowed heavily. From the look of the sky, she might not be home for several days unless she rode in pretty quick. Lem had bought her a gentle bay mare, which he called Rose. Roberta rode the mare back and forth to town, stabled the horse when she had to spend the night at her girlfriend's. Lem didn't know the woman, just her first name, Ernestine. Roberta said she worked for Kroger and was a widow, lived alone.

"I don't care," said Morgan, interrupting Lem's thoughts. "I just want to shoot this beautiful rifle."

Lem knew how Morgan felt. He remembered his first rifle. It was so heavy he could barely lift it, but there was power in the holding of it. There was even more power in the buck and roar of it when he had touched it off for the first time.

Morgan called the dog.

"Here, Tut. Come here, Tut."

The beagle rounded a corner of the house, snow flying from his paws, ears flattened against his neck.

"Well, he's about ready," said Lem.

"Pa, that hound's plumb ready," said Morgan, stretching himself to be tall next to his father.

"Let's set us some kindling wood to shoot at," said Lem. "See can we find us a place to stick 'em. Grab a bunch of them little ones off the pile." Lem pointed to the stack of kindling next to the woodpile. Morgan scurried off, Tut hard on his heels, to grab several pieces of kindling.

Lem picked up several three-foot, unsplit logs, carried them in back of the cabin. He made a square, cabinlike structure two feet high. He began to pile snow inside. Morgan saw what he was doing and joined in. They heaped snow up and then Lem started poking kindling sticks in the snow at three-inch intervals.

"Those be our targets?" asked Morgan.

"Yep. We're going to start you off at twenty yards."

Lem walked off twenty yards, Morgan tagging along in his tracks. Tut, the beagle, scratched a bed for himself, digging through the snow until he struck solid ground. He kept busy at that, widening it, until it was big enough for him to plop down and make it warm.

Lem cradled his rifle and pulled the peg out of the primer

horn with his teeth. He sprinkled powder in the pan, blew on it to get rid of the excess. Morgan handed his rifle to his father.

"Do mine," he said.

"We got to get you a horn, boy."

"Yes sir. I got to get me a horn. Two of 'em like you got."

"You need a heap of things, Morgan. There's one thing you ain't asked me about. It's real important."

Morgan cocked a squinched eye and looked at his father, then at the new rifle. A puzzled expression etched furrows in the boy's forehead, knitted his brows. Then, his face softened and he cried out.

"Lead ball!" he shrieked. "I don't have no ball to shoot."

Lem grinned, dug into a pocket of his coat. He pulled out a handful of .035 balls.

"I cast these when you was asleep," he told his son. "Got you a mold, too, at the smith's. And you can use my patches 'til you cut some for yourself. Let's load you up. You watch what I do and do it that way ever' time."

Lem showed the boy how to measure the powder. He put a ball in the center of Morgan's palm, poured powder from his big cowhorn on top of the ball. When enough grains had trickled to cover part of the ball, he took the ball away.

"Pour that down your barrel, son. Don't spill any."

Morgan set his rifle butt in the snow, made a funnel of his hand. He poured the powder down the barrel. Some of the powder stuck to his palm. He rubbed it off on the muzzle.

"Now, pick up your piece and whack it a few times just above the lock to shake that powder down all the way."

Morgan did that.

"Now for patch and ball," said Lem.

Lem laid a strip of greased patching across the muzzle of Morgan's rifle. He placed the ball on the cloth, poked it down inside the barrel until it was flush with the muzzle. He took a patch knife from his belt and cut off the excess material. He rammed ball and pouch six inches down the barrel with a short starter. Then he took the ramrod and seated the ball.

"I can do that," said Morgan.

"Here, take my little horn and prime your pan. Point the barrel toward the ground and away from you. Once you've put powder in the pan, you've got yourself a dangerous weapon."

Lem watched as Morgan poured fine powder into the pan. He poured too much.

"Now, blow gently on it. You've got so much powder in there you'll burn your face off when that flint strikes sparks. You want just enough to cover the bottom of the pan."

Morgan blew away the excess powder.

"Now, take aim at that stick farthest to the left," said Lem. "When you're 'most ready, pull back the cock until she clicks. Make sure the frizzen is down. Hold the rifle snug to your shoulder and catch you a little breath and hold it. When you've got your barrel steady, you squeeze the trigger. Real smooth and easy."

"I'm ready, Pa."

"Go on then and make some thunder."

The boy stepped up to the imaginary firing line and faced the target as he had seen his father do many times. He set the cock back full and shouldered the small rifle. Lem watched him, saying not a word. He noticed how the boy lined up his sights on the target, held steady. He saw Morgan take a shallow breath, hold it in without strain.

Morgan squeezed the trigger. Fire and smoke belched from the muzzle of the .36 caliber. Lem's eyes tracked to the target. The stick snapped in two.

"I got it, Pa," said Morgan. "Looky yonder."

"I see it, son," said Lem. He touched the boy's shoulder, gave it a gentle squeeze. "You're a right smart shot, less'n it was just luck."

"Warn't no luck to it," said Morgan. "I saw that stick and I held on it real steady."

"Umm, you did that." His father hoisted his rifle, pulled back the cock until the sear engaged. He aimed for the second stick from the left, but it was all one flowing motion. Cocking, aiming, firing. The stick broke in half. White smoke blew back on the boy and his father. The shot echoed in the snowy hills, then faded into nothingness.

"Good shot," said Morgan, his voice thin as a girl's. His breath mingled its vapors with the smoke.

"Maybe you got the gift," said Lem. "Maybe you've got the hawk-eye. Let's reload and see can we scare up a hare or two before noon."

"A rabbit? Oh, Pa, I can't wait."

Tut whined.

Man and boy reloaded their rifles. This time, Morgan did it all himself. Lem watched him carefully. The boy made no mistakes. He would, Lem knew, but for now, he was mighty careful.

They started out for the woods. Tut ranged back and forth in front of them, crossing and recrossing the rabbit and bird tracks that threaded the open pasture. Soon, he gave throat to his hunting cry and dashed off on a fresh spoor trail. The dog disappeared in the woods. His high-pitched yelps carried on the clear winter air.

"Tut's got him a rabbit trail," said Morgan.

"If he's good, he'll run the game our way. You be set, son. You see the rabbit, you start your aim behind it. Swing your rifle on the same line, squeeze off a shot just as the muzzle blocks out the rabbit. Foller on through as if you ain't shot yet."

"I been practicin' that with my wooden gun, Pa."

Lem swelled up with pride. The boy could barely straggle along through the snow. His trousers were wet to the knees, yet he was game, game as any boy might be. It was plumb cold and there wasn't a trace of a shiver in the boy.

Tut's yelps unraveled like ribbons to a higher pitch. They faded only to grow loud and piercing again. Lem and

Morgan drew closer to the edge of the forested hill where Tut had begun tracking the rabbit. Lem put out a hand as Morgan caught up with him.

"We'll wait him out," said his father.

Morgan nodded, his dark eyes glittering. He gripped the rifle with mittened hands, a thumb on the dog cock of his rifle. The beagle's yapping grew more excited. Then, the rabbit broke from cover, angled out of the woods on a line that would bisect the open field.

"Take him," said Lem.

Morgan thumbed back the cock. He shouldered the rifle. He aimed at the running rabbit. The snowshoe hare bounded in erratic patterns, zigzagging away from the two hunters. Morgan fired and the rabbit changed course. A puff of snow erupted several yards behind the animal. Tut broke from the woods, short stubby legs flying, in full cry.

Lem shouldered his rifle, tracked the darting rabbit, squeezed off a shot.

"Just like on a string," he said aloud as the rabbit jerked up short, flew straight up in the air, then fell to the snow in a furry heap.

"You got him!" screamed Morgan. The boy raced toward the downed rabbit. Lem laughed and slogged after him.

Tut reached the rabbit first. It was still kicking. The beagle bellered as if it had been cuffed, circled the twitching hare as if he had gone mad.

Morgan snatched the rabbit by the hind legs, held him proudly aloft.

"You was way behind him," said his father.

"I know."

"Know what you done wrong?"

"I think I stopped swinging the rifle barrel."

"Likely," said Lem. "You'll do better next time."

"Well, you sure got him, Pa. He's a big 'un too."

"Want to gut him out?"

"Do I?"

"Take my knife. Get his entrails. You can skin him back to home."

"Can I have his fur, Pa?"

"You got to tan it yourself."

"Oh, I will, I will," said the boy, excited.

"Think about this one next time you shoot. Think about how hungry you could get and have only one ball. You might depend on a rabbit's meat for your supper one day."

"We got plenty of meat, Pa."

Lem frowned. He handed Morgan his knife, butt first. The boy took it eagerly.

"Might come a time when a rabbit's all you got. You miss him and use up all your powder and ball it would sure do powerful bad things to your disposition."

"I won't miss next time, Pa. I promise cross my heart."

Lem laughed. The boy made a mess of gutting out the rabbit until his father showed him how to make a clean gut.

"Don't saw at it. Keep your knife sharp and slit your game from asshole to rib cage."

Morgan made a sound raspy with disgust.

"Reach in and pull out the guts, just strip 'em out. If you was really hungry, you'd clean them entrails and fry 'em. Save the gizzard and the heart."

The boy watched his father deftly remove the entrails, slice through the windpipe, crack the anal cavity open. Lem washed the insides with snow. He stuck the rabbit inside his shirt at the back. It made a bulge along the small of his back.

They heard a sound.

"Listen," said Lem.

"Them's sleigh bells, Pa."

"Right enough. Somebody's a-comin'."

"Might be Calvin. Or Mrs. Bickham, maybe."

They knew the sleighs by the sounds of their bells. The woodcutter's used the heavier, clanking bells. The Bickham sleigh used the smaller, higher-pitched bells. Lem and

Morgan started walking toward the road that bordered the field. Lem's leased property stood west of Bickham's, well off the main road to Lexington.

"Wonder why somebody'd be comin' here," said Lem. He and Morgan had only seen the Bickham sleigh on the main roads.

"I don't know, Pa."

As they crossed the open field, the sleigh came into view where the hedgerow and the forest parted and the road came through. It was drawn by a single dray horse wearing blinders.

"Can you see who it is?" Lem asked his son.

"Calvin, I think. Only one person near as I can figger."

The boy was beginning to sound like him, Lem thought. "Sure enough."

Lem waved. The sleigh veered from its course and headed straight for them, across the snowy field. The snow was wet enough to pack. The sleigh left parallel tracks in its wake. The bells crackled like crystal, making sweet music. Tut started barking.

"Shut your gob," said Lem.

"Shut up," said Morgan and the dog crept away, its tail drooping.

The sleigh pulled up a few yards from the man and the boy, its runners hissing underneath the sound of bells.

"Whoa, Ben," said the driver, Calvin Moon. The horse slowed to a stop.

"Calvin," said Lem.

"Mista Lem, Mizriz Bickham says to come quick."

"Something the matter?"

"It's your Mizriz. She come to the house and done fainted I s'pose. Mizriz Bickham says to take you there in the sled."

"Go on back home, Morgan," said Lem.

"But, Pa—"

"Don't you argue with me, boy. You take this rabbit and Tut and get on home. I'll be back directly."

Lem took the rabbit out of his shirt, handed it to Morgan. The boy looked as if he was going to cry. He took the rabbit by the hind legs.

"You got you a nice hare, Mista Lem," said Calvin.

"Pa," said Morgan.

Lem climbed up on the seat next to Calvin. He did not look at his son, but nudged the slave in the side.

Calvin slapped the reins against Ben's rump. The horse took up the slack in the traces. The sleigh began to move. The horse turned in a wide circle, headed back the way it had come. Soon, the new tracks blended into the old.

"What's the matter with my wife?" asked Lem when they were out of earshot of the boy.

"She pretty sick, Mista Lem. Her face all pale and white like a ghost and she having trouble breathing. Mista Horatio, he done gone hisself for the doctor."

Lem said nothing. He looked back and saw Morgan still standing in the middle of the field. He looked so small and alone out there. Tut sat there on his haunches like an andiron, next to the boy. The sleigh bells jangled mindlessly and a few flakes of snow began to fall. Calvin Moon took the buggy whip and snapped it over the rump of the horse. The sleigh picked up speed, the runners gliding over the packed snow of the road, the brassy tintinnabulation of the bells settling into a steady, frantic, annoying monotony.

13

Lem handed his coat to the black woman. A little black boy dusted the snow from Hawke's trousers and moccasins. The woman shook out his coat.

"You can go inside now," she said. "Mizriz Bickham, she's with the doctuh."

"I'll show you where they is," said the little boy.

Lem felt strange entering the Bickham house. He had never been inside before. Calvin had stopped the sleigh by the back door. Lem followed the servant boy through the hallway and into a large kitchen with the biggest stove he had ever seen. Utensils hung from hoops attached to the ceiling. The house was two stories and looked bigger than a barn from the outside.

"This year's the parlor," said the boy. "I'll tell Mizriz Bickham you's here."

The boy disappeared. Lem looked around the room. The furniture was elegant, probably expensive. There was a Philadelphia Chippendale side chair made of gleaming mahogany with a matching hassock, a scroll-ended English couch, a cabriole armchair, a walnut desk and chair. The carpet felt soft and velvety to the soles of his moccasined feet. It was still light out, but the snow was falling faster and heavier now and the room was growing dark. He hoped Morgan had sense enough to bring more firewood in and to put logs on the fire.

Lem heard voices. One was Horatio Bickham's. Another belonged to a man he didn't know. He heard Nancy Bickham's soft voice underneath. He heard the Negro boy's high-pitched squeak, then footsteps broke the conversation, grew louder as they approached.

"Lemuel," said Nancy, entering the parlor. "I'm so glad Calvin found you. Come with me."

"What's the matter with Roberta?" asked Lem.

"The poor dear. She collapsed right at our doorstep. I don't think the fall hurt her. Calvin was right there."

"She fell?"

"From her horse. The doctor's here, talking to Horatio. We'll find out more from him."

Lem felt queasy. His stomach shrank and quivered. He and Mrs. Bickham entered the foyer of the house. Horatio

Bickham stood at the foot of the stairs, listening to a short stub of a man wearing a wrinkled coat. His collar was soiled, unpressed, his shoes were unshined, muddy and damp from melted snow. He held a small leather satchel by its handle. The satchel was marred by wrinkles and minor rips and tears.

"Ah, here's the woman's husband now," said Bickham.

The man turned to look at Lem.

"Doctor Guenther, this is Lemuel Hawke," said Nancy.

"Your wife had a spell. I gave her some powders. You may take her home in a few moments."

"What's wrong with her?" asked Lem.

The doctor sniffled, wiped his nose with a handkerchief.

"She's going to have a baby," said Guenther. "In another two or three months, I'd say. I'd advise her to avoid the tippling houses until she's had her child." He turned to Bickham. "Horatio, I'll be going now."

"Thank you, Kurt," said Bickham. "I'll show you out."

"What a minute," said Lem. "My wife don't go to no tipplin' house. She's a temperate woman, same as me."

"Whatever you say, son," said the doctor.

Lem watched them walk to the door. Bickham stepped outside with the doctor.

"Do you want to go upstairs and see her?" asked Nancy.

"I don't understand," said Lem, dazed. "He said she was going to have a baby. And, what did he mean by sayin' Roberta's been intemperate."

"Perfectly natural. About the baby, I mean. And we did smell spirits on your wife's breath. The aroma was quite strong and unmistakable."

"Yes'm," said Lem. But he was puzzled about both matters. He had never known Roberta to take or want strong spirits. And he had not shared Roberta's bed in more than six months. The queasy feeling in his stomach did not go away. He fought down the sickness, swayed inwardly for balance on the pitching deck of his imagination.

Three months later, Roberta gave birth to a baby girl. She named it Chastity, which puzzled Lem more than a little. More startling than the child's name, however, was her shock of red hair. The girl was thin and sickly. She died six weeks later of strangling colic. It seemed to Lem that the infant had no will to live. She cried all the time and did not take to the milk of her mother's breast. Roberta acted restless and inattentive, seemed almost relieved when the baby turned blue during a choking spell and expired in Roberta's arms. Lem dug a grave on the corner of his leased property and made a small coffin out of maple. Morgan didn't understand what had happened to his baby sister. Lem tried to explain death to him, but he couldn't tell if Morgan understood. Roberta sank into a deep depression after Lem interred the child.

She took to her bed for a week. He and Morgan waited on her, fed her soup and broth, tried to cheer her up. A week later, she announced she was going back to work. She also told him that she was going to move into town.

"But this is your home," Lem said. Morgan was making a snowman out by Chastity's grave.

"No, Lem, it's your home. I can no longer bear to stay in this squalid hut."

"You're just walkin' out?"

"You can live in town, if you want. You'll never amount to anything staying here. There's jobs aplenty for a man with gumption, for a man who wants to better hisself."

"This is good land, good soil. In a few years, I ought to be able to buy it from Bickham."

"You couldn't meet his price," she said.

"Well, somewheres else, then."

"Lem, don't you understand? I don't want to be a

farmer's wife. I want to wear fine clothes and be gentry. I want to improve my lot in life."

"Well, by God, you are a farmer's wife. You can't just walk off and leave Morg and me. Hell, what do you think I'm working for? It's for you, Bobbie. All of it's for you."

"Well, I don't want it. Not this. I want to have a life."

"Can't you just be patient?"

"I've tried that."

"Bobbie, there's somethin' else to it."

"Damn you, Lem. Isn't that enough for you?"

"How'd you get that baby? It warn't mine." As soon as he had said it, he was sorry. He had gone too far. It had just slipped out. But, the thought had been buried in his mind, buried and rising up out of its grave every night to torment his sleep, to make him wake up angry every morning.

She slapped him, then, and he saw the rage in her eyes. He saw, too, the loathing she had for him, a look like none other he had ever seen. It cut through him, cut deep, and hurt like a knife driven into his heart. He stood there, not feeling the sting of the slap, but hurting so bad he wanted to die in his tracks.

"Don't you ever accuse me of anything like that again," she said, her gaze fixed on him so tight, her eyes flickering so dangerously, he stepped back. Her face was a bloodless mask, chalk white with rage. He wanted to protest, but his voice caught in his throat and the moment was gone as she wheeled away from him. He stood there, transfixed, as she packed her satchel, saddled up Rose and rode away without a word. Little Morgan saw her going, came running in from the field. He called to her, but she never spoke.

"Where's Mama goin'?" asked Morgan as he ran to his father, breathless.

"She's goin' to live in town for a while."

"She is?"

"You come on inside now, boy. We got to do some thinkin'."

"What about, Pa?"

But Lem couldn't answer him. Something had happened, but he didn't know how to explain it, neither to himself nor to his son. Roberta had gone crazy when the baby girl had died. That was the only thing that made any sense. Maybe it was just temporary. Maybe she would get over her anger in time. That was all he could hope for because she left him no room for anything else. He had never seen such a look of pure hatred in another human being's eyes. For a moment, he thought she meant to kill him, would have killed him in some way, if she could. That terrible look in her eyes still gave him the shivers.

Lem and the boy ate a quiet meal that evening. Morgan started to ask again where his mother was, but his father shook his head and there were tears in his eyes. Lem jumped at every sound. He kept hearing the sound of hoof-beats, a footfall on the snow, a faint tap against the door. He tried to shut out all the sounds by banging the plates and utensils when he was cleaning up after supper. He threw more logs on the fire. He turned the lamp in the front room up high and kept the curtains open so the light would shine out. He went out, late, and looked at the snow glistening in the moonlight and let the cold numb him, deaden his thoughts until they were like frozen wood and empty of all but a bitter, distant pain.

"Pa, you comin' to bed?"

Lem turned, saw the boy and Friar Tuck silhouetted in the doorway. Saffron light splashed on the snow outside.

"I'm a-comin'," said Lem, a catch in his throat as if he had swallowed sand.

His moccasins crunched on the snow. In the far woods, he heard the throaty crow of an owl and the faint ribbons of laughter from the sugar camp on the ridge. The beagle wagged its tail as he approached. Morgan shivered in his pajamas.

"It's cold outside," said Morgan. "Mighty cold, Pa."

Lem said nothing. It was cold inside, too.

It was another six months before Lem saw Roberta again. Spring came and he and Morgan did the planting, working long hard days from dark to dark, plowing, seeding, cutting poles for a corral he put together at odd moments, mending harness at night. He went on lone hunts for quail and woodcock in the canebrakes, called the turkey gobblers down off the hardwood ridges, shot a 10-point whitetail buck at the steaming pond one glistening morning in April. Morgan missed his mother and Lem promised him that he'd go looking for her when he could find a clear day. But, in truth, he dreaded seeing her again. He never wanted to see that look in her eyes again.

But in early summer, when the meadow larks called from the fence posts and crows ragged a sleepy barn owl in the hayloft, Lem decided it was time to talk to his wife. It was early June in 1807 when he summoned the courage to go into town. Morgan was thirteen, growing like a thistle, his hair down to his shoulders, his cowlick drooping like a leafed-out willow branch.

"I could cut your hair, boy," said Lem, "but we might hunt us up a barber in Lexington."

"Oh goody," said Morgan, his eyes bright as coppers in a stream.

"You be ready tomorrow, early," said his father. He said nothing about going to find Roberta.

The next day, shortly after dawn, with the chores all done, Lem saddled Hammerhead, tied the beagle, Friar Tuck, to a crossbrace on the new corral he had finished putting up a few weeks before. He set out pork scraps and bones to keep the dog happy, filled a wooden pail with water, tied it to a pole with rope so the dog wouldn't spill it. He donned his best linsey-woolsey shirt, cotton trousers, slicked up his moccasins, brushed his wool felt hat free of lint. He saw to it that Morgan was neat and his hair combed and greased enough to keep his cowlick from spiking up in the back of his head. Lem carried a few pounds and some loose shillings in a small possibles pouch he draped over his wide leather belt.

"Come on, boy, let's look up your ma," said Lem as he climbed into the saddle. He had thought about telling Morgan all night. No sense in fooling the boy. "Get you a haircut too, maybe."

Morgan's face lit up with excitement. He took his father's outstretched hand and flew up behind the cantle.

"Hold on," said Lem.

"I'm ready, Pa."

It took them an hour and a half to ride to Lexington for they didn't dawdle along the way. They waved to travelers, other farmers, Calvin Moon, Nancy Bickham, but they didn't stop to explain their mission. Lem kept looking at his fingernails. He had trimmed them down with his patch knife and dug most of the dirt out. Morgan held onto his belt as he bobbed up and down like a sack of potatoes on the back of the horse.

Quail piped in the fencerows and martins flickered like feathered darts as they scooped insects above the summer ponds. Morgan laughed at a funny scarecrow in one of the fields they passed.

"It looks like Calvin Moon," said Morgan.

"It sure does," agreed his father.

Lem was surprised at how Lexington had grown. Everywhere he looked, new buildings were going up and they all seemed to be made of brick. Men hammered and sawed; hod carriers hefted their loads, streamed like ants back and forth between brick piles and structures, groaning under their heavy loads. Morgan stared at the workmen in silent fascination.

"Where we goin', Pa?"

"Why, to where your ma works, son. To Kroger's print-ing establishment, I reckon. This is Tuesday and she ought to be hard at work."

"Where is it?"

"I don't rightly know," replied Lem, "but we'll find it."

"I never saw so many big buildings," said Morgan. Block after block of finished brick buildings clustered around the center of town. The streets were broad and hard-packed. The store fronts became a bewildering maze. Lem had never seen so many different shops and he struggled to sort them out. Finally, at the courthouse, he dismounted and asked a young man for directions.

"Where might I find Kroger's Printing Shop?"

"Why, they was over on Third and Broadway," said the youth. "On Third, yes sir. Since last year."

"Can you p'int me?"

"Yonder," said the boy, extending an arm. "You can't miss it. Center of the block. Biggest building there."

Carriages wheeled through the center of town; men and women scurried from every direction, all seemingly in a hurry with urgent business to transact. Men yelled at dray horses pulling wagons loaded with cotton and pottery and farm implements. Morgan's eyes widened. He had been to Lexington before, but never on such a busy day, and not for more than a year. Calvin usually brought out supplies on his regular runs into town. Since his mother had left home, his father had shown no interest in going into town. It had been lonesome with just the two of them. The work had made the time pass, but the nights were long. Often, Morgan wept into his pillow, holding back so his father wouldn't hear him, burying his face in the pillow until his eyes grew tired and the sadness left him hollow inside.

Somehow, Lem found his way to Kroger's. The sign over the large brick front said KROGER'S PRINTING COMPANY in huge letters painted black with yellow gold trim.

"Is that it, Pa?" asked Morgan when they pulled up to the hitching post sticking about two feet out of the ground.

"Looks sure enough like it."

He tied the reins to the hitch-ring. Morgan slid off Hammerhead's rump, landed squarely on both feet. He followed his father as Lem entered the shop.

Behind the long wooden counter, a man and a woman worked at facing desks, leafing through sheafs of papers, spindling some, putting others in square boxes. The girl wrote something in a ledger, then looked up.

"Good morning," she said. "May I help you?"

"I'm a-lookin' for my wife," said Lem.

The young man looked up then, regarded the pair at the counter. Morgan had to stand on tiptoes to look over it. The girl, in her early twenties, smiled indulgently and stood up. She walked to the counter, her summer dress flowing gracefully from her hips, hugging her thighs and waist. She had light sandy hair, blue eyes, dimples.

"Does she work here?"

"Yep. Her name's Roberta. Roberta Hawke."

The girl turned to the young man. Beyond the door, the presses made loud whispers.

"Anyone with that name work here, Stephen?"

"Used to," said Stephen, once again absorbed with the papers on his desk. He dipped a quill pen into a well, signed a document with an exaggerated flourish.

"I'm afraid she doesn't work here any longer," said the girl.

"Well, she surely does," said Lem. "Roberta Hawke. You got to be mistook."

Stephen looked up at Lem, shook his head.

"She hasn't worked here for six or seven years. She went to work over at B & J Hatters a long time ago."

"Where's that?" asked Lem.

"Fourth and Main. Right around the corner. Broadway's the next street over, and you go one block up."

"Thanks," said Lem.

"Ain't Ma here?" asked Morgan.

"No, she ain't," said his father.

The girl went back to her desk. Stephen looked across at her and winked.

"If that's Mrs. Hawke's husband, he is in for a surprise," he said.

"What do you mean?"

"She's taken up with Barry O'Neil. Scandalous, Marie, quite scandalous."

"Well, I hope that man's not the jealous type."

"If you hear screams, you let me know."

Stephen scrawled a note on a piece of foolscap. Marie tried to busy herself in the ledger, but her thoughts were on the little boy peering over the top of the counter.

Lem left Hammerhead hitched in front of Kroger's. He and Morgan walked over to Main, then up to Fourth. The large building stood out from the others because the wooden frame was being replaced with new brick.

The storefront had large doors that were open in clement weather to display the company's hats on shelves and staggered wooden racks with pegs. Small glass display cases featured other headwear on attractive wooden trees.

A young man approached Lem and Morgan as they entered the display room. He wore a high starched collar, drooping ribbon tie; was thin and vestless. His hair was coiled with foppish curls.

"Something for your head?" asked the clerk.

"No, I'm lookin' for Roberta Hawke."

"Miss Hawke is not in, sir. She just left a few moments ago."

"She works here then?"

"Yes, she's our top model. Mr. O'Neil's personal favorite."

"Mr. O'Neil?" Lem felt the back of his neck prickle.

"Yes, Mr. Barry O'Neil, one of the owners. I believe you'll find them at Worthington House in an hour or so." The clerk pulled a brass watch from his pocket. The watch was on a chain. He opened the lid elaborately, looked at the time. "They have a noon showing there and a tea, later this afternoon."

"What's 'at?" asked Lem, bewildered.

"Worthington House is one of our finest hotels and restaurants, sir. It's quite elegant and one must dress to dine there." The clerk looked haughtily at Hawke. "If it's about furs you wish to sell us, perhaps I could—"

"Nope, it ain't about that. Where is this Worthington place?"

"Worthington House is on First and Walnut. You can't miss it. Just go down to First and it's three blocks from Broadway."

"I'll find it," said Lem. "Where is she now?"

"Why, she and Mr. O'Neil went to meet someone, another model, I believe."

"Where?"

"Why, that I don't know, sir. Perhaps it would be best if you spoke with Mr. John O'Neil."

"No, I reckon I can find my wife," said Lem angrily.

"Why, I didn't know Miss Hawke was married," said the clerk.

"Maybe she's forgotten it too," said Lem. He turned on his heel and left the hatters, Morgan chasing after him.

"Where did he say Mama was?" asked Morgan when they were back on the street.

"Some fancy hotel," said Lem, scowling. "Let's get Hammerhead and go a-lookin' for her."

"I bet she's lookin' for us, too," said the boy. Lem looked down at his son. Morgan was probably as bewildered as he was himself.

Lem put Morgan up on the horse, climbed into the saddle. He rode to First Street, turned right. Worthington

House dominated one corner of Walnut, its massive columns supporting a stately roof, looming over a wide veranda. Crepe myrtles and roses of Sharon bloomed in the yard. Huge mimosas flanked a magnolia tree that provided shade for the walk and the porch. A small ornately lettered sign proclaimed that this, indeed, was Worthington House.

"What is it?" asked Morgan.

"That's where your ma is supposed to be," said Lem, as he stalked up the cobbled walk. Hollyhocks bordered the bricks, all neatly trimmed, the blooms just starting to fade. Lem and his son climbed the steps. The door opened and a black man dressed in livery stepped out.

"Mistas," he said, "you done come to the wrong do'."

"I'm lookin' for somebody," said Lem.

"You'uns'll have to go around back," said the servant.

"No, we ain't," said Lem, pushing by the Negro.

"But you can't go in there."

Lem ignored him, but he blinked his eyes in the dimness of the foyer. Beyond, down a long hall, he saw a smartly dressed man standing at a podium by a doorway. Lem headed for him, Morgan running to keep up.

The servant trailed after them, his hands uplifted in helplessness.

The man standing on the podium, a small platform adorned with carpeting, turned to face them. He held a large book in his hands.

"What is it, George?" he asked the black man.

"Mista Blevins, I couldn't stop these two. They just busted on by me."

Blevins, the maitre d'hotel, looked down at the man in the linsey-woolsey shirt, the urchin at his side.

"What is the meaning of this?" he asked.

"I'm lookin' for my wife," said Lem.

"Well, she most certainly is not in here," said Blevins, from his haughty perch. His sickly smile stopped just short of being a sneer.

"I was tolt she was," said Lem.

"Well, you have been misinformed. We don't cater to your class here."

Lem glared at the man, then reached out and grabbed Blevins by the shirtfront. He jerked him from the platform and spun him around. With a heave, he shoved the hapless man into George's arms. The two staggered backwards, fell down in a heap.

Morgan stared at the two men in wonder.

Lem walked into the large room. Tables with bright white cloths and set with glasses stood at intervals from one another. Plants helped to break up the expanse of room. Waiters hurried in and out of a pair of double doors at the far end. A few diners looked toward Lem and Morgan as they swept into the room. In a far corner, Lem saw Barry O'Neil sitting at a table by a window. There was a woman with him, but he couldn't see her face.

He headed in the direction of Barry's table. A waiter came toward him, looked at Lem's face and veered off. Morgan's feet thumped on the carpeting as he hurried to keep up with his father.

The woman looked over Barry's shoulder as Lem came up to the table.

It was Roberta, and she was dressed in a fine black dress, her lips and cheeks rouged so that she looked like one of the women in the tippling houses. She held a glass of spirits in her hand.

"O'Neil," said Lem, "what are you a-doin' with my wife?"

"Why, she works for me," said Barry.

"Bobbie, you come on back home with me," said Lem.

"Oh, don't be silly, Lemuel. You have no right to order me around."

Her words were slightly slurred. Lem knew she had been drinking.

"Mama," said Morgan, "Mama, we come to see you. Pa's gonna get me a haircut."

"Is that your son?" asked Barry, turning to Roberta.

"No, it's his son," she said, and her eyes flashed a hidden bitterness. "Leave us alone, Lemuel."

"Yes, I believe the lady wishes you to go," said Barry.

"You comin', Bobbie?"

"For the last time, no," said Roberta. "Get out of here. I never want to see you again."

With that, she leaned toward Barry, slithered an elbow-length glove around Barry's head, pulled his lips toward hers. She kissed him, long and lingeringly, then released him with a flourish.

"You bitch," said Lem.

Barry stood up, pulling his sleeves back.

That's when Lem hit him. He doubled up his fist and drove it straight into Barry O'Neil's jaw, knocking the small red-haired man backward into his empty chair. Barry's eyes rolled up in their sockets and then crossed as he collapsed and sank to the floor.

Roberta stood up and screamed hysterically. She began to throw water glasses at her husband. She threw the glass pitcher at him, splashing water all over the table and carpet. She began to throw silverware, cursing like a dockworker.

"Get out! Get out!" she screamed. "You filthy bastard."

Spittle formed on her lips and her face whitened to a floury mask.

Lem took Morgan's hand, backed off.

"Whore," he whispered, and turned on his heel. The maitre d'hotel and the liveried doorman stepped aside as Lem and Morgan stalked past them. The diners sat frozen, their mouths open, their eyes fixed on the pair who had caused so much commotion on a quiet morning.

"I hate you!" Roberta screamed. "I hate you both!"

Morgan began to cry. Lem knocked the front door off its hinges as he kicked his way outside.

"Son, no need to shed no tears over a woman like that,"

Lem said as he reached the street where Hammerhead stood hipshot in the shade of a mimosa.

"But she's my ma," whined Morgan.

"Not no more she ain't," said Lem, and he knew they were the saddest words he had ever spoken.

The truth was, he wished he could cry himself.

14

Lem looked at the first snow of winter falling, dusting the hills and fields with flour, the flakes swirling in the rising chimney smoke. Morgan stood with him at the corral where the new horse pranced in a circle, blowing steam through his nostrils. The horse was a chestnut sorrel, gelded, six years old, fifteen and a half hands high. Lem had traded two pair of buckskins and ten bushels of corn for him.

"What should we name him, son?"

"He's sure pretty, Pa."

"Hammerhead's gettin' old. Might not be around much longer."

"He's got gray whiskers, ain't he?"

Lem chuckled. The boy was observant. He looked to be growing tall. It had been two years since they had last seen Roberta. A constable had ridden out one day and served Lem with papers he could barely read. Then, another man had come out and told Lem that his marriage was formally dissolved by the court in Lexington. A year ago Roberta had sent a present for Morgan back with Nancy Bickham, a little coonskin cap, and no word from her since. He had heard the other day, from Calvin Moon, that she and Barry O'Neil had gone to Nashville, Tennessee, to open a haberdashery and sell hats, furs and clothing to a fashion-conscious clientele.

Lem had been numb inside for so long that he seldom thought about Roberta. But, with Morgan's birthday coming up in October, the next month, he had begun to think of his wife again, wondering how she could leave her flesh and blood behind without so much as a fare-thee-well. It pained him to think of Morg growing up motherless and nigh to sixteen years old. He had gotten some schooling from Nancy Bickham and her kids, could read, write his ciphers, knew the alphabet and how to add and subtract numbers, do simple multiplying. That wasn't much, but the boy seemed taken by hunting and fishing more than schooling.

"You go on and name him," said Lem. "Might be I'll let you ride him."

"Can I? Oh, I want to, Pa. When can I?"

"Soon's you give him a name."

"Well," said Morgan seriously, "he looks like a big fox, and his stockings make him look like he's got on boots. I think he should either be called Fox or Boots."

"You call it," said Lem.

"Well, I don't think he's a fox. He's not sneaky or anything and he don't chase chickens. So, I think his name is Boots."

Lem laughed.

"Good name," he said. "You get a bridle on him and I'll help you get on him."

"Oh, bully, bully," said Morgan. He ran into the small barn he had helped his father build. A few moments later, he came out carrying a bridle. Lem held the horse's neck down while Morgan slipped the bridle on, tied it under his chin and behind his ears. Lem lifted his son onto the horse's back, stepped aside.

"Well, you're pretty tall, Morg. Think you can handle Boots?"

"I can handle him."

"Don't run him hard. Just let him get used to you."

Lem watched as Morgan rode out into the snowy field,

Friar Tuck barking as he raced to catch up on stubby legs. The horse had three gaits that he knew of, was saddle broke, seemed gentle enough. A wave of sadness, like hearing a fiddle play a mourning song, washed over him. Snow tinked against his face, melted on the sun-leathered skin. He had taken to growing a winter beard and the stubble that shadowed his face was already a quarter-inch long, dark as hog bristles.

Morgan rode to the edge of the field where a rabbit broke from cover. Friar Tuck cut off his pursuit of Boots and Morgan, took after the rabbit, into the woods. Morgan rode the edge of the field, put the horse into a gallop as he cut back toward the house.

Lem smiled as Morgan rode up, grinning wide as a wolf.

"He's a beauty, Pa. I really like him."

"Well, you put out some feed for him and rub him down good. I'll get us some supper."

"Can't I ride no more?"

"Be dark soon and I 'spec by mornin' we'll have us a snowfall. Chores'll take longer."

"Aww."

"Put him up, boy."

Lem turned and walked back to the house. He'd had a fair crop and had given Morgan some coppers to save when they sold the last of the corn. Next month, he might buy the boy a rifle. He was already at work on some buckskins that ought to fit him. Morgan didn't know about them. Lem worked on them late at night after the boy was asleep. Morgan was the only thing that kept him going, but his son could not fill the emptiness he felt whenever he thought of Roberta and what she had done to them.

That night, after supper, Morgan went to bed early. Lem stayed up, working by lamplight on the trousers of the buckskins. He felt like an old woman at such times, sitting there with the awl, sewing like a granny. But, it was something to do; something to pass the time.

* * *

The October hills were dusted with an early snow, the trees gaunt and leafless, the hollows drifted in wavelets from the wind like floury oceans. Lem and Morgan had been gripped by cabin fever during the freak storm, snapping at each other like children, pacing the floor, looking out the window, hoping the storm would break. It had started out as rain, turned to sleet, then hail, then back to rain again. Just before morning, the temperature dropped and the rain turned to snow. When dawn broke, clear and cold, Lem took his rifle, primed it, and told Morgan to bring his new one, the birthday rifle, a lean Kentucky of .41 caliber, with fancy brass furniture, an English lock, blade front sight, buckhorn rear.

"We goin' huntin', Pa?"

"Might be time for you to get you a buck," said his father, slipping his possibles pouch over his shoulder. He wore buckskins, warm enough for hunting with the woolens under them, a coonskin cap like Morgan's. The buckskins he had made for the boy fit pretty well. The sad thing was that he would outgrow them in less than a year. Lem had left some bottom in them to let out, some waist as well, but he couldn't do much about the length and the lad's shoulders would break out the seams in the shirt if he kept growing.

"You got your woolies on, Morg?"

"Yep. Just like you, Pa."

" 'Member all I taught you?"

"I truly do. I can shoot me a buck."

"Got your horns and pouch?"

"I'll fetch 'em."

Lem felt a pang of pride at the boy's eagerness. Morgan draped himself in powder horns and hunting pouch, checked the lacing on his boot-length moccasins. He stood there, rifle at his side, as his father slipped some biscuits into Morgan's pouch.

" 'Case we get hungry later on. Your rifle loaded?"

"It's loaded, Pa. I ain't primed the pan yet."

"Time enough when we get a piece away from the house. Better put Tut up so's he won't run the deer."

"I got him tied up in the barn," said the boy.

"Well, let's see what we might see," said Lem, smiling.

"Yes sir, let's see what we will see," mocked the boy.

Friar Tuck yelped from the barn as Lem and Morgan stepped outside.

"Pay him no mind," said Lem.

The boy and his father walked across the field, Morgan following the trail Lem broke. They entered the woods, climbed to the top of the nearest ridge. Lem pointed out deer tracks, most of them small, does and yearlings, as they went deeper into the hardwoods.

A startled squirrel chittered from a hickory tree, and the ground was laced with his brethren's tracks. They also saw the tracks of birds, rabbits, fox, and finally, the deep spoor of cloven hooves in a briar thicket.

"There's your buck," said Lem, in a low whisper.

"Big 'un," said Morgan.

"Umm. We got to go careful. You foller, stop when I stop, step real soft. Watch them twigs brushin' against your 'skins. Don't do no talkin'."

"Ought I to prime my pan now?"

Lem almost laughed, but held it in. He nodded, watched as the boy took the small powder horn, jerked the stob out with his teeth and poured fine powder into the pan. Morgan blew away the excess as his father had taught him, closed the frizzen.

"You ready?"

"Ready, Pa," Morgan whispered.

Lem circled the thicket, picked up the buck's tracks on the other side. The tracks were fresh, less than an hour old. Farther on, Lem found a pile of droppings. They were still steaming, had partially melted the thin snow. A doe had left a yellow stain and the buck had added some urine of his own. Lem pointed out tufts of deer hairs stuck to the oaks and hickorys, a fresh rub where the buck had stripped a sapling of bark as he raked it with the tines of his antlers.

Morgan was thrilled at everything he saw. He tried to do everything his father did, step where he stepped, stop when he stopped. He held his breath when they halted to listen.

The buck stopped following the doe and his tracks veered off, heading toward a deep hollow.

Lem stopped, leaned against a tree. He hunkered down and Morgan squatted next to him, a puzzled look on his face.

"That buck knows we're a-trackin' him now," whispered Lem. "We got to get ahead of him or figger out if he's a-goin' to circle us."

"How do we do that?"

"You stay put right here, Morg. I'm going to cut way off and make a wide circle. I figger he'll come back this way to pick up that doe's track. You be ready. Hold on him just behind the shoulder, squeeze off your shot when you got him in range."

"Pa, what if I miss?"

Lemuel put a hand on Morgan's shoulder, looked him square in the eye.

"Son, when you're a-huntin' you don't think about missin'. A deer ain't nothin' but a overgrowed rabbit. You just hold yourself steady and think about that ball a-goin' into his heart."

Morgan crinkled his face in a weak smile. Lem chucked his son on the arm and strode off at an angle away from the buck's tracks. It seemed to the boy that the path his father was taking was all wrong, that he would never intercept the buck. He was sure his father was widening the distance with each step. He watched until his father disappeared. He stood against the hickory tree and blew into his cupped hands. The silence welled up around him.

Lem made a wide circle, keeping the ridge between him and the hollow where the buck had gone. He moved faster than he could have with Morgan following him. He did not intersect the buck's tracks on that side, so he knew it was likely the deer was still in the hollow, perhaps pawing the snow for acorns missed by the squirrels and deer in the fall. When he had covered a half mile, he looped back toward the hollow where he knew it opened onto the flat. He crossed to the opposite ridge, stayed low, near the brush in the thin end of the hollow. He stalked carefully now, stopping every few minutes to wait and listen.

He moved from tree to tree, using them for cover. He scanned the snow for tracks that would show him the buck had come out of the hollow and gone to higher ground. He saw deer tracks, but none that matched the buck's and none of them had climbed up to the ridge.

He moved carefully the closer he got to where he had left Morgan. He leaned against a tree for ten minutes, listened to every sound. He heard the brush rattle, higher up the hollow. Listening carefully, he heard the sounds of a deer working a sapling, pawing at the snow. The buck snorted, and Lem knew he was preoccupied making a scrape, perhaps a rub as well.

"We got us a hot buck," he said to himself.

Lem moved up the hollow, staying closer to the brush than before. He hunched over, stopped to listen at intervals. The sounds of the buck worrying the snow with its hooves, its rack twanging the saplings, grew louder.

Lem knew that if he entered the hollow, he wouldn't be able to see. The buck could run down it, taking the natural escape route, or take either ridge. Or the buck could run straight up the hollow to the saddle that bridged the two ridges. If the deer ran anywhere but down the hollow, Morgan had a good chance for a shot. But Lem had to make a

decision. Should he cut the buck off from the downhill retreat by going into the hollow, or should he try to drive the
buck directly toward Morgan? He would be working blind.

He would have to take the chance.

Lem slipped down into the hollow, cutting toward the
sounds at an angle. It was slow going. The brush was thick,
the second growth tangled with thorny briar that could trip
a man, grab his clothing like clutching fingers. If he moved
careful, the thorns slipped noiselessly over his buckskins.
He made less sound than a deer would make, he thought.

Now, he heard the buck, pinpointed his location. The
deer was in the broadest part of the hollow, somewhere in
a grove of hardwoods. Lem worked his way through the
snow-limned brush, staying downwind. It took him twenty
minutes to stalk within sight of the animal.

The buck was big, with a majestic rack. It stood under a
low-lying limb, pawing the snow out of curiosity, rubbing
its back with the limb. Every so often, it would stop, sniff
the air, twist its ears to pick up sound. The slight crosswind
was in Lem's favor, Morgan's as well.

Lem saw the deer plain, no more than sixty or seventy
yards away. He did not move, breathed so that his breath
did not show when he exhaled. His blood raced with excitement. It was an easy shot. The buck's flank was fully
exposed, his black-tipped tail flicking nervously.

He wished now that he had brought Morgan with him. But
he realized that had he brought his son on this track, they
never would have gotten so close. No, this was better. Let
Morgan get the buck on his own. Let him feel the thrill of
bringing down a running buck for the first time. It would
be a moment he would remember the rest of his days.

Lem stood up and yelled his son's name.

"Morgan!"

The buck stiffened for a split second before its muscles
bunched up and it wheeled away from the sound of the
human voice. It hunkered low and broke into a run up the

slope, toward Morgan's stand. Lem ran after it, making all the noise he could.

"Here he comes!" he called to Morgan.

The buck's white tail flared like a flag just before it disappeared, flying and bounding toward the ridge where Morgan waited, in perfect position for a running shot. Lem stopped, out of breath, hoping his son remembered to lead the animal, aim for the heart.

Morgan jumped a foot inside his skin.

He heard his father's shout, then heard the buck crashing through the brush, headed his way. His heart stuttered a rapid tattoo as he thumbed back the cock, waited for the buck to appear.

His mind flooded with thoughts. He tried to picture the buck in his mind, foretell where it would top the ridge. But the sounds were confusing. Time slowed to a bewildering crawl. He thought the buck might be running the other way; then he thought it must be a few feet away, so loud were the sounds of its hoofbeats. Panic skewed his thoughts; his palms slickened with a sudden flood of sweat. His mouth turned dry and a pulse in his throat began to beat out of control.

The buck scrambled up the slope, its russet coat like fire against the whiteness. Snow flew off its sharp hooves as it struggled for footing. Morgan swallowed a mouthful of air, blinked in wonderment. A feeling of calm suffused him as he saw the magnificent buck, its head held regally high, its antlers symmetrically formed, majestic in their sweep.

Morgan's eye fixed on the buck's side. He brought the rifle to his shoulder. The buck saw the movement, bolted away. Morgan had the deer fixed in his mind. He led it in one clean motion from its rump, swinging the barrel past the target spot behind the left foreleg. When the spot disappeared as the muzzle passed over it, he squeezed the trigger and kept swinging. The rifle bucked against his shoulder. A stream of orange flame and sparks spewed from the barrel. A puff of white smoke billowed from the muzzle, blotted out the racing deer. The shot reverberated in the snow-flocked hills, the report so loud Morgan was temporarily deafened by the explosion.

The white smoke hung in the air and Morgan felt wrapped in a cocoon of silence, an emptiness where he could neither see nor hear. Dazed, he stood there, a tendril of smoke coiling out of the barrel, his cheekbone hurting where the comb of the stock had bruised it in recoil.

Then, the smoke cleared and he saw the buck lying in the snow, some sixty yards beyond the place where he had shot it.

Morgan began to shake as if gripped with a fever. He stood rooted to the snowbound earth, unable to move. His hands shook so that he thought he might drop his rifle. His knees trembled and his teeth began to chatter. He saw his father trudge up over the hill and stop, staring at him.

"Morg?"

Morgan squeaked, unable to speak.

Lem looked at the deer, ran to it, his tread slow through the snow. He approached it warily from behind, his rifle aimed at the animal, his finger on the trigger, his thumb on the cock. The buck didn't move. Lem leaned over it, grabbed an antler, lifted up its head. He dropped it with a thunk and slit its throat with his knife to let it bleed.

Morgan swallowed, trying to free up the lump in his throat. He saw his father trotting toward him, but he was still frozen there, quivering in every muscle.

"What's the matter, boy? Got you the buck fever?"

Morgan tried to shake his head. Nothing moved. He lowered the rifle slowly; swallowed air. He began to breathe normally again as his father came up to him.

"That was a fine shot," said his father. "Wish't I could have seed it."

"Oh," said Morgan, the squeak fading.

"When did you start to get the shakes?"

"A—after I saw it. Dead. The blood . . . Pa . . . I . . ."

Lem put a hand on his son's shoulder.

"Better you get it afterwards, son. Same thing happened when I killed my first deer."

"It did?"

"Sure enough. Took me a half hour to quit a-shakin'. Come on, let's gut him out. You got yourself a fine buck."

Morgan took a deep breath, smiled wanly.

"Yeh," he said. "I did."

Lem and Morgan reached the fallen buck. Lem took out his knife.

"You watch me do this, so's you know how next time you make meat."

Lem knelt down, stuck the blade into the deer just in front of the genitals, slit back to the anus. He reversed the blade and sliced from aitchbone to breastbone, up the buck's belly, heard the carcass sigh as steam belched from its bloody cavity. He worked the knife past the breastbone and up to the neck. Always, he worked the cutting edge of the blade away from him, in case he slipped with the knife. He squeezed the bladder gently, since it was full, and emptied it of fluid. He cut around the anus to clear the intestines from the pelvic arch, the aitchbone. He reached down into the loins, drew yards of entrails into the body cavity.

Morgan watched in fascination, his eyes glittering. He was no longer cold. The quivering had passed.

Lem turned his head slightly to avoid the fecal stench, drew a shallow breath before continuing to gut out the deer.

Lem probed inside the deer's abdomen at the breastbone, cut the membrane, freeing the innards. He was careful not to slash the stomach or intestines. He cut the windpipe and esophagus, jerked downward, pulling the mass of cartilage and gristle down into the mid-section. He took out the heart and liver, set them aside. Then, he turned the deer over and

shook the innards out into a gut-pile. He propped the deer's
loins apart with a stick.

"We got to carry it back to the house, hang it up, skin
him," said Lem.

"Can I tan the hide, Pa? I want to get me a couple more
and make my own buckskins."

"You've really growed up all of a sudden, ain't you,
Morg?"

Morgan grinned.

"If you say so, Pa."

"We'll take turns a-draggin' him back. He'll weigh out
to a hundred and fifty, I reckon."

"I feel real good, Pa."

Lemuel looked at his son. He felt the pride glowing in
him like cherry coals. Morgan did not resemble his mother
so much anymore. He was growing tall, filling out. There
was a sureness about him that had not been there before. It
made Lem feel old. Why, Morgan was nigh as old as he
was when he married the boy's mother. A few more years,
he might be taking a wife of his own. He hoped Morgan
had better luck. His pride turned to bitterness when he
thought about Roberta. He shook out the images in his
mind, took a deep breath.

"I know how you feel, by God," said Lem. He grabbed
a tine and began dragging the buck. "Best load up again
whilst I'm haulin' this here deer. Never know what we
might see twixt here and home."

"Yes, Pa. I'll spell you when you want me to."

"Well, that won't be too long. Buck's heavy all right. Got
him enough points you might want to save his horns."

"Oh, I do, Pa," beamed Morgan.

That night, they both skinned the deer by the light of the
lantern. Lem could not help notice that the top of Morgan's
head just came nigh up to his pa's shoulder. The boy would
be tall, sure enough, taller than his pa.

Morgan sawed the antlers off the buck himself. He took them inside the house that night, put them at the foot of his bed where he could look at them.

Lem said good night and took to his bed. He blew out his lamp, lay in the dark, thinking.

What would happen to him, he wondered, when Morgan grew up and went away on his own? What would happen to him? Where would he go? What would he do?

The sadness came on him again. A different sadness this time. This one smothered him, drowned him. He had lost his wife; he could not bear to lose his son. The night, he thought, was not as dark as the darkness in his heart just then. He turned over, cursing Roberta, cursing all women, cursing them until sleep pulled him down below all thought, all feeling.

15

Morgan Hawke crept up to his favorite tree, sat in the hollow of the earth he had made himself by sitting there so much and leaned back against the oak, his rifle across his knees. He looked down toward the den tree, waited for the light to come. He had made little sound coming through the woods, but even if he had, he knew the squirrels had short memories. Pa had taught him that. Fifteen to twenty minutes. He had tested it himself. If he made noise coming into the woods, the squirrels would all run up their trees and hide. But, if he sat still for fifteen minutes or so, they would come back, forget all about him.

It was a warm morning, the warmest of the spring, and he wanted to bring in at least four squirrels before helping Pa with the chores. He had already set out grain for Hammerhead and Boots, fed Friar Tuck, the chickens, slopped the hogs, brought in the eggs. He could do a lot in the dark, but he had used the lantern this morning because he wanted to get up to the hardwoods before the sky lit up.

From his perch, he could see the house and road. It made him feel like a king to look down on the fields and the house that way, to watch the long road that stretched to the back parcel of the Bickham place.

He saw smoke rising from the chimney at Bickham's. He heard a sound, the scratch of claws on bark. His father had taught him to shut out everything when he was in the woods, just to lean against a tree and become part of it, sit there so long you just became part of the forest and once you had gone into it, you would see and hear things nobody else could hear.

A squirrel stuck its head out of the hole in the den tree. It gave a bark. Then, it was quiet for a while. Morgan closed his eyes and listened. He heard an answering chitter from another part of the woods. The squirrels were waking up. The sun began to peach over the land. A thin scar of cream appeared like a rent in the sky. He liked to watch the woods wake up, see the trees and bushes light up slow and see the leaves take on definition. Stumps and rocks took on color, were no longer blobs of shadow.

The squirrel inched down the trunk of the tree, its tail twitching, its eyes peering everywhere. Morgan sat very still and waited. He had not hunted this tree since last fall and he knew there were other squirrels inside.

Morgan watched as the squirrel leaped to the ground, then rustled through the leaves as it ventured forth in search of food. Another squirrel peeked out of the den hole. Mist began to rise in the valley as the sun rose in the east. The first squirrel came toward Morgan, oblivious to his presence.

The second squirrel scrambled out of its den, scampered down the tree.

Morgan put the rifle to his shoulder. He held the trigger

in slightly so there would be no click as he pulled back the cock. He tracked the squirrel with the sights aligned until it stopped on a fallen log. When it sat up, he held his breath and squeezed the trigger. The rifle slammed against his shoulder, spewed flame and white smoke out of the barrel. Morgan didn't wait for the smoke to clear, but stood up, grasped his powder horn. He poured an estimated 30 grains down the barrel, tamped the stock, reached for a patch and ball, seated them on the muzzle. With his short starter, he shoved the ball until it was flush with the barrel end. Quickly, he cut the surplus patch away, then rammed the ball six inches down the barrel. He snatched his wiping stick out and seated the ball on the powder. He primed the pan, started looking for the second squirrel. It had scrambled back up the den tree, was clinging to the bark next to the hole. Morgan cocked his rifle, took aim.

He fired again, saw the squirrel twitch, then fall to the ground.

Morgan let out a breath. He picked up the first squirrel next to the fallen log. The other was still kicking at the foot of the den tree. He picked it up by its hind legs, dashed its head against the tree.

Deftly, Morgan gutted out the two squirrels, stuffed their warm carcasses in the back of his loose shirt. He started to walk up to the top of the ridge and hunt the other side, when he saw a rider emerge from the mist below. Curious, he stood there, gazing downward, as the man and horse slowly made their way up the road. He wondered who could be coming to see them at this hour of the morning.

There was something peculiar about the man. He wore an odd hat, something odd on his head, anyway, that might have been a hat, and his buckskins were decorated with bright colors. As the sun rose behind him, the rider seemed illuminated in the ground fog. Morgan stared at him transfixed, wondering who he was and why he was riding up their road. There was a bedroll, or pack, on the man's saddle, and a rifle in a buckskin stocking laid across the man's lap.

Morgan forgot about hunting squirrels and made his way slowly down the slope toward the road. He caught occasional glimpses of the rider through the trees, which had not yet begun to bud. As he drew closer to the road, he hid behind a tree so that he could observe the rider more closely. As the man loomed larger, Morgan's pulse began to race.

The horse was old, swaybacked, its hide scarred, its winter coat marred with bare patches. Morgan noticed that the horse wore no shoes and made very little noise. The man riding the bony horse had no face. It was hidden behind a brushy beard that was streaked with white slashes. He was a thin man, as bony as the horse, but fearsome. Morgan blinked to clear his vision, for he had never seen a man dressed as this one was. His buckskins had swatches sewed to them that were blue and red and yellow, black and white. Morgan wondered whether they were made of cloth or painted leather.

Morgan huddled tight against the tree as the horse got close enough so that he could hear its hooves on the ground. He drew his arms in close to his sides, held the rifle straight up and down.

"You, boy, I know you're ahind that tree. Come on out where we can get a look at you."

Morgan's heart seized in his chest.

He peeked from behind the tree. The rider sat his horse not twenty yards away.

"Well, come on, son. I ain't a-goin' to bite ye."

Morgan blinked sheepishly, stepped out from behind the tree.

"Hello, sir," he said. The man was even stranger up close. His buckskins were white as snow and his moccasins had those same colored patches on them. They, too, were white, and the most beautiful he'd ever seen. The man's hair was long, past his shoulders, and his beard was so bushy it was hard to see his eyes. He wore a tomahawk and a knife on his belt and a pistol jutted from his wide belt. He looked, Morgan thought, like some kind of warrior. His hat was made of the shiniest fur, red and golden and russet, and it had an animal's face on the front, all squinched up. But he could tell it was an animal from its eyes and ears. He thought it might be a fox, but he was shaking inside so much he couldn't tell for sure.

"Sir? My, ain't we the polite chile? What's your name, son?"

"M-M-Morgan, sir. My pa taught me to address older men that way."

"Oh, he did, did he? Morgan, you say? Now, Morgan's my name, boy. Don't seem likely they'd be two with the same name in the same spot, does it now? You don't reckon somebody stole it from me and give it to you?"

"That was the name my pa give me."

"Then I reckon he's the one what stole it."

"My pa don't steal," Morgan said, a hard edge of defiance to his tone.

"Who's your pa?"

"Lemuel Hawke."

"Well, I'm Silas Morgan and I'd sure like to talk to this Lemuel Hawke what stole my name. That his hut yonder?"

"Uh huh. It ain't no hut, though. It's our house."

"Well, take me to him, young Morgan. We'll just talk to Lemuel hisself about this business of stealin' a man's name." Silas didn't smile and Morgan thought he was dead serious. "I seed you shot you a couple squirrel up there. You cook?"

"I can skillet fry 'em."

"Well, get to goin' then. I've got a gut thin as a spring b'ar's. You ever et elk?"

"No. I ain't never seen one. What is it?"

Silas Morgan threw his head back and laughed.

"Why it's a most fearsome animal, big as my horse here, with sharp horns wide as a wagon."

Morgan didn't believe him. He snorted and started running toward the house. He looked back and Silas was just jogging along, like before, in no particular hurry. He didn't know what to make of the stranger, but up close he saw that he had little fur tails growing out of his buckskins and those colored patches that weren't cloth and weren't beads. He wondered what they were.

"Pa, Pa, wake up!" Morgan yelled as he ran up to the house, breathless. "Somebody's a-comin'."

The door opened.

"I'm awake, Morg. What're you hollerin' about?"

"There's a man says you stole my name from him. He's a-comin'. He was telling me about a elk. He eats 'em."

Puzzled, Lem stepped out of the cabin. His face was lathered with soap. He was bare-chested, his cotton trousers dangling a pair of galluses. He held a straight razor in his hand; his face was half-shaven. Morgan pointed to the man on horseback.

"Don't seem in no hurry, does he?"

"Better get your gun, Pa. He says you stole my name from him."

"Well, if he's who I think he is, I did steal your name from him."

"You did?"

"Did he tell you his name?"

"He said his name was Morgan too. Silas Morgan."

"Well, damn me for twenny seconds in hell, if that ain't your namesake, Morg."

"Huh?"

"That's the galoot I named you after. He taught me more'n any man alive, I reckon. Boy, your ma sure kicked up a fuss when I called you that."

"How come, Pa?"

"Oh, your ma didn't like Silas none. She thought he was the devil's own son."

"Is he?"

Lem started to wave at the rider. Silas waved back.

"Huh?"

"Is he the devil's son?"

Morgan walked over to stand beside his father and peer out at the oncoming Silas Morgan.

"Why that's just a sayin', son. Look, I got to finish parin' my face. You tell Silas to light down and bring him on inside."

"Truly, Pa, I don't know what to make of that man. He looks like a pirate or a murderer."

"Well, he ain't neither. You make him welcome."

His father disappeared, leaving him alone outside with the rapidly approaching man on horseback. He heard the door slam shut.

"Well, was that yore pa?" Silas asked as he rode up.

"Uh, yes sir. He said to—to . . ."

Morgan froze as Silas fixed him with a beady stare. He thought of the devil and wondered if his ma wasn't right about the man looking down at him. He looked right fearsome. He expected fire and smoke to spew out of his nostrils if he looked at him too long. As it was, he was sure, in his imagination at least, that Silas' eyes were shooting sparks right at him. Sparks straight out of hell.

"Well, spit it out, boy. What'd yore pa say?"

"He said, uh, tolightrightdown'ncomeinthehouse." With that, Morgan turned on his heel and went inside the house.

Behind him, he heard Silas laugh and it made Morgan's face flush hot with shame.

Lem finished wiping off the last of the lather from his face. He slipped into a wool shirt and slid his galluses over his shoulders.

"What's got into you, boy?" he asked. "Where's Silas? You should have tended to his horse."

"I reckon he can take care of his horse, all right. He come this far by hisself, Pa."

Lem looked at his son, wrinkled his nose in puzzlement.

"You don't like old Silas? Why he's my best friend."

"He eats elks," said Morgan, unsure of himself.

"Why that's just an animal. I heard of 'em plenty."

"I don't know what to say to him. He gives me the fidgets."

"Well, you just come outside and stop actin' like a damned fool, 'cause Silas is a sight for tuckered eyes."

Morgan followed his father outside, still suspicious of the strange man.

"That you, Silas?" His father's voice was reassuring.

Silas had dismounted, was looping his bridle reins around a hitch post Lem had sunk into the ground.

"It ain't Brown the tax collector," cackled Silas. He turned, flashed a grin through his thick beard. He walked over to Lem, slapped him on the back. "Boy, I been ridin' a month of hard Sundays to find you. Never thought you'd still be a-farmin'."

"Silas, I got to take your word for who you are," said Lem. "You done hid your face from me. Or are you a-wearin' fur to keep the cold winds from burnin' your pretty cheeks?"

"Haw. I growed me a beard for that very reason and you just as skinny as ever. Got you a pup, too. Mighty skittery, ain't he? What's he sulled up for?"

Lem looked at his son. Morgan's face was as dark as a thundercloud.

"Morgan, shake hands with Silas."

Morgan just stood there, transfixed. Silas held out a hand toward him.

"Lordy, I do believe he thinks I'm goin' to bite him," said Silas.

"Morg, shake the man's hand," ordered his father.

Morgan crept out from behind his father, tentatively stretched out his hand. Silas took it, shook it vigorously, as a man would shake another's. Morgan tried to keep his teeth from rattling. He thought Silas was going to wear out his arm or pull it from his shoulder.

"There now, warn't so bad, was it?" Silas smiled.

"He's pleased to meet you, Silas. And, I'm mighty glad to see you. Come on inside and set. I can burn some vittles for you. Do you take coffee? I got me some beans that are some ripe."

"Well, now, Lem, I could chew me some meat and swaller some coffee bean juice or p'izen."

Lem looked at Silas's skins, touched the colored patches that had dumbfounded Morgan earlier.

"What're them?" he asked.

"Quillwork. Porkypine quills. Inyun gals mash 'em up, twist 'em, and paint 'em. Right purty, ain't they? Some of 'em uses beads and I got me some mokkersons what's got the purtiest colors you ever seen."

"What are them little furs?" asked Morgan, regaining some of his courage.

Silas lifted up a long slender piece of fur, tweaked it.

"Ferrets' tails, some of 'em. Some of 'em's minks."

Silas followed Lemuel inside the house. Morgan almost stumbled trying to keep up. He didn't want to miss a word that Silas Morgan might say.

"Got somethin' to show you by and by," said Silas as Lemuel pulled a chair out for him.

"How'd you find me?"

"Ran into Roberty down to Nashville," said Silas, and there was a silence in the room dark and heavy as a rain cloud. No one spoke for several seconds. Lem stoked the firebox in the stove, cleared his throat. Morgan stood stock-still, his mouth open like a frog's fly trap.

"How—how's she a-doin'?" Lem asked, trying to act unconcerned about it.

"Pore gal is kinda peeked. She tole me you warn't hitched no more and I let it go at that. I asked her where you was and she tole me. Figgered I could find you. No need to bother the pore woman no more." Silas paused, hacked at something in his throat.

"Poor woman?" asked Lem. "Hell's fire, Silas, Roberta was livin' high on the hog when she left here, workin' for that damned hatter, Barry O'Neil, swilling down whiskey in fancy tippling houses like a sow. Wearin' clothes more dear than anything I ever seen." Lem looked at Morgan apologetically.

Morgan stiffened, tried to fix the wan smile on his face.

"She ain't wearin' fancy clothes no more. She's workin' in that hattery all right, sniffin' that glue what makes you crazy. Warn't no fancy tipplin' house I seen her in last, neither."

Lem sat down at the table opposite Silas. He was as rigid as Morgan a few moments before. Morgan sucked in a quick breath, stood there hanging on Silas's silence like a boy on a cliff.

"She ain't no model or nothin'?"

"Nope," said Silas. "She works same as the other gals there, makin' hats out of beaver." He turned to Morgan. "Son, kin you go out and bring me that blanket roll on my saddle? Got somethin' to show you."

Morgan blinked, then wheeled, ran from the room as if he'd been hurled from a sling. He dashed to the horse, untied the leather thongs, freed the heavy bundle from behind the cantle. He carried it triumphantly into the house and laid it on the table in front of Silas.

". . . went to see for myself, talk prices with Barry O'Neil," Silas was saying. "Ah, thank you, young Morgan." Silas unwrapped the plain woolen blanket. Morgan hung close to the table, eyes big as a great horned owl's.

"What you got there, Silas?" asked Lem.

Silas did not show everything inside the blanket roll at

first. He extracted an oilcloth from the folded blanket, un-wrapped it. He held up a shiny dark pelt.

"This here's the reason I come to Kentucky," said Silas.

"What is it?" asked Lem. "Groundhog?"

Silas laughed.

"This is a prime beaver pelfry, Lemuel. Caught him my-self up on the Wind River, a mighty powerful place in the Rocky Mountains, a place what makes a man feel small and big at the same time. This here's what they make hats out of, makes rich men out of farmers and thieves and the likes of me."

Silas tossed the pelt to Morgan, who jerked back in sur-prise. But the boy held it and stroked it, turned it to let the morning light drench it in freshets of silver, ripple with shadows and golden threads. The beaver seemed alive in his hands, seemed to radiate a pulse of faraway places, seemed to glow with the promise of sudden wealth.

"Lemme see it, Morg," said Lem, reaching for the pelt. Morgan reluctantly gave it to his father.

"It's so soft," said Morgan.

"I worked on this one special, so's you could see how purty it shines. Beaver don't look like that right after you tan it. Fur's all coarse, hide's rough and slick with beaver grease. Underneath, it's like silk wool, real soft and warm."

Lem examined it, turning it over and over in his hands.

"I never seen anything like this," said Lem. "How do they make a hat out of this?" He looked at Silas's fox-skin hat.

Silas shook his head.

"Nope, not like this fox, though they be some who keep 'em and wear 'em like this 'un. That's personal. Them hat-ters they go to a mighty lot of trouble to make felt. They shave that coarse hair from the pelfry, then the thick wool. The hatter sells the bare hide to a glue maker, then blows the hair and wool with a little bellows. Got to get 'em sep-arate. He throws away the hair, keeps the wool to make felt."

"What's felt?" asked Morgan.

"Why it's what they make hats out of. Felt stays stiff, not like this fox." Silas took his hat off, handed it to Morgan. "See? Limp as a preacher's pecker at a dunkin'. Felt now, it stays hard and water don't do nothin' but run off it like it does on a beaver."

"How do they make this into felt?" asked Silas.

"I seen 'em do it at O'Neil's in Nashville. It's real interstin'. They got this copper cone with a lot o' little holes in it. It spins around and sucks that loose fur up ag'in' it. The gals and fellers pack it down whilst this hot water's a-sprayin' on it. They keep addin' fur to the cone and packin' it until it gets real hard. When they got it all done, they take that felt, which looks like a hood at that p'int, and then put it in a mold what shapes it. While the felt's still soft and warm, they got this plunger that shoots shellac into it from inside the mold. Then they take some of the real fine fur and dab it on the hat. They use more hot water to do that. Then, at the last, to make it shine real purty, they put the hat on a spinning block. Whilst it's a-goin' around, they smooth it all out with sandpaper, irons, velvet and such. It comes out looking real glossy, glossier'n this here beaver pelfry."

"Sounds like a lot of foolishness just to make a hat," said Lem. Morgan's face reflected his rapt fascination with the story.

"Well, they's people who will pay to own a fine beaver hat. A' course all that glue and shellac makes them hatters plumb crazy. Addles their brains."

"Is that what happened with Ma?" Morgan blurted out.

"I reckon," said Silas sadly. "Most of them hatters walk around like they been into the hard cider."

"I'll stay with the farming," said Lem.

Silas looked at Morgan, tweaked his beard and smiled.

"Maybe not. I got more to tell you. Lem, I never saw a land such as what I seen out West. A man can't get enough of it, and it fills you up. First time I seen the Rocky Mounts I felt like a ant. And then I swolled up inside until the tears just boiled outen my eyes."

"This is good land right here," Lem said stubbornly.

"Good enough for a little man," snorted Silas.

"Huh? What you mean by that?"

"Man stands on a mountain, he's pretty tall. He goes up short, comes down taller'n any."

"You ain't growed none."

"To me I growed a whole lot," said Silas.

"What else you got in that blanket?" asked Morgan, craning his neck.

Silas smiled.

"I was a-savin' the best for last. Somethin' for you, young feller. Fetch me your powder horn."

"What do you want it for?" asked Morgan.

"Just fetch it."

Morgan looked at his father. Lem nodded. Morgan went over to his bed while Lem stood up, added kindling to the firebox, started to grind coffee beans. Silas drummed his bony fingers on the table, licked his lips.

Morgan laid his powder horn on the table in front of Silas.

"That it?"

"That's the horn my pa made for me," said Morgan.

"Well, I got you somethin' better. Made by the Crow Inyuns. They tell me it's got powerful medicine."

"Medicine?" Morgan cocked his head.

"Spirits. Make a man strong. Make him powerful 'gainst his enemies."

Lem poured water in a pot, shook the ground beans into the water. He put the pot on the stove, added a chunk of wood to the main fire. He clanged the door shut, walked over to the table.

"What's this talk?" he asked.

"I brung your boy this powder horn, Lem. I hope you let

him keep it. I brung it a long ways. Was goin' to sell it until Roberty told me you had a son. Medicine's better you give it to a young man. Better for me, better for him."

"Let me see it," said Morgan eagerly.

Silas reached into the blanket roll and grabbed something. He drew it slowly from the blanket.

"Aww!" exclaimed Morgan.

Silas held the horn up high. It gleamed like black ivory in the sunlight streaming through the windows. It was gracefully curved, slender, with a thick butt, narrow point. Light glinted from its polished surface.

"There you be," said Silas softly, his voice laden with reverence. "That be your medicine horn, Morgan."

Morgan reached for it, closing his eyes for a moment as if saying a silent prayer. He felt strange when he touched it, as if there was magic in the horn, magic that coursed through him like the tingle he got sometimes when lightning struck near him. The hairs on the back of his neck stood up and his arms crawled with goosebumps.

"My medicine horn," he said, and there was a strange husk in his voice as he touched the smooth horn with his trembling fingers.

16

Morgan Hawke held the medicine horn in his hands as if it was bone china. He looked at the strange markings on it, their indentations whitened as with chalk. It had no powder in it, was light in his hands. It had a wooden peg at the pouring spout, a wooden butt that was flat, inset, and varnished to a dark sheen. There was something mystical about the powder horn, something ancient and timeless and mysterious.

"What do those markings mean?" asked Morgan, his voice cloudy with rapture.

"Them is Crow sign. Some calls 'em the Blue Bead People. Bear Foot, the Inyun what give it to me, said they was a heap of power in 'em. I don't rightly know what they mean exactly."

The coffee pot boiled. Lem rattled a pair of tin cups, set them on the table.

"What you want to eat, Silas?" he asked as he poured the cups full. The aroma of boiled coffee beans filled the room.

"Boy there got him a couple of squirrel."

Morgan's face rippled with surprise.

"Oh, I forgot." He reached behind his back, felt the squirrels inside his shirt. "I'll skin 'em right away. Got me two of 'em, Pa."

"That ain't hardly enough to feed a hungry man, let alone two and a boy," said Lem, but there was approval in his voice. Morgan reluctantly laid down his powder horn and scampered out the door. It closed behind him, but there was a fresh cool in the room.

"Mighty fine lad you got there, Lemuel."

"He's a-growin' fast."

"Wisht you two 'ud come out west with me. I got to make tracks, get to the mountains afore the snow flies."

"I don't know, Silas. We're pretty much settled and all."

"I seen a heap of country," said Silas, reaching into the blanket roll once again. He pulled out another oilcloth, unwrapped it. He handed Lemuel a fine beaver hat burnished to a glistening black. It was round and had a bill made of beaver tail, cured and shellacked until it was hard as a tortoise shell. "This is for you, Lemuel. To 'member me by."

Lemuel took the hat, held it at full length as he admired it.

"Why, it's a mighty fine hat, Silas. I thank you."

"Try it on your pate."

Lemuel put the hat on. It felt alien to him, but was soft inside, fit right.

"I don't know where I'd wear such a hat, Silas."

"In the mountains, that's where. Plenty more where that'n come from."

"I ain't no animal trapper."

"Easy as sin. Lord, it's a life, Lemuel. I seen sights and Inyun gals purty as any you ever did see, and b'ilin' streams churnin' white and foamin', trees bigger'n anything back here, taller, straighter. Everything a man needs can be found in the big mountains."

"They have towns there?"

"No, an' that's the beauty of it. Forts and such along the Missouri and up the Yallerstone, along the Platte, most ever'where a man goes. They's wide places and small, but room for a man to move 'thouten people gettin' in his way."

"You make it sound like . . . like I don't know what. Paradise. The Garden of Eden."

"Waw! That's just what it's like, Lemuel. Ye gods, you got to see it just once. You don't like it none, you come on back to your plow and hogs."

Morgan returned with the two squirrels, cleaned and wet down, heads and feet cut off, ready to fry.

"I'll get the skillet hot," said Lemuel, taking off his hat. Morgan stared at the hat in awe. "Morg, you better fetch some deer meat from the springhouse."

"What's that?" asked Morgan.

"A pure beaver hat," said Silas.

"Did you catch it?"

"I trapped him up on the Yallerstone last winter. Two of 'em jest alike. I sewed 'em together so's you can hardly tell it. It sure do shine, don't it?"

"You bet a shilling it does," said Morgan. "Can I touch it, Pa?"

"Sure, put it on, Morg," said his father. He banged an

iron skillet on the stove. "Get them vittles in here real quick now."

Morgan picked up the hat, put it on. It fell over his eyes. Silas and Lemuel both laughed. Morgan took off the hat, rubbed his hands through the soft fur.

"It's beeeyoutiful," he drawled.

"Deer meat," said Lemuel, smiling.

"I'll fetch it," said Morgan and he was gone again, leaving the two men alone.

"What're you tryin' to do, Silas?"

"Seeds, Lemuel. Plantin' seeds is all."

"My boy and me, we got us a good life here. I aim to see him grow to be a man on land I bought and paid for."

"You own this land?"

"Not yet," Lem gruffed. "But I aim to buy it."

"Boy's nigh a man already. He might think different."

"He won't think no different. I'll learn him what he needs to know."

" 'Pears he's already learned a lot."

"What're you aimin' at, Silas?"

"Nothin'. I notice he fetches right well. Probably does the chores right good, too."

"You leave us be, Silas. I got plans for that boy."

"Wal, I reckon," said Silas, and took out his pipe and a tobacco pouch made of antelope hide. He filled the bowl. He walked over to the stove, took out a small firebrand, touched it to the tobacco. He drew deeply, exhaled blue smoke. "I can see you and the boy are all set here." Silas looked around the room, sat back down.

Morgan returned with a leg and hindquarter of cured venison, gave it to his father. Lem savagely sliced off several large chunks of meat, tossed them in a greased skillet. He poured more coffee for Silas and himself.

"You want to see my dog, Mr. Morgan?"

"What you got?"

"A beagle. His name is Friar Tuck. He's number two. His pop died, but we got a pup to 'member him by."

"After I get some vittles in my innards," said Silas.

Lem cut the squirrels up, added them to the skillet. He banged the pot on the griddle, rattled the iron stove handles. He grinned maliciously as the meat sizzled, spit and hissed. Morgan took his medicine horn over to his bed, sat down to admire it away from the din. There was something different between his pa and Silas and he didn't know what it was. But he felt it. Silas just sat there, smoking quietly, and his pa wrestled with the hot skillet as if he wanted to burn the meat to a crisp and get it over with.

S ilas stayed there for two days, telling Lem and Morgan about the things he had done, the sights he had seen. He spoke of prairies and rivers and game. He told them of seeing buffalo herds so huge it took them days to cross a river.

"I seen elk in herds of two, three hunnert," he said. "I kilt antelope what come up to me out of curiosity, shot 'em dead at less'n twenty yards."

"What about the Indians?" asked Morgan.

"Some is bad and you got to fight 'em. Some is good and will trade with you, let you sleep in their lodges. You got to keep your wits about you, son."

"Morg, you ask too many questions," said his father.

"But, Pa, I want to know what it's like out there."

Lemuel frowned and said nothing, but Silas smiled at the boy and gave him a furtive wink.

When Lem was plowing, Morgan followed Silas around, listened to his stories of Indian fights, trapping, hunting, fishing, running from grizzly bears. He heard mention of Lewis and Clark, of John Colter, Manuel Lisa, Louison Beaudoin, Jacques Clamorgan. To young Morgan, the names sounded strange and heroic.

The morning came when Silas bade farewells. Lem was

anxious to see him go. He had seen a change in Morgan that he didn't like. The boy had taken to daydreaming, staying up late at night with Silas, talking of beaver like they was big as cows, Injun nonsense. Morgan was paying more attention to Silas than he was to his chores.

"Well, Lem, I done wore out my welcome, I 'spect, but it were worth it. I got to meet your boy and see how you growed. I'm back to the mountains and the trapper's life."

"Been good to see you, Silas. Thank you for the hat."

"And for the medicine horn," said Morgan.

"Ain't nothin' to that. You change your mind 'bout comin' out west, you look me up in St. Louis. Most ever'one knows Silas Morgan. You ask. I could use a partner. I'd give you traps and such the first season."

"No more talk about that, Silas. Best you be on your way."

"I will and thank ye for the hospice." Silas rumpled Morgan's hair. "Be seein' you, young Morgan."

"Good-by, Silas," said Morgan, surprised at his own boldness in using the trapper's first name. But he felt grown around him. Silas didn't treat him like a kid.

"Silas, you ride careful," said Lem.

Father and son watched Silas mount his horse and ride to the road. The first sarvice trees were starting to bloom and there were flashes of white, like gunsmoke, in the woody hills. The air had a sharp apple tang to it, and the morning wind blew strangely warm. Lem went to the barn to shoe Gideon, but Morgan stood there watching Silas until he disappeared from sight. Only the ring of hammer on iron broke his revery, brought him back to the present. As Silas was riding away, Morgan dreamed that he was going with him, all the way to the far mountains, where the beaver played in deep, dark pools, and elk roamed the high meadows, bugling like lords in the king's forest.

There was a sadness in Morgan when he realized Silas was gone and that he probably would never see him again.

*   *   *

In the spring of Morgan's sixteen year, the Bickhams' house caught on fire. The conflagration started on the back porch when a spark from a stump Calvin Moon was burning blew into Nancy's washbasket. The spark apparently smoldered for hours while Nancy was busy shaking out blankets and beating rugs and Mr. Bickham was in town buying mules and new harness. Late in the afternoon, the porch erupted in flames. The wind came up and spread the fire. The Bickhams' house burned before anyone could get a bucket brigade started. Sparks spread to the hayloft and the barn exploded, spewing sparks and fireballs in every direction. The trees along the road caught fire and the wind whipped the fire across the fallow fields and down to Lem Hawke's place.

Before he and Morgan could do anything to stop it, the fire burned the barn and corrals. They managed to get the two horses, with their bridles, out, but the mules burnt to a crisp, their horrible brays chilling to hear. Friar Tuck Two barked until he was hoarse, ran around in circles until he collapsed in exhaustion. The Hawkes got their rifles, powder, ball, possibles pouches, horns and a few other things out of the house before it caught fire.

"You stay well away," Lem told Morgan. "Keep them horses from runnin' back to the barn."

Morgan led them to the field where their few goods lay in a heap. Friar Tuck followed, tail drooping, eyes swollen and red from the smoke. Morgan snatched up his medicine horn and held onto the bridle reins as his father dashed from the well to the house, carrying a bucket of water.

Lem stood on a wagon throwing water on the walls, but the flames scorched him so badly, he had to run to the well and dowse himself. Morgan stood by in the field, tears streaming down his face, watching the house burn to ashes. He held his medicine horn tightly in his hands until his father had to slap his face to bring him out of his sobbing fit.

All around them, smoke made the land dark, choked them. The fire raged into the hills, hungry flames licked at the hardwoods, snuffed out the beautiful white blossoms of the sarvice and dogwoods, the pale pink blooms of the redwood trees. Lem watched everything he owned burn, watched the woods blaze and belch columns of smoke into the sky until the sun was blotted out. The wind hurled the flames in all directions.

"We'd best go," he told Morgan. "Gather up your things and get on Boots."

"Pa, what'll we do?"

"I don't know, son. Better check on the Bickhams first. Then we got to find us a place to stay."

"My eyes hurt and it's hard to breathe."

"I know, Morg. We got to get out of the smoke."

Horatio Bickham met them on the road. His slaves were all huddled together trying to get the children to stop crying. Nancy's eyes were red from the smoke and her face blackened with soot.

"How's it down at your place, Hawke?" Bickham asked.

"All burnt," said Lemuel.

"Jesus."

"Anythin' I can do, Mr. Bickham?"

"Not now. We'll try and build it back someday. But not now. Jesus."

"Yes sir," said Lemuel. "Could I leave Friar Tuck with Calvin? Don't want him runnin' around town."

"I'll take care of it. C'mere boy."

Morgan carried Friar Tuck over to Bickham, gave him the dog. He patted Tut's head, whispered something into his ear.

"I'll be back for him, Mr. Bickham."

"We'll put him up in the empty hog pen," said Bickham.

Lem and Morgan waved good-by and rode into town. People lined the roads looking at the smoke and when they called out their questions he told them what had happened.

Soon, people began to load their wagons up and ride out to see the destruction.

That night, Lem and Morgan sat in a hotel room, looking at their few pathetic possessions.

"I got my money outen the house before she went," said Lem. "We can get by."

"Are you goin' back, Pa?"

"Back? To what? A burnt-down farm. A coupla dead mules."

"We could go out west. Try and find Silas."

Lem looked at the boy, saw that he was serious. He shook his head, slumped with a weary resignation. He thought of the hard work that must be done, the money it would cost to buy new lumber, the time it would take to rebuild. He would still have to plow and plant, buy new stock. There was just him and the boy now. When he had begun the farm before, he had had Roberta and the unborn child to think about. He had wanted the farm then. Now, it seemed so useless. Morgan was growing into a man, filling out. He would be a help if he started up farming again.

"What do you want to do, Morg? Want to start up the farm again? Build us a house? It'd be hard. Plumb hard."

"What for, Pa? You don't own the land. It belongs to Mr. Bickham, you told me so. We could find Silas."

"Dammit, leave Silas out of this!" Lem didn't mean to shout, but there were things that fire had smoked out of him and maybe something burning inside him that he couldn't put out so easy. "Just tell me what you want to do."

"I don't want to go back there, Pa."

Morgan took a quick breath to keep from shaking. His father's scorching stare was making his face hot. But he was glad he had said it out loud. Ever since Silas had come to see them, he had been thinking about going out west, been thinking about those big rivers and the prairies and the beaver. He wanted to see what an elk looked like. He wanted to hunt antelope and see a prairie chicken strut when it was mating season. He wanted to see a grizzly bear up close and stand on top of the world and look down at it like the tallest person alive.

"You don't want no more of farmin'?"

"No," said Morgan.

"Why?"

"I don't know, Pa. It just seems like we don't get no place there. We do the same thing ever' year and then a big fire comes along and burns it all up. Don't make no sense to me. I want to see what Silas seen. I want to trap beaver."

"Be hard, boy. Awful hard. Did he tell you about how cold it gets and about standin' in shiverin' water tryin' to set a trap when your fingers is hard and cold? Did he tell you how dangerous it was? There's Injuns and they ain't no fun. I know. I kilt me a couple and it got a lot of innocent people kilt."

"You kilt Injuns, Pa?"

"I did and I ain't proud of it. It was necessary."

Morgan looked at his father with a keen interest. He felt something like pride swelling in him, something making his heart beat faster.

"Well, I'll fight 'em. You ain't got to worry none."

"Brave talk," said Lem, but he was pleased with his son.

"Let's go, Pa. Silas asked us to. Can we? Can we, please?"

"I'll think about it. It's a mighty big chunk right now. A fur piece to go, just on one man's say-so."

"We could do it, Pa. I know we could."

Lem sighed. What was it Silas had said? Seeds? Well, some more had been planted this night. He looked at Morgan, tried a feeble smile. Maybe the boy was right. Maybe they should move on, try something else. He had no close friends in Kentucky. He had done well, but he would have to start all over again.

"You go to sleep, Morg. I'll study on it awhile and do the same."

"I hope you make up your mind to go, Pa. I truly do."

"We'll chew on it some more in the mornin'."

Morgan grinned.

Later, when he fell asleep, his heart raced. Maybe they would go, he thought. Maybe they would see Silas again and go to the mountains with him.

In the morning, Morgan woke up in an empty room. It took him several moments to realize where he was. And then he remembered the fire.

"Pa?"

There was no answer.

He felt a tug of fear, a queasy swirl in his stomach. What if his father had left him? The room was strange. He scrambled out of bed and dressed quickly. He walked down the stairs and through the lobby of the hotel. Out on the street, he looked both ways, hoping to see his father.

There were a few people on the street. A two-wheeled cart lumbered by. Somewhere, a dog barked. Morgan's heart sank like a stone.

Then he saw his father emerge from the livery stables down the street. He was leading Hammerhead and Boots, and they had new saddles on their backs. Well, they were not new, but Morgan had never seen them before. His heart soared. He ran to meet his father.

"Where we goin', Pa?" he yelled. "Where we goin', huh?

Lem smiled.

"Why, we're a-headin' west, Morgan, to see if we can find old Silas. After we pick up Friar Tuck and say our good-bys to the Bickhams."

"Oh, Pa! Oh, Pa!" Morgan jumped up and down. He wanted to do handstands and cartwheels, but he chained his exuberance by pumping his arms up and down and just hopping around like a fool. But he felt real good and he wanted to hug his father and maybe peck him on the cheek.

"Settle down, Morgan. We got a heap to do afore we can

leave. We'll need food and canteens and somethin' to sleep on and under and a whole lot of stuff."

"I know, I know. Oh, Pa, I can't wait to go."

"We might stop by and see your ma, too. Tell her we're goin'."

Morgan fell silent. He had forgotten about his mother. But she would want to know, he reckoned. Maybe. She might not like it, neither.

"Let's just tell her real quick and then go on our way," said Morgan.

"We won't linger none," said Lem, and the bitterness welled up in him again. He was leaving a lot more than Kentucky, he thought. He was leaving a life that had gone bad on him for no good reason. Maybe Morgan was right. Maybe it was time to move on and forget about the past. He had money. He didn't owe any taxes.

For the first time in his life, Lemuel Hawke was beginning to feel truly free.

17

Friar Tuck ranged the post road out of Lexington, sniffing at every clump of grass, peeing on trees, jumping quail out of the thickets, chasing rabbits across wide, fresh-plowed fields, disappearing in the bluegrass that was just high enough to hide most of him. The Hawkes, father and son, left the town behind them as they headed southwest on the post road. The sun spangled the green buds with gilded spray, splashed goldenrod pollen on the winter-bare pastures, laced the ponds with ripples of molten honey. Meadowlarks piped on the fencerows as Morgan and his father, their horses loaded down with bedrolls and saddlebags bulging with foodstuffs, looked one last time at the hills and hollows they were leaving.

Morgan's stomach jiggled with the flutter of butterfly wings. A terrible feeling of homelessness overwhelmed him, but there was another, more elusive feeling as well. He dreaded seeing his mother, not so much for his sake, as for his father's. He had heard his father moan in the night and call her name aloud in his sleep. "Bobbie, Bobbie," his father had called, and Morgan awoke with an eerie feeling that she was in the room with them, come back to lurk in the shadows like a ghost. He had slept fitfully after that, and when they had said good-by to the Bickhams, Mrs. Bickham had broken down and cried, then run away to call her children together and tell them the Hawkes were leaving.

It had pained him to see Mrs. Bickham cry that way and he wondered if his mother would feel the same way when his pa told her about going out to the West.

Morgan slowed Boots some to ride behind his father. He looked at Lem's strong back, his long hair burnished dark by the sun. He knew that his pa still loved his mother. He had often heard him sob in his pillow at night and call out for his lost wife and it stabbed Morgan like a knife to hear his father weep for the woman who had deserted them both. He missed his mother, too, but he kept seeing her with that other man, Barry O'Neil, and the smirk on her painted face, the blurred look in her eyes. He kept hearing her scornful laughter and it tore at him like razors, left him bleeding inside with dozens of tiny wounds that hurt like black locust thorns.

After they had said good-by to the Bickhams, to Calvin Moon and the children, he and his pa had returned to town and bought goods for the trip: fry pans and boiling pots, wooden canteens, powder, ball, extra flints, smoked bacon, sacks of beans and flour, coffee, tobacco, blankets, rope, an axe and hatchet, a few tenpenny nails, some tinder and used cloth for making fires.

They had slept in the hotel one last night, his pa telling

him they'd be spending their nights on hard ground once they left Lexington. Morgan looked at the stars a long time that night, standing at the window until his pa had called him to bed. He went to sleep wondering where Silas was at that moment, whether he was still in the mountains or if he had come down to the plains with his furs.

His father turned in the saddle to look at him. Morgan bowed his head for he did not want his pa to see what surely must be on his face.

"You tired, son?"

"Naw."

"Som'pin' wrong?"

"Nope. I was just thinkin'."

"Well, come on up and ride beside me."

Morgan tapped his heels into Boots's flanks, caught up with his father.

"What you been thinkin' on, Morg?"

"Ma, I reckon."

"Well, she might be glad to see you, seein' as how you've growed some."

"How come she to leave us, Pa?"

"I can't figger it. She got sweet on that Barry O'Neil, I reckon."

"You pine for her, don't you?"

"Some," said Lem, and drew in a breath, let it out in a barely audible sigh. "Was a time I thought she was the prettiest thing I ever saw. She was, too. I get to pinin' for them days now and again."

"I don't hardly remember her anymore," said Morgan, but that wasn't what he wanted to say. He didn't remember her as his mother, just as a woman who had been drunk and sent them away so's she could be with another man. Morgan hated her for that. He couldn't remember her touch, or whether she had ever put her arms around him or hugged him. Those were the things he wanted to remember, but he could never summon them up to his mind.

"Sure you do, son. Why, she used to dote on you."

"Did she?"

"On both of us," said Lem, and then he was silent, re-membering little things that he had almost forgotten.

Lem thought of those lazy afternoons back in Virginia when he wanted her so much he had to come in from the fields and tease her, coax her into bed. He remembered her shy giggles when he wrestled with her, and burned her cheeks with kisses, smothered her with his youthful lust. He remembered the glow in her brown eyes when he made love to her, and how they lay back and lingered on the beauty of their passion, awestruck at the wonder of it. Her hair smelled of lilacs and her mouth tasted of crushed mint. He remembered how she made him feel good inside, how his awkwardness would go away when she kissed him back as good as he had kissed her. Those were the thoughts that wrenched him now, made him realize how much he had lost when Roberta had left him.

"I hope she's glad to see us," said Morgan, breaking into his father's thoughts. "But, I hope you don't auger none to stay."

"She won't want us to stay," said Lem.

"And we won't anyway," said Morgan, so curtly his father laughed aloud.

"No, we won't stay. Once you cut loose, you don't let nothin' stop you from goin'."

Morgan grinned, rode off chasing after Friar Tuck with a whoop and a holler.

After camping for one night in the woods and riding half a morning of the next day, Lem and Morgan rode into the Cumberland Valley where the post road intersected another road running east and west through Gallatin. They headed south to Nashville, passing a number of tippling houses, some of them new. They came to the town just after noon. They passed fields planted in cotton and tobacco that butted up to the narrow Cumberland River with its deep brown waters. They looked up, saw small houses clinging to the edges of a bluff like boxes nailed to a wall. Lem put Hammerhead into a trot as the road steepened, rising up above the river. There, atop the high bluff that commanded the wide valley, stood the town of Nashville.

"Small, ain't it?" said Lem, looking at the houses and buildings.

"Not as big as Lexington," said Morgan.

They kept to the main road, looked at the houses lining both sides of the unpaved streets. At the center of town, Lem marked the public buildings as his gaze swept the business district. There had been earthquakes during the winter; they had seen wrecked buildings in Lexington and along the way. Here, the damage seemed worse; they passed brick buildings that had cracked open like eggs, chimney bricks strewn in the weeds beside collapsed houses. In the center of town, there were downed scaffoldings, teetering walls and scattered piles of rubble everywhere they looked. There was a jail, a courthouse, a post office, and a large market house. The side streets were all crowded with people at market, and they had passed two noisy inns just before reaching the square.

At another, the Red Lion on a corner of the square, a man hailed them. His cheeks, nestled in a thick, woolly beard, glowed like cherry coals. He stood outside the inn, holding a fired-clay jug.

"Pilgrims," he called, "light down and wet yore thoats."

The man was dressed in grimy buckskins that were almost orange and most of the fringes had rotted or been torn away. He packed a large skinning knife on his wide belt, and a hunting pouch and a matched pair of powder horns hung from his shoulders.

Lem shook his head, but the man stepped onto the road and blocked their way.

"You farmers?" he asked.

Morgan shook his head. Lem nodded.

"Well, which is it? One is and one isn't."

"We been farmin'," said Lem, holding Hammerhead back with the reins pulling on the bit.

"I been trappin' the Great Lakes and the Ohio Valley, eatin' bear meat and wolf. Good season too, when we wasn't fallin' down from the quake."

"We got to get on," said Lem.

"Not 'thout havin' a tipple with Nat Sullard, you don't," said the man.

"My boy don't drink," said Lem. "And neither do I," he lied.

"That yore boy? Wal, now, Pilgrim, 'bout time he tasted the critter. Me 'n my pard's quittin' the Ohio and headin' west to the big mountains."

"You been there?" Morgan just blurted the question out.

"Nope, but they's a feller over to the market sellin' the purtiest furs you ever seen what he got in a place called Yallerstone. Me 'n him're hookin' up, and my pard's a-goin' with us. Light down and come inside. The boy can have ginger beer, won't hurt him none."

"We got things we got to do," said Lem.

"Pa, can't we? Just for a little while?"

"Why, shore, Pa," mocked Sullard. "Come on and meet some of the trappers. We done sold our goods and we aim to drink Nashville dry afore we set out for the mountains."

"We'll come back," said Lem. "We got business."

"Wal, now, you and the boy come back. Me'n Charlie Pack will be in the Red Lion swallerin' grog."

"Oh, Pa, can't we go in now?" asked Morgan.

"We'll be back," said Lem.

"Promise?" asked Sullard.

Morgan looked hard at his father.

"Promise," said Lem tightly, slacking up on the reins. Sullard stepped aside and the Hawkes rode slowly by him.

From inside the Red Lion Inn, they heard a burst of laughter, and someone yelled exuberantly above the noise.

"We'll be back, Mr. Sullard," said Morgan, waving to the trapper, who was already weaving his way back inside the tippling house.

"Morgan, you got a lot to learn," said his father, as Hammerhead broke into a trot.

"Look, Pa," said Morgan, pointing to the big market across the quad. "That's where the other trappers are!"

Buckskinned men sat on bales of furs, or leaned against two-wheeled carts. Clumps of men crowded the makeshift counters out front, pawing through loose pelts, holding them up to the light.

"Trappers," said Lem, riding toward the bustling throng of marketers and fur traders.

Morgan grew excited when he saw a man standing atop a large crate, waving a beaver pelt like the one Silas had shown them.

"They got beaver," exclaimed Morgan, clapping his heels to his horse's flanks. Boots galloped ahead of Lem's horse, heading straight for the trader's market. Men looked at the boy and a constable waved a wooden stick at Morgan, warning him to slow down his horse. Morgan reined up and waited for his father.

A trapper argued with a fur buyer over the quality of his catch. One of the buyers wiped perspiration from his brow with a swatch of broadcloth. The trapper had a faint accent. He was burly, muscular, with a dark shock of hair coiling from under his light voyageur's cap. He was dressed in cotton trousers, wore a bright red sash under his belt, a loose-fitting muslin shirt that bore the grime of a working man. He carried a large knife on his belt, wore moccasin boots that laced to his knees. His most striking feature, however, was that he wore a smile, even though he appeared to be angry.

"But you are cheating me," said the trapper. "Deez are prime fur, you bet. O'Neil, he give me one pound."

"That's my price, Jocko," said the buyer, a reedy-voiced man in his midtwenties. "Barry's bought up. Half a pound."

"Pah! You take dem, you cheater sumbitch," said the trapper, still smiling. "You give me twenty pound."

"Nineteen and the half," said the buyer.

"Twenty."

The buyer sighed, pulled out a roll of banknotes. He counted out twenty and handed them to the trapper. The trapper, still grinning, counted each bill and stuffed them inside his sash. He swaggered toward Lem and Morgan.

Lem swung down off his horse.

"Sir," he said to the trapper, "could I have a word with you?"

"I got no more fur to sell." The trapper smiled pleasantly.

"I'm wondering where I can find Barry O'Neil," said Lem.

"That sumbitch. He don't show his damn face. He send that cheater Wally, eh? O'Neil, he got better t'ings to do."

"Where can I find him?"

"He got a store just down that street." The trapper pointed. "Big store. He buy plenty fur cheap. I go see Big John. He owes me money. Then, I go to St. Louis. No more cheating this damn place."

"You goin' to the mountains?" asked Morgan, his eyes lit up like firebrands.

"You bet," said the trapper. "Ever'body he go to the mountains. Dis be last time I trap those damn big lakes."

"That's where we're a-goin'," said Morgan. Lem gave his son a dark look.

"You meet the Major?" asked the trapper.

Morgan shook his head.

"Come, you follow Jocko to see Big John O'Neil. He owes me some money, eh? Then we go to that Red Lion whiskey store, see Major McDougal."

"Who's he?" asked Lem.

"He works for Missouri Fur. He make you a good offer, I think. Me, too. We go to see that Major, listen to what he has to say, huh? He sell plenty prime fur for top dollar."

"We'd be mighty obliged to go with you to O'Neil's," said Lem. "I got business with Barry."

"Ah, Barry, he ain't no count," said the trapper. "Mighty good bootlicker for his uncle, I think."

"What's your name?" asked Morgan, not realizing it was considered impolite.

"Hah! I'm Jacques Decembre. They call me Jocko DeSam. And you, young feller, what they call you?"

"I'm Morgan Hawke."

DeSam turned to Lem.

"And this is your papa, no?"

"I'm Lemuel Hawke, the boy's pa."

"You're not trappers?"

"No," said Lem. "But we aim to go west, see someone we know."

"This Morgan, he look pretty young."

"He's broke to the plow," said Lem, some testiness in his voice.

DeSam laughed. He slapped Morgan on the shoulder.

"You come with Jocko. We get the business done and see Major McDougal. He make you both a good offer. Plenty of money in the fur, I think, but in Tennessee, they are all thieves. Big John O'Neil's the biggest thief of all."

Lem mounted up. They followed DeSam to the street he had pointed out. Halfway down the block, Jocko stopped in front of a large building. Workers were filling in chinks where bricks had loosened during the winter earthquakes. The big sign over the entrance proclaimed:

TENNESSEE HATTERY
JOHN O'NEIL, PROP.

"Used to be called different," said Lem.

"He big-time hatter now," said Jocko. "He make the best damn thief." DeSam smiled when he spoke, as if everything was a big joke to him.

The three entered the store, stood peering about the large showroom. Men and women shoppers browsed among the hat displays. Male clerks fawned over the women and Barry O'Neil held a mirror up to a female customer's face while she admired a beaver felt hat. A tall man at the rear of the store pulled down a hatbox, handed it to a man at the foot of the ladder.

"That's Big John back there," said DeSam.

"Me'n my boy'll speak to Barry, that red-headed feller over yonder," said Lem.

Jocko strode toward the rear of the store, making a bee-line for Big John.

Barry looked up, saw Lemuel and Morgan. He smiled at the woman, handed her the mirror. He stepped away, waited. Lem jostled a man aside. Morgan followed in his wake.

O'Neil swaggered to meet them, the barest curl of a smile at one corner of his twisted mouth. Morgan felt his muscles tauten as he looked at the man he'd last seen with his mother. He could not help thinking that he was already as tall as the man his father hated.

"Hawke," he said. "It's been a long time. I hope you came to buy a hat." Beneath the overt cordiality, there was a faint trace of nervousness, a slight quivering in O'Neil's voice.

"I come to talk to Roberta," said Lem tightly.

"She hasn't worked for us in some time," said O'Neil.

"You know where she is?"

"Last I knew, she was staying at Miss DuMont's Boarding House. Over on Central." O'Neil held up his right hand, curled the fingers as if examining the nails. He regarded the Hawkes with a diffident air.

"Why ain't she a-workin' here?" asked Lem.

"That's none of your business, Hawke."

"Maybe it is. You fire her?"

"We had to let her go. She, ah, she has a fondness for barleycorn whiskey."

"If she does, you put her to it."

"I think, Hawke, whatever she has, she brought it with her."

"You sonofabitch," said Hawke quietly, a seething hatred in his tone.

O'Neil turned on his heel, took a step before Lem caught him by the collar. He spun the hatter around. Barry's mouth widened in surprise.

"Somethin' to remember us by, O'Neil," said Hawke. He drew back a fist and shot it straight to Barry's jaw. There was a sharp crack and O'Neil's eyes rolled backward in their sockets. His neck snapped backward and he reeled away, crumpled into a hat tree. The tree and O'Neil went down with a resounding crash.

"Golly damn!" exclaimed Morgan, swearing for the first time. "You busted him good, Pa."

John O'Neil, hearing the commotion, broke away from Jocko, sweeping him aside with a brawny arm, headed toward the scene of the ruckus. DeSam, angered that he had not yet finished the argument to his satisfaction, recovered his balance and set off at a strong lope to catch the elder O'Neil.

Barry groaned and pulled himself to a sitting position. Lem braced himself, his hands still balled into fists, and glared at the fallen O'Neil. He did not see Big John eating up floor with long, determined strides.

Big John O'Neil was not the puny spectacle of manhood his nephew Barry was, but an oversized brute with muscular arms, powerful broad shoulders and a neck thick as a nail keg. He stood six foot six in his socks. His massive brow jutted over crisp blue eyes, set off a jaw square as a plumb-bobbed slab of granite. The only resemblance between him and his nephew, Barry, was the thick sheaf of red hair that graced his pate like a lion's mane.

Morgan looked up and saw the giant redhead striding straight toward his father.

"Pa, look out!" he called.

Lem turned around, but not in time.

Big John, for all his size and weight, was quick and lithe on his feet. He grabbed Lemuel Hawke by the scruff of his collar and hauled him toward a ham-sized fist hurtling toward the smaller man's jaw with the impetus of a 16-pound maul. John's fist landed square on Lem's chin, propelling him from O'Neil's grasp and into a woman's bustle. The woman screamed in terror and went down. Lem slid across her rump and into a cabinet stacked with hats.

Morgan threw himself headlong at Big John's legs, tackled him. It was, he thought, like trying to bring down a scaly-bark hickory with twenty-foot roots. Big John didn't budge and lashed downward with one of his gigantic hands. He grabbed Morgan's hair and jerked the boy upward like a kicking puppet.

DeSam waded into the melee with both fists swinging. He caught Big John in the side with a roundhouse left and banged his right into a kidney. It was like hitting a slab of cold beef hanging from a butcher's rack.

Barry O'Neil scrambled to his feet and raced from the store, screaming at the top of his voice.

"Constable! Constable!" Barry yelled, and the store, filled with screaming women and confused men, emptied like a factory at the closing whistle.

Morgan broke free of Big John's grip and fell to the floor.

Big John turned and warded off another of DeSam's blows and slid an uppercut under Jocko's right arm and compressed his chin with a solid, smashing fist of considerable force. DeSam blinked like a snared rabbit and staggered around in a little circle on rubbery legs.

Lem crawled from under a pile of hats and ran back for another chance at Big John, as the latter swung a bruising fist in Morgan's direction. Morgan ducked and felt the rush of air over his head. The fear that knotted his innards oozed away with the rush of anger that filled his veins with needles. He saw his father jolt into Big John's midsection like a charging bull. Big John, caught off balance, staggered a half-foot off his spot. Morgan saw his advantage and plowed into him, arms flailing like a pair of rugbeaters. His fists grazed Big John's cheek and bounced off his barrel chest. Jocko stepped in, drove a fist into Big John's solar plexus with little noticeable effect. Big John smacked Morgan in the temple. Morgan went down in a heap, but grabbed one of O'Neil's legs. He pulled himself close enough to bite him as Lem and Jocko increased the fury of their twin attack. Morgan bit Big John in the calf and felt the muscle cord up and harden like a chunk of pig iron.

The next thing he knew, Morgan felt a shoe crunch his stomach flat and he lost all the air in his lungs.

Three constables rushed into the store, each grasping a polished bung-starter. On their heels, Barry O'Neil gripped a chunk of two-by-four lumber snatched from the construction platform outside.

Big John went down, to his knees at least, under the onslaught from Lem and Jocko. But, the constables came up on the fight just as both men were about to deliver the *coup de grace* and started clubbing them mercilessly with the bung starters. Barry O'Neil swung his two-by-four club on Morgan, thumping him soundly on the temple. Lem and Jocko went down, blood streaming from their scalps, thickening in their hair, blinding them in a crimson rush.

"Arrest them, arrest them," Barry screamed, and one of

the constables shoved him aside and spoke in a thick Irish brogue.

"Sure, and that's just what we'll be doin', Mr. O'Neil, if you'll stop your squawkin' and leave to us the immediate corporal punishment of these divils."

Barry took one more whack at Morgan, hitting him in the gluteus maximus with the flat side of the board. Morgan never felt it. He was out cold, a lump growing on his temple to the size of a darning egg.

Within a half an hour, Lem, Morgan and Jocko were all painfully regaining consciousness in the Nashville jail.

18

Morgan heard the soft tread of footsteps outside the jail cell. Thin morning light streamed ashen through the single high window in the log wall. He shivered in the chill, rubbed his grit-clogged eyes. His pa and DeSam were asleep in opposite corners. His father had moaned during the night, whimpered sporadically in his dreams. The three of them were the only prisoners and no one had come by since one of the constables had turned the key on them the day before, locking them in. No one had fed them and Morgan's stomach rumbled with hunger.

He stood up, his joints stiff from sleeping on the hard dirt floor of the cell. His neck and shoulders ached. A shot of pain stabbed his chest. He peered hard at the woman standing in front of the iron bars.

For a moment, she looked like a statue, or a scarecrow. Morgan felt an odd tingle at the back of his neck, a slender moment of fear that he could not explain.

Roberta stood to one side of the cell door looking frail and emaciated in her loose-fitting cotton dress. She wore a faded bonnet that failed to shield her gaunt face. Her eyes drooped with weariness and resignation. There was no depth in their murky brown pupils; they appeared glazed and lifeless.

"Ma?"

"Is that you, Morgan?"

He walked a few steps toward her, trembling. He felt dizzy, lightheaded.

"I—it's me, Ma," he stammered. The shock of seeing her so close, and after so long, made his throat go dry.

"Come here," she said, "so I can see you."

"Yes'm," he said, and walked a few paces toward her, then stopped.

"Come closer."

He stepped up to the bars, quaking inside with that nameless tingle of fear still probing his spine.

"My, look at you. Nigh full growed." She paused, looked at him oddly. "I was beautiful once," she said.

"Yes'm," he said, looking down at his feet. He felt her eyes scouring him from head to toe. He thought it was strange for his mother to say that. He remembered her as being beautiful. She still was, in a way. There was just something peculiar about the look in her eyes.

"What has your pa done to you?"

"Nothin'."

"Fightin' and such. The whole town's talkin' about it."

"That Barry O'Neil, he started it. Then, his uncle got into it and them constables come in and started hittin' us. Throwed us in jail."

"What does your pa want in Nashville? Have you seen my mother? She was not beautiful. No, not in the least, I tell you." A savage tone crept into his mother's voice. Morgan swayed back on his heels, but he did not move away.

"We come to say good-by to you," said Morgan. He looked up at his mother, then. She reached through the bars and touched his hair. He drew back. His pa stirred at the back of the cell.

"Lemuel," said his mother, looking past her son.

Lem moaned. Morgan turned, saw his father rise to his feet, sway on wobbly legs.

"Bobbie? That you?" Lem's voice rasped and he cleared his throat, wobbled toward Morgan.

"It's Ma," said Morgan, some of the fear going away. His pa walked up, stood beside his son.

"Come to gloat?" asked Lemuel. "That chicken gut O'Neil got us into this fix."

"Well, Lemuel," she said softly, "you and the boy turned out as I expected. A couple of common ruffians."

"Bobbie," said Lem, pulling himself up straight. "We—we come to see you, say good-by."

"Is this the way you do it? The whole town's talking about the way you and Morgan attacked Barry and John. You never saw me, Lem. I was there, but you couldn't see me like I was. Like I really was."

"What the hell you talkin' about, woman?"

Morgan heard a sound, looked over his shoulder. Jocko was awake, but his face was a lumpy mass of dried blood and his hair was matted with dark tangles. His lips were swollen and cracked and his eyes were just slits behind puffed mounds as if he had been stung by a swarm of hornets.

Morgan's father looked just as bad, with a tattered and bloody ear, black-and-blue eyes, his mouth crooked and lumpy as unkneaded dough. Lem's shirt was torn and his face stippled with dark bristles.

"You don't know, Lem," said Roberta. "You just don't know. You never did. I wasn't in the dirt. I was in the trees like a beautiful bird. You just couldn't see me."

"I just come lookin' for you," said Lem, awkwardly. He wondered what Roberta was talking about. She sounded crazy.

Roberta stepped closer to the bars, looked down the hallway. She spoke in a deep whisper.

"Well, Big John wants to put all three of you in the stocks. I've come to warn you. Can you pay your fine? I've already spoken to Constable Parkhurst. If you pay five pounds apiece, he'll let you go. Barry is a murderer. He will murder you."

"I ain't afraid of no O'Neil," said Lem loudly.

"Shh! I'm serious, Lem. If they put you in the stocks, someone will sneak up on you after dark and put a bullet in each one of you. Barry plowed me like a field. He dug everything up and then—then he squatted on me and left a smell. He—he scattered all my seeds. He will put you in the stocks and squat on you."

"You think so?" Lem didn't know what to make of Roberta. One minute she seemed sane, the next she drifted off and made no sense at all.

"I heard talk of it," she whispered. She narrowed her eyes and lowered her head. "There are skulls buried out there."

"Pa, let's pay the money and go on out west," said Morgan quickly. He, too, knew that his mother seemed touched in the head.

"You're going west?" asked Roberta.

"We are."

"Then, you'd best be on your way quick," said Roberta. "Before he robs you, too. He will take everything away. He taketh, he taketh." Her eyes rolled in their sockets and she swayed on her feet as if about to topple backwards, but she recovered from her spell and glared at her former husband and her son.

"We'll pay," said Lemuel. "And we thank you for warning us."

Morgan breathed an audible sigh.

"Good," said Roberta. "I'll tell Mr. Parkhurst."

She turned to leave. She stopped, looked back toward Lem and Morgan.

"They'll all burn in hell, Lemuel. All of 'em."

"Wait," said Lemuel. "Can we talk some place?"

"No, it's best you leave town. Your horses are in the Pine Street livery. I'll say good-by now. He loved to touch my breasts and we drank champagne and we lived in clouds, in dark clouds. It was smoky and we floated all over."

She looked at Morgan, drew in a deep breath.

Morgan winced at the sadness he saw in his mother's eyes. She was whispering something and it made no sense. He listened to her words and knew that she was mad. He saw the sugar-hot light in her eyes, the flare of lightning when she talked of strange things she saw in her mind and he knew that she was addled. He did not understand why or how, but he knew she had gone mad as sure as he knew a rabid skunk when it came hunting chickens and spraying the night air with an acrid foulness that stung his nose and blistered his eyes until they watered with unwilling tears.

"Godspeed," she sighed.

Before Lem could stop her, Roberta was gone. He heard voices and a few moments later one of the constables came down the hall. He carried a key attached to a large ring.

"You got the money?" he asked.

"Fifteen pounds," said Lem.

"Twenty."

"I thought—"

"Make up your mind, me bucko. It's twenty pounds. Be higher if you make me wait."

Jocko rose to his feet, lurched toward Lem and Morgan. He reached into his belt, extracted a wad of notes.

"Just open up that door, turnkey," he growled. "We pay you the damned money."

Lem took off a moccasin, pulled out some bills. Morgan watched the two men in fascination as they counted out the banknotes.

"Let's see that key go in the door first," said Lem.

The constable opened the cell door. Lem and Jocko slammed money into his palm, brushed past him. They walked through the office and out the door into the feeble sunlight. Jocko blinked and winced in the glare. Lem squinted.

"Point me to them stables," he told DeSam.

"I don't know who that woman was, but she knows Big John and his damned nephew," said Jocko. "Them two work real good in the dark."

"You heard what she said?"

"I did, sure."

"You goin' west, then?"

"Soon as I can get my traps," said DeSam.

"Maybe we'll meet up with you," said Morgan.

"You know the way?"

"We do," said Lem. "It's a fur piece."

"Maybe I see you in St. Louis," said Jocko. "You go down this street to the next one yonder and turn right. Stables be back of Blevins Dry Goods."

"Thank you kindly," said Lem.

DeSam flapped an arm in farewell, plodded off in the opposite direction. Morgan watched him get smaller and smaller, then realized his father was already walking away in the direction Jocko had pointed.

Within an hour, Lem and Morgan were finished with Nashville. They heard talk of war with Britain at Blevins's store, where they bought extra shirts and a coffee pot. The clerk mentioned a man named Andrew Jackson, who was recruiting a militia, and Blevins himself said they ought to go over to the courthouse that night and hear a young lawyer named Thomas Hart Benton talk about defending the southwestern frontier of Tennessee. Lem had told both men they were leaving the country, heading for Missouri Territory. Morgan noticed the odd looks as they carried out their goods.

"How far to St. Louis, Pa?" asked Morgan as they rode along the Cumberland River.

" 'Bout three hunnert mile," said Lem.

"How do you know the way?"

"A long time ago, Silas told me about it. I guess it plumb stuck in my craw all this time."

Morgan beamed.

"I'm glad we're goin'," he said. Neither of them wanted to mention that they now had another reason for leaving. Morgan kept thinking about his mother and the scary things she had said. He knew his father was thinking about her too. He was as solemn as a preacher.

"You tell me that next week, Morg. Silas said St. Louie was just about the hardest place to get to he ever seed."

"How come?"

"Well, you just can't go straight to it. We got to ride the Natchez Trace to the Mississippi River. What I hear, it's a fearsome wilderness. We'll have to keep our eyes peeled and locks primed."

Morgan's face glistened in the cool wash of sunlight. He touched the medicine horn slung on his shoulder and felt a surge of excitement. With the horn and his rifle, he was ready to face the most horrible dangers he could imagine. He looked forward to anything that would stop him from thinking about his mother and her madness. He hardly noticed when his father turned southwest, heading, it seemed, in the opposite direction of where they were bound.

After waiting five days in Natchez for a boat to carry them up the Mississippi, Lem and Morgan Hawke thought they'd never live long enough to see St. Louis. Morgan did not mind the slowness. He loved the feel of the rolling river, the tide surge of the mighty waters that made the deck rise and fall. He felt a sense of power watching the land go by and when he saw game, mostly deer, he took imaginary aim as if holding his rifle and squeezed off a killing shot. They learned, from others who waited, that they could have ridden post roads from Tennessee across Kentucky and up into Illinois and saved a lot of miles. But,

Lem did not rue the trip. They had seen a lot of country, had no trouble with Indians or robbers, and now, at last, they were in Missouri Territory.

They unloaded the horses at the small settlement, sniffed the garbage piled in the street along the waterfront. A clutter of whitewashed buildings shone like disheveled swans in the sun. Beyond the foul-smelling sandy levee, the rolling countryside sprawled invitingly toward the distant horizon.

Stevedores wrestled cargo on the docks, swearing in French and English. Boats of all sizes bobbed at anchor or jostled for position at one of the wharves, and the gulls wheeled above the fishing boats like papers fluttering in the wind.

"Where do we go now, Pa?" asked Morgan.

"Find us a place to bed and board, I reckon."

"Will we look for Silas?"

"I reckon." Lem's bruises had faded and most of the stiffness had gone, but he still had a few aches in bone and muscle. He had gotten sick on the boat, but Morgan had scampered about like a swashbuckling pirate, calling out each new sight as if he was Christopher Columbus. Sometimes, Lem thought, the boy's enthusiasm was downright disgusting.

The long trip had hardened Morgan's muscles. His hair had grown thick as a mane and his handsome face was bronzed by the sun. He would be seventeen in October, and he was almost as tall as his father, though not as muscular. They unloaded their gear, packed it aboard Boots and Hammerhead, rode past Front Street and up Olive to the center of town on Fourth Street. They found a stone building that housed a hotel, whitewashed like the others, on Fourth and Laurel, and a stable at the end of the street where they could board their horses. They shared a small second-story room at Lescoulie's Hotel; two cots, a small table and two chairs, a small highboy dresser. There was a privy out back and for sixpence, they could bathe in a wooden tub in a back room on the first floor. Pierre Lescoulie told them about the stables, owned by his brother-in-law, Emile De-Balaviere. Board was a shilling a day.

"It's better you pay in coin," Pierre told Lem. "They's some as will take banknotes, English not American, but most all will take Portagee coin, Spanish bits and pieces, French, too."

"We got mostly coin," said Lem.

"Best get the paper changed," said the innkeeper. "You talk to Emile."

Emile, a stocky Frenchman from New Orleans, had been in St. Louis since 1803, when the Louisiana Purchase made it part of the United States. He had visited the city before, when the Mississippi was a dangerous river, infested with cutthroats and pirates. Emile's father, Etienne, had partici-pated in *L'Anee des Dix Bateaux* (the Year of the Ten Boats) in 1788. The crews of the boats had traveled up-stream from New Orleans and met the pirates in savage combat, driving them from the river.

"Since I come here," Emile told them, "ever'body he make a lot of money from the furs. But, there is always much trouble on the levee, the fighting and killing. *Mais*, there are many fine and beautiful homes here, even so."

Emile told them where they could change their pound notes into hard coin. Lem had no American money. Paper currency issued by the Continental Congress had been worthless since it was first issued in '92.

"Where might we find a trapper by name of Silas Morgan?" Lem asked Lescoulie.

"Ah, I know this Morgan. He drink at the King's Boar and he eat at Spanish Jack's. These places are on Third Street. They stink. Too close to Bloody Island for me, eh? Too many men killed there."

"Bloody Island?"

"That whole levee, the waterfront. They call it that. They

fight the duels, they bet the cards, they fight the cocks. Gamblers, the freebooters, adventurers, they like cats at night. They look for fights and trouble, no? Eh, I tell you what they say. They say they can do anything they want. God he don't never cross the Mississippi, they say."

"You know Silas Morgan?" Lem asked.

"He work for Missouri Fur. He trap the mountains. So many now. Yes, I know him. He part Indian, I think, part bear. He stay too long in the mountains. Go there too many years."

Emile walked away from them, shaking his head, still talking to himself.

Morgan smiled.

"Let's go find Silas," he said to his father.

"We'll look for him, I reckon," said Lem, hitching up his worn trousers. "Maybe we'll eat supper at Spanish Jack's, ask about old Silas."

Morgan grinned wide enough to make his eardrums pop.

Spanish Jack's, on Third Street, was crammed between a jumble of other buildings. Lantern light spilled onto the dirt street, buttered the wooden platform that served as an entrance step.

Lem and Morgan stood out front, listened to the clank of metal plates, the tink of clay mugs, the rattle of eating utensils, the low hum, and occasional eruption, of multilingual conversation.

"Let's eat," said Lem.

"I'm sure hungry, Pa."

The two entered the eating establishment, blinked in the yellow-orange light. Heavy tables crisscrossed the room, benches and tables stood near the walls to accommodate larger parties. A serving wench looked up at them, a waiter whisked away through a doorway in the back. The aroma of food assailed Morgan's nostrils and he felt a tug in his stomach.

The waitress cocked her head toward an empty table.

"Pa? There's a table over yonder."

Lem didn't move. Instead, he stared at a man seated with another in one corner of the room.

"Pa?"

Lem stood there, transfixed, looking into the eyes of a man he believed dead.

19

Morgan looked up at his father, saw the startled expression frozen on his face. He tugged at Lem's sleeve. The serving girl waved an arm at the empty table while continuing to stare at the elder Hawke.

"I'm lookin' at a ghost," said Lem.

"Huh?" Morgan followed the path of his father's stare. He saw the man at the far table with that same look in his eyes.

"We got to get out of here," choked Lem, but he remained rooted to the spot, unable to move.

"Who is he, Pa?"

"Someone who's dead."

"He looks alive to me," said Morgan.

The man at the table rose up and Lem's face blanched like an early morel. The man's chair scraped as he pushed away from the table. He started walking toward Lem and Morgan, head cocked to one side, an eyebrow arched in puzzlement.

Lem made a gurgling sound in his throat.

"G-get away from me," he croaked.

"That you, Hawke?" The man hunched over, peered intently at Lem's face. "Aw, shore, it is you, Lemuel Hawke."

Lem gulped in air. His eyes popped from their sockets as the man drew closer. He seemed changed, but there was no mistaking that face. It was older and more cragged than he remembered. But it couldn't be. The man with that face was dead, long dead. Dead and gone.

"Haw, it's me, Dick Hauser. 'Member? Hell, you got to recollec' me. Back when you kilt them two Injuns? When we was all a-goin' to Kentucky, huh? Me and Ormly skelpt 'em, took their rifles."

"No," said Lem and he struggled to lift his foot, but he couldn't force himself to turn his back on the apparition that stalked him.

"Haw, now, Lemuel. I didn't get kilt. Did you think them Injuns kilt me and Ormly?"

"Jesus," rasped Lem. "I plumb thought you was dead. I just knew you was." In his mind, Lem saw the bodies of those who had been killed. The women and children, the men. All of 'em. Ever' damn one of 'em.

Dick Hauser stepped up close to Lem, clapped him on the shoulder. Lem didn't faint, but he felt giddy. Morgan braced himself to fight the stranger. For some reason his pa was afraid of him. Had they been in a fight? Did his pa think he'd killed this Dick Hauser?

"Pa, want me to hit him?" asked Morgan.

Hauser looked, then, at the boy.

"This one of your'n? Looks some to resemble you, Lemuel. Come on, I'll buy you a cup and tell you my tale. It's long and fearsome, but I got out alive and stand here fit and hearty to tell about it."

"Christ, Dick," said Lem, shaking his head in disbelief. "I surely thought you was dead. I mean—"

"I know. They kilt ever'one, my poor wife and kids, and Ormly's family. Come on, set with us. The boy might like a good story. What's your name, son?"

"Morgan Hawke."

"Good name."

"Come on, Morgan," said Lem, recovering his composure. "We'll set with you, Dick. If it's really you."

"It's really me. Luckiest son of a buck what ever walked this earth. C'mon."

Puzzled and curious, Morgan followed the two men to the back table. The serving girl gave the boy a funny look and shrugged. When they reached the table, the other man looked up at Lem Hawke without smiling.

"Doc, this here's Lemuel Hawke, the one I told you about. Some older an' I hope not much bolder, but here he be."

The man at the table scowled. Morgan took him to be likkered up. His breath reeked of strong whiskey and his eyes were red-rimmed. He was dressed in simple clothes, like Dick Hauser. He wore a shabby linsey-woolsey shirt, the cuffs dirty. His eyes were pale blue and he had a mole on the tip of his bulbous nose.

"Well, well, well," said Doc. "The big brave Indian fighter. Never mind that you cost the lives of a dozen people, mister. You got your stinking scalps and left behind a lot of women and children to rot like carrion."

"Haw, he don't mean nothin'," said Hauser. "Doc's just drunker'n six pounds and six bits. He come off his first year of trappin' and he's still trying to thaw his pizzle. Gets damned cold a-settin' traps in them high mountain cricks." Hauser paused. "Set, Lemuel. You too, Morgan."

Lemuel was not appeased. He sat down, glared at the man called Doc. Morgan sat down eagerly. He looked at Dick Hauser and Doc in a new light. They were trappers. Dick wore a dyed linsey-woolsey shirt, heavy trousers, and boot moccasins. He packed two lean Spanish pistols stuck inside a beaded sash tied around his waist. A large knife with a massive handle dangled from his wide leather belt. He had deep-sunk lines and scars on his face, a patch of hair missing in the front. He had combed over it, but Morgan could see the pink circle where hair had once grown. The man was lean as a slat.

"I kilt them Injuns in fair fight," said Lem to Doc, "and

I gave the scalps to Dick here, or Ormly one. They was only two and I didn't know the whole damned tribe would come huntin' them folks. Lord knows I tried to warn 'em. Them two was a-tryin' to sneak back and draw more blood, that's for damned sure, mister."

" 'At's right, Doc. Fact is, Lemuel, givin' us them scalps was what saved our puny asses. Them Injuns thought we'uns was the ones what kilt their brothers and onliest reason they didn't kill us was to show us off to their kinfolk. Hell, they paraded us around their camp like we was high-kickin' prize mules. They let the women beat hell out of us and the kids crack us with sticks and th'ow rocks at us, but they was proud to capture us, they was. The bucks treated us like we was heroes."

The serving girl came over to the table with a slate in her hand. She sailed it onto the table. It landed in front of Lemuel. The girl scrutinized Morgan, made a slight moué of her mouth. She was dressed in a one-piece cotton dress, gray, high-bodiced, with a black apron. Her hair was auburn, her eyes brown. She looked to be about nineteen, with a fresh-scrubbed face, a ribbon threaded through the bun where her long hair coiled at the back of her head. She wore no rouge, nor charcoal. Her eyes sparkled like shiny beads.

"Eat, drink or both?" she asked.

"Bring my friends here whatever they want," said Hauser.

"We have ale, whiskey, and whatever's writ on the slate," said the serving girl.

"I'll have ale," said Lemuel. Morgan picked up the slate and read the items: boiled beef or antelope, potatoes, fish, beans, turnips.

"I'll try some of that antelope and some 'taters and turnips," said Morgan.

Hauser and Doc laughed.

"Boy, you don't want to eat any of that antelope," said Hauser. "Tough as a Britisher's boot and tastes like buckskin broiled in brine."

Morgan flushed beet red.

"The beef is right tasty," said the girl, nudging Morgan. "By the way, my name's Willa."

Lem frowned at the girl and grabbed the slate from Morgan.

"Bring him the beef, then," he said curtly. "I'll have the same, 'cept beans 'stead of turnips."

"Bring us more whiskey," said Hauser, pointing to Doc.

"Just as you wish," said Willa, deliberately rubbing her hip against Morgan's arm.

"Looks so that gal's got her eye on you, Morgan," said Hauser. "She 'pears to be sweet as honey on a biscuit."

"He'll have none of that," snapped Lemuel. "Damned women, anyway."

"Why, whatever happened to your missus?" asked Hauser.

"None of your business," said Lem, curtly.

Morgan gave his father a look, then his gaze followed the serving girl as she went to the serving bar, put her foot on the iron rail underneath and leaned forward. Her buttocks thrust tight against her dress. Morgan felt a stir inside him. He had begun to look at women and girls. It didn't make any difference how old they were; they fascinated him. There had been a girl about his age on the boat that brought them up from Natchez. She was about sixteen and shy as a titmouse.

One day, when he was sitting on the pitching deck, holding onto a davit, she came up behind him and sat down next to him. She asked him if he'd ever kissed a girl. He told him he hadn't. She asked him if he'd like to kiss her. He had become embarrassed and stricken with a sudden case of the tongue-tied.

The girl had suddenly leaned over and thrown her arms around him. She found his lips and planted a wet kiss on them. She wouldn't turn loose and they were like that when his pa had come up on them. He grabbed Morgan by the ear and pulled him out of the girl's arms. She gave a shriek and jumped up, scrabbled across the wildly tilting deck. Morgan got to his feet to avoid having his ear pulled clean off. He glared at his pa.

"Don't go messin' around with trash," his father had snapped.

"Pa, she was just a girl. We wasn't doin' nothin'."

"All women are trouble," said Lem and he had stalked away, leaving Morgan with a stinging earlobe and a considerable amount of his pride damaged. The boat had rolled just then and Morgan had to grab the rail to keep from going overboard.

While his pa hadn't mentioned it again aboard the boat, he kept a watchful eye on Morgan and the girl kept her distance. Morgan thought of her now as he looked at the serving girl.

"Ain't much to St. Louis," said Lem, looking around the room.

"It's small, but wild," said Doc. "Easy place to get killed or skinned."

"Keep away from the Masons and the Choteaus," Hauser said to Lem.

"Huh?"

"Free trapper. Onliest way to be," said Hauser.

" 'At's right," echoed Doc. "You'll starve a lot quicker that way." His speech was slurred and he had trouble focusing his eyes.

"What you drivin' at?" asked Lem. Morgan stopped looking at the girl. He was getting uncomfortable with his thoughts. He kept wondering what she would look like without her clothes on.

"Masons is tryin' to organize here and get in on the money," said Hauser. "Them Choteaus got a company, Missouri Fur, and got 'em a store. They want to hog it all just like them damned Masons. They might not make you an offer first time out, but you bring in furs, they'll want to put cash in your pockets and give you traps you'll pay dear for when you come down in the spring."

"Who are the Masons?"

"Bunch of secretive pilgrims," said Hauser bitterly. "Hard tellin' who's one and who ain't. I just ask and if they's Masons, I don't sell to 'em or buy from 'em."

"And Choteau?"

"They's a bunch of 'em. They got money. Auguste, anyways. Young Cadet, he's the smart one. Pierre. He got him a license to trade with the Great and Little Osage. Didn't do too well, but Pierre's pa, Auguste, is the Injun agent up there and he did the Mandans a favor once't. You got to get thick with the Injuns, you wantin' to trap, but you got to be careful."

"You do all right, did you, Dick?" asked Lem.

"Not at first. We had some fights with Hudson Bay trappers and with Missouri Fur time and again. Arikaras tried to take our mules, traps, guns and hair once't. You learn."

"But you make good money?"

"You work hard for it," said Hauser.

Willa brought the ale and drinks. Men kept coming into the eatery, buying drinks at the bar. The conversations, in French, English, Spanish and Portuguese, sometimes in German, rose to a noisy pitch.

"War's broke out," said Willa.

"Huh?" asked Hauser.

"They're talking about it. Andy Jackson's gone to New Orleans to fight the British."

"Don't say," said Hauser. Willa shrugged, glanced at Morgan and smiled.

"I'll fetch your vittles," she said to Lemuel, who had that look in his eyes that Morgan dreaded. "A lot of men are goin' to fight in the war," she added, before she left the table.

"Well, I ain't a-goin'," said Hauser. "I've had my fill of the States."

"Fuck the British," said Doc, swilling down a mouthful of whiskey.

Lem didn't say anything and Morgan wondered what his father was thinking. Morgan didn't know what war was, but there had been talk of it back in Nashville and in Natchez. Some said the Mississippi was going to be a mighty busy river.

Willa brought the food and when she served Morgan, she leaned over him so that her breasts rubbed against his back. Lem didn't notice it, but Doc did and he winked at Morgan. Morgan's face felt hot and he knew it was red. He felt the burn of her breasts long after she had gone. He ate in a daze, trying not to think of Willa's breasts, listening to his pa and Hauser talk about trapping in the mountains.

"You got money, Lemuel?"

"Some."

"Might be you could buy some traps cheap from Eshelman. Whatever you buy here in St. Louis is a heap cheaper than what you'd buy up in the mountains."

"I don't know much about trappin'," said Lem, wolfing his food.

"Ain't many gonna tell you much, neither," said Dick. "I learnt from the Injun, some Ojibway I met up north after I got away from Chief Yellow Roach's Tuscarory band of cutthroats. Learnt more when I got to the Rocky Mounts. Beaver's dumb, but they got good noses and you got to fool 'em."

"How do you get to the mountains?" asked Morgan.

"Wal, now," said Hauser, "you can walk, ride or go up the Missouri in a bullboat or such. Easiest way is by water, but you got to lay down more coin on the barrelhead. They's a way through Taos, but you got to watch out for Mexican so'jers and bandits. Lots of Injuns and thieves 'twixt here and yonder, but it's short and straight."

"Anyplace I can get maps?" asked Lem.

"You can get 'em, but don't trust 'em much. I got lost first time I used one I got here in St. Louis. Damned near got kilt."

Hauser ordered more drinks from Willa. Lemuel cleaned up his plate, belched loudly. Morgan still toyed with his food and when Willa brought the drinks she brushed up against him again and he felt his blood heat up and boil up to his neck and face.

"There are some dangerous rivers to cross," said Doc. "It's a long hard way and the Indians might not want you riding through their lands."

"You'd best carry least two rifles apiece," interjected Hauser, "and keep a brace of pistols loaded and primed. Carry a big knife and take lots of powder and ball. You'll need pack horses or mules for your traps and such."

"How long a trip?" asked Lem.

"Ridin'? Two months, maybe three. When you get to the high country it'll take you two, three days to get your breath. Ain't no air up there some places."

Morgan's eyes brightened.

"Me'n Doc here, we take the river. Stay to the forts and stay alive, I say."

"Crowded up where you go?" asked Lem.

"Gittin' thataway," said Hauser. "But them mountains is plumb big and wide. We was workin' up on the Yallerstone and back up in the Absorkas. Run into a brigade now and again. Some places they's trappers run in packs."

"Like wolves," said Doc, his eyes blearing. He took out a twisted cigar, bit off the pointed end and stuck it into his mouth. He reached behind him to another table and grabbed a candle. He touched the gnarled end of the cigar to the candle and his cheeks sank to hollows as he drew air through the tobacco. He put the candle back and sucked the cigar until the end glowed orange.

"Like goddamned wolves."

"You haven't said nothing about your friend Ormly," said Lem, after a silence.

"Ain't seen hide nor hair of him." Dick took a swallow of whiskey, beckoned to Willa, who was across the room. "He had him a little red maid he was sweet on. When we got to the point where we knew we could excape, he said he wanted to bring Little Thrush along. I told him we'd never make it. I had been savin' up powder and ball for when we could run off. Injuns sent me out to hunt, give me one ball. I'd take it out, cut it in half, hide the other half. They never caught on to it. When they gave me powder, they poured it in my hand. I always tucked back a mite and never did use no full load. Ormly did the same, I reckon. They kept us apart, but we got so we could use numbers and some sign to tell each other what was what."

"How'd you get away?" asked Morgan.

"One day Yellow Roach said we had to move. They was Rangers in the woods or somep'n. I gave Orm the high sign and he nodded. We knew what direction them woods-beaters were a-comin' from, so when the tribe started to move, I run toward 'em. Ormly and I split up when some of the braves started to chase us. I had one on my tail, waited until he come up on me and I let him have half a ball in his heart."

"You shot that good?" asked Lem.

"Surprised me, too. That half ball went straight."

"And what about the other feller, Ormly?" asked Morgan.

"I heard some shots, but I didn't stay with that dead buck to find out what was what. I just kept a-runnin'."

"Did you run into the Rangers?" asked Morgan.

"Never saw 'em. I made my way up the Ohio and just kept a-movin' north and west. I worked some settlements, got me a poke and went to trappin' up in the north country. I run into a bunch of Americans in a town called Vincennes on the Wabash. A woman there told me about a trapper name of Lisa what had gone to someplace called Mound City in Missouri Territory. That's right here. I come out in aught-three. Then Lewis and Clark come through and come back and I listened to all the tales. Heard about the mountains and rode with some fellers in a keelboat up the Missouri. That was in aught-seven, I reckon. Not many trappers then. I went up there with Manuel Lisa, John Colter and George Drouillard. We didn't get up until late and they started to build Fort Raymond up where the Yallerstone and the Big Horn rivers joined up. Lisa went into Crow country and Colter went somewheres, up in the Wind River country, I reckon, and I come on back. It was too late to trap."

"Then what?" asked Morgan eagerly.

"I got them mountains in my blood. I come back the next summer and roamed around. They was startin' to build tradin' posts along the Missouri. Lisa had been tradin' with the Crow and such. I run into some other lookers and we trapped that winter and I made a few dollars. I stayed away from Drouillard and them. I heard he was a killer and maybe Lisa, too. Them companies. You got to do what they say or . . ."

Morgan sighed.

Willa brought more whiskey and Lem joined in the drinking. Hauser talked of the mountains and Morgan hung on every word like a moth at a lamp chimney.

Doc seemed not to get any drunker. He drank more, but he kept his wits about him. He smoked his cigar down to ash and made dry comments from time to time. Men came and went, talking of the war. Willa rubbed against Morgan every chance she got and their eyes met more than once during the conversation at the table.

Morgan got up to relieve himself. He walked out the front door onto the street, looked for a dark place. He peed against one of the buildings and as he was walking back, Willa met him.

"Uh, hello," said Morgan.

"I come out to talk to you," she said. Her face was in shadow, but the light from the lamps in Spanish Jack's made her hair glow.

"I got to get on back."

"I like you," she said. "I've got a room upstairs. Would you like to come up? I get off in a few minutes."

"I don't know," he said.

"Please. There's some stairs out back." She moved close to him and he stood there, wondering what to do. She touched his hand, ran her own up his arm. She kissed him and it was not like kissing the girl on the boat. Willa sent sparks through him, made his lips warm. He felt a stirring in his loins, an embarrassment because she was so close. "Ummm," she moaned and put her arms around him. She kissed him harder and he put his arms around her. He closed his eyes and the heat from her body warmed him, warmed him all over and she was soft, so soft, she made him giddy.

Morgan strangled on words of protest, choked them down because he did not want to say them.

She took his hand and led him to the back of Spanish Jack's. She pointed to the dark stairs.

"First door on the left," she whispered. "Go on up. I'll meet you there in ten minutes."

"God, I don't know."

"Yes, yes," she said, and he knew he would go up the stairs. She touched the part of him that was hard and he knew he would go up there and wait for her.

She left him there, scurried around the building. Morgan took a deep breath and started for the stairs. His feet were leaden and he cringed when the board on the first step creaked.

He walked up the stairs, counting the seconds in his mind, wondering why time went so slowly now.

20

Morgan opened the door to Willa's room. Stepping inside, he closed the door quietly. He groped in the dark until he found a chair. He didn't dare light the lamp, didn't know where it was. The chair creaked when he moved and he was sure that people downstairs could hear him. Gradually, the dim light of stars seeped through the window, gave fuzzy shape to the objects in the room. Pale outlines of a bed, a table, a dresser, began to appear. Morgan sat on the chair, listening to the ripple and thrum of voices filtering from below up through the flooring. He heard the clink and tinkle of glasses and plates, the ebb and flow of laughter washing through the walls, rising and falling like waves on a sea of air.

Morgan stopped counting the seconds and waited for the slow minutes to pass. Every time he heard a sound, his heart jumped and a throb of fear pulsed at his throat. Finally, he heard a footfall and his blood seemed to freeze in his veins. He saw a light flicker under the door. The door opened and Willa entered, carrying a candle on a pewter saucer. She moved toward him, in shadow, and the light splashed her pretty face, made her eyes glitter like obsidian beads. She slid the chimney up on a lamp, turned the wick up. She touched the candle flame to the wick and the oil burst into flame. She adjusted the intensity of the blaze and blew out the candle. A thin tendril of smoke lingered in the still air of the room. Willa walked back to the door and slipped the bolt through its slot.

"Hello, again," she said, a thrill to her voice, a lilt that made his heart jump.

"Hello," he said, a thick husk in his voice.

Willa took off her black apron, tossed it across the room, toward the bed. She fluffed her hair and moved toward Morgan. He rose from his chair and took her into his arms. She embraced him eagerly and he felt the softness of her hair brush his chin.

"Mmmm," she breathed. "You don't know."

"Huh?"

"The kind of men who come here. They paw me and try to lift my dress. They're crude and smelly and mean."

Morgan said nothing. She looked up at him, small and comfortable in his arms. He pressed close and his manhood stirred, began to swell.

"I-I ain't n-n-never done nothin' before," he stammered.

"You'll learn," she whispered, and pulled his head down toward hers. She kissed him and her tongue streaked across his lips. He felt a stab in his genitals and the lump hardened, strained against the crotch of his pants.

She rubbed his back with eager hands, stroked him as she moved her lips against his. He wanted her then, wanted to plunge into the heat that he knew was there, wanted to bury himself in the heat, inside her and he lost all reason in that moment when tumescence peaked in his manhood. The heat blinded him and made his brain swell and the other swelling made him want her bad.

"Oh God," he breathed when she broke the kiss and he felt her hot breath against his face.

"Yes," she said. "I feel you. Do you want me?"

"Yes."

"The bed," she told him. "Let's lie down and take our clothes off."

He followed her dumbly across the room. She slipped out of her dress so fast he wondered how she had done it. Her breasts were beautiful in the lampglow and she stooped slightly to take off her panties and then he saw her, saw the dark thatch between her legs and the nipples on her breasts. He saw all of it and felt the wonder of her womanhood, the mystery of her sweeping through him like a storm. There was a pride in him that she let him see her and it was like being in a dream or in a trance because he had never seen a naked woman before and he was so close to her he felt faint.

"Hurry," she said, and he fumbled with the buttons on his shirt and his fingers lost their deftness so that she had to help him. She peeled his shirt off and her hands dove to his pants and she slid his trousers down and he blushed because he stuck out and she could see the hard bone of him jutting out and leaking the clear fluid of desire.

She pulled him onto the bed and slid beneath him. He looked down at her and swallowed. Her hips were dotted with small bruises the size of thumbprints. Her breasts, too, were blotched with yellow-purple blemishes. His breath came in short gasps as he touched a breast, roamed his hand over it, touching the nipple and feeling the little brown bumps around the dark aureole.

"Does it hurt?" he asked, an almost reverent tone in his voice.

"No," she said. "It feels good. Kiss me. Touch me between my legs."

He leaned down, kissed her on the mouth. His hand crept to her leg, slid into the wiry thicket of her sex. He felt her body quiver and he probed the soft lips between her legs, felt surprise at the delicate sponginess of that part of her. She pushed upward and moaned.

"Do it to me," she said, moving her head to break the kiss.

"I—I don't know what to do," he said, but he knew; he was just afraid to do it wrong.

She opened herself to him and drew him into her. He shuddered and closed his eyes. It was like being suddenly hooked up to a lightning bolt. Phosphorous explosions lit up his brain. His body coursed with savage pulsations, electric jolts that rendered him mindless. It was all over in a rush, but in that brief moment, universes opened to him, ecstasy suffused his body, a great mystery dazzled and tantalized him. He rode the bright heavens and strode the earth like a god. Just for that one fraction of a second, he knew the awesome power in his loins, felt the magnificence of creation when his seed burst forth in a mighty spume like some divine fountain.

Lem was getting drunk. Not roaring drunk, but drunk enough so that his vision wavered and his tongue thickened. He looked at the cracks in Hauser's hands, around the knuckles, wondered about them.

"Cold water, hot sun, dry thin air," said Dick, holding his hands up as if he was wearing rings. "Got the same thing when I used to milk cows back in Virginny."

"It looks like you've got leprosy," said Doc. His hands were smooth, the flesh around the knuckles tight.

"How come yours ain't that way?" Lem asked Doc.

"He rubs 'em with grease ever' night," said Hauser. "He still thinks he's a surgeon."

"You a real doctor?" asked Lem.

"None of your business," said Doc. Dick gave Lem a look, shook his head slightly.

Lem drank another swallow of whiskey, felt its glow as it went down. He looked around the room.

"Hey, where's Morgan?"

"He went outside," said Dick.

"Oughta be back by now."

"I wouldn't worry none," said Hauser. "He looks like he can take care of himself."

Lem drew a deep breath, drew himself up straight to correct the slump of inebriation.

"Damn kid," he said.

Doc got up from the table, headed for the door. He was surprisingly agile and gracefully dodged a drunk who teetered into his path. He seemed more sober than any man in the room. Lem watched him cross the room and marveled at Doc's ability to hold his drink.

For a moment, Lem forgot about Morgan. He turned to Dick after the door closed behind Doc.

"What's he got in his gullet?" he asked.

"Doc?"

"Yeah, him. Damned sourpuss barber."

"He ain't no barber, like a lot of 'em," said Hauser. "He was a surgeon, a pretty good one I hear tell. He don't do no cuttin' no more, but he carries them sharp tools around with him. I only seen him use 'em once, when he got a Ree arrer stuck in his leg. Took 'em out and cut out the arrerhead 'thout ever blinkin' a eye. Salved it up and bound it. Them Rees was mighty disappointed. So was Doc, I reckon. I guess he blames hisself for when his wife died."

"Huh? How'd she die?"

"Way he told me, she had a busted appendix. He went to cuttin' on her and she up and died. Broke him right in half, he said. He quit surgeryin' and come west to try and drink up all the whiskey he could get his hands on."

"How come him to go a-trappin' with you?"

Hauser fixed Lem with a blistering eye, keen as a Spanish dagger.

"Well, Doc just don't care no more about hisself—I reckon he wants to die, but is too God-fearin' to take his own hand to it. He don't much favor one way over another, neither. Just so's it's hard and real painful like his wife done."

"Jesus," said Lem, momentarily sobered. "No woman's worth that."

"This'n was, 'cording to Doc."

Lem said nothing, but he was thinking about Roberta and the alcohol fueled dead thoughts, made them swirl and boil in his mind like rocks and sticks caught up in a whirl-wind. And then he thought about Doc and the thoughts got all tangled up and driven by the fierce winds of his own personal hatred. Doc's wife had died and even in death she was tormenting the man, wouldn't leave him alone. A woman was trouble, sure enough, and had been since Eve gave Adam the apple in God's own garden.

"What's Doc's real name, anyways?" asked Lem, trying to break out of the foul mood brought on by his dredged-up thoughts of Roberta.

"Henry McIntire," said Hauser, "but you'd best not call him that 'lessen he asks you. He don't want to be nobody."

"Damned women," snorted Lem and he would have gone down into his dark thoughts again, if he had not seen movement out of the corner of his eye.

A man in his late thirties, wearing a grimy apron and carrying a wooden tray came up to Hauser's table.

"You gents need anything here?" he asked.

Hauser nodded. "Three whiskeys," he said.

Lem looked up at the man, brought him into blurry focus.

"Hey, where's 'at gal what was here? Wilma."

"You mean Willa Montez?" asked the waiter.

"Willa, Wilma. Gal 'at was a-servin' us," said Lem.

"She's gone upstairs to her room. She's off at ten of the clock, and it's a good quarter past that." The waiter was very polite, with a northeastern accent. He looked out of place in the room full of rowdy, rough men. His hair was neatly slicked with grease and trimmed, his shirt pressed.

"She live here?"

"She has quarters upstairs, as do I," said the waiter. He glanced at Hauser. "I'll bring your whiskeys promptly, sir."

The waiter left. Dick finished off his cup and banged it on the table.

Lem's brows wrinkled in thought. He swept the room again with a searching glance, contracting his pupils to bring faces into focus. He looked at the door as it opened. Doc was just coming in, listing slightly to one side, but he straightened and wove his way to the back table.

"Ah," Doc said, as he sat down, "a muggy evening, with the scent of raw piss on the air, the stench of rotting fish and yesterday's garbage disgusting as ever. St. Louis is a stink hole. No wonder we go to the mountains and endure hardships beyond human bearance."

"Aw, Doc," said Hauser, "you ought to go east where you belong."

"Never," said Doc, emphatically. "To live back there is to die slowly of indolence and boredom. I much prefer to meet my end in an adventurous way. I'll hie back to the mountains and pray for the swifter death from the Rees' hatchet or the grizzly's violent hug. If we stay here, we'll suffocate in the fecal atmosphere of an open-air latrine."

Lem didn't understand a word Doc had said, but he knew what was bothering him. He lurched to his feet, extended his fingers to the table for support. He swayed there until the room stopped spinning.

"I'm goin' to look for Morgan," he announced, and when Dick put a hand on his arm, Lem tore away from him and staggered toward the bar.

"The man's looking for trouble, I suspect," said Doc.

"He's carryin' him a load," said Hauser.

"I know exactly what you mean," Doc said, and his stare went vacant. He sat there, soundless as stone.

Lem saw the stairs, aimed himself toward them. He took the first step, faltered as a strong hand squeezed his arm.

"That's as far as you go, pilgrim," said a faintly accented voice. "There is nothing up there for you. Piss outside like everyone else."

Lem turned around, looked at the man who had stopped him.

"I aim to find that gal Wilma," Lem told the man.

"She's occupied."

"Occupied?" Lem asked drunkenly. "Occupied? What the hell's that mean?"

"That, *señor*, is none of your business."

"And, who in hell are you to tell me my business?"

"I'm Jack Montez and Willa is my daughter."

"Well, she'd better not have my son up in her room with her," said Lem and pushed Jack backward with a flathand slam to the man's chest. With that, Lem took four steps in a single bound and disappeared at the top of the stairs before Spanish Jack could stop him.

Lem tried each of the four doors. All were locked. The last one had a glow of light seeping from under the door. He pushed and banged on it. The door wouldn't give. Spanish Jack appeared at the top of the stairs, started toward him. He carried a bung starter in one hand.

Lem banged on the door again. He heard the soft pad of footsteps. The door opened. Willa stood there with a nightgown held against her naked body. Lem saw Morgan on the bed, pulling at a pillow to hide himself.

Jack Montez raised the bung starter overhead and charged Lem. Lem ducked low and sailed his right fist into Jack's gut. Spanish Jack doubled over and gasped for breath. He waddled backward on the heels of his boots as Lem swept Willa aside and entered the room.

"Pa!"

"What the hell are you doin' with this woman?" asked Lem.

"Pa, don't start no trouble now."

Willa went to her father, put her arms around him.

"Papa," she said, "let me talk to the man."

"Aquel hijo de mala leche," swore her father in Spanish. She pushed him back, pleading with her eyes. Then she reentered the room.

Lem turned to her.

"You slut!" he spat. "What did you do, you harlot?"

"Please," said Willa. "We don't want any trouble, sir."

"I'll give you trouble, you fornicating bitch."

Morgan watched in horror as his father lunged at Willa. She staggered backward to avoid his rush. Spanish Jack came into the room, still carrying the bung starter, as his daughter spun away. Willa screamed as she crashed into the bureau. Lem followed after her, yelling at the top of his voice. Morgan dashed up just as Spanish Jack brought the bung starter down hard on Lem's head.

As Spanish Jack's momentum spun him around, Lem accidentally struck Willa in the mouth. Blood spurted from her lips. She screamed again and Lem turned to fight off Spanish Jack. Morgan leaped into the fray, naked as a frog, trying desperately to reach his father, pull him away from the fight. Jack tried to hit Lem with the bung starter again, but he was too close. Lem cracked the Spaniard on the jaw with a crossing left. Spanish Jack's knees buckled. Morgan grabbed his father. Lem stiffened his son with a straight right to the temple. Morgan collapsed, his eyes rolling backward in their sockets.

Willa screamed and started flailing Lem's back with her fists. Lem turned on her and pushed her away. She smashed his nose with a roundhouse swing. Blood gushed from both of his nostrils, ran down his cheeks like the juice of a crushed tomato. Jack tackled Lem and wrestled him to the floor. Morgan struggled to regain his senses. He sat up groggily and watched his father lay into Jack with both fists pumping. Jack went down, blood seeping from a half dozen cracks on his face. The lamplight flickered on his battered features, gave his visage a grotesque cast.

Lem was still beating Jack when Doc and Dick Hauser stormed into the room, dragged him off the unconscious man. Willa whimpered and fell down beside Morgan. Morgan put his arm around her, fought away the fog in his brain.

"Enough, Hawke," said Dick. "You already done enough."
He steadied Lem with an armlock around Hawke's neck.

"That two-bit slattern," growled Lem. "She done guiled my boy."

Morgan looked at his father in bewilderment. Hauser forced Lem to his knees. Lem lashed out ineffectually. Doc stood in front of Lem, fists balled, ready to put Hawke down by force, if necessary. Spanish Jack groaned, but he was still out.

"Pa," Morgan said, "you . . . you hadn't ought to have come up here. Now look what you done."

"What did you and her do?" Lem croaked.

"It don't make no difference," said Hauser. "What was done was between him and the girl. Now, steady down or I'll have to choke you, drag you out of here like dead meat."

Morgan, keeping a wary eye on his father, got up and slipped back into his clothes. Willa, still sobbing, wiped her face and breasts with a towel she retrieved from a nail by the bureau, put her dress back on. A couple of curious men looked into the room, then left hurriedly.

"Let me up," said Lem.

"You aim to leave this be?" asked Dick.

"No more trouble," said Lem.

Hauser and Doc exchanged looks. Doc nodded. Dick released his grip on Lemuel's neck. Doc knelt down next to Spanish Jack, felt for the pulse at his throat. He began to gently slap Jack's face.

Lem kept looking at Willa. Morgan saw the look, shuddered inwardly. There was hatred in his pa's eyes, an intensity he'd never seen before. Something cold balled up in Morgan's stomach and made him sick. He looked at Willa. There were streaks of tears she had missed with the towel.

Morgan's muscles were stretched taut with tension. The adrenaline still raced in his blood. Confused feelings stormed his thoughts. He had never seen such a rage in his father, such a killing rage. Willa stood there, trembling, in a paralyzed state of shock. She looked at Doc, who was trying to bring her father back to consciousness. She looked at him with a doll's dead eyes and she shook ever so slightly that Morgan wondered if she was not on the verge of going into a fit. It scared him and he wished he could do something to comfort her. But he would not touch her again while his father was in the room.

"He goin' to be all right?" asked Dick, looking down at Spanish Jack.

"Might need some salts to bring him around," said McIntire. "Concussion, maybe."

Lem said nothing. He kept staring at Willa.

"You got any smellin' salts, Doc?" asked Dick.

"No. You'd have to find an apothecary."

"Hell, don't know if there is one in St. Louis."

"Probably not," said Doc. He peeled back one of Jack's eyelids, bent over to look at the pupil more closely.

Willa broke her gaze, looked at Morgan. He caught the movement, met her glance.

Lem saw it and something broke in him again. He saw the look and he thought of Roberta and Willa became his wife, turned into her in the soft light of the flickering lamp, turned into the girl he had married, the woman who had deserted him. He roared, uttered terrible sounds that sprang up from his throat and shattered the stillness of the room.

All of the pent-up anger of the months and years rose up in Lemuel Hawke and he bunched his muscles, gritted his teeth and charged Willa, snarling like some wild beast.

Hauser reached out to grab Lemuel, but his grasp fell short. Willa screamed and dashed toward Morgan. Morgan pushed her aside and braced himself for his father's charge. Lem crashed into his son and the two fell toward the lamp on the small table near the bed. The lamp went flying, smashed against the wall. Particles of fiery oil sprayed in all directions. The glass chimney shattered. Fresh oil splat-

tered on the bed, the floor and the wall. Little patches of
fire turned into tongues that raced along the splatter-path.
In an instant, the wall and the bed erupted in flames. The
dry wood floor exploded in a wall of flame.

Doc tried to lift Spanish Jack up, but the man's dead weight
was too much for him. Lem grabbed Morgan and hauled
him away from the burning bed. Willa crawled toward the
door. Hauser's shirt caught on fire and he began beating
his sleeve with the palm of his hand.

"Get out!" yelled Lem, dragging Morgan toward the door.

Willa ran to her father, grabbed his feet. Hauser put out
the flame on his sleeve and went to help Doc and Willa.
The flames surged upward, devoured the wallpaper. The
small table burst into flames. Wood crackled and popped
as the hungry fire lapped new fuel. The room became an
inferno. Smoke billowed from every corner and seared the
lungs of everyone in it.

Lem and Morgan shoved Doc and Hauser toward the
door. Morgan broke away from his father and he snaked
an arm around Willa's waist. Doc and Hauser staggered
from the room, choking and gasping on the smoke.

Lem turned and pulled at Morgan's shirt, hurling him
toward the open door. He stepped aside and shoved Willa
and his son outside.

Doc yelled. "Fire!"

He and Hauser staggered down the stairs. No one in
Spanish Jack's moved.

"Fire!" Hauser choked, and the people in the eatery
saw the smoke clinging to the hall ceiling, wisps curling
around the corners. The room boiled with men jumping
up from tables, scrambling for the front door. The bar-
tender and waiter both yelled and ran into the melee. Men
packed together, fought to get out as the fire burst from the
room and filled the hall with smoke and flames.

"Papa!" screamed Willa and Morgan had to shove her
down the stairs.

Flames licked at Lem's back. His shirt caught fire and he grimaced in agony. He shoved Morgan and Willa ahead of him down the stairs.

"There a back door?" he yelled above the din. His skin had turned black from the flames.

Willa nodded.

At the bottom of the stairs, she turned to the right and Morgan followed her.

The men in the restaurant milled and shoved. Their weight pushed part of the wall surrounding the door away and they streamed out into the night.

Willa opened the back door. She and Morgan fled outside, followed by Lem. He dashed past them and threw himself on the ground. He rolled to put out the flames. Behind them, the fire raged.

"Oh, Papa," Willa wailed.

Lem put the fire out and stood up, smeared with dirt. The back of his shirt was burned away and blisters started to form on his flesh.

"I'm sorry," Lem said.

"My papa's in there," said Willa. "Can't you do something?"

Morgan started to go back in, but Lem grabbed his arm, restrained him gently.

In seconds, the entire building was engulfed in flames. The three of them backed away from the heat, powerless to do anything. They heard shouting from out front.

"Get buckets!"

"Form a brigade!"

With a deep sense of shock, Lem realized that the other buildings could catch. But he stood there, rooted to the earth, watching Spanish Jack's burn. The fire roared and sent tongues of flame up into the blackness of night. It rouged their faces and illuminated the stark horror in their eyes.

Willa collapsed in a swoon and Lem stooped to grab her, break her fall.

Morgan knocked his father's arms aside.

"Don't you touch her," Morgan said. "Don't you ever touch her again."

Lem winced as he saw the look in his son's eyes.

It was a look he would never forget.

21

Lem sat on the edge of the bed, slumped forward, his head in his hands. He was covered with soot, his face smeared with dirt and ash, his clothes laden with grime. He could not get the smell of smoke out of his nostrils, the sickly sweet stench of burning flesh. He and the others had worked for hours to put out the blaze, keep it from spreading to the other buildings next to Spanish Jack's. In the excitement, no one noticed when he had finally slipped away and come back to the room. He had not seen Morgan or Willa after leaving them in the alley, but Morgan's things were gone from the room. His possibles pouch, his rifle, his bedroll, the medicine horn—all gone. Lem felt as if something had been wrenched out of him, some part of him stolen and lost so that he could never get it back.

So, the boy had come back, and he had gone off somewhere with that girl. She had started it all, damn her. If it wasn't for her, none of this would have happened. Now, he had to live with it, by God, but he was right about her. About all women. They were the source of man's troubles, had been since the beginning of time. The Bible even said so.

He was sorry about Spanish Jack. He hadn't meant to hit him that hard. The damned fool. Him and his daughter, two of a kind. She hadn't ought to have jezebelled Morgan that way, the little trollop.

Lem straightened up, lay back on the bed, too tired to wash up. He lay there, his mind squirming with thought, wondering what to do. The knock on the door jarred him out of his tormented reverie. He leaped from the bed, opened the door.

"Morgan. . . ."

It was Dick Hauser, and he looked like an apparition from hell. His face was black with soot and his eyes red-rimmed. His hands looked like lumps of coal.

"Gotta talk to you, Hawke."

"I thought you was Morgan," Lem said lamely. "He's done picked up and gone."

"That's what I come to talk to you about. You got any squeezin's?"

Lem shook his head. He closed the door, waved Hauser to a chair. The last thing he wanted was whiskey. His mouth tasted of rust and rain water; his stomach was knotted and raw. A distant throbbing in his skull reminded him of the whiskeys he had had earlier.

"No matter. Look, Lemuel, you done me a favor once't and I figger I owe you. I ain't got much but advice to give you, but it's good advice."

"What's on your mind, Dick?"

"Well, they ain't much law in St. Louie, none at all, I reckon. But Spanish Jack had him friends and they're talkin' about puttin' a ball in you or makin' you a rope collar. Was I you, I'd make tracks for somewheres right quick. Bunch of 'em is drinkin' at the King's Boar right now and decidin' how to make you join Spanish Jack in the local cemetery. Word ain't got to the town yet, but it'll spread by mornin'. Best leave the country, go somewheres until this blows over."

"Where's my son, Dick?"

"Him and Willa is safe. Nobody blames them for what happened. But Morgan don't want you to go lookin' for him. The gal's pretty broken up. All she had was her pa. Her ma died five year ago and she ain't hardly over it yet. She didn't have much of a life, but she put a fair amount of stock in her pap."

"Christ, I'm sorry Dick. I just—"

"Hell, I know you didn't mean nothin', Lemuel. But, folks is folks, and they's some as got blood in their eyes. You'd best pack out of St. Louie right quick."

"Where would I go without Morgan?"

"Likely he'll get over his mad someday."

Lem tried to hold it back, tried to stay the ache in him that made his eyes crinkle up and start to leak tears. He couldn't help it, though. He thought of Morgan, that last terrible look he had seen in his son's eyes, and he broke down. He rolled over onto his belly, put his head in his hands. His body shook with sobs, his throat boomed with the wrenching sounds of his weeping.

Dick rose from the chair and left the room quietly. He did not say good-by.

Lem didn't hear him go.

Emile DeBalaviere shook his head.

"The boy, he take his horse last night. He did not say where he was going, *non*. But, he had no girl wit' him. He was alone, eh?"

Lem sighed, finished tightening Hammerhead's cinch.

"I'll need me a mule or two," he told the Frenchman. "Some advice about trappin' the mountains."

"Ah," said Emile, eager to provide information. "I have the best mule, eh? The Mexican, he make the best."

"How much?" asked Lem.

Emile squinted at an imaginary ledger in the palm of his hand. He scratched a spot just behind his right ear.

"One mule or two?"

"Two, I reckon. I got to carry traps, grub and such."

"*Oui,* two of the mule. You have the coin?"

Lem nodded.

"Silver?"

"I got silver."

"I will sell you the mule for thirty Mexican pesos apiece, and you can buy traps and trade goods from Eshelman."

"Trade goods?"

"If you want to buy the bevair from the savage, you must trade him the pretty things, *non?* You buy the ribbon, the little mirror, the beads and the cloth. You must take the whiskey and the axe, the skinning knife, eh? Eshelman, he tell you what to take, I think."

"Look, Emile, if I give you some money, will you give it to my son? To Morgan?"

Emile scratched his head again. It seemed a ponderous question to him.

"I don't know if I see him, eh? He don't tell Emile where he go."

Lem was almost certain Emile was lying.

"But you might see him?"

"Eh? Maybe."

Lem counted out the silver. He did not have enough pesos, but he had shillings and Spanish silver.

"This is for the mules," he said.

"You will have to buy the pannier to pack the goods, *non?* Eshelman have the good ones, I think."

"This is for Morgan," said Lem. "You tell him I'm a-goin' up to them Rocky Mountains."

Emile's eyes widened at all the coins.

"I will do this," said the stableman. "Ah, if I see the boy, that is. Now, we get the mules, eh?"

Lem led the two jacks up to Eshelman's on Fourth and Market as the sun was just clearing the levee. There were a few people about, but they paid him no attention. Dogs searched the edges of buildings for scraps, roaming in and out of the shadows of morning like skulking robbers. He hitched the mules and Hammerhead to the rail out front of Eshelman's. He knew the store. This was where he had changed his money.

Eshelman and two clerks were stacking blankets as Lem entered. Another clerk was rolling a barrel out of the back storeroom.

Lorenzo Eshelman nodded to Lem.

"I will be with you soon," said the storekeeper, a German with only a faint trace of a Pennsylvania accent.

Lem started toward the back of the store.

Two trappers stood at the counter looking at jars full of trade beads. They were attired for the trail, possibles pouches slung over their shoulders, knives on their belts, pistols jutting from their sashes. They wore light clothing, tattered and patched, boot moccasins. Both were young and bearded. Lem had not seen them before, but he walked toward them now. Eshelman continued to separate and stack blankets on a square boxlike table along one of the aisles. The store was lined with shelves, crates and tables stood in rows facing each other. One small section of wall served as a display for traps, knives, hatchets, tomahawks, lanterns and other hardware. Behind the counter, prominently displayed, a sign painted on a flat section of two-by-twelve proclaimed NO CREDIT.

The clerk who had rolled the barrel in finished positioning it next to the saws and double-bit axes in a corner and walked behind the counter as Lem came up alongside the two trappers.

"Mornin' gents," said the clerk, young, dough-faced, with jutting ears and pomaded hair that glistened like sweat on a black horse. "See somethin' you need?"

"Need a dozen six-inch candles and two dozen of flints," said one.

"Gimme a gross of them blue, red and yaller beads," said

the other man, "and ten pound of middle fine powder, a chunk of lead, say ten, twelve pound, three dozen assortments of them buttons."

"Surely," said the clerk.

Lem cleared his throat.

"You goin' to the mountains?" asked Lem.

"No, we're goin' to a Sunday picnic," said the candle-and-flint man. He was chunky, with a moon face lumped with fat, a little cherubic mouth and tiny blue eyes swallowed up by puffy cheekbones. He looked as wide as he was tall and his legs were as bowed as barrel slats.

"None of my business," said Lem, "but I'm headin' there myself and need to know a good way to get there."

"You ridin' or floatin'?" asked the bead man. There was something familiar about him. Lem knew he had seen the man before. He was only slightly less chunky than the other trapper, but taller, with apple-round cheekbones, crafty hazel eyes, sandy hair still tangled from sleep. His clothes had more patches on them than a quilt. His hands had scars like those he'd seen on Hauser's.

"Ridin'. I got me two mules and a horse."

"They's a whole lot of mountains," said the first man, "and a whole lot of ways to get to 'em. Fust time me'n my brother Leo come here in aught-seven, we follered the Missouri clear up to the Yallerstone. Next year, we follered the Osage to ther South Platte and follered it on into the mountains. Last year, Leo and I trapped south of here on the White and my brother drownded in a flood. You ain't agoin' to get lost if'n you foller the Injun trails, head toward the sunset and stay close to the big rivers."

"But not close enough you get in any one's way," said the other trapper, the one who looked familiar. Lem was trying to place him.

"What?" asked Lem.

"He means huntin' Injuns," said the first man. "Say, what's your name, pilgrim?"

"Lemuel Hawke."

"I'm Bill Letterman and this year's Nat Sullard. He don't say much 'ceptin' when he's drunk."

"He don't look the same sober, neither," said Lem, grinning at Nat Sullard.

"Do I know you?" asked Sullard.

"You offered me a drink at the Red Lion in Nashville," replied Lem. "You said you was with a man name of Charlie Pack."

Sullard squinched up his eyes and regarded Hawke with a scathing look of interest. Recognition flickered in his eyes.

"You 'n the boy," said Nat. "Farmers. Hoo boy, you got a good mem'ry. Me'n Charlie was out to drink up all the whiskey in that tipplin' house."

"Wasn't you the ones got into a fight with Big John O'Neil?" asked Letterman.

Lem winced inwardly. He cocked his head in assent.

"Nat tolt me about it," said Letterman. "I was there. Finally got him an' Jocko and Charlie convinced to come out here and trap the Rockies with me. The Major is takin' a brigade up in a day er two for Missouri Fur."

"MacDougal?" asked Lem.

"You know him?" asked Nat.

"No. We met up with Jocko DeSam and he said I ought to meet MacDougal."

"Meanest bastard you ever saw," said Bill. "But he knows them mountains. Chouteau puts a lot of stock in the Major."

"You might be able to get on," said Nat.

"No, I reckon I got to go my own way," said Lem.

Evidently the two trappers hadn't heard about the fire the night before, the death of Spanish Jack. It was just as well. He didn't know how he could explain such a thing. It was still unreal to him, like a bad dream.

"Free trapper, eh?" said Bill. "Mighty hard. You can't get credit and you got Britishers and British-bribed Injuns after your scalp. Mighty hard."

"I got to try," said Hawke lamely.

The clerk finished packing up the goods the two trappers had ordered.

"Anything else?" he asked.

"That'll do 'er," said Letterman. He turned from the counter, called to Eshelman. "Lon, what're you gettin' for your traps now?"

"Four dollar," said Eshelman without batting an eye.

"Whooee," said Letterman. He turned to Hawke. "They was a dollar seventy when I first come out here and that was in the Injun territory. Last time, it was three dollars American. Be five or better at the forts."

Lem's heart sank.

"How many traps you figger a man needs?" he asked Letterman.

"You can run a line with half a dozen, but you better square that, just in case."

"Two dozen would be better, still," interjected the clerk.

Eshelman walked over. He was a burly, drum-chested man, with a thick black moustache, black hair and neatly trimmed sideburns. He had a wide forehead, a sturdy, though crooked, nose and deep-set brown eyes, fleshy lips. He looked darkly Teutonic with his square, determined jaw and muscular build.

"You get a price on four dozen," said Eshelman. "Three eighty-five the trap."

"Well, Lon's going to sell you the store, Hawke," said Letterman. "We'll be goin'. Pay the man, Nat."

Nat plunked down coin.

"Before you go," said Lem to Bill Letterman, "would you know a man by name of Silas Morgan?"

"I knowed him," said Bill.

"Is he dead?"

"No, I reckon not. Seed him over the winter, up on the Yallerstone."

"Would he be in St. Louis?"

Letterman laughed.

"Nope," he said. "Old Silas, he got him a Crow squaw. He's been livin' with 'em. Part Crow hisself by now."

Lem was crestfallen. Silas living with an Injun woman? It didn't seem possible. Silas was—was, well, he was a dyed-in-the-wool bachelor, he was. Always had been.

"Are you certain sure?" he asked Bill.

"Sure as I'm a-standin' here, Hawke. Silas got him a squaw purty as any I ever seed. They call her Blue Shell."

Bill laughed again, slapped Hawke on the back and the two trappers left the store. Lem felt more alone than he had since he'd left the room at Lescoulie's hotel. He hadn't a friend in the world and no son anymore. It was enough to break a man's heart and mash it into pulp.

Lorenzo Eshelman took charge of Lem, showing him the various breeds of traps, axes, beads, cloth, blankets, knives and "necessaries." Lem bought two sturdy panniers and some rope.

"I'll need a good pistol," said Lem. "Cheapest you got."

"I got 'em from two dollar on up, Spanish breed, or Portagee, English or Pennsylvania-made."

"I'll look at the Pennsylvanias," Lem told him.

He ended up looking at all of them. He wanted one that had a sturdy lock, would not fail him when he needed it. The Spanish locks were big, brutish, and the English locks not much better. He finally settled on a Pennsylvania-made road pistol in .58 caliber. Eshelman said his brother, living in Lancaster County, had made it. The lock was tight, the workmanship better than any of the others he had looked at. It had a heft to it and a good feel to the walnut grip. The stock was all of a piece, the inletting precise and smooth.

"You made a wise choice," said Eshelman. "Those pistols do not stay long in stock."

The merchant sold Hawke a hide-vial of castoreum for two bits and by the time Lem left the store, he was down to a few dollars American with which to buy food staples. But he left with something even more valuable than money. Lon Eshelman had copied for him a crude map showing the trails, the rivers, the major fords, the forts. The fords would change, Eshelman told him, as rivers always changed.

"Likely you'll run into trouble on the upper Missouri," Eshelman told him. "Manuel Lisa left early this spring, prepared to do battle with the British agents who are stirring up the Indians. You look out for the Blackfeet and the Gros Ventres."

"Are them tribes of Injuns?" asked Lem.

"Devils," said Eshelman, and Lem had left with his thoughts, his doubts, his considerable worries about Morgan. It crushed him to leave like this, an outcast, a murderer.

At LaValle's River Market, Lem bought flour, beans, coffee, buffalo jerky in thick, lumpy strips, half a smoke-cured ham, sugar, and salt.

Marcel LaValle and his wife, Denise, chattered like French magpies as they filled his order. In English, they mentioned the terrible fire and asked him if he was heading west. Denise said that he was so young and it was so dangerous in the mountains. Marcel asked Lem if he was with one of the fur companies. He was a sprightly man, thin as a beanpole, with dark Gallic features, a pince-nez perched on his aquiline nose, ears that jutted from his head like jug handles.

"Nope," said Lem. "I'm goin' alone."

"Which way you go?"

Lem had already decided to go to St. Charles and follow the Osage River to the Platte.

He told LaValle.

"Ah, that is a very dangerous way," said Denise in her precise English, the vowels soft and drawn out. "And you go alone. Tss, tss."

"Well, I think some go alone and do not come back," said Marcel, "but some go with other men and some of these do not come back, either. So, you go with God, young man, and I hope you can shoot straight."

"You tell us your name and we will wait for word of you," said Denise.

Hawke told them his name, feeling very itchy about it. They both smiled as they talked and the talk was light, but their words gave him an uneasy feeling, nonetheless.

After fiddling with his packs longer than necessary, graining the mules and Hammerhead until they could hardly walk, Lem set out from St. Louis with a heavy heart. He looked long and hard at the map again and decided against traveling up the Missouri. It was a longer way and the Platte, either South or North, looked like an arrow pointing to the mountains. He headed north to St. Charles where he knew he could pick up the Osage River, heading southwest.

He kept wanting to turn back and look for Morgan, but he knew his son was filled with hatred for him. Maybe it was best this way, he thought. Morgan could find his own way. He was almost a man, sure enough.

A bittern, startled by the horse and mules, jumped up from the shore of the Mississippi river, flapping ungainly to gain altitude. It flew downstream, screaming in protest, crying out so forlorn Lem felt as if the bird was talking to him, expressing what Lem felt inside. The echoes of the bird's scream lingered in Lem's mind and the silence only deepened the numbness of his grief, a grief so complicated and deep he couldn't explain it to himself.

Lem's heart was stone heavy and hurting as he followed the river, the well-rode prairie trail north to St. Charlies. Beyond, to the west, lay an unknown land, the future. He kept looking back, every so often, but there was nobody there and the emptiness inside him kept widening like the blue sky, the endless sea of grass that stretched to the west, to the distant horizon.

22

Morgan sat in the chair that leaned against the wall. He ran his fingers over the medicine horn, just the touching of it was a comfort to him. The feel of the hard polished surface somehow soothed him. He looked at Willa lying there on the bed in the small, bare room in Emile DeBalaviere's house. There was no table, only a single chair, a long box made into a chest of drawers, a small stool fashioned from a nail keg. Emile was at the stables, but he had come up to the room that morning, given him the money his pa had left for him. At first he had wanted to refuse it, but he didn't have a shilling or a note to his name. Willa hadn't even awakened when Emile had come. She had not awakened since she fell to the bed, exhausted, and cried herself to sleep.

And Morgan was too keyed up to sleep. His thoughts raced and darted like tadpoles in a pond.

He could not stop looking at Willa, thinking about her. She was still a wonderment to him. There was something so beautiful about her form as she lay there. Like a fine woodcarving, graceful and smooth like his buffalo horn, but more than that, more mysterious, more puzzling. Her dress clung to her thighs and legs and he imagined her naked underneath, imagined being with her all over again. But his imagination would only carry him so far. He remembered only parts of it and it seemed like dreaming, as if he had dreamed some of it, or all of it, and when he tried to think of being inside her, of exploding his seed inside her, he couldn't remember how it had been. But his flesh remembered it and he wanted her again, wanted to go into her and become part of her, sink into her until his senses drowned and soared at the same time.

Willa stirred and Morgan's breath caught in his throat. He felt guilty, a-spying on her like that, lusting for her when she was asleep. Wanting her when her pa was dead and his pa had caused it. He got mad every time he thought of his pa coming up there and hitting her. He had no right to do that. He shouldn't have done it. Look what had happened. But that, too, was like a dream.

Morgan stood up, walked over to the bed.

"You awake?" he asked.

Willa groaned and her eyes fluttered. She blinked, then her eyes opened.

"Where am I?" she asked.

"Emile, he give us this room."

She shook her head, sat up, her dress falling back, snugging wrinkled against her thighs.

"I remember," she said. "Oh God, I feel awful."

He sat down, tried to put his arms around her. She pushed him away.

"What's the matter?" he asked.

"I don't want you to touch me," she said, and there was anger in her voice, loathing in her tone.

"Why? What'd I do?"

"What'd you do?" she asked, and her voice rose in pitch, hovered on the edge of hysteria. "My papa's dead and you ask me what did you do?"

"Willa, I—I'm sorry, really sorry, but I didn't have nothin' to do with that fire."

She laughed harshly, swept her tangled hair back with a violent rake of her hand. She fixed Morgan with an icy glare and her lips curled in a contemptuous sneer.

"You bastard," she said. "When I look at you, I see your goddamned worthless father. You're both the same. You even look like him, act like him. Get out, get away from me."

"Willa, don't," he said. "It ain't that way. My pa's done gone and I want to take care of you. I mean you give me somethin' last night, somethin' I ain't never had before and I want to make it up to you, your pa dyin' and all."

She spat at him and Morgan recoiled, startled. Willa's face turned ugly, then, and left him bewildered. Gone was the pretty face of the girl he had lain with the night before. The night-soft contours of her face had been replaced by the hideous visage of a witch.

"You can't bring him back," she said, a snarl edging her voice higher on the scale. "You goddamned dumb pilgrim. You can't do anything right, you stupid farmer. Where's Doc? Have you seen him?"

"Doc?"

"Didn't you know? I was just makin' up to you last night to make Doc jealous. Doc's my man and he—he made me feel bad."

"You mean you didn't want me?"

"Oh, little boy, grow up. I want a man. Like Doc."

The enormity of what Willa was saying sank into Morgan's mind like a lead sash weight. He felt like a fool.

"Did Doc put them bruises on your body?" Morgan asked.

"He's very strong."

"God, Willa, you—you make me sick."

"Is the little boy going to cry?"

"I ain't no little boy. You done me wrong, Willa. You done my pa wrong, too. You was playin' with me. Look what it done to your pa. I felt sorry for you, but I don't no more. You—you just can't do people like this."

"You wanted it. Like a lovesick puppy. Now, get out. I never want to see you again. You and that stupid powder horn."

The coldness of her words knifed through him. He

gripped the medicine horn more tightly in his hands. He wanted to brain her with it, wanted to smash her face until it bled. He wanted to lash out and hurt her as she had hurt him. His face darkened and his eyes narrowed to slits. He shook with the repressed violence that gripped him.

"I'm a-goin'," he said. "I hope you and Doc are real happy together. He's a damned drunk and you're nothin' but a whore."

Willa laughed. She laughed at him and that hurt worse than anything she had said to him. Morgan turned, angrily, and grabbed up his rifle, possibles bag, bedroll, all of his meager possessions. He stormed through the door, slamming it behind him. One of the leather hinges ripped apart and the door sagged to one side. Willa's laughter increased in intensity and the sound followed him as he stalked through the house, fighting down his anger.

Neither Emile nor his wife were home. He looked for them, but they were gone. Morgan walked to the little barn where he had hid Boots. The horse whickered when Morgan entered the darkened stable. Friar Tuck was still tied to one of the posts. He started wagging his tail when he saw Morgan.

"Tut, you doin' all right, boy?" Morgan untied the rope. The dog squirmed and groveled as Morgan walked over to the horse. Boots bobbed his head as if he wanted to prance.

Morgan saddled him and rode through town, a purpose in him now. Tut barked at everything in sight, but didn't stray far from Boots and kept looking up to see if Morgan was still riding the horse. It was nigh noon and there was something he had to do before he left St. Louis.

The King's Boar was an outpost on Fourth and Laurel, a log structure that had been enlarged with wood and limestone. Its shingle creaked on rusty chains, stirred by a slight river breeze. Horses and mules stood hipshot at hitching rings and rails, each with its own pile of steaming droppings. Some of the mules were loaded down with diamond-hitched packs as if ready for a journey. A couple of bearded men dressed in trapper's garb sat in the shade outside, drinking from tankards, smoking pipes. Morgan did not recognize them, but they laughed throatily as he dismounted and stalked to the door, packing only his medicine horn.

"Give you a dollar for thet buffler horn," said one.

"I'll give you two," said the other man.

"It ain't for sale," said Morgan. He entered the tavern, blinked in the smoke, the hazy darkness. He saw only dim shapes of men, a face or two in slanted sunlight that streamed through a pair of partially curtained windows on the sun side.

"Hawke!" called a voice, and Morgan recognized it as Jocko's. He peered through the gloom, saw an arm waving at him. He walked toward it.

Jocko DeSam sat with a couple of trappers Morgan didn't know and the man he and his father had seen outside the Red Lion tavern in Nashville.

"Hear tell your pa's done gone and left," said Jocko. "He no take you with him?"

"Me'n pa had some words," Morgan said laconically.

"I hope you got more sense than him," said one of the men Morgan didn't know.

Morgan felt a testiness beginning to prickle him like a stinging nettle.

"Mister, my pa's got sense enough for bothen of us."

"Now, don't you get your hackles up, sprout," said the man. "I mean looks like he's gone off by hisself up the South Platte and if a man values his hair, he don't take two mules and goods into that country by hisself."

"How do you know this?" asked Morgan.

"Saw him at Eshelman's and LaValle told me that Hawke was headin' over St. Charles way to catch the Osage trail to the South Platte."

"Morgan, set," said DeSam. "This here's Braggin' Bill

Letterman talkin' to you, eh. And this here's Pappy Roth, recently down from the north bringing pipestone he stole from the quarry. He makes the good pipes. And this is Nat Sullard what trapped with me up on the Ohio."

Morgan did not sit down, but he looked at Letterman, Roth and Sullard. Roth wore a round bushy beard threaded through with gray hairs. He smoked a pipe that was pink, carved out of a stone Morgan had never seen.

"I recollec' you, Mr. Sullard," said Morgan.

"Why you're the farmer boy, sure," said Sullard. "I saw your pa, too, a-buyin' trinkets and such at Eshelman's."

"I'm a-lookin' for someone," said Morgan.

"Who might that be, young 'un?" asked Letterman, the talker in the bunch.

"Doc. Name of McIntire I think. He might be with a man named Hauser. Dick Hauser." Morgan looked around the room. There was a balcony and he saw silhouettes of men up there, heard their talk and laughter.

"Doc's here," said Pappy Roth. "Hauser, too." He gestured with his pipe toward the balcony. "You don't want to see him, though, I reckon."

"Why not?"

"Drunker'n a hive of smoked hornets," said Roth, "and gettin' him a mean up worse'n a she-griz with pups."

"I don't care how drunk he is," said Morgan.

Roth stood up. "Maybe I better go up there and see how he is," he said.

"You tell him I want to see him," said Morgan.

"I'll do that, son, but you might think on pickin' a better time."

Roth went up the stairs.

"Set, Morgan," said Jocko. "No use you goin' up there."

"Yes, there is," said Hawke.

He started to leave, go up the stairs, but Jocko grabbed his arm.

"Sit with us, Morgan. We're fittin' out to trap for Missouri

Fur. I might can get you on, get you some advance monies. We're packin' out today or tomorry for Missouri Fur."

"Ain't int'rested," said Morgan. He pulled away from Jocko.

Jocko shrugged. His eyes blinked like an owl's.

"You change your mind, eh, you come see me," said DeSam.

"Hell, Chouteau ain't gonna take on no boy," said Letterman.

Morgan ignored him and headed for the stairs, the medicine horn banging against his side with a dull thud.

The tavern reeked of stale beer and fresh whiskey fumes. Upstairs, the tang was even stronger. Morgan saw that the balcony was really a large upper story, open, with a separate serving bar, benches along the walls and tables where men could drink or play cards.

Morgan looked for Dick Hauser, saw him hunched over in conversation at one of the tables near the side of the room. Doc was with him, and another man Morgan didn't know. Pappy had scooted a chair close to their table. Doc had a small wooden keg in front of him. Dick and the other man held copper tankards in their fists.

Doc looked up as Morgan approached. His face broke into a wan smile that curved into a smirk the closer Morgan got.

"Now, would you look at who's here," said Doc. "Young Master Hawke and he's got blood in his eye." Hauser rose out of his slump. The other man turned his head.

"Uh oh," said Dick. "He looks mad."

Morgan stopped at the table, his hands balled into fists. He glared at Doc.

"What's on your mind, sonny boy?" asked Doc, with a taunting sneer. "Did your daddy run off with your sugar teat?"

"Easy, Doc," said Hauser. "Go easy on the boy. You got

you a snorter full of firewater and it ain't hardly past noon yet."

Morgan felt something harden inside him. He didn't know what it was, but it calmed him down, made him feel strong. He looked square into Doc's eyes and he saw a man afraid, a man hiding in the whiskey, swimming in it, swimming in the hopes he might drown. Willa had said Doc was a man, a real man, but Morgan couldn't see one there. He saw only someone cruel enough to hurt a woman and let another man take blame for something he did.

"I ain't never hated no one before," said Morgan, his voice low and steady.

"Huh? What're you saying, boy?" asked Doc. "You hate me? Why, whatever for? What harm have I ever done you? I don't even know you. Don't want to know you. You're nothing but a pimple on a gnat's ass, still wet behind the ears, still suckin' on a woman's teat. Didn't Willa give you some of that cunnus of hers? Didn't charge you, did she? She usually gets at least six bits for bedding a man and she doesn't care about the color of his epidermis. She told me she was going to give it to you for free."

"You know about it, then," said Morgan. He held back, wanting to make sure. There was time. He wanted to savor the moment when it came. He wanted to feel something course through him that was like when he spilled his seed with Willa. He wanted to feel good about what he meant to do to Doc.

"Knew about what?"

"Willa takin' me to her bed."

Doc threw back his head, roared with laughter.

Hauser frowned.

"I don't like this," he muttered.

Pappy Roth sucked a lungful of smoke from his pipe, let it out like a belching chimney.

"Did you?" Morgan asked again and there was a deadly

tone to his voice that made Doc stop laughing. He seemed to sober up in that instant.

"I knew she was making a play for you, sonny," said Doc. "She made it quite clear. She's just a common trollop. One pecker is much like another to her. She was just a receptacle to me, something to piss in."

Morgan drew back his fist then. Doc saw it coming. He made no move to avoid it. He closed his mouth and seemed to brace himself, to stiffen.

Young Hawke drove his fist into Doc's nose. He felt the bone and cartilage crumple under the impact. Blood spurted from Doc's nose like a squashed raspberry. Doc fell backward, still in his chair, hit the floor with a resounding thump.

McIntire didn't move. He didn't make a sound. He lay there like a corpse. Hauser leaned over and looked at him. Doc was conscious, but he didn't move. Pappy Roth rose up and craned his neck to look at Doc, too. He shook his head and sat back down.

"That was for my pa," said Morgan. "He's a damned sight smarter than any of you."

Hauser straightened up, looked at Hawke with something like respect in his eyes.

"Is that it? You just gonna hit him once? Hell, I thought you was mad."

"I'm not mad," said Morgan. "I just hate what Doc done, not only to my pa, but to Willa. She's real sweet on Doc and he done kicked her like she was a dog. Ain't nobody ought to be treated like that. Nobody."

Morgan turned to leave.

Hauser rose from his chair.

"Where you goin' boy?"

Morgan turned. His eyes seemed to burn a hole through Dick's skull.

"I'm a-goin' after my pa. Me and him are goin' to trap them Rocky Mountains."

"Hell, neither one of you got the brains of a turnip," said Hauser.

"Well, you're some such to talk about brains, takin' up with the likes of Doc there. He ain't no man, and neither are you if you call him friend."

Morgan left them there. Dozens of eyes fixed on him, followed his movements as he left the tavern. There wasn't a sound until he was outside and then the talk rose up like a cloud of insects on a dusk pond, a chattering din that shattered the ears of every man in the King's Boar.

Dick Hauser caught up with Morgan as he was leaving LaValle's River Market with food supplies. It was late afternoon, would be dark in a few hours. Tut rose up from his bed in the dirt under Boots's belly, started barking.

"Morgan, hold up."

"I got to get a-goin', Mr. Hauser."

"Call me Dick. Look, I know Doc's got something a-gnawin' at him. He's a mean bastard. Tipples a mite too much. But, he's got reason."

Morgan packed his goods in his saddlebags. He was anxious to leave. The LaValles had told him his pa was heading for St. Charles, leading two mules. He ought to be able to catch up with his pa if he hurried.

"I got to go, Dick." He turned to Tut. "Stop your barkin'." The dog cringed and backed away, whimpering.

"I know, I know. Look, your pa done me a turn once. I feel sorry about what happened 'twixt you and the gal and with Spanish Jack gettin' burned up like that. I told your pa it might be best if'n he got clean away from St. Louis. Jack's got kin, a brother down to New Orleans. I'll see what I can do about settin' things straight."

"That's mighty kind of you, Dick."

"Morgan, your pa is a good man, better'n most. You tell him I sent greetin's to him. And you, you young whelp, keep your rifle clean as a whistle, your tomahawk sharp, carry plenty of powder and ball. You keep your eyes peeled. Act like you was a-sneakin' up on a deer. Injuns got a way of sneakin' up on you when you're plumb tuckered or busy at somethin'. You and your pa take turns a-sleepin' at night. Don't cross no rivers by a regular ford. Somebody tracks you, you circle around, come up ahind 'em. And, if you get attacked by Injuns, don't stand up. Get off your horse if you're ridin'. If you're a-walkin', get on your knees, lie down, hide ahind a rock or a tree."

"You sound like you know what you're a-talkin' about, Dick."

"Son, I been to the mountains. It's as hard a-gettin' there as it is a-stayin' there."

"I ain't afeard. I got me a good rifle and my medicine horn here." Hawke patted the powder horn. It gleamed black and regal in the sunlight.

"I reckon you'll be all right," said Dick.

Morgan climbed aboard Boots.

Hauser slapped the horse on the rump.

"I'll be seein' you, Morgan, maybe by and by."

"Maybe so," said Morgan. He put his heels to the horse's flanks.

"Just foller the river," yelled Hauser as Morgan rode away, headed north.

Boots stepped out, prancing, flicking his tail. Friar Tuck, tongue lolling, tagged along in the horse's wake, merry-eyed, as if glad to be going somewhere in particular.

Morgan did not look back. He had seen enough of St. Louis to last him a lifetime.

Morgan caught up with his father at dusk of the following day. He had ridden Boots hard and the horse was weary. He had carried the dog some of the way. Tut's little legs had given out on him and his footpads were cracked and bleeding.

He saw the mules first, then Hammerhead, just over the

horizon. A few minutes later, he saw the small fire, his pa hunched over it, feeding it sticks of driftwood. The Osage River shimmered in the glow of the long sunset, its ripples ruddy with the splash of color from the sky.

"Pa!" Morgan called.

Lem stood up. The fire crackled and sputtered. A pair of swifts darted by, streaked across the river, their shadows rumpled on the moving waters.

"Morg? That you?"

"It's me, Pa."

Morgan rode up, swung out of the saddle. Tut squirted out of Morgan's arms and dashed toward Lemuel. The dog leaped up in the air and tried to lick Lem's face. Boots heaved a heavy sigh and switched his tail at the blowflies. Hammerhead whickered a burbled greeting. One of the mules cleared its nostrils, yawned.

"You rode hard, son." He patted Tut's head, pushed him away.

"Wanted to catch up to you," Morgan said breathlessly, beaming a wholehearted grin.

"Glad you did."

"We're still a-goin' to the mountains, ain't we?"

"I reckon so," said Lem, grinning. He put his arm around his son's shoulder. "You hungry?"

"I could eat the south end of a northbound horse."

"Good. Me, too. Strip Boots there and I'll get to fixin' the vittles. You and Tut look plumb starved."

Tut was sniffing every square inch of the camp, mindless of his sore feet, belly full of river water.

Morgan let out a long "ahh" of relief. It was good to be with his pa again, just the two of them, heading west.

That night, they sat on the bank and listened to the river. They looked at the stars spangled in the waters. Lem was smoking his pipe. Morgan tapped on his medicine horn, listened to the tiny reverberations at the spout end, the dull thump at the thick end.

"Dew dust," said Lem, after awhile.

"Huh?"

"Them stars in the water. Heard it called that once. An old man told my pap that when you saw stars in the water, it meant a heavy dew come mornin'."

"You never told me that before, Pa."

"Never thought of it till now."

"It's mighty pretty."

"Sure is. Man in St. Charles told me we got to watch out for the Pawnee. Them are bad Injuns and we'll likely run into them on the Platte."

"You know where we're goin', Pa?"

"I thought we'd take the north fork of the Platte. Got me a map. Looks shorter that way. Feller what spoke of the Pawnee told me about going to a place called South Park. He made a circle on my map where it's at. Said beyond them big mountains, they's plenty of places what ain't trapped out, game aplenty so's a man can live."

"Yes," said Morgan, a dreamlike quality to his voice, "I think that's the best place to go."

Morgan picked up a small stone and chunked it into the river. It made a sound and the water wrinkled the starshine and then it was quiet again.

The two men sat there for a long time, without speaking. But Morgan felt as if they were talking, even so. His chest swelled with a good feeling and he could hear his father's voice as he talked about the journey to the mountains. He could see all the rivers and hear the elk bugling in the high meadows. He could see the beaver swimming and leaving wide wakes in peaceful streams. He saw the immense land in his mind and his father was telling him that wherever they went, the land was theirs.

"Seems like you growed some since I last seen you," said Lem.

"I reckon I have, Pa."

"You're almost as tall as me."

"Almost." Morgan grinned. Lem grinned back at him. They looked like a pair of raccoons. The fire died away and coals pulsed like something alive and breathing.

Later, the moon came up and Morgan knew it was the same moon that shone over the Rocky Mountains.

Both of them looked up at the moon.

"Be closer when we get up high," said Lem.

"A lot closer," said Morgan.

The two men laughed softly in the dark.

Their journey had begun.

Trapper's Moon

For my son Vic

Strange, that people can find so strong and fascinating a charm in this rude, nomadic, and hazardous mode of life, as to be estranged themselves from home, country, friends and all the comforts, elegances, and privileges of civilization; but so it is, the toil, the danger, the loneliness, the deprivation of this condition of being fraught with all its disadvantages, and replete with peril is, they think, more than compensated by the lawless freedom, and the stirring excitement, incident to their situation and pursuits.

—W. A. FERRIS
Life in the Rocky Mountains

1

Lemuel Hawke and his son, Morgan, were lost.

Morgan had known it for at least the past two hours, ever since they had passed an abandoned hunter's shack after following a trail from the river through thick, tick-infested woods. They were back at the river now, heading west, but Morgan knew they were lost.

Lem didn't believe it yet, but Morgan had a sick feeling in his gut. He was a strapping lad of fifteen, with crystal blue eyes, square shoulders, curly locks burnished golden by the sun. He was already taller than his father, who was thirty-three, lean as a barrel slat, with dark hair and coffee-brown eyes, a thin, ascetic face. Both men wore buckskins, but Morgan's shirt was off and his skin was tanned by the sun. Lem wore a linsey-woolsey shirt, but his arms and face were wind-burned and just as dark as his son's.

"You been follerin' the wrong river," said Morgan.

"No, I ain't," argued Lem, reining up Hammerhead, his blunt-nosed horse. The two mules stopped as the lead rope slackened. Morgan brought his horse, Boots, up close, halted him. The horses switched their tails at summer flies. Morgan's dog, Friar Tuck, caught up to them, sat down, his tongue lolling from his beagle mouth. The black-and-tan dog panted noisily, then began to bite at the woodticks on his rump, working his teeth through the fur like pinking shears.

"Let me see that map, I'll show you."

"Morg, I've looked at that map until I'm blue in the face."

"Maybe it's time you let me see it, Pa. You been holdin' onto it like it's a secret. Where'd you get it, anyways?"

"Feller in St. Louis give it to me. Lon Eshelman, the storekeeper. Drew it for me on a piece of paper."

"I bet he's never been out here before in his life."

"He tolt me it was a good map to the fur country."

"Let me see it," Morgan insisted.

"Dang it, Morg, what in Jupiter do you know about readin' maps anyhow?"

"I got eyes," said Morgan. He had caught up to his pa a week ago and had been blindly trusting his father's judgment, until now. But he had been counting miles and by his reckoning, they had come 135 miles from St. Charles. Which was fine, but Morgan was sure that he had started out on the Missouri, while his father was convinced that the Osage River drained into the Mississippi at St. Charles. They had argued about that for two days, but not so seriously as now. Morgan was still walking on eggshells around his pa after running away from Lem in St. Louis, taking up with a tippling house girl that he had thought pure and sweet, but was just a tramp like his father had said.

"What do you mean by that?" asked Lem, fishing the map out of his possibles bag.

"This ain't the same river we started out on."

"It's the Osage. Supposed to lead us right to the Missouri."

"That was the Missouri we were on, Pa. The Osage drains into it, what I heard."

"Where'd you hear that?"

Morgan took the map from his father. He had to pull it out of Lem's hands, so tightly did his pa clutch it.

"In St. Louis. Somewheres. They was talkin' about taking a turn to the north where the Osage comes into the big river. That'd be about thirty mile or so back."

"The hell you say."

Morgan studied the map. Lon Eshelman had drawn the

map a little too quickly. There was a line drawn from the Osage River clear to St. Charles, but Morgan knew there had been only one river and it was a sight bigger than this one. There was no fork on the map, which instead showed the Missouri running parallel to the Osage and coming into the Mississippi closer to St. Louis.

"This danged map ain't no good," said Morgan. "You know where we passed that fork last night?"

"I seed it," said Lem, sulking. He picked a crawling tick off his neck, crushed it between the thumbnail and forefinger of his left hand. Each night, he and his son had to strip out of their buckskins and hunt each other's flesh for burrowed-in ticks. There seemed to be no end to the woods that bordered the river and fought the prairie grasses for domain.

"I wanted to take it, but you said that was where the Osage come in."

"That's what the map shows."

"No, it don't," said Morgan. "Somebody got it back'ards."

"I don't believe it."

"This'll lead us to the trail that goes to Santa Fe, but it's a plumb dangerous way to go. Let's go back, before we lose any more time."

"I figger we'll hit the Missouri any hour now."

"Pa, we done hit it and passed it. That was a fork back there some thirty mile ago."

Lem dug out a twist of tobacco from his possibles pouch and cut two inches from it with the blade of his skinning knife. His shirt was soaked through with sweat and his neck hurt from being burnt by the sun. He stuck the chaw in his mouth, worked it around to the side. He shaded his eyes with his hand and looked upriver. It wound through tree-flocked prairie, over rolling land. The grass was high and the trees so thick neither he nor Morgan could see very far ahead. The air was heavy with the promise of rain. They followed a wide game trail laced with old sun-hardened elk tracks that had grown over. They had seen no fresh tracks and that bothered him some.

To the west, the sky was dark, turning darker. The breeze had freshened from the north in the past few minutes, and when Lem looked in that direction, he saw even more clouds lumbering in, closing off the horizon.

Morgan could be right. The map might have been drawn wrong, either deliberately or ignorantly. The country was new to him. He had never seen so much sky all at once as during the past week or so, and not a sign of any other humans in a long while. Yesterday, he had seen faded tracks of an unshod horse, but even these were more than a month old. There were always deer and other game tracks along the river. Morgan was right about one thing. If this was still the Missouri, it threatened to peter out. It was scrawny as a creek and wouldn't float a light raft, much less a bullboat.

They hadn't seen another human since leaving the settlement at St. Charles, and Lem knew there were trappers heading westward. Maybe the Osage Trail wasn't the way to go, after all. Maybe nobody wanted competition in beaver country.

"Looks like we're in for some weather," Lem said, spitting a stream of tobacco juice at the ground. Tuck got up off his haunches and trotted over to inspect the stain in the grass. He sniffed and backed away.

"Tuck, boy," said Morgan. The dog stopped biting ticks and wagged his tail.

"He's plumb wore out," said Lem.

"He's chased ever' rabbit for better'n a hunnert mile," said Morgan.

"And caught nary," said his father.

In the distance, they heard the first rumblings of thunder.

"Looks like we'd best find some shelter," said Lem.

"Way I figger it, Pa, we wouldn't have to go back the way we come. Just head north. Bound to hit the Missouri in a half day, maybe less."

"What if you're wrong, son?" Lem fixed Morgan with a sharp look.

As always, when Morgan was worried, he touched the black buffalo horn hanging at his side. It had been given to him by his namesake, Silas Morgan, the trapper who had first told them about the shining streams and the beaver in the Rocky Mountains. Silas called it a "medicine horn" and Morgan had treasured it as something special ever since he first held it in his hands. There was a comfort in its presence, as if it truly held magical powers, what Silas had called "strong medicine." His fingertips traced the Indian symbols etched into the hard dark shell of the horn.

"We'd know soon enough, I reckon. This ain't the way to go to the mountains. There ain't been a man ride this way for months."

"Eh? That's so. We may have been given a bad way to go. Well, we could head north. It's worth a try. But from the sound of that thunder, I'd say we can't outrun the hard rain in those black clouds. Plenty of trees yonder. We could hole up until the storm passes."

Morgan looked westward, saw jagged lightning slash the clouds. He counted the seconds until he heard the thunder, trying to figure how far away the storm was. It was something his pa had taught him back in Kentucky. Lem told him that it took time for the sound to travel overland and if a man counted off the seconds, he could get a pretty good idea of how soon they'd get rained on.

"Ten miles away," said Morgan.

"More like fifteen," said Lem.

Morgan laughed. He was beginning to like his father again, after the trouble in St. Louis. When the fight broke out over the girl, Willa, at Spanish Jack's, Morgan had thought about killing his father. But, it turned out that the girl was no good and had just made a fool of him. When her father had died in a fire that burned Spanish Jack's tavern to the ground, some blamed Lem for that. Morgan hated St. Louis now. He had thought he'd never see his pa again and it had taken some hard riding to catch up with him. He was glad now he had come. His pa was smart, but he was following a bad map. Morgan was sure of that.

The wind picked up and the horses and mules caught a whiff of the storm. Their ears sharpened to cones and twisted in semicircles to pick up sound. Friar Tuck barked as a dry brittle leaf rattled past him, kicked up by a gust of wind.

The clouds rolled toward them faster and blotted out the sun. The air grew suddenly heavier, and both father and son could taste the tang of dampness on the air. Then, the wind died suddenly, and it grew strangely quiet. The songbirds went silent. Not a breath of air seemed to be stirring.

"We'd better find us some shelter quick," said Lem.

Morgan looked at the strange, low-flying clouds scudding overhead. They seemed to drip, to hang there like shrouds. There was a strange cast to the light part of the sky, to the north and east of them, a dusky yellowish glow that seemed eerie in the stillness. In the distance, he heard a roar like nothing he had ever heard before.

"Pa, what's that?"

Lem straightened in the saddle. His face drained of color.

"Sounds like a hurricane. I saw one once't in Virginny, 'long the coast. Blew everything to smithereens. Come on, let's get in them trees yonder."

The mules balked when Lem took up the slack in the lead rope. Friar Tuck yipped and Boots bucked, kicking out both hind legs. Morgan hung on, brought the horse under control.

"What's the matter with the mules?" Morgan asked.

"Scared," said Lem, jerking on the rope. He dug his heels into Hammerhead's flanks and the horse pulled the mules into movement. There was a large open sward of prairie to cross on a low hill before they could reach the woods. The noise from the west grew louder. Morgan saw the black clouds swirl and form into a conical shape. It looked like a huge, twisting snake as the cloud mass moved toward them.

Lem saw the funnel too, and just then the winds stiffened and blew hard, rattling the fringes on his buckskins, making his shirt flap.

"Go on, Morg. Hurry!" Lem yelled as the roaring turned him deaf to all but the wind.

"Lordamighty!" cried Morgan, but his utterance was snatched away by the fierce wind. The funnel cloud grew darker, edged still closer, and the roaring in his ears was so loud it terrified him.

Boots galloped ahead. Raindrops began to spatter the river, and then they hit like millions of needles, stinging Morgan's face, blinding him as they raked his eyes. He bent over in the saddle, felt the wind tugging at him with an almost unbelievable force. It seemed as if he was being held in place by the wind, but the horse moved forward toward the woods, struggling, too, against the powerful, invisible barrier.

Lem fought to hold the rope as the mules bolted in another direction. He felt his arm almost pull out of its socket as he went one way, the mules another. Hammerhead halted and Lem, blinded by the lancing rain, cursed at horse and mules until he realized he'd drown if he kept his mouth open. In seconds, he was soaked to the skin. Hammerhead turned, started after the mules. Lem tried to turn him back toward the woods, but the mules headed south, away from the brunt of the storm.

Morgan reached the edge of the woods, turned to look back. He saw the dim shape of his father, Hammerhead, and the pair of mules. They would hit the woods further down. Without thinking, Morgan turned Boots and chased after his father. The wind at his back, he rode fast, but the hard rain pelted his bare skin. The savage roar of the tornado seemed right behind him.

Lem gave Hammerhead his lead, knowing they'd hit the

woods on their present course. He was glad they hadn't headed for the river. He didn't see Morgan until the boy rode up alongside him, shouting something Lem couldn't hear above the brutal blare of the twister. He looked over his shoulder, braving the slashing raindrops battering his eyes and saw the funnel getting even closer to them. It seemed gigantic, towering over the woods like some ominous black dragon.

The twister zig-zagged, struck the river and sucked up volumes of water in its angry throat. It stuttered at the river, then gathered momentum and crawled across the open prairie. It began to jerk trees from the earth, rendering them to splinters as it roared with violent winds. It smashed trees in its wake, picked up stones and hurled them in all directions as it danced toward the south like some maddened dervish, a slow, mindless beast that flattened everything in its path.

The tornado broadened its path, seemed to grow wider as it carried the river waters in its maw, hurling them with cyclonic force at Lem and Morgan.

The two men rode into the fringe of the woods, the tornado following them with an ear-splitting, terrifying roar.

"Get off your horse and run!" Lem shouted, but he knew that Morgan could not hear him. He managed to ride next to his son and gesture to him. "Get down, find cover!"

Morgan nodded, swung out of the saddle.

He tried to hold onto his reins. A moment later, his father appeared at his side. The sky was now totally dark, almost pitch, and both of them could see the twisting funnel cloud getting wider in girth and closer to them.

"Leave Boots be. Find a hole! Quick!"

Morg released his grip on the reins. He saw, out of the corner of his eye, his pa's horse bolt away, followed a moment later by Boots. The mules were nowhere in sight.

"Where's Tuck?" yelled Morgan into his father's ear.

Lem shook his head, started running, pulling one of Morgan's arms.

Morgan tried to see in the darkness, but the rain burned holes in his eyes and he lowered his head, following blindly in his father's path. Lem headed for a large oak tree, scrambled behind it and fell flat on his stomach. Morgan joined him a second later. There was barely enough room for them.

"Is it safe here?" Morgan said at the top of his voice.

"I don't know!" Lem screamed at his son.

They stopped trying to communicate with each other as the booming voice of the monstrous storm grew so loud neither could hear. They listened to the sound of trees being uprooted and smashed; the leaves around them rattled with stones that sounded like buckshot.

Morgan felt his stomach muscles tighten. He knew, in his heart, that it was the end of the world. Nothing could live in such a storm, nothing in its path would escape destruction. He had seen trees swirling around on the edge of the twister just before he ran into the woods, and he could hear them now, battering the standing trees, knocking them down as if they were straw.

The darkness enveloped them and they braced themselves for the final smash of the tornado.

Rain poured down on them like water from a millrace. They couldn't hear it above the ghastly thunderous clamor of the twister, but they felt as if they were being washed away by a tidal wave. They dug their fingers into the earth as the winds tore at them. The tree behind them shuddered as if struck by a colossal force. Lem thought the oak would be uprooted, leaving them at the mercy of the tornado. He turned to his son and Morgan put his arms around his father. He knew that this was probably the end for both of them. He, too, heard the big oak shudder and thought he could hear it straining at its roots.

"Pa!" he shouted, but the word tore away with the wind and Morgan felt as if the air had been sucked out of his lungs.

"Hold on, Morg!" screeched Lem, holding his son more tightly. Around them, he heard the thrashing of trees and brush as if a giant was scything down everything around them. The oak still shuddered and its treetop whipped in the winds, snapping limbs, dropping them down on the two men with thumping force.

The tornado swerved toward a different course, wending southeasterly just as it hit the fringes of the woods. It seemed to be seeking open ground. But its edges were dangerous, and as it turned, it flayed trees to shreds, hurled rocks and debris through the forest.

Morgan heard the terrible howl of the wind, heard the smashing trees, the whistling rocks. He clung to his father, sure that he was going to die. The oak shuddered under a mighty blast of air and strained at its moorings as the tornado made its wide slow turn.

Then, as suddenly as it had touched down, the funnel retreated back up into the clouds. Lightning crackled in its black belly and thunder boomed and cracked. Rain rattled on the leaves, but the roaring sound was gone.

Lem released his hold on Morgan. Morgan reluctantly let loose of his father.

"I-I thought G-God was a-goin' to take us," stammered Morgan. "Did you?"

"God don't take part in such devilment."

"Mother always said He was almighty powerful and could smite us all in a twinklin'."

"Your ma had a lot of queer notions. My pa and ma were God-fearin' folks and I never understood it. One time they'd say he was merciful, next time they'd say he was vengeful. Like the time a flood come through Virginny and kilt folks right and left. The preacher said it was God's will, punishment. But there was babies and good old folks and young 'uns what never did nobody no harm. Didn't make sense to me."

"I never saw no storm like that one," Morgan said, still awestruck. Rain drenched them both, but they were glad to be alive. They stood up and looked around them. Trees lay strewn like jackstraws everywhere, their trunks and limbs split apart, their fibers shattered to bone white pulp. Blown leaves were plastered to tree trunks like flattened green ornaments. Lightning lit the sky with thin silver wires every few seconds and the thunder made them jump.

"Still some buckshy, ain't we?" said Lem.

"I reckon," said Morgan, grinning.

"Welp, best we start huntin' down the stock."

"I wonder if Tuck made it."

"No tellin', son. I'll bet he's one scared hound, though." Morgan laughed.

The wind still blew hard, dashing freshets of rain against their faces as boy and man stalked through the devastated forest, looking for horses and mules. All around them were signs of the terrible destruction inflicted by the tornado.

"Look, Pa," said Morgan, pointing.

"Sure enough."

A manmade log, hewn from oak, lay against a fallen tree, poking the sky like a ship's mast.

"Must be another hunter's cabin somewheres around here," said Morgan.

Lem traced a path in the direction he had seen the horses and mules run. The ground looked as if something had exploded at its center. Trees were stripped of bark. One tree, exploded by lightning, sent tendrils of soft gray smoke spiralling into the air.

A piece of sodden driftwood, carried from the river, lay atop a pile of broken trees. A stump lay in the center of a clearing, its roots still clogged with fresh dirt.

"Pa, there are folks livin' about. That's a fresh hickory stump yonder."

"Sure enough," said Lem. "But, we got to get them animals back or we'll be walkin' plumb to the mountains."

The rain beat at them, hammered their faces, ragged their eyes. In another part of the woods, they came across the mules, still tied to the lead rope, which was tangled in a briar patch. Lem waded into the briars, hacking at them with his knife. Morgan followed by a different path. The mules began braying, kicking at the brush.

"Hold on, Jack," said Lem, trying to calm them. "Morg, you take holt of that jenny and hold her whilst I pull old Jack out of here. She ought to foller."

They heard a horse whicker. A few moments later, Hammerhead trotted out from between a pair of trees, reins trailing, saddle slick with rain.

"I see he didn't lose my rifles," said Lem.

"Now if we can find Boots and Tuck," said Morgan, as his father led the jack out of the brush. The jenny followed docilely, Morgan patting her neck, talking to her in soothing tones.

"Here, you hold this jack tight while I catch up Hammerhead. Lead 'em out in the open. I'll look for your horse."

"What about Friar Tuck, Pa?"

"Oh, he'll find us, if he's able."

"Danged dog," said Morgan, trying to conceal the worry he felt. He knew Tuck had to be scared. He hoped he had gotten out of the way of the twister. He dreaded to think what would happen to such a small creature in such a fierce wind.

As his father rode deeper into the woods, Morgan led the mules back out into the open. He saw a dead rabbit, then, its eyes popped out of their sockets, staring blindly into the dark sky, the rain pelting them so that they moved, looked alive.

Morgan shuddered. The rain was coming down in ragged sheets now as the wind gusted, sometimes stopping him in his tracks it blew so hard. The mules brayed mournfully and loud, as if they were being beaten mercilessly. That's when he saw the snakes.

Cottonmouths and copperheads, rattlers and king snakes slithered across the sward, through the grasses, over the downed trees and castaway logs. They came from the direction of the river, gliding faster than Morgan had ever seen a snake move before. The mules made even more racket as snakes squirmed under their legs. None of the snakes struck, but disappeared into the tall grasses, into the woodpile and the woods.

Morgan shivered, turned his face away from the wind and the rain. The rain was cold on his bare flesh and he wished he had his horse back and dry clothes—if any were still dry. He heard a sound, then, a small cry, and lifted his head, trying to peer through the slashing rain.

Out of the corner of his eye he saw movement. Turning, Morgan saw a droopy, sag-tailed Friar Tuck cowering in the rain, but waddling toward him like a whipped pup.

"Here, Tuck, here boy!" Morgan called. Friar Tuck tried to wag his tail, but the effort seemed too much for him. Instead, he gave another little yip and gained speed on tired little legs.

Morgan stooped down, took Tuck into his arms, brought him close. The dog lapped at Morgan's face, squirming, whining pitiably.

"It's all right, Tuck. Good boy."

Morgan embraced his dog, squeezed him, grateful that the beagle was still alive.

Friar Tuck began licking Morgan's ears and neck in gratitude. Morgan set him down and the dog whimpered and cowered as the rain pelted him. Morgan patted the dog's head, spoke to him reassuringly. The mules began to settle down, seemingly reassured by the sight of the little dog.

Morgan had no idea how much time had passed, but it seemed his pa had been gone a long time. The rain battered him as he knelt by the dog. Friar Tuck was still shivering;

his tail no longer wagged, but quivered involuntarily with each hard gust of wind.

The wind increased in velocity and Morgan longed for shelter from the spearing lances of rain. If he took to the woods, he was afraid his pa couldn't find him right off. The longer they stayed in the open, the more the animals would suffer. He heard a voice through the raging downpour.

"Help! Help!"

Morgan's blood froze.

"Pa?" he called.

"Godamighty, please help!"

It was not his father's voice. Morgan stood up. Friar Tuck cowered and whimpered as Morg released him.

"Who's there?"

"Over here!" yelled the man.

Morgan turned, saw a strange sight. A man, his clothes soaking wet and in shreds, staggered across the clearing. He was barefoot and bareheaded with a long, full beard. As he drew closer, Morgan saw that he was a white man. He was bleeding from a wound on the head and his face was drenched with blood and rain.

"Oh, God, please help me!" the man pleaded.

Morgan stood transfixed as the man stumbled and fell. When he arose, Morgan saw that he clutched something in his hand. It was then that he noticed it was a hand. The other arm ended at the wrist, white bones, washed by the rain, sticking out of a mass of raw flesh.

Morgan felt his knees go weak. He backed away in horror as the man lurched toward him, holding up that lifeless hand.

Friar Tuck growled and the mules brayed mournfully as the wind blasted their eyes with sharp stinging needles of rain.

"Help me!" the man screamed.

But Morgan couldn't move.

2

Morgan stepped backward as the screaming man fell to his knees like a beggar.

"Please, for God's sake, help me. I'm plumb bleedin' to death. My hand . . . Jesus, look at my hand."

Morgan stopped his retreat. Something in the man's voice, something in the way he knelt there in the rain touched Morgan, touched him deeply. That tone of utter despair and supplication wrenched at his heart, made him see beyond the horror, made him see the child in pain, the little boy with fingers burned in the fire. A flood of compassion rose up in him and he found his voice, strangled as it was by fear and that loathing reserved for cripples by men whole in mind and body.

"I—I don't know w-what I can do," he said. "What happened? How'd you lose your hand?"

"The storm—that twister, God, can you sew it back on my arm?"

Morgan couldn't answer. He could not look at the man's severed hand without feeling revulsion. Could he sew it back on? He didn't think so. He was about to vomit and his mind raced with images of disfigurement, torn flesh and ruptured blood vessels. Now, as he looked closer, he could see that the man's mutilated arm was bleeding profusely. It was hard to see in the rain, but blood was spurting from the stump so fast that its darker hue made him realize the man was in shock.

"I—I'll see what I can do. Just stay there. I—I'll have to get something to tie off your arm so you won't bleed no more."

"Oh, thank God. I don't want to die. God knows I don't want to die."

"Hold on," said Morgan. Friar Tuck sought shelter in the pile of debris as Morgan started trying to untie the diamond hitch on the jack mule. The wounded man moaned and whined. Morgan tried not to think about that hand, that bloody stump of an arm.

The young man found some strips of leather and a few patches of cloth they had brought along for fixing holes in their shirts. He dug deeper and found an awl and some heavy thread they had carried out from Kentucky. Lem had done a lot of mending after Morgan's ma run off with that Lexington hatter.

The wounded man was mewling pitifully when Morgan knelt down beside him.

"Give me that—that bad arm and let me see can I stop the bleeding."

"You got needle and thread? You take this hand and sew it back on."

"Not yet," said Morgan, steeling himself for what he had to do. He still couldn't look at that bloody, lifeless hand.

Three antlerless deer galloped out of the darkness, eyes fearful and wild as they raced through silver curtains of rain silent as ghosts.

Morgan began wrapping a thong around the man's bleeding arm. The man screamed in Morgan's ear, screamed louder than the wind-blown rain tattering on the leaves.

L em heard the horse whinny in terror. He knew it was Boots. He could not see in the driving rain, but he shielded his eyes from the stinging downpour and followed a course toward the sound.

Hammerhead threaded his way through a jumbled pile of hewn logs, overturned trees and broken pieces of furniture. The howling wind lashed Lem mercilessly as he gave the horse its head, guiding him only when he veered too far away from the path to the screaming horse.

On the other side of the rubble, Lem made out the lower part of a log cabin. A crumbled chimney of rock lay strewn about one side of the structure. A few yards away, a man was pulling on the reins of a horse, cursing the animal. The horse was Boots and it was frantically trying to escape.

"Hold on there!" Lem shouted, but the wind snatched his words away.

He dug moccasined heels into Hammerhead's flanks, rode up on the stranger. He grabbed the reins from the man's hands. Boots collapsed on his haunches in mud and water.

"What you doin' with this horse?" shouted Lem.

"Man, I need it. I got to get my woman out of here. She's bad hurt."

"Woman? I don't see no woman."

"In there." The man held up an arm, the shirtsleeve plastered to it. He was young, with long hair, a full beard masking his face. His clothes were sodden; he was barefoot. He pointed toward the smashed log cabin.

"What you doin' livin' way out here?"

"Hunters. Me and my bub. He got his hand sliced off when that twister hit. Axe come off the wall and cut his hand clean off. He run off somewheres."

Lem looked down at the wild-eyed young man. He had never heard such a story before. In the screeching wind, he thought the man must be mad, crazy as a loon.

"Where's your own horse?" Lem yelled.

"Gone. I got to get out of here. My woman."

"You married?"

"No, not exactly."

"What the hell's that mean?"

"I got me a squaw-woman. She's bad hurt, mister. Can you help us out?"

Lem looked nervously toward the shattered cabin. He saw no one.

"I got troubles of my own," Lem said, but the man didn't hear him. Instead, they both heard a loud, animal-like cry from the remnants of the cabin. They turned, saw a young girl standing up. Blood streamed over her face from a cut on her scalp. One of her arms was broken, dangled crookedly at the elbow. She wore a tattered buckskin dress, slick with rain.

"There she is," said the stranger.

"That ain't but a girl."

"She's about twelve, I reckon."

Lem's jaw tightened. He remembered Willa, the young girl at Spanish Jack's in St. Louis who had seduced his son. He remembered his own wife, Roberta, when they were both young and the way she cuckolded him, took up with that hatter, O'Neil, in Lexington. Women were trouble, all of them, and this Indian girl was no different.

"You help her yourself," Lem said tightly, his voice gravelly, husk.

"Goddamn you!" The stranger leaped up, grabbed the fringes on Lem's buckskin shirt, jerked him out of the saddle. Lem felt the reins flow from his fingers as he lost his balance, tumbled toward the soggy earth. He could smell the foul breath of the stranger as he hit the man midway to the ground.

Hands locked around Lem's throat. Fingers tightened around his neck, blocking off his air. He brought up his own hands, rolled to the side, the stranger gripping him tightly. Lem pulled the man's hands away, gulped in a deep breath. The man clawed at him, reaching for his neck. They wallowed in mud and water, each searching for an advantage.

Lem's fingers slipped as he tried to grab the stranger's hair. He felt something hard smash into his cheek. He shook off the pain, kicked out with both feet, hoping to strike the man's groin. He heard a grunt in his ear as he felt a jarring impact on the soles of his feet.

Lem stiff-armed the man, pushing him away with his left hand. He smashed a fist into his attacker's temple, heard a sodden *smack*. The man went limp for a moment and Lem pressed his advantage. He rolled over atop the man, pinned his arms to the puddled ground. He heard a noise behind him, turned, saw a shadow looming over him. The Indian girl raised a stone war club in the air.

Lem gave a choked cry and released one of the pinned man's arms to ward off the blow. The Indian girl struck. Lem grabbed her wrist, twisted it. She never made a sound as he bent it so far back it snapped at the elbow. Lem heard the loud *pop* and watched her crumple. The man beneath him squirmed and wriggled, trying to get out from under Lem's weight. Lem drove a hard fist into the man's nose, felt it crunch, turn rubbery. Blood streamed from the man's nose. The man gurgled as blood filled his throat. Lem hit him again and again until the man no longer struggled.

The girl tried to rise, but could not with both her arms broken. She scooted around in a circle, kicking up water as the rain hammered down, blown hard by the wind.

Lem lurched to his feet, looked down at the stranger. He was young, not much older than the Indian girl. He wondered what they were doing living way out in the wilderness. Hunters, he supposed, but where was their market?

The girl grabbed his buckskin trousers.

"You take," she said in English.

"No," said Lem.

"Me good girl."

Lem jerked his leg away from her clutching hand.

"You're filth," he spat. His face froze into a mask of hatred. "Nothin' but a goddamned animal."

She shook her head, raised her broken wrist toward him, begging him silently to take her with him.

Lem turned his back on her, caught up Hammerhead and mounted the horse. He rode down Boots, picked up the trailing reins. He rode away from the crumbled cabin without a backward look, the anger in him still seething. The rain seemed to steam as it struck his buckskins, spattered into fine mist.

Morgan couldn't touch the mangled hand, though the man held it out to him. He gave the tourniquet-thong one last twist and shook his head. The bleeding had stopped for the moment, and he could think no further than that. His hands were shaking so badly he knew he couldn't even sew the wound shut, much less attach the severed hand.

"That's all I can do for you, mister," Morgan said loudly to the other man.

"Please."

"I ain't got nothin' to sew it on with. 'Sides, it ain't agoin' to work."

"I don't want to be a cripple."

"I ain't no barber, neither."

"You sonofabitch," yelled the stranger. He threw his mortified hand in Morgan's face, reached down to his waist and pulled out a skinning knife. He slashed at Morgan, narrowly missing his neck. Morgan rocked back on his feet, the hackles stiffening on the back of his neck. He heard the whisper of the blade as it passed beneath his chin. The man, his face twisted into a hideous glower, came after Morgan, crawling on his knees. The young man slid backward, tried to gain his footing on the slippery, watery ground. His heels could find no footing and slithered out from under him. His rump plopped into a muddy puddle.

The man scrambled forward on his belly toward Morgan. The makeshift tourniquet slipped off his wrist stump, but he seemed not to notice it. Blood gushed from the wound, spurted onto Morgan's buckskin pantsleg.

"D-Don't," said Morgan. "Keep away."

"I'll gut you like a toad," snarled the stranger, his lips wet with rain.

"You're bleeding again," said Morgan, scooting away, trying once again to get his legs underneath him. He felt as if he was in a mud wallow. Everytime he moved, he slid through water and slimy earth.

The stranger got up on one knee, then stood straight up, towering over Morgan, the knife ready to strike. Morgan's fingers sought his own blade. The buckhorn handle was slick and his hand slipped off. He kept scooting backward as the stranger stalked him, eyes glistening with madness and pain.

"You can't get away," the stranger croaked.

Morgan realized that the man was right. He could not get away as long as he was on the ground. He grabbed for his knife again, but he was sitting on the scabbard. The blade wouldn't come loose.

Morgan hurled himself sideways. He crawled quickly toward the pile of rubble, toward the comparative safety of the mules. Behind him, he heard the wet plop of the stranger's feet striking the ground as he broke into a faltering run. Something roiled in Morgan's stomach and fear gripped him like talons at his throat.

Panting, Morgan lashed out, grabbed a chunk of a shattered tree limb. He pulled himself up to one foot, turned. The killer hurtled toward him, holding the knife in his good hand, ready to thrust.

"Stay away," Morgan yelled into the teeth of the wind, into the ferocious gale that whipped rain into his eyes, stung them blind. He jerked his knife free and braced himself.

Then, a strange calmness overcame him. The wind died out in his ears as if he was in the eye of a hurricane. The fear dissipated in a sudden wash, the panic flooded away as newfound sudden strength flooded his veins.

"Come on, then," Morgan said softly and he gripped the handle of his knife, held it close to his belly. "Come on, you crazy bastard."

Lem rode out of the woods, leading Boots, and let out a sharp cry.

Morgan didn't look at his father. Instead, he kept his eyes fixed on the stranger, watching his every move. As the man drew close, drawing his knife back, the young man stepped in under it and shoved his knife straight at the older man's belly. He felt the blade strike the skin, part it and sink into soft flesh.

He heard the man utter a gasp, then a long sigh. The stranger collapsed and the knife fell out of his good hand, glanced off Morgan's shoulder and splashed into a pool of water.

"Morgan, don't!" shrieked Lemuel as he saw his son grapple with the man, saw his son's blade, saw the man crumple—but didn't see the stranger's knife.

Morgan felt the weight of the man, jerked his knife free and stepped back. The stranger pitched forward, fell on his face.

"Godamighty, Morgan, what have you gone and done?" Lem said as he dismounted and dashed toward his son.

Morgan looked up, saw his father's face through the shroud of blowing rain, saw his eyes wide in the hollows of their sockets.

"I reckon I kilt him," he said calmly.

"Christ. Why?"

Lem looked down, saw the man's slashed wrist, saw that the hand was missing.

"Did you cut off his hand? Or kill him?"

"I didn't cut off his hand. I tried to fix it. Then, he come at me, Pa, honest. He come at me with a knife."

"I don't see no knife."

Morgan looked around. He didn't see it either.

"It's down on the ground somewheres."

Lem knelt down, turned the man over. Rain spattered into the open mouth, razed the dead glassy eyes. The look on his face was hideous, the look of a man slain in violence, frozen in a final agony.

Morgan kicked through the puddles until his moccasinned toe struck something.

"This here's his knife," said Morgan, holding it out to his father.

"This must be kin to the one I tangled with back in the woods."

"You run into trouble, too?"

"That storm caused a heap of damage. We better make tracks. No tellin' who these people are. This un's deader'n a doornail."

"He was goin' to kill me, Pa. I sure enough didn't want to hurt him none."

Lem stood up, looked at his sopping wet son, his hair slicked down, blood on his knifeblade, on his wrist. The rain was already washing it away.

"Put your knife away, son. Cotch up Boots and we'll get those mules, get on out of here."

"Shouldn't we—bury him?" Morgan looked down at the dead man.

"Hell, let his own kind bury him. He warn't no good nohow."

"What happened to you?"

"Nothin'," said Lem. "Nothin' as serious as this."

"Pa, I feel funny."

"Killin' a man?"

"Uh-huh."

"Don't feel too good."

"Nope."

"It was you or him, Morg." Lem slapped his son on the back, spraying water droplets in a wide circle.

"I reckon."

Lem took the dead man's knife from Morgan, stuck it inside his belt. Morgan sheathed his own blade. They caught up their horses, untied the mules and rode away from the clearing, back toward the river, both hunched over in their saddles against the brunt of the wind.

Morgan felt a strange tingle course through his veins. For a few moments he felt a kind of exhilaration, then his hands began to tremble slightly. He drew in a deep breath and his hands steadied. His thoughts were all tangled, jumping, skittering, winding around in his mind so that he could make no sense of them. He remembered the terror he felt when the man came after him, and he remembered the blade sinking soft into his gut. He remembered the man letting out the last of his breath in one long final sigh. And, then, he remembered the dead look on his face, the staring eyes, the slack, open mouth, the rain falling into it.

So, that was death, he thought. One minute, someone's alive, the next they're gone.

Then, he felt strange again, and powerful, for some reason. As if he had done something no one had ever done before. But, he knew that was not true. His pa had killed Indians. And some said he killed Spanish Jack, but that was an accident.

Killing wasn't as hard as Morgan thought it would be. But it sure made a man feel powerful strange.

3

All day long, Lemuel looked over his shoulder, stopped to walk around, lay facedown on the prairie, put his ear to the ground. His coffee-brown eyes shimmered with light as they widened, then narrowed again. At times, Lem would pick up a handful of dirt and sniff it, as he once did when they farmed in Kentucky.

Morgan noticed that Friar Tuck was fidgety, too, and the horses and mules seemed just as nervous. He supposed they were still skittery from the storm. At least they had found the right river, finally. They were on the Missouri and heading the right way. His pa had ought to feel pretty good about that.

Maybe his pa was wondering if another twister was sneaking up on them. For most of the morning and half of the afternoon, his pa hadn't said anything. Lem would just look back at the long prairie miles behind them and squint and shade his eyes and wrinkle up his nose like he had got a whiff of pig dung. Friar Tuck hadn't barked once, and he slunk along the river sniffing at every clump of grass, every little bush and bone of root sticking out of the bank of the Missouri.

"Pa, what you lookin' back yonder for?" asked Morgan.

"Shadows, I reckon." He said "shadders," in his soft Virginia accent.

"Shadows? You don't mean black clouds, do you?"

"I seen something back there in those cottonwoods where we fixed up them panniers on the dadblamed mules, and then I seen something out of the corner of my eye out on the prairie."

"I didn't see anything," said Morgan. He had his mother's blue eyes and they crackled in the burning daylight like sharp-cut diamonds.

Lemuel hauled on the reins, pulled Hammerhead to a stop. The old blunt-nosed horse tried to shake out the bit, shivered from forelock to tail as if telling his master he wanted out from under the saddle, too.

Morgan's arms were brown from the sun, his face bronzed from the prairie winds, his hair tawny from the golden light of the long, wending days through high grasses under endless blue skies.

Friar Tuck ranged so far ahead Morgan hadn't seen him for the better part of an hour.

Up ahead, less than another day's journey, was Independence, and beyond that, the Platte. Somewhere along the

way Morgan knew Lem hoped to find other trappers heading overland for the Rockies and learn all he could about
this new country.

"Well," said Lem, "it worries me some. Man don't want
to be seed, he skulks, and that 'un back there is some shy."

"Why don't we wait on him, Pa? Find out who he is."

"Might be more'n one. Might be a Injun."

Morgan felt the hairs on his scalp prickle. Something
knotted in his throat. A muscle quivered in his stomach.
He wiped a sweaty palm across the front of his buckskin
shirt, touched the hammer on the flintlock rifle lying across
his calves. He grasped the throat of his medicine horn.
Although it held coarse powder for Morgan's flintlock
rifle, it was a comfort to him during times of worry.

"We ought to hide someplace," said the young man.

"Hell, I ain't hidin'," said his father.

Morgan kept looking toward their backtrail, but he didn't
see anyone. Tuck burst from a clump of bushes, ran toward
them, following rabbit trails through the grasses, beagle tail
whipping back and forth like a divining rod.

Morgan's horse, Boots, whickered softly and his ears
twisted, trapping a faroff sound, the fine hairs glistening
in the sun like golden threads.

"Well, we could wait till he cotched up with us," said
Morgan.

"He's had plenty of time to ride up," said Lem laconically. He checked the pan on his flintlock, saw that it was
black with fine grains of powder. He closed the frizzen,
kept the hammer on half-cock. "All I saw was a speck at
first, now I make it to be a man a-horseback."

"Likely he don't mean us no harm."

"Likely," said Lem, but he kept looking back more often now, and when he looked ahead, he sought out cover
in case they had to make a run for it. Blackbirds took flight
as they passed a gravel bar, wheeled in a ragged formation
as the flock sought a landing in a different place. They had

seen little game along the way, but plenty of sign, both of travelers and critters.

Friar Tuck veered off, gamboled across a stretch of greensward.

"Tuck, here boy," called Morgan. The dog ignored him. Young Hawke watched as the dog romped out of sight, hot on the trail of whatever had passed through and left scent.

"He's havin' him a time," said Lem.

"I reckon."

They rode another two miles, marveling at the bluffs along the river.

"Sorta spooky, ain't it?" asked Morgan when his father stopped.

"Whatcha mean, son?"

"Looks like Injuns could stay atop them bluffs and see everything comin' upriver."

"Sure could." Lem reached into his possibles pouch, pulled out a twist of tobacco. He cut off a chaw with his skinning knife. He was lean in his buckskins, weathered and tanned. He had four days of beard, giving him the look of an ascetic!

Morgan stood up in his stirrups, looking back over their trail.

"Somebody's comin', Pa."

"I know. Ain't the same one I seed."

"How can you tell?"

"Other feller was big, settin' a pony. This here one's ridin' a big horse and pullin' a mule."

"He sure is," said Morgan.

"We'll wait on him."

Morgan sighed with relief. He hadn't seen another human being in a hundred and fifty miles. Any company was welcome.

"Maybe he knows who was a-follerin' us, Pa."

"Mmm."

A half hour later, they saw the stranger as he drew near.

He rode a chestnut sorrel with a buckskin mane and tail, splotches of white on its face and threaded through its coat like gray hairs. The man was dressed in buckskins, had two rifles hanging from elkskin scabbards on either side of his saddle. A full beard hid his face; he wore a beaver hat with a beavertail bill. A beaded possibles pouch hung just below his waist and two powder horns dangled on either side of his chest, a small one for the fine priming powder and a larger one that held a coarser grained powder for the ball propellant. He had a black leather patch over his left eye that bore a colorfully beaded Indian thunderbird symbol.

"Pilgrims," called the stranger, "either of you seen that red nigger of mine?"

"Can't say as I have," said Lem. "You talkin' about a Injun?"

"A damned Delaware buck. Come all the way out to the big mountains with me in ought three from the Ohio Valley. 'Bout as trustworthy as a skinny snake, he be, and damned if he didn't run off a while back."

"Pa, maybe that's who was a-follerin' us," said Morgan.

"Eh, what's that you say, young feller?" asked the mountain man.

"Pa, he seen somebody a-skulkin' on our backtrail."

"That'd be that red heathen, Looking Loon. I calls him Loonie, 'cause he's tetched. He didn't steal nothin' from you, did he?"

"We didn't see him," said Lem. "I saw somebody a-ridin' a pony, but couldn't make it out ner his rider neither."

"Well, likely Loonie's gone on ahead. We got to get to rendezvous at Independence. Makin' camp yonder for t'night. You'uns is welcome to jine us."

"Obliged," said Lem.

"Who ye be, Pilgrim?"

"I'm Lem Hawke. This is my son, Morgan."

"They calls this old coon Patch. Dave Sisco's the name

I was borned to, but since I lost this eye to a Pawnee, they just calls this hoss Patch."

"We'll ride along with you," said Lem. Sisco was thirty-seven years old, but looked ten years older than Lem, who was only four years younger. Lem was wiry and lean, with no soft fat on him. Patch had girth to him, but he was what Lem would call "big-boned."

Morgan smiled. It was good to have company and Patch seemed likable enough.

Patch grunted. He clapped moccasined heels to his horse's flanks. The mule he was leading jerked to a start as the tether grew taut.

"Well, now, Lem Hawke, be you the man what burned down Spanish Jack's in St. Louie?"

"It was pure accidental," said Lem.

"Josie Montez, now, he thinks you did it deliberate after rubbing out Jack."

"Who's Josie Montez?"

"Why Spanish Jack's own brother, come up from New Orleans to mourn and pick over the leavings."

"Well, he's damned sure got it wrong," said Lem. "I never meant no harm to Spanish Jack." Lem looked at his son. Morgan was scowling. It was a touchy subject between the two. It had started over a young woman, Jack's daughter, Willa, who worked in the saloon. She seduced Morgan, and Lem had seen red, then gotten into a fight with her and Spanish Jack. A lamp had been knocked over and set fire to Willa's room. Lem had gotten the girl out, and Morgan, but Spanish Jack was unconscious. The flames spread so fast, the tavern had burned to the ground before he could get Spanish Jack out.

"Might be," said Patch. "But Josie's got blood in his eye and you might want to watch your backside ever' now and again."

"I'll do that," said Lem.

Morgan said nothing, but he could see that his pa was worried. Dick Hauser had warned Hawke that Spanish Jack had a brother who might want to take up the fight where it left off. Lem had met Hauser and his partner, Ormly Shields, on the Wilderness Trail when a member of another party had been killed by a band of Tuscaroras. Hauser and Shields had been captured, but managed to escape. Hauser, a trapper, had turned up later in St. Louis, much to Lem's surprise.

Long shreds of clouds floated like an armada of white-sailed galleons across the western sky as the sun lengthened the shadows of men, horses and mules across the afternoon prairie. Three swifts darted downriver, silent as wraiths. A lone hawk screamed like a baby, hovering over a patch of ground with quivering wings until its pinions collapsed and it fell like a stone from the sky.

Morgan looked around for Friar Tuck, but the dog was nowhere to be seen. The old man, Patch, chewed quietly on a chunk of tobacco, his eye taking everything in without seeming to make any effort, as if it was habit.

"You and the boy goin' to the big mountains?" Patch asked as the sun began to level off just above the horizon.

"Yep," said Lem.

"First time?"

Lem nodded.

"Figgered so. Might prove intrestin'."

"Huh?"

"Going by yourselfs, are ye?"

"Just me and Morg there."

Morgan was listening intently.

"Mighty lot of changes since ought three. Them red niggers ain't so hospitable no more. They's some as likes white men's scalps a-danglin' from their lodgepoles and lances. Take the Blackfeet, now. Time was when a man could trade with 'em and get some might fine pelts. But, now, you just don't never know. The Oglallies is the same."

"We aim to stay away from the Injuns," said Lem.

"Haw!" exclaimed Patch. "That ain't likely. They's a sight more of 'em than us. Beggars and thieves both. Might be you ought to learn the trappin' and tradin' from coons that knows them mountains."

"Do you trap with someone?"

"Waugh! Not this coon. But I trapped with some when I come out, first time or two so's I wouldn't lose my hair to the Rees. Once't I larnt to make sets, skin and cure, I trapped free. The companies come in and buys trappers till they own a man, lock, stock and bar'l. Me and Loonie, we stays to ourselfs. We ain't owned by nobody."

"Well, we never done it," said Lem.

"Wal, you got a heap to learn," said Sisco.

"Pa, tell him about Silas," Morgan offered.

Patch looked at the boy more closely.

"You talkin' about Silas Morgan? Why, sure. That's your name, ain't it? Any kin?"

"Nope," said Lem. "Knew him back in Virginny. He's the one what put the idee in my head to come out to the mountains."

"Pa named me after him. Silas, he give me this medicine horn," said Morgan, holding up his powder horn. "He got it from the Injuns."

"Well, if old Silas said he got it from them, I reckon he did. Last I saw of him, he was livin' with the Crow. Had him some Crow woman name of Blue Shell. Right purty woman, she was. You'd be findin' him up on the Yallerstone, I reckon."

"Might be we'll look him up," said Lem.

"Likely," said Patch.

They rode on in silence, watched as the sun went down.

"Pa, I reckon we ought to stop. I'm gettin' hungry."

Patch, who had been studying Morgan, broke in.

"That red nigger'll have some supper for us. He knows where we always camp. I like to ride into Independence fresh. Be there come mornin'. But Loonie will have some-thin' a-roastin' for us—rabbit, sage hen, prairie chicken or goat."

"How do you know?" asked Lem. "Maybe he run off."

"Oh, he does that. But, he knows I'll want vittles when I get to camp."

"How much farther?" asked Morgan.

"Why, I can smell somethin' now." Patch made a show of sniffing the air. Morgan sniffed, too.

"I smell it, too. Makes my stomach plumb jump," he said.

Lem laughed. He, too, could smell something roasting.

They rounded a bend of the river and saw a small fire near the bank. The Delaware's horse was hobbled. He was squatted next to the fire, a small animal spitted just above it.

Morgan stared at the Indian. Looking Loon was tall and lanky, with dark red skin. He wore moccasins, leggings, and a breechclout. His head was shaved except for a roach that split his skull in the middle. He looked fierce until he gave Morgan a lopsided idiotic grin. He touched his hand to the spitted carcass and turned it over the flames.

Patch did not say anything to the Indian when they rode up, but stripped his mule of its packs, unsaddled his horse and hobbled both animals. Lem and Morgan tended to their stock, leaving the horses and mules on long tethers to graze.

"Come on, boys, fill your bellies!" called Patch.

Lem and Morgan walked over to the fire, carrying pewter plates and forks. Patch was tearing off a haunch with his bare hands. Loonie had one side of a ribcage and was gnawing on it, grinning widely.

"Set," said Patch. He handed Lem one of the hindquar-ters, tore off the other one.

"Smells good," said Morgan.

Lem tore the chunk of meat in half, handed some to his son.

Morgan set his teeth to the flesh, bit off a mouthful. As

he chewed, he looked at Loonie, fascinated by the strange-looking Indian, oddly thrilled to be so close to one.

Patch tore at his food savagely, spoke out of the side of his mouth.

"You done good, Loonie," said the old trapper. Looking Loon signed with one hand, then the other.

"Don't he talk?" asked Lem.

"Nope, 'cept with his hands. Jesuits cut out his tongue, he says, when he was just a young buck." Patch made sign with his hands, sticking out his tongue and knifing across it with one finger.

Loonie nodded and grinned, grunted low in his chest. He opened his mouth as if to show Lem and Morgan that there was nothing there but teeth and a gaping hole.

Morgan winced as the image of a knife cutting out a man's tongue became vivid in his mind.

"Lordamighty," he said.

Patch laughed. "You'll pick up sign, too, you talk with Injuns much. They got different tongues, but they can talk with their hands easy as can be."

Morgan watched in fascination as Patch moved his hands, fluttered them like birds. The young man could make no sense of the silent conversation as Looking Loon replied with hand gestures of his own. There was something strange and poetic about such talk, though, and Morgan vowed to learn the language.

"Loonie says he hopes you like the meat," said Patch.

Loonie grinned and patted his belly, moved fingers to his mouth as they were doing with their forks.

"I can understand that sign, Pa," said Morgan. "He wants us to eat, fill our bellies."

"Why, shore," said Patch. "That's what Loonie was a-signin' all right."

The Delaware made some other signs to Patch and the trapper grunted as he tore into a piece of meat, bit off a mouthful.

Morgan was hungry after the long ride and he ate voraciously. Soon, there was nothing left but bones.

"Hey, Pa, I just remembered. Friar Tuck. He'd love to have some of these bones."

Lem looked around.

"I wonder where he went to?"

"You missin' somebody?" asked Patch.

"My dog," said Morgan. "He run off and I ain't seen him in a while."

"He'll be along," said Lem, as he tossed a bone onto the heap.

Loonie belched.

"A little dog?" asked Patch.

"A beagle," said Morgan, standing up. He started to walk away, then turned back to Patch.

"You seen him?" he asked Sisco.

"No, I reckon not. Ain't likely to, neither."

Morgan stiffened.

"What's that supposed to mean."

"Why, Loonie there loves dog," said Patch. "That's why he was so confounded proud of the vittles tonight. Didn't you see what he told me?"

"I don't understand hand talk," said Morgan.

"Well, what you think we et tonight, Pilgrim? Antelope? Jackrabbit?"

Morgan felt sick.

"I don't know," said the young man. "What was it?"

"Loonie there said it was dog. Ain't no finer food, he thinks. Eats 'em all the time. Warn't bad, was it?"

"That was my dog we ate?" asked Morgan.

"Likely," said Patch. "Dogs is scarce as hen's teeth in these parts. Wild Injuns eat 'em, too."

"Pa?" Morgan turned to his father.

Lemuel shrugged.

"I'm a-goin' to kill him," said Morgan, looking at Loonie. But he thought of the meal they had eaten and felt his stomach buck. He doubled over and vomited, tears streaming from his eyes. He staggered away from the campfire, deathly ill.

"Shame to waste a good supper like that," said Patch.

Lem stood there helplessly, watching his son retch.

"I'd be mighty careful of what you say to Morgan about that dog," said Hawke. "He could be a mite touchy about what he et."

Looking Loon laughed soundlessly, his hands weaving curious images in the air as the sun died in cold flames over the horizon.

4

Morgan stopped vomiting, finally. His face flushed and the veins stood out like ruddy ropes on his neck. He balled up his fists, wiped his mouth with his sleeve. He glared at Looking Loon, a rage flaring in his eyes.

"Morg," warned Lemuel.

"You sonofabitch," said Morgan, breaking into a run toward the Delaware.

"Whoa there," said Patch, sticking out a buckskinned leg. Morgan didn't see the barrier in time. He pitched forward, fell straight into the fire, skidded through it in a boil of sparks, scattered chunks of flaming wood and cherry-red coals.

"Yow!" exclaimed Morgan as a hot coal burned his stomach.

The Delaware rose to his feet, put a hand on the buckhorn handle of his skinning knife.

Lem reached for his own knife, but did not draw it.

Morgan turned over on his back, flailed at the sparkling coals on his belly.

"Simmer down, boy," said Patch, still sitting by the fire.

"Loonie there'll slit your gullet and think no more of it than squashing a bug."

"He kilt my dog," said Morgan, struggling to his feet. He brushed soot and ashes from his buckskin shirt.

"He didn't know it was your dog," said Patch. "And he didn't mean no harm. Fact is, he was a-tryin' to do some good, give us all some vittles to fill our empty bellies."

"It ain't right," said Morgan, still glowering.

"Sonny, you got some lessons to learn," said Patch softly.

Lem said nothing, but he kept his eyes on the Delaware, who still gripped the antler handle of his knife.

"Whatcha mean by that?" asked Morgan.

Patch stood up slowly, careful to make no sudden move. He stood where he could watch Lem as well as Looking Loon and Morgan. Sparks still glittered in the dry grasses around the fire and tendrils of smoke rose from some that had caught fire briefly, died out.

"Well, now, that little dog of yours, he was a civilized dog, warn't he?"

"I reckon," said Morgan sullenly.

"My guess is he never would have made it to the mountains, nohow. They ain't no laws out here and there's lots of Injuns what love dogmeat. And, if Loonie there hadn't of et him, then somethin' else would have made a meal of him. Might of been a griz or a timber wolf or a painter, but sooner or later that dog would have wound up in one belly or another."

"I could of took care of him," argued Morgan.

"I can see that," said Patch, smiling.

"Ain't no need to rag the boy," said Lemuel, his voice stony hard.

"Didn't mean no harm," said Patch. "A dog ain't worth a man's life, nor a boy's either."

"I ain't no boy," said Morgan.

"No, I reckon you ain't, but you ain't all haired over yet neither. Ain't no rules out here, Morgan Hawke, 'ceptin'

those you make as you go along gettin' snakebit and ball
froze and clawed and chased and shot at. Them's the rules
you live by or you don't live long."

"Well, dammitall," said Morgan, "he ought to pay me for
my dog."

"Morgan," said Lemuel.

"Pay you?" asked Patch. "For what? For fixin' your supper? Fillin' your belly?"

"I lost my supper," said Morgan.

"Ain't Loonie's fault. He did what he thought was right.
Now you back off and do some thinkin' on this. That Injun might not talk, but he sleeps with one eye open and he's
meaner'n a cornered painter when his back's up."

Patch made a sign to Looking Loon. The Delaware
laughed soundlessly and took his hand away from his knife.
He held up his hand, palm out flat, in the sign of peace.

"He wants to make friends with you, Morgan," said
Patch. "All you have to do is hold up your right hand to
show him you ain't got no weapon."

"I ain't a-gonna do it."

"Morgan," said Lem again.

"All right." Morgan held up his empty right hand. The
Delaware grinned. He made signs with both hands, but neither Lem nor his son understood.

"Loonie thinks you got sick on the meat. He still doesn't
know that was your dog. He's sorry if his cookin' don't
agree with you."

"What?" asked Morgan.

Lem started to laugh. Patch joined in. The Delaware
bounced up and down, shoulders shaking in silent laughter.
Morgan saw the idiocy of it and began to laugh, too. He
pointed to Loonie, then rubbed his belly. Loonie rubbed his
own belly, then acted out the vomiting sickness. He danced
around, showing them all what had happened to Morgan.
Patch howled with glee. Lemuel doubled up, gasped for
breath. Morgan laughed until tears came to his eyes.

Later, as he lay in his blankets, Morgan looked up at the stars. He could hear Patch snoring softly. His father was asleep beside him in his own bedroll. The Indian lay in a sitting position with his back against his saddle. Morgan didn't know if Looking Loon was asleep or not.

He thought about Friar Tuck and the things that Patch had said. Perhaps the dog would not have survived the journey to the mountains in any case. But, it was sad to think of the dog in his last moments, probably wagging his tail and trying to make friends with the Indian. He hoped Loonie killed him quick, but he didn't want to think about that. He would miss the dog, but he'd get over it, just like he got over his mother. Almost.

L em, Morgan, Patch and Looking Loon rode into Independence the next morning. Camped just outside the settlement were several groups of men, some of them drunk, most of them noisy and full of ginger. Some shot off their fusils and shouted a greeting to the newcomers. But others stood around in morose groups, strangely silent, smoking their pipes like mourners at a funeral.

"Somethin's up says this chile," said Patch.

The Missouri was over its banks, its waters raging, tossing chunks of driftwood and trunks of trees in its turbulent maelstrom. A keelboat lay on its side, well off the bank, its hull caved in, a large gaping hole below the waterline. Several men encircled a man lying on his back. Two men were pushing on his chest and belly, slapping his face. The man on the ground was soaking wet. He appeared to have drowned.

"Pa, is that man dead?" asked Morgan.

"I dunno," said Lem. "He don't look alive."

"Deader'n a stump," said Patch. He and Looking Loon spoke in quick sign.

"There's Jocko DeSam," said Morgan, pointing to a buckskinned trapper at the edge of one group.

"I thought he was long gone up that river," said Lem.

"Ain't nobody goin' up that there Missoura," said Patch. "Look at that keelboat stove in."

A tall man walked away from the group surrounding the dead man. He was smartly dressed in fringed buckskins, a brace of pistols tucked in his sash. The shoulders of his shirt were gaudily decorated with quillwork and his moccasins were colorfully beaded. He carried a large, knife, possibles bag, powder horns. The man looked at the newcomers and frowned.

"Who's that?" asked Lem.

"That tall feller? Major Angus Llewellyn MacDougal is what he calls hisself. Slick as a buckhorn blade, wily as a timber wolf. That's one of his boats a-lyin' there. He had him three last I knew."

"There's the other two," said Morgan, pointing upstream. "They're busted up, too."

Lem saw the boats. They were even more badly battered than the one close by. One of them had a tree driven through its hull. The other didn't look like a boat so much as a pile of broken lumber.

As they rode closer, the noise of the river increased, roaring in their ears like a flood. Men were climbing over the broken hulks of the keelboats, salvaging their packs, food, weapons, traps, odds and ends. Several of the men onshore were clad in sodden buckskins, hatless, their hair flattened with dampness. The waters of the Missouri boiled with angry gray and black water. A man looking through the debris cursed in several tongues, angrily threw his tomahawk against the hull of a keelboat, where it stuck.

A man spread out his blankets to dry in the sun, shook his head as he looked at the destruction around him.

Morgan and Lem saw DeSam arguing with a taller man, shaking his fist.

"Same old Jocko," said Lem.

Lem and Morgan could not hear the voices above the

roar of the river, but Jocko DeSam stopped shaking his fist at the taller man and turned toward them.

Morgan lifted his hand in a tentative wave.

Jocko turned from the man, waved back. In a few moments he called out to them.

"Bienvenue, mes amis," called Jocko DeSam, walking toward them. "You have come, at last. There has been much rain up on the river, look what she do to our boats. We have lost several horses and mules. Some men have gone to look for them upstream. But I saw a dead mule float by a few minutes ago, *sacré bleu!"*

"It's a mess," said Lem. "What will you do now, Jocko?"

"Ah, some will fix the boats, but I am going to walk, no? It will not be so fast, but *c'est la vie, non?"*

"We been lost," said Morgan.

"Maybe that is good, *non?* The wind she blow and the twister, she tear everything up."

Several of the villagers stood next to trader's tents, jabbering in low tones.

"Light down," said Patch. "Looks like there's goin' to be a pow-wow."

"What's that?" asked Morgan.

"Talkin'" said Patch. "Them as figger to use the river are going to have to go overland, either up it or straight acrost to the Platte."

"What about you?" asked Lem.

"All the same to me. I didn't figger to find room on a keelboat nohow."

Lem and Morgan dismounted. Jocko DeSam, whose real name was Jacques Decembre, shook Lem's hand. The Hawkes had first met the French trapper in Kentucky. All three had shared a jail cell together after a brawl in a hatter's establishment.

"Where can we ford?" asked Lem.

"Where did you come cross the river?" asked DeSam. He showed no trace of the anger he had shown the tall man, who now seemed to be barking orders at some of the other trappers.

"Way down yonder where the Osage feeds in. We just hopped from gravel bar to gravel bar."

"Ah, the gravel bar. She is always big trouble for the boats. But, I think we go up the river, *non?*"

Lem and Morgan exchanged looks.

"Ain't that where you broke up?" asked Lem.

"But the storm she has passed, *non?* The river she will calm down like a woman when she is petted and we will find a place to cross. Even if we do not, we can always climb the hills like goats, eh?" Jocko laughed. The Hawkes failed to see the humor. They were going into a great unknown, and so far, they had seen that unknown turn savage.

Jocko beckoned to them. He walked back to the rubble and picked out his horse and pack animals. Dick Hauser emerged from behind a broken keelboat and waved to them. Men looked at Jocko as if he had gone insane.

"Wait'll I get my horse," said Dick. "I'll ride with you."

"Ha, you are one crazy man, Dick," said Jocko. "We go without the boat."

"I ain't stayin' around here," said Hauser. "That god-damned Scotsman's plumb crazy." He jabbed a thumb toward the man the Hawkes had seen arguing with Jocko. Hauser was a lean, scraggle-bearded man, five foot nine or so, with a chaw of tobacco bulging one cheek. His buckskins were worn smooth, black from charred wood and streaked with grease from past meals on the frontier. "He thinks he's God almighty."

Lem smiled wanly. He felt nervous around Dick Hauser. He was a man he had thought dead, killed by Tuscarora Indians back in the Cumberlands, only to turn up alive and seasoned in St. Louis. His partner, Ormly Shields, hadn't been seen, but Dick said that he had survived the war party as well.

A tall man, dressed in a light capote, buckskin trousers and leggings, separated himself from a party of men working on one of the damaged keelboats. He walked towards Jocko and the Hawkes as Dick caught up his horse and pack mules.

"Uh-oh," said Jocko, "we are going to get the argument. Do you have your licenses?"

"Who's that?" asked Morgan, staring at the broad-shouldered man DeSam had been shaking a fist at moments before. The stranger carried a big knife thrust in a studded leather scabbard in his sash. The man wore a wide-brimmed hat with a large eagle feather jutting from its beaded band. He carried a long flintlock rifle. It looked like a toy in his oversized hand. The man wore a neatly trimmed beard, large sideburns. His hair was thick and shorn just above the shoulders. A large birthmark colored his forehead like a swatch of rust or faded vermillion.

"That is the Major," said Jocko, sotto voce. "Old Angus himself."

Jocko had mentioned the Major before, back in Kentucky when they had first met.

"Do you work for him?" asked Lem.

"Not anymore," said the Frenchman bitterly. "Shusss! Be careful. He's now the booshway."

Before Lem could ask Jocko what he meant, Major Angus Llewellyn MacDougal was upon them, taller than the horses.

"Och, Jocko, do you leave us with the boats to go on ahead?"

"Mais oui," said Jocko DeSam. "We ride the river."

"Who is this boy?" demanded MacDougal. "I hope he's here to see one of you off, because he's much too young to go to the mountains. And you," he said to Lem, "if you're going past this point, I'll need to see your license."

Lem took papers wrapped in oilcloth out of his possibles pouch.

He had obtained his trapper's license from the French bourgeois, the "booshway," just before leaving St. Louis. But Morgan had not been with him, and Lem had not gotten a license for his son. Usually, the brigade leader saw to it that all his men were licensed, but Lem had spoken to Pierre Choteau, Sr., and gotten a license through the St. Louis Missouri Fur Company.

Lem handed the license papers to the Major. MacDougal looked at them, frowned, then handed them back.

"Those are just for you. The boy cannot go."

"He's my boy," said Lem. "And he's a-goin'."

Angus scoured Lem with a raking look, cocking one eyebrow so that it arched up into his scarlet birthmark.

"Aye, and you'll bury the lad somewhere between here and the land of the Crow. How old are ye, laddie?"

"I'm fifteen," said Morgan, bristling as he thrust out his chest. "We come all the way from Kentucky, my pa and me."

"Then you must be the scalawags who burnt down Spanish Jack's and raised such a ruckus in St. Louis. Aye, I've been hearin' tales of you Hawkes all the way from Nashville from Jocko here and Nat Sullard and a dozen other flapmouths."

"Warn't my fault," said Lem, taking an instant dislike to the Major.

"But it shows a bungling that will give ye a grave marker in a land that tolerates no mistakes, am I right, Jocko?"

"He will make his way," said Jocko quietly. "He can trap on his father's license—or I have an extra one."

"Then, you've decided not to come with my brigade, is it, Jocko? Well, you still owe me beaver from last year."

"I will pay you, Major. I do not wish to have you cheat me with the furs."

The Major's eyes flickered dangerously.

"Aye, laddie, be careful what you say now. I expect an honest day's work and a fair tally. I take what's me due, no more, no less. And, you are making a big mistake not coming with my brigade. I can make trouble for you."

Jocko said nothing, but the battle lines were drawn.

"Come," said DeSam. "We go."

"I'll not have you talkin' to my men," said MacDougal. "Stay to your own grounds. If I catch you with furs taken from my creeks, I'll tack your French hide to a willow hoop."

"I trap where I please," said Jocko, kicking his heels into his horse.

"Mind it's not where I please, then, Jocko laddie."

The Major's voice was pleasant enough, but there was an undercurrent of threat in his tone. He doffed his hat to Lem, scowled at Morgan.

"Mind I warned you, Hawke," said Angus. "That lad's not dry behind the ears yet and there's perils ahead, perils enough for a man grown and seasoned. And, if he takes fur, he'd better have a license. I ought to throw you both in irons as it is."

"I can take care of myself," said Morgan defiantly, but he urged Boots to a trot just to get away from the man.

"I don't like that Scotsman," Lem told Jocko. "He pure puts a burr under my blanket."

"He's a hard chunk of rock," said DeSam. "I see how he cheat me, so I do not trap with him this year. And, now he is the booshway for the dam' government. Well, maybe he is not so smart. But, he knows the beaver, eh? He is one hell of a fighter, *non?* He speak with Indian in Indian talk, and they think he plenty brave."

"I ain't afraid of him," said Morgan, looking back over his shoulder.

Angus MacDougal was still standing there, staring at Morgan, shaking his head.

5

Calvin "Pappy" Roth and Nat Sullard joined DeSam's bunch. Major MacDougal watched the men go, the only sign of his anger a clenched fist that he quickly flexed back to normal once everyone had seen it. He smiled to himself with the secretive smile of a man who has just set a concealed trap.

As the small band of men and Hawke's boy, Morgan, rode from sight, Angus walked over to a man working on one of the keelboats. Fletcher Bancroft was a short, muscular man with sloping shoulders, a heavy beetled brow, hair matted and tangled to his shoulders. He was bare to the waist and carried a ten-pound maul in his gnarled left hand. He had been knocking at the pins of a deck cannon.

"We lost the bow gun, Major," said the man.

"Never mind that. How long before we're in the water?"

"Two days, three maybe."

"I want one boat loaded and ready to sail on the morrow."

"Too damned soon, Major."

"Not soon enough, Fletch. Tomorrow. Put all available men on a single craft. You pass the word, then there's something I want you to do."

"What might that be, Major?"

"I want you to get three men and go after Jocko. Bring him back to me."

"He won't like it none."

"He knows too much to go on ahead. I don't want him as competition."

"You want me to kill him, Major?"

"That would be an acceptable alternative."

"How's that?"

"Yes, if you can't get him back here without trouble, put

his lamp out. Oh, and bring the lad back here, too. I'll not have a young 'un muckin' up the year's work. We'll put him in irons and send him back to St. Louis."

Fletcher grinned. He threw down his maul and started calling out to the men working on the keelboats.

"Hear ye, hear ye!" he yelled. "Gather 'round and listen up, you mangy bunch of gap-toothed louts. We got work to do!"

Angus smiled that strange slow smile of his. There was no warmth in it. It was the smile of a mourner at a funeral where his worst enemy was going six feet underground.

A few yards away, Patch Sisco slunk back behind a stack of barrels. He had gone there to piss and had heard every word between Major MacDougal and that worthless scoundrel, Fletcher. But something about the Major's behavior made him wonder if Angus wasn't up to something. He had the odd feeling that he had just seen a man step out onto a stage, give a speech and then go off the boards to laugh at everyone in the audience.

Dick Hauser joined Jocko, Lem and Morgan as they rode away from Independence.

"Feller tolt me they was some pirogues cached up yonder and some feller put a bullboat in the bushes thirty mile upriver."

"That is good," said Jocko. "I will bet the prime beaver plew we can find a keelboat with some room if they put the boat to shore when the storm she hit."

"We might get lucky," said Hauser.

"We couldn't fit all these goods in a pirogue," said Lem.

"No, but the river could carry some of us until we find a big keelboat. There were three or four boats ahead of us."

"Seems like a lot of fuss. Horse can take a man anywhere."

"Ah, but not like the boats, eh? In the boats, a man can

look for Indians and sleep at night with both of the eyes closed, *non?*"

Lem laughed wryly.

"I think I'd rather be on dry land," said Morgan.

"We will see," said Jocko cryptically.

Morgan rode away from the others, swelling up inside with the immensity of the country, feeling dwarfed by the sky. Cottonwood trees marked the serpentine course of the river, green beacons cutting a swath through wild prairie. Morgan glutted himself on it, watching every waterbird take flight, gazing in awe at the bluffs that seemed like monuments built by some ancient giant. He saw eagles and hawks, the lazy carousels of turkey buzzards, floating in circles on invisible currents of air. He heard the *yawp* of a blue heron and watched its ungainly stride as it flapped across a sandbar, disturbed from its fishing by the passing horsemen and pack animals. Morgan felt his own muscles strain until it finally gained flight and soared above the trees, majestic at last.

That night, they camped below some bluffs some fifteen miles upriver from Independence. Jocko explained that they'd have to take turns standing guard.

"With the rocks behind us, we do not have so much to watch, eh?"

"You think Indians will attack us?" asked Morgan.

"I do not think so, but sometimes they are very quiet and when they do not want to trade, they like to take the hair and the goods for free." Jocko laughed at his joke. Morgan looked at his father. Lem only shrugged and began to strip the mules of their cargo.

Morgan thought it would have been better to have ridden to the top of the limestone bluffs where they would be able to see and hear anyone approach, but he said nothing. There were signs that others had been to this place before. There were burned rocks and flattened grasses, remains of firewood. For such a big country, it seemed to attract a lot of travelers. However, he knew that once someone left the river, or rode away from a creek, such country would swallow them up. Anyone who rode into the country had to stay close to water, or die.

The dank smell of the river wafted on the close summer air as dusk drew the shadows long and thickened in the grasses and on the ground. The littoral cacophony of insects shattered the silence and a great horned owl hooted like a rooster with laryngitis, its bass notes quavering in the distance.

"No fires," whispered Pappy Roth, as he strode up to the Hawkes. "Jocko says to stay quiet."

Pappy turned on his heel and went back to where the others were making camp for the night.

"Pa, do you think we'll see Indians?"

"No. Jocko probably knows what to do. Just keep your eyes open and don't make no noise."

Morgan finished stripping Boots and helped his father unload the panniers from the pack saddles. He and Lem hobbled their horses and put all the stock on a single tether line, anchored it to a cottonwood in sight of their camp. They broke out their bedrolls, set them head-to-head as they had done each night along their journey.

"Let's us find us a spot to ourselves, Morg," said Lem, taking one of the wooden canteens and a leather pouch that they carried their "day grub" in. "Get some food in us and talk, just you and me."

Morgan grinned. Sometimes his pa made him feel full growed.

They walked to a spot down the bluff where there was a slight depression, almost a cave. Lem hunkered down and searched through the "day grub" pouch for some dried elk and fried dough.

"Set," he told Morgan.

"What you wanta talk about, Pa?"

Lem handed his son a chunk of brisket and an oblong piece of fried dough. He held an index finger to his lips.

"Well, we done started," said Lem, biting into another quarter pound of dried brisket, "and so far not much has gone right. I got me a bad feeling 'bout this bunch."

"You don't like 'em, Pa?"

"Didn't say that, son. It's just that it seems that Major feller back downriver didn't like us all goin' none. And, they's got to be some reason these mountain trappers go in such big bunches."

"Indians, likely," said Morgan, chewing a morsel of sun-toughened meat.

"Likely. So, I think we better watch ourselves, ever' step of the way. DeSam has got him a grudge with that MacDougal, and if you notice, he keeps watchin' over his shoulder."

"I noticed."

Lem swallowed a half-chewed wad of elk meat. His Adam's apple bobbed and rippled like a snake swallowing a field mouse.

"We stay together all the time, you and me, Morg. Don't trust nobody too much."

"Aw, Pa. . . ."

"You just mind your P's and Q's, like I say."

"I will, Pa."

"I got me some funny feelin's," said Lem.

"Like what, Pa?"

"I can't rightly say. But, I got me somethin' pricklin' at me like a itch."

"Maybe it's because we don't know where we're goin'," said Morgan.

Lem nodded. They spoke no more until they had finished washing down the last of their supper with the warm water from the canteen.

DeSam called all of them together just before dark.

"We all have the fatigue, no?" he said. "But, we do not all sleep at once, eh? Maybeso, we draw the grasses to see who take the turns standing guard. I will take the watch nobody else wants. We do the four watches. Dark to the tenth hour, the tenth hour to the midnight, the midnight to the third hour and the third hour until the light she break. We start with the longest blade of grass. Does it not make the sense?"

All of the men nodded. Pappy Roth cut several blades of grass with his knife, handed them to Jocko. Jocko turned his back on the assemblage and bit the grass stalks to various lengths, counted out four blades.

He fisted his hand, held the jutting grasses to each man. He skipped Morgan.

"We got us an extry two men," said Dick Hauser.

"We will have the two men on the last of the watch," said DeSam.

"I want to draw one," said Morg.

"Non," said Jocko softly.

Morgan's face reddened and he started to rise. Lem put a hand on his shoulder, pressing him back down.

"But, Pa . . ."

"When you get a little more experience," said Lem.

"Aw, but . . ."

Lem silenced him with a narrowing of his eyes, a slight shake of his head.

Dick won the eight to ten watch, Pappy the ten to midnight, Nat Sullard had the next shortest. Lem got the morning watch.

"Is there anybody who wants to make the change?" asked Jocko.

They all shook their heads.

"I will take the last watch with Lem Hawke," said DeSam.

"I could do it with you, Pa," said Morgan as the two walked toward their bedrolls.

"I know, son. Let Jocko run it his way until he gets to know you better."

"But, I want to watch, too."

"Why don't you ask Dick if he needs some he'p?" said Lem.

Morgan's eyes flashed with light. He ran off to talk to Hauser while Lem laid out his rifle and pistols, checking the pans and flints.

Dusk crept over the camp, shawling out the last of the western light. Frogs croaked in the river bottoms, and insects sawed a cacophony of sound. Lem sat there on his bedroll, listening to a whippoorwill yammering from a nearby tree.

Morgan came back, a hangdog expression on his face.

"Dick didn't want no help," he told his father.

"Set, then. If you're a-itchin', best you start lookin'. I done kilt four ticks and swatted two of the biggest 'skeeters I ever saw."

Lem scratched his leg, probed inside the tops of his moccasins. He dug a tick out of his flesh and put a thumbnail to it. Morgan reached back over his shoulder, put a hand inside his shirt. He, too, found a tick and sliced it in two with his fingernails.

"Likely, there's more," said Lem.

"I can feel the little boogers," said Morgan, searching in earnest now, under his armpits, around his back, in his crotch. Lem slapped at a mosquito. His palm smacked against his cheek.

"Critters'll eat a man alive," he said.

"They don't bother me," said Morgan proudly.

"They just ain't seen you yet," said his father.

A few moments later, Morgan heard a buzzing in his ears. He slapped his face, but missed. A second later, a mosquito was drawing blood from the welt.

Later, the two stopped their bug hunt, having scratched themselves raw and slapped their faces long enough.

"I don't like it here, none," said Lem softly.

"Why, Pa?

"Dunno. Just a feelin'."

"Feels kinda closed in," said Morgan.

"This close to the river ain't good."

He was remembering the storm, thought Morgan. He could hear the river now, almost like a whisper underneath the other sounds. It sounded far away, but he could imagine it in his mind, see its forbidding muddy waters swirling past the cottonwoods, nibbling at the banks, moving earth, turning it to silt and sand. It was a powerful feeling he had about that river. It meant a journey to him, but it also meant adventure and danger. The river was everything and it was not tame. He had already seen its power, what it had done to the keelboats.

"Best turn in," said Lem, sighing.

"I reckon," said Morgan, but he sat there for several moments until he heard his father's soft snores. Then, he lay on his bedroll, found the right position, closed his eyes.

The night sounds soothed Morgan to sleep.

Later, he was awakened roughly, and he thought he was dying.

Morgan felt a hand over his mouth, smothering him. He struggled to rise, but powerful hands pinned him down. He smelled the foul breath of a man as he leaned down in the darkness.

"Don't make a sound, son. I come as friend."

Morgan whipsawed furiously, trying to break free.

"Be quiet or you might be dead," said the voice. He recognized it as belonging to the trapper they had met downriver: Patch. "Here's your sack of possibles. I've got your rifle."

Morgan stopped struggling.

"We got to get you out of here quick. Just foller me," said Patch, taking his hand away from Morgan's mouth.

"Where's my pa?" whispered the young man.

"With Loonie. Come on, follow me."

"I don't—"

"Shh!" said Patch.

"Where's my horse?" Morgan whispered as Patch guided him through the darkness.

"Taken care of. Don't talk no more."

Puzzled, Morgan allowed himself to be pushed along blind. His mind was still foggy from sleep and he wondered where Patch was taking him.

Morgan stumbled and Patch had to pull on the youth's arm to keep him from falling. Morgan knew they were climbing up the bluff.

Patch shoved Morgan down behind an outcropping of rock and handed him his rifle.

"You set real still, young 'un. If your teeth get to chatterin', you bite down on a stick. No noise."

Morgan nodded. He shivered, but he knew it was not from the chill. He heard the soft pad of Patch's moccasins and then it was still. He knew the trapper had gone back down the spine of the bluff. But why?

It was quiet for a few moments. Then, Morgan heard a moccasin scrape on stone. Something rustled in the brush down below, where the trappers were camped.

Gradually, Morgan's eyes adjusted to the darkness. Clouds hid the moon and stars, but there was enough light that he could distinguish shapes. He could not tell what the shapes were; he could only guess. The night changed everything, and he was always fascinated by it. At times, back in Kentucky, when he was in the woods late, he would watch the shadows take shape and try to guess what they were. Or, when he went into the woods early in the morning, when it was still dark, he would mark each shape. Often, they resembled the heads or bodies of animals. Then, in the light, he would see that they were only trees and bushes, leaves and stumps, or rocks.

He made no sound as he looked around. He thought he

might be alone, but he heard someone breathing a few feet away. The silence took on an eerie aspect. He wished whoever was there would say something. Anything. He felt as if he was being watched. But he couldn't see anyone's eyes. He couldn't even see a face in the pitch-black hood of night that pressed on him now with a slow, suffocating terror.

Morgan slid his right hand down his side, searching for his knife. He touched the handle, then something moved close to him and he felt iron-hard fingers close around his wrist. His heart bumped as it skipped beats and his throat froze with a terrible lump that had not been there before.

He felt a man's hot breath on his face and then a hand clamped over his mouth. He felt himself being pushed backward, toward the edge of the bluff. He wanted to fight back, to kick his attacker, but the man straddled him, pinning his legs to the ground.

He wriggled to free himself from the grasp of whoever had hold of him, but the man only increased the pressure.

Morgan couldn't see who it was, but he knew that in another few seconds he would be shoved over the bluff to fall to his death far below in the empty, mindless dark.

6

Morgan heard footsteps crunching softly on the loose stones atop the bluff. He heard a branch brush against a deerskin legging.

"Leave him be, Loonie," said Patch softly.

Suddenly, Morgan felt a release of pressure over his mouth as the Indian took his hand away. He felt himself being pulled roughly away from the edge of the precipice back to a sitting position.

"I told you not to move, kid."

"Damn you, Patch," growled Morgan. "If your nigger ever touches me again, I'll gut him."

He knew Patch was laughing because there was a change in the man's breathing, but the laugh wasn't out loud. He saw two shapes dimly silhouetted against the black sky. He felt that both of them were probably laughing at him.

Patch knelt down next to the boy.

"Looky yonder," he whispered into Morgan's ear.

He felt a hand at the back of his head. Patch turned the boy's head to the east.

"What is it?" Morgan asked, his voice barely audible. He saw flames dancing in the darkness. On the river, or near it.

"Torches," said Patch in his ear. "Them coons was comin' to grab you up and take you back to MacDougal."

"How come?"

" 'Cause the Major's got forty kinds of bat in his belfry, that's how come. He wanted them niggers to cotch Jocko, too, and drag him back."

"I don't understand."

"MacDougal don't have all his hinges in place, son. Now, you just set and keep your flap shut."

Morgan watched the torches disappear and reappear through the trees. There were three of them. If he had felt odd before, he was deeply bewildered now. It was as if he was not really there, sort of dreaming. He felt as if he was watching something strange and evil and was powerless to do anything about it.

"Where's my pa?" he asked.

"I got him in a tree. Jocko's in another. You just sit tight, son. You be quiet as a dead beaver or I'll put the butt of my rifle to your skull and put you to sleep."

It was quiet for a long time after that, except for the incessant sawing of mosquitoes. Morgan watched the torches until his eyes burned in their sockets. Then, they winked out. He thought the men might have dowsed them in the river, but he heard no hissing sound. The only sound was in his mind and it wouldn't go away.

Lem listened harder than he had ever listened before, trying to shut out the whine of a mosquito in his ear. He, too, had seen the torchlights, knew what they meant. Patch hadn't told him much, only that some men from the Major's brigade were coming to do them harm. He sat in the crotch of a cottonwood tree, a portion of his butt dead and bloodless. He didn't dare move, though he felt the sting of a mosquito's needle on his cheek. He could not see Jocko DeSam, but he knew that he was sitting up in another tree like a raccoon, not twenty yards away.

It was so quiet for such a long time that Lem thought he was no longer breathing. That everything in the world had disappeared or come to a halt.

Then, he heard it. The soft rustle of moccasins on the grasses, the quiet rasp of 'skins brushing against bushes, the faint tink of rustled leaves.

The noises stopped. Then, he heard a low whisper. He scanned the ground below, thought he saw someone skulking toward his bedroll. A second later, he saw shadowy movement, then heard a loud crunch.

Lem brought his rifle to his shoulder, careful to make no sound. As the shadow bent down, he drew a bead from memory, for he could not see his sights in the darkness.

Suddenly, without warning, Lem got the shakes. He hadn't had those since he was a boy, the first time he saw a buck in his iron sights. And he hadn't had them since. But he had them now. He couldn't find a target, didn't know whether he was shooting a bear or a man.

Sweat beaded up in his brows, dripped downward, stinging his eyes.

Then, the night exploded with bright orange blossoms

and the thunder of big bore rifles. Lem heard the deadly whisper of flints striking steel, the low *whoosh* of powder igniting in the pan. The camp lit up with dark shapes as men scurried out of the crossfire. The leaves rattled in the trees, lead balls thunked into limestone and burnt bark from cottonwood trunks. Lem tried to find a target, but the light faded, leaving his retinas glowing with fiery sparks.

Lem heard men shouting, running.

"Goddamnit," he muttered. Stuck in the tree. Helpless as a pig on an iced pond.

"Get the hell down out of that tree, Hawke," yelled Dick Hauser.

"By gar, they get away." Jocko's voice.

Lem listened to the crash of men running through brush, the crackle of small limbs, the thrash of leaves. Rocks rattled down from the bluff and the dank breath of limestone assailed his nostrils, mixing with the heady scent of the mud and sand-laden river swirling past banks thick with vegetation clinging to fragile moorings.

Hawke dropped from the tree, bent his knees to absorb the shock. He gripped his rifle tightly, rocked back on his heels until he regained his balance.

On the ground, he could see even less. The noises were drifting away. He stood there, not knowing what to do, wondering if he'd knocked all the powder out of his pan when he jumped down from the tree.

"Hawke, come on," said a voice.

"Who's that?"

"Hauser."

Lem felt a hand touch his elbow.

"Dick? Where we goin'?"

"After them bushwhackers."

"Hell, I can't see a thing."

"Foller me."

Dick stepped into the darkness and Lem had to jump

after him to keep up. He followed Hauser more by sound than sight, but knew they were heading toward the river. Ahead, they heard shouts and the sharp crack of a rifle.

Blindly, Lem raced after Dick Hauser. Sapling limbs slashed at his face, brush tugged at his leggings. He tripped, cursed silently. His breath burned hot in his chest and he gulped in air as the pace quickened.

He wondered how Dick knew where to go in the darkness. Then, he saw dark sky, the silhouettes of trees growing along the river. A few moments later, Hauser stopped at the bank of the Missouri. They heard men talking in low, gruff tones. Then there was another rifle shot, followed, in quick succession, by two more. Bright flashes of orange light sprouted from barrels downriver.

"Hooowaaay!" shouted Jocko DeSam.

"Come on," said Hauser. "It looks like they got 'em."

"Who in hell are they?"

"Damned if I know. Thieves. Scundrels."

Dick walked downriver, Lem right behind him, holding his rifle at the ready.

Nat Sullard and Pappy Roth stood looking down at the ground. Jocko was on his knees, turning over one of the men he had shot. There were three men stretched out, their chests soaked with blood. One had been shot in the groin as well.

Lem's breathing settled down and the fire in his chest subsided. His nostrils filled with the smell of dank river water and death.

"One got away," said Jocko, standing up. He stood his rifle on its butt. His powder horn rattled as he brought it to the muzzle. "Goddamn dark. Can't see no goddamn thing."

He poured powder down his muzzle, going by instinct and feel. Then, he pulled a strip of patching from his possibles pouch. He stretched the cloth across the muzzle, fished a ball from his pouch and centered it, thumbed it down the barrel until it was flush. Grabbing his patch knife, he cut the excess patch away. With his wiping stick, he eased the ball six inches down the barrel, then rammed it home atop the ninety or one hundred grains of powder he figured he'd poured. He seated the ball, then primed his pan, blowing away the excess powder, shoved down the frizzen plate over the pan.

"Dick, strike us some light," said Nat Sullard. "Let's see who we got here."

Hauser stepped away from the bunch and knelt down. Lem heard the clatter of a tin box, the rattle of flint and steel. Dick scratched sparks from the steel, set the tinder afire. A few moments later, he had a small fire. Jocko tore cattails from the river, set them afire. He swung the torches over the faces of the dead men.

"Know 'em?" asked Lem.

"That one, he's Lucien LeBoef," said Jocko with solemnity. He kicked the corpse in the side, muttering *"Merde."*

"This 'uns Dave Trask," said Nat, pointing to the middle man.

"And that other'n, he be Ernie Parsons," said Dick Hauser. "Warn't none of 'em no account."

Lem sucked in a breath. The men looked like lifeless husks, their faces gaunt in the fireglow, the eyes vacant, the skin pallid as if the blood had drained out of their heads. He felt queasy.

Jocko DeSam looked over at Hawke, muttered something to Nat Sullard. Nat spoke to the others. Lem heard them stripping the dead men of their possibles pouches, moccasins, knives, stacking their rifles. A moment later, he heard a splash and turned around. He started toward the men coming after the second body, when Jocko stopped him and braced him by the shoulders.

"What in hell are you doin'?" asked Lem.

"That be as good a-buryin' as they deserve, eh, *mon ami?*"

"Goddamnit, Jocko, you just killed three men. Why?"

"Ah, it is a long, long story, eh?"

"Well, maybe you better start explainin'."

"Ah, *oui,* maybe so, it is a good time to talk of this and of other things. Come, we find Patch and Loonie and your boy. We hold the pow-wow, *non?*"

There were two more splashes and Lem shook his head.

"There was another man, Jocko. I seen him," said Sullard.

"Yes, he is not here. Patch told me it was Fletch."

"Who's Fletch?" asked Lem.

"Fletcher Bancroft," said Dick Hauser. "A damned snake, that one. I shoulda figgered this was his handiwork, skulkin' up to our camp in the dark, sneakin' up on us."

"I just don't know if I want anymore of this," said Lem. "All this killin', this treachery."

"Ah, *mon ami,* this is nothing," said Jocko. "These men were the vermin, eh? They kill plenty men before they get the number come up, *non?* This MacDougal, he give Jocko the double cross and now he want to rub me out, put the grass in my mouth."

Lem didn't understand what Jocko was saying, but it was something to hold on to while he tried to settle his senses. He could not get the images of the dead men's faces out of his mind, and he thought of the man Morgan had killed and wondered if he was not bringing his boy into a worse world than they left back in Kentucky.

"Bring the torch," said Jocko to Hauser. "We will light the fire and make the big pow-wow. We will smoke the pipe and make the talk, eh? Maybe we burn the woodtick, is it not? Come, Hawke, you listen to Jocko DeSam, eh? He tell you plenty." Jocko scraped a tick from the back of his hand, pinched it deftly between thumb and forefinger until blood oozed from its flattened body.

Jocko tugged on Lem's sleeve. They followed the torch back to the disrupted camp through the eerie shadows it cast, single-file, like men going to the gallows, silently, each with his own thoughts about the night's foul work.

Morgan followed Patch and the Delaware down the bluff. His brain was teeming with questions, but he was having too much trouble with his footing. The Indian and the trapper made no sounds with their moccasins, but Morgan kicked stones loose and he felt as if the bluff might slide out from under him and pitch him into the blackness below.

At the bottom, clouds of mosquitoes rose up and enveloped Morgan's face. He swatted blindly in front of his face to keep from breathing them in.

He heard the other men coming back to the camp, their voices low-pitched, throaty with manly rumbles.

Patch and Loonie disappeared in the shadows of the bluff, leaving Morgan alone by his bedroll.

"Hallo the camp," called Hauser.

"We'uns be here," answered Patch. Moments later, the band of men stalked into view, single-file shadows carrying rifles.

"Dick, make us the little fire, eh?" said Jocko. "The smoke she will make the mosquitoes go back to the river. Nat, you keep the eye out, *non?*"

"I reckon I kin," said Sullard.

Morgan slunk over to his father, whispered a question into his ear.

"What happened, Pa?"

"I'll tell you later," Lem said quickly.

Hauser soon had a small fire ablaze. The light flickered on the men's faces. Sullard stood a few yards away, behind an Osage orange tree, his rifle nestled between a fork in the limbs, pointed toward the river.

"Why would that damned Scotsman send those killers after us?" asked Lem, looking directly at DeSam.

"Ah, it is the politics," said Jocko. "It is the goddamn fur, *non?* Eh, these company, they kill for what they want."

"We don't work for no company," said Morgan, feeling his father's anger, sensing that his pa was all by himself, that something had changed between him and the other men. "We ain't done nothin' to them."

"That's right," said Lem. "Was it you they was after, Jocko?"

"Eh, mebbe so," said DeSam, shrugging. He waved a hand through an antic scrim of mosquitoes. The other men slapped their faces at random, scratched at woodticks crawling into their moccasins. "Maybe he also want the boy." He pointed to Morgan. Young Hawke's expression of consternation showed his puzzlement. His eyebrows knitted in a sudden scowl and he blinked like a barn owl.

"Me?" Morgan asked.

"You tell him, Patch, eh?" said Jocko.

Patch walked over to the fringe of the glow thrown by the fire, hunkered down on his haunches. His hand slid down his rifle barrel and stopped at the brass trigger guard.

"The Major, he's got him some conscripts," said the grizzled old trapper. "Young 'uns he totes up to the mountains. He buys 'em, trades for 'em, don't pay 'em much er nothin' 'tall. I reckon he had his eye on your boy all right."

"You mean he wanted to steal Morgan?" asked Lemuel.

"Likely he wouldn't call it stealin', more like teachin'. Slavery's what I calls it. Cheap labor. He's cheated more'n one lad and a few growed ones, too, I reckon."

Morgan swallowed an imaginary lump in his throat. He looked at his father.

"Well, he better stay away from my boy," said Lem. "He even looks at Morg cross-eyed, I'll lay him out cold."

"I think we meet the Major again," said Jocko. "I think he work for that bastard Astor."

"Time was you was askin' me to hook up with him," said Lem.

"I did not know him so well, eh?" replied DeSam. "I worked for him, I see him cheat the trappers. So, I cheat him."

"He don't like Frenchy none," said Patch, referring to Jocko.

"The Major don't like nobody much," said Hauser. "I worked for him a season, too."

"What is this about Astor?" asked Lem. "Who's Astor?"

"Ah, he plenty rich man," said Jocko. "He owns American Fur Company. I think this Major he work for American Fur."

"And who do you work for?" asked Lem.

Jocko did not answer right away. Sullard and Hauser looked at Lem, shook their heads, as if telling Hawke that he had gone too far.

Patch stared at Jocko as if demanding an answer.

DeSam heaved a sigh, shrugged.

"It is late," said the Frenchman. "I will take the first watch." To Lem Hawke, he said privately, "Do not worry yourself over these little politics, eh? You trap the beaver and let Jocko take care of the business, my friend. You and your son will make fine trappers, eh?"

"Are you asking me to work for you?"

"Well, do you have the license?"

"Yes. I got a license from Missouri Fur."

"Ah, then, do not worry. You trap, you work. Jocko will see that you get the fair deal."

Jocko slapped Lem on the back, winked at Morgan. He walked over to the fire and kicked dirt and rocks on it to put it out. The men wandered off to their bedrolls. Patch and Loonie disappeared into the darkness.

"Pa?" Morgan called from his bedroll.

"What?"

"Do you like Jocko?"

"I dunno," said Lem. "Makes no nevermind."

"How come?"

"We mean to go trappin' anyways we can. Jocko knows the way. He can learn us how to do it."

"He might cheat you."

"He might," admitted Lem. "But he'd only do it once."

"Then what?"

"He wouldn't do it no more."

"How come?"

"He'd be dead or cripped up so bad he wouldn't want to do it no more."

"Maybe we should go back home," said Morgan, his voice lazy with sleepiness.

"We don't have no home no more, son. This is home. Wherever we be is home."

"It don't feel much like home."

"I know," said Lem. "Get some sleep, son. Hard as this day was, tomorrow's bound to be harder."

"Good night, Pa."

"Good night, Morg."

Morgan looked up at the pulsing silver stars. Mosquitoes buzzed around his head. He felt a tick burrowing in his leg. He was too tired to scratch it. The buzzing lulled him to sleep as soundly as if he had been drugged. He saw dead men in his dreams. One had the face of the man he had killed during the storm. Then the face changed and became the Major's. And the face was laughing.

7

The Missouri River still boiled, its writhing waters a yellowish brown, contrasting sharply with the slate-gray seethe of the Mississippi. Fletcher Bancroft and another trapper tugged on the boat hook. The body of Dave Trask slithered over the rail. His sodden pantleg caught on a davit. Fletcher jerked the pole attached to the hook and Trask's remains landed on deck with a thud.

The river rats had gotten to Trask's face, had dug out the eyes and eaten into the sockets. Part of his nose was chewed away. Major MacDougal joined the group of men looking at the waterlogged body of the dead trapper.

"I told you to take care of this yourself, Fletch," said McDougal, stepping close to whisper in the trapper's ear.

"They had us outnumbered, Major."

Fletch dragged the body away from the gunwale and spread the linsey-woolsey shirt.

"Square in the breadbasket," he said, pointing to the hole in the dead man's stomach.

A man stepped up close to the Major. He had swarthy skin, eyes black as raw coffee beans and a thin scar bleeding away from one eye as if a large tear had left a track. His lips had been mashed by countless fists and heavy objects. Some of his teeth were missing, the others carious.

José Montez was dressed more like a sailor than a trapper, but he had been both.

MacDougal nodded to the Spaniard, his eyes as cold as cave rocks.

"That one of 'em you sent after Jocko?" asked Montez.

The Major nodded.

"You sure that Hawke sumbitch was with DeSam?"

"And his whelp," said the Major. "I swear I'll have all their hides stretched on willow withes before I'm finished with this expedition."

"Them Hawkes is mine," said the Spaniard.

"Montez, you have all the hair you want of the pap, but that boy looked to be prime goods. He didn't have a hand in killing your brother, anyway."

"He's a nit from a louse," said Montez. He looked at the bank as the keelboat slipped past, guided by men poling the boat, two on the rudder. Ahead, other men kept the horse herd moving overland. The square sail on the forward mast snapped in the breeze, its long cordelle dangling like a tree snake from the masthead to the deck.

Another boat followed, its goods stacked amidships in a long boxlike structure, lashed down tight, forty-odd men aboard. Montez had ridden up the evening before, just as the men in the Major's brigade were loading the two keelboats.

The men had pulled into the landing stages that same morning, early, cursing in the dark, shadowy figures in the swirling fog. Montez had gotten aboard the lead boat in time to help cast off the lines and set his shoulder to a pole. Then, one of the trappers had spotted the body of Trask, bobbing next to the bank, a leg caught by an exposed cottonwood root.

Montez puffed on a thin cheroot, his eyes glittering with the feral brilliance of a man who started every day with a shot of gut-wrenching whiskey. His small-billed seaman's cap sat atop a shock of thick, black curly hair. His loose homespun shirt was unbuttoned at the neck, revealing more curls on his chest, coiled tangles that looked like wire springs. His hands were rough, the joints knotty, the fingers gnarled as twisted manzanita roots. Buckskin trousers, smoked over greasy campfires, snugged tight against his lean hips. He carried a Spanish flintlock tucked in his bright red sash; a large knife hung from a wide belt with an ornate brass buckle.

By then, everyone aboard the keelboats knew that Montez was the brother of Spanish Jack and that Lem Hawke had been responsible for burning down the tavern in St. Louis. Spanish Jack hadn't made it out and had ended up ash and bone. His daughter, Willa, had told her uncle the whole story when Montez arrived from New Orleans. Now, Montez wanted revenge for his brother's murder, for that's how he figured it. He meant to rub out Lem Hawke at first sight.

The Major had known both Montez and Spanish Jack. Like everyone else, he knew the story of the fire at Spanish Jack's tavern. Lem Hawke, angry at Jack's daughter for seducing Morgan, had started a fight in Willa's bedroom. During the brawl, Lem had either knocked over or thrown a lamp. The fire had spread quickly. Jack's daughter, Morgan and Lem had gotten out, along with all the patrons downstairs in the saloon, but Spanish Jack had perished in the flames. Willa told the story that Lem had knocked her father out cold and had deliberately set fire to Spanish Jack's.

"Fletch, throw that corpse back in the river," ordered MacDougal. "Big 'Un, get 'em movin'."

Big Mike Finnegan, patroon of the two keelboats, stood atop a large cargo box and yelled lustily: "You thar. Set poles for the mountains." His clean-shaven head, his enormous girth and thick neck gave him the look of a hydrocephalic mushroom. Josie tossed his cheroot over the side just as Trask's body splashed back into the river. He grabbed an oar and joined Fletch and four other oarsmen forward of the cabin. They swung their oars over the side, braced for the first thrust. Forward, twenty polemen poised to port, preparing to shove off with their long, iron-clad poles.

Mike swung the helm with one mighty arm, lifted the hunting horn hanging from a thong lacing his chest and put the mouthpiece to his lips. He blew the signal to start, a throaty mellifluous moan that increased in pitch and ended up in a vibrant tremolo that hung in the air like thick fog.

The six oarsmen dipped their oars in unison. The polemen, facing the stern of the keelboat, slid their poles into the murky water, set them against the river bottom, threw the muscle and sinew of their shoulders against the curved sockets at the tip of the poles. They heaved, shoving the boat away from shore and upstream against the current. They slogged their way, in single file, toward the stern.

Mike began singing a sea chanty and the polesmen

picked up the melody. When they reached the stern, the patroon yelled "Ho!" and the men all turned quickly, raced
back to the bow, rammed their poles back to the bottom
again and once more braced themselves against the sockets and pushed. The boats slid upstream, lumbering against
the tug of the current.

Major MacDougal stood by the cabin watching the men
strain against the Missouri. His face bore no expression,
but he looked at the eyes of the young men with the poles
as they lunged aft and his eyes glittered like coals fanned
by a whispering wind. They were strong young men, most
coming back for their second season of trapping.

On the western shore, the men with the horses and mules
paced themselves, letting the animals graze and drink
along the shore. Some of the men looked at the sky, dread-
ing the next spring storm. Others rode off, singly and in
pairs, to seek game for the brigade.

MacDougal nodded silently in satisfaction as the keelboats gained headway. They were headed for the mountains, and among the men in his brigade, with its many
internal factions, there were some he trusted, some who
served as his eyes and ears. None but he knew who they
were. He suspected that Jocko DeSam would prove a prob-
lem later on. Those who had gone with him were of the
same ilk, not to be trusted. In the fur trade, the Major knew,
beaver were not the only animals that must be skinned;
competitors, be they few or several, were fair game. He now
considered Jocko, Patch and his crazy Indian, the Hawkes,
and the others who had ridden off with the Frenchmen to
be competitors, possibly spies for a rival fur company.

He looked down at Josie Montez, now just another
oarsman earning his keep. That one could prove useful,
MacDougal thought. Montez wanted to kill Lemuel Hawke.
Perhaps he would consider killing the others who followed
Jocko DeSam.

As the work got harder, the men stopped singing, but Big

'Un kept up a steady chant as he steered the keelboat up-river, guiding the helm with one hand, swatting at mosquitoes with the other.

"Put your muscle into it, boys," sang Mike. "Bear a hand there, Paddy. Let's see your neck bow, Harold me boy."

The unwieldy keelboat, a hundred feet long and twenty feet wide, gained headway mainly through the efforts of the *voyageurs*. With their necks bowed, their heads nearly touching the track of the running board, they pushed with all their might to the stern. They followed the patroon's commands to return to the bow for each new "set." With its shallow draft, the keelboat did well on such a river as the Missouri. When the boat gained deeper water, the oarsmen took over the work of propelling the boat upriver and the sweat-soaked *voyageurs* could relax for awhile as they watched for treacherous snags, sandbars, floating trees.

When they were well underway, Big 'Un ordered Fletch to set sail and they caught the wind and the men rested as the boat cleaved through rushing muddy waters, listening as the occasional thud of a log or tree branch turned to flotsam by a storm struck the hull. The mast stood a third of the way down from the bow and the sail was a tall square piece of heavy cloth. There were not many stretches on the Missouri where the sail could be used, since the river writhed like a giant snake through bluff-dominated prairie and there was often a terrible surprise waiting at each dramatic bend.

And MacDougal, setting the glass to his eye, scanned the horizon beyond both banks and looked ahead for any sign of Jocko DeSam's renegade party. He wondered if they would try to go to the Rockies by river or travel overland, out of sight, but not out of his raging, vindictive mind.

Morgan Hawke was glad that they had left the river and were riding well away from the clouds of mosquitoes that had plagued them ever since breaking camp that morning. Morgan could see the trees that marked the river's banks, the way they twisted through the stark, beautiful land, with its high bluffs like castle fortresses. Beyond the river, the land rolled gently, high grasses waving gently in the morning breeze that was fanned by the heat from the rising sun. Jocko had decided, for all of them, that it would be better if they did not try and find a keelboat ahead to take them on. Instead, he said they would follow the river at a distance until they reached one he called the Platte.

"There's a man keeps lookin' over his shoulder," Lem told his son later that day.

"I noticed it," said Morgan softly. He and his father rode alone, following well behind Jocko, Loonie and Hauser. They had been delegated to handle the spare horses and pack mules. Jocko had said they would all take turns. Patch was well ahead of the party, followed by Nat Sullard. Pappy Roth had gone off hunting.

"Seems like he done changed his mind oftener'n his shirt."

"You mean about the Major?"

"Him and a lot of things."

Morgan wondered what his father was driving at. His pa was a hard thinker sometimes; slow to speak, but when he did say something it was more like a riddle than fact.

"Where are we going, Pa? I mean did Jocko say?"

"Some river."

"He knows this country then."

"I reckon."

"How come Patch is ridin' so far ahead?"

"Figgers to see we don't get no big surprises."

"Indians?"

"Maybe. Nat tolt me this was all Injun country, but big enough so's you might never see 'em."

"I hope we see some."

"Son, you don't want to flap your mouth like that. Injuns,

from all I hear, is trouble. All of 'em's pure mean, 'cordin'
to Hauser and Sullard."

"You talked to them 'bout it?"

"This mornin' whilst you was packin' up."

They heard the sharp crack of a rifle far off and then
the quiet rushed in giving the day a special silence for
a few moments. The wide game trail they followed was
trackless after the rains. To the north, the sky was more
black than gray and the air seemed laden with moisture.
The sun, wherever it was, sent a heavy sweaty heat down
on them.

"I'll go see if he needs help," said Lem. "You stay put."

Lem rode off, leaving Morgan to follow Jocko and the
others on a march that roughly followed the river. Boots
kept nipping at the rump of one of the mules. Morgan finally
got tired of it and slapped his horse's neck. Boots' ears
went flat for a moment and he shook his head. The mule
brayed as if he was the one who had taken the blow.

The country was strange to Morgan, so unlike any he
had ever seen. Missing were the vast forests of Kentucky
and Tennessee, replaced by tall trees wrapped in wild
grapevines. When he glimpsed the banks of the river, he
saw the trees rose out of tangled brush that was too thick
to walk or ride through, and he avoided those places, swinging wide with the pack animals to avoid the fallen trees,
huge giants that blocked his path. He looked in amazement
at a place where several trees had fallen on top of one another. They were overgrown with shoulder-high nettles. He
rode too close, once, and the nettles struck at him, stinging his wrists, burning into his skin like the sharp cuts of
a whip. He got tangled in the climbing roses and buckthorn,
and vowed never again to ride or walk anywhere near such
dangerous plant life. Boots began to buck with the gouge
of thorns before horse and rider were free of it. Morgan was
covered with ticks, and though he brushed off those he
could see, others burrowed into his flesh. Mosquitoes,

swarming from fetid ponds created by the flood waters, found him, covered him with burning welts.

A buck deer, flashing a white tail like a flag, burst from a thicket and Morgan stifled the urge to cry out to those ahead. Instead, he was caught up with the beauty and grace of the buck as it bounded through places too thick for a rabbit to hop and disappeared into a swallowing darkness of thicket and vine.

He heard the faroff crack of a rifle and wondered if his father had found game. Perhaps his pa had seen the big buck with its fourteen-point rack, but the buck had not gone that way. Morgan found the image of the deer lingering in his mind and he wondered then why he heard no birds calling. Suddenly, a wave of lonesomeness swept over him like a silent tide and he felt alone and friendless, fatherless as well.

Then, Morgan heard the distant hammering of a woodpecker and thought of the forests of his boyhood in Kentucky.

Sometime during the afternoon, when still he had heard no birdsong, Morgan was surprised by a loud screeching. Ahead, he saw hundreds of what he took to be flying leaves, all flittering from branches like butterflies. As he drew closer, he saw the birds, wild parakeets startled by the riders ahead, dozens of them, flying erratically through the tall trees like leaves before the wind.

As he watched the green birds dart from tree to tree, creating the worst racket he'd ever heard, Morgan lost sight of the horses and mules. Moments later, he realized the animals had gotten ahead of him. He put moccasin heels to Boots' flanks, rode two hundred yards around a bend in the treeline. The herd was not there.

The other riders were nowhere in sight, either.

Panic rose in Morgan's throat, squeezed it tight. He felt a sense of suffocation. He stood up in the stirrups, trying to see far enough ahead to spot the others, or the animals in his care. It seemed suddenly quiet, with only the sound of his heartbeat thrumming in his ears.

Dark clouds were moving in and Morgan felt a soft spray of rain against his face. The parakeets stopped their raucous screaming now that he was away from their habitat. The wind lisped in his ear, a whisper from the northwest, not yet heavy but freshening, cooling.

Morgan wanted to call out, but the stillness, the emptiness of the land seemed too forbidding. He saw the swath through the grasses where the horses and mules had gone and kicked Boots again to hurry him along. He felt a pang of embarrassment that he had let the herd get away from him. He did not want the others to know that he had neglected his duty.

On he rode, the anxiety in him increasing with each moment. He looked at the darkening sky, watched the clouds float like silent barges until they shrouded the sun. The trail petered out, as if the herd had scattered. There was no single swath any longer, but tendrils of paths recently trod, fanning out in bewildering directions as if someone had scattered the animals.

The panic in him changed to fear. He clutched his flintlock, realized he had unconsciously folded his hand over the pan after the first kiss of rain. Now, he fumbled in his pouch for a blackbird's wing quill that fit the touchhole. He stuck it in the hole, kept his hand over the pan. He looked down, saw the fine patina of powder lining the tiny bowl and felt its dryness. He looked toward the hidden river, the tall trees. If the horses or mules got into that, well, he wouldn't know how to get them out.

Morgan followed a single trail and then he lost it. He stopped Boots and drew in the first deep breath he'd taken since losing sight of the pack animals.

His throat went dry. He heard the rain begin to spatter and Boots began to sway his head in annoyance as heavy drops stung his eyes. Morgan felt the darkness closing in

on him. Ahead, he saw the distant horizon flash with lightning and seconds later heard the thundercrack booming
like a cannon shot.

The wind stiffened, but it was a warm wind and heavy
now with moisture. Morgan went on, but he saw no track,
no sign that anything had passed his way. Another staggered flash of light in the sky and the thunder boomed
closer, warning of danger.

Five minutes later, the rain burst over him like a waterfall
and he could no longer see the trees. It was a steady, soaking
rain, blinding, wind-driven, blotting out the land, driving
it away from his eyes until he knew he was all alone, lost
and caught in the open where the lightning could fry him
like a moth caught in flame.

Morgan felt suddenly, strangely, calm.

He turned Boots to the right, toward the river, seeking
shelter from the storm that broke over him with a ven-
geance.

The fear was gone, but the loneliness, like a smothering
blanket, left an ache in his chest as if his lungs had been
singed.

He wondered if his pa even knew that he was lost.

Morgan slackened the reins, gave Boots his head.

"Find us a place, Boots," he said, patting the horse's
neck. The rain soaked the powder in his pan, wilted the
blackbird's quill in his touchhole until it drooped limp as
a rag.

But Boots turned away from the river and Morgan heard
it roar like a maddened beast as the raging water collapsed
banks and snatched trees from the shore, snapped them like
string beans and gobbled them into its maw.

There seemed, just then, no safe place to go as lightning
streaked the sky with silver lace and thunder cracked so
close Morgan jumped inside his sodden buckskins.

And the horse stopped dead in its tracks, lost and blinded
by the surging, pelting rain.

8

Morgan realized why Boots had balked at going on. The horse had probably saved his life.

Flooding waters roared through a deep gash in the land a few yards ahead. It seemed as if the river had changed course, gone wild, lashing angrily at everything in its path along an old dry wash.

The flash flood cut a swath twenty feet wide, four or five feet deep, tearing chunks out of the bank as it streamed past, widening the ancient streambed. He heard, above the din, the scream of horses, the hysterical braying of mules, the shouts of men like ragged pennants of sound flapping and fading in the angry lash of the rain. The sounds were eerie, almost unearthly. So, too, the din of the boiling torrent that devoured the land as it rushed toward the big river.

Morgan rocked backward in the saddle, the fear in him suddenly palpable, an iron thing so cold he could taste it in his mouth, so hard he could feel it pressing against his senses, numbing them like whiskey hot in the veins.

He knew that if he stayed there, the flood waters would take the ground from beneath him, snatch him up like a rag doll and hurl him to a watery death, bury him in a grave no one would ever find.

Turning Boots, Morgan felt the ground pull away from the horse's hooves. Currents he could not see, burrowing under the earth, were nibbling a new course for the sudden stream. He dashed toward Boots; The horse moved as Morgan tugged on the reins. His eyes swept the terrain, squinted against the pelt of rain. He reined the horse in a tight circle, clapped moccasined heels to the animal's flanks.

With the roaring of the floodwaters in his ears, Morgan sought high ground, knowing there was little likelihood he'd find any the horse could climb. The only high ground he'd seen had been steep bluffs bordering the river. Beyond those, the land was as flat as a pine board.

As he rode away from the flooded creek, Morgan saw someone waving to him. Just a shadow with the shape of a man, but enough to catch his attention. Turning Boots, Morgan guided the horse to the solitary figure. The man was afoot, stranded on a tiny island amid raging waters.

"Ho, boy. Help!"

The man calling to Morgan was Nat Sullard. His face was streaked with mud, his buckskins torn and sodden. Something seeped from under his hairline, something that looked like blood.

Morgan felt Boots fighting the bit as he drew closer.

Then, the horse stopped.

Another outlaw creek had formed, bursting through a new channel, slashing a separate course from the other, winding toward lower ground. Nat Sullard stood alone between two floods, horseless. All around him water surged, ravishing deep passages in the plain.

"I—I can't get no closer," shouted Morgan. "Look at it. It's ever'where."

"You got a rope?"

"Nope."

"Come on, Morg. We didn't mean nothin'. We was just jokin'."

"Huh? What're you talkin' about, Mister Sullard?"

"Just funnin' ye. Now, come on now. It's real important." Nat's voice quavered with fear. Morgan could sense the man trembling, shaking inside. Nat seemed to have lost his reason.

"I don't have no rope. This horse won't come no closer."

"You got to help me, Morgan. Your pa would want you to."

"Where *is* my pa?"

"I don't know. That water come down on us 'thout no

warnin', God. Drownded, maybe. Morgan, you got to get me outta here."

"If you can get acrost that one stretch," said Morgan, "I can help you. Give you a ride out of here."

"Hell, I can't swim, Morgan."

"Me neither."

"Dammit, boy, this ain't no time to be holdin' grudges."

"I don't know what you mean, Mister Sullard."

"Oh, shit," said Nat.

"Where's your horse? Maybe I could go and fetch it."

"Swept off when it hit. Damn, boy, you goin' to come get me?" Nat's voice rose to a hysterical pitch.

As Morgan watched helplessly, Nat Sullard looked all around him. Water lapped at his moccasins. The island began to shrink. The lone trapper began to blur before Morgan's eyes as the rain fell harder than before. Wind-driven, the downpour lashed at Morgan's face, stung his eyes.

"Jesus," said Sullard.

"Maybe it ain't as deep as it looks," said Morgan, but he knew that was a lie. The water was deep and getting deeper. In another minute or two, he would have to ride away or the flash flood would sweep him up in its grasp. "You want to try and jump it, maybe grasp the stock of my rifle."

"Too danged fur," said Sullard.

"Where's everybody else did you say?"

"Scattered ever' whichaway," said Nat. "Hell, boy, we didn't mean nothin'. We was just a-pullin' yore leg."

Morgan had no idea what Sullard was jabbering about. He wondered if Nat blamed him for his predicament. The man sounded plumb addled. Morgan started to say something, when he heard a sound that sent spiders scurrying down the nape of his neck.

Just then, the waters surged and widened. A sudden rolling tide rushed toward the hapless Sullard. Like a battering wall, a two-foot-high wave careened from a point behind him, seeming to come from nowhere as if a giant had thrown out a bucket of water.

"Look out!" called Morgan.

Sullard yelled something, but Morgan couldn't hear him above the roar of water. He held on to the saddle horn as Boots turned, began to gallop away through the sheeting rain.

"Whoa boy," said Morgan, hauling in hard on the reins.

Morgan saw the wall of water hit Nat in the back of his knees, pitch him forward into the swirling maelstrom. There was a terrible force in the water, an energy that belied its small size. The way it hit Sullard, cut him off at the knees, told young Hawke that. That small wave was more powerful than a span of horses. Morgan's stomach knotted as he saw Nat flailing his arms, helpless against the surge of the flood. He wondered if Boots would be able to swim the swollen, surging wild creek. He slapped the horse's rump and withers with the reins, dug his heels into its flanks. Boots kicked and sidled, but he would not go near the flooding waters. Morgan knew that if he threw himself into the rampaging waters, both he and Nat would go under. Helplessly, Morgan stopped beating the reluctant horse. He turned in the saddle, saw Nat swept away, farther and farther from where the island had been until he disappeared where the twin creeks converged once again.

Morgan's senses were jumbled, spun with fragments of distorted sensation, as if something was snatching at his mind, clawing all his thoughts to shreds. Seeing a man go like that, down and under and away . . . a terrible thing. Morgan felt helpless, small, powerless, as if he was anchored in stone.

And, he felt something else, too, the odd feeling that someone was watching him. Maybe God. God or someone was watching him. He looked around, tried to look up into the rain, but the water blinded him.

He tried to shake off the spooky feeling, tried to erase

the image of Nat Sullard's arms flailing against the force that plunged him to his death. It was hard to breathe as he thought about Nat trying to suck in air and getting only lungfuls of water.

"I—I'm sorry, Nat," he whispered, and then felt ashamed that he had said such a thing. To no one.

No, he had the curious feeling that *someone* had heard him.

Boots galloped to the west, away from the boiling, rampaging waters. Morgan gave him his head. Maybe the horse knew a safe place to go.

Morgan let the rain wash away his tears, slumped in the saddle, broken by the death he had witnessed, beaten down by the maddening drum of the rain, scourged by the hard wind that drove needles into his back, flayed his face, stung his eyes.

He hated the country at that moment. Hated it as if it were a living thing.

But what about his pa? He could see his father swept away like Nat, helplessly trying to swim, going under, drowning. But, he had heard voices, hadn't he? Maybe his pa and the others were still alive. Maybe they were stranded, too, cut off from high ground by the flash flood.

He tried to remember from which direction the shouting voices had come when he had first heard them.

He knew he couldn't go back to the creek. Boots wouldn't go anyway.

Still, he had to do something.

Angrily, Morgan turned the horse, headed him on an angle that would take him toward the flooding creek higher up. He had no real sense of direction, could only bore into the rain using dead reckoning, hoping he would find a place above the wash where he could cross to the other side.

He had heard of flash floods before. His pa had told him about one he'd seen coming over the Cumberland Gap from Virginia when Morgan was growing in his mother's belly.

Pa said it was mighty powerful and they were lucky he and his ma were on a hill when it swept through a big gully, washing away trees, wagons, everything in its path. His pa had told him about a family that had got caught in it.

"You ever see one, get to high ground fast," his pa had told him.

But where was high ground? The earth smelled dank, stank of dead animals and rotted vegetation. The land seemed flat, but from the saddle, he knew that there were small undulations in the surface.

Boots did not fight him, so Morgan knew he must be headed in a safe direction.

Then, he heard the voices again. Men shouting. Their voices sounded muffled in the incessant splash of rain. They faded and resurfaced on the wind currents. Boots jumped ahead at Morgan's prodding.

"Hold on to 'em!" someone shouted.

"Damn you, Hauser, grab that rope!"

"Hawke, come quick!"

At first Morgan thought they were shouting at him, but as he rode closer, he heard the horses and mules clamoring with frenzied voices. The mules brayed in terror and the high-pitched whinnies of the horses screeched on the wind like a thousand hawks in full cry.

The men floundered in mud, their horses caught in the quagmire. Some of the pack animals were belly deep in the sinkhole. Patch and Loonie were trying to pull their mule out of the bog. Jocko was whipping his horse to no avail, trying to pull a pack mule onto dry ground.

Dick Hauser, more muddy than the others, was twisted up in three ropes, horses pulling in opposite directions, panniers and packs askew, mud up to his knees.

Morgan's pa was trying to find a dry patch so that he could help Hauser, but he kept slipping on slick, boggy soil. Lem was covered with mud from head to toe, literally, and Morgan scarcely recognized him through the gauze of rain.

"Turn loose of 'em!" yelled Lem. "Dick, dammit, cut 'em loose."

Hauser, bewildered, tried to move, but the animals hemmed him in. They were terrified at being caught in the muck. Dick fell and got up again, even more encumbered than before.

Finally, Lem clambered over to Hauser, grabbed one of his arms and jerked him free of the bog and the tangled reins. He dragged Dick up to high ground as the stock clambered to gain footing in the mire.

Jocko DeSam floundered in mud up to his thighs. He cursed in French as he tried to catch up his horse. Packs were scattered on the edge of the quagmire, panniers rode cockeyed on the backs of the mules trying to find shelter in a grove of cottonwoods.

Looking Loon and Patch Sisco dragged a foundering mule from the edge of the swampy bottom onto higher ground, both pulling on a thick rope wrapped around a water oak's trunk. Morgan rode over to them and dismounted. He helped pull the jenny out, then shouted through the rain.

"Gimme the rope, Patch. I'll help Jocko."

"Take it, son," said Sisco.

Morgan loosened the loop around the mule's neck, gathered up all the slack. He ran to the other side of the slough and threw the looped end to Jocko.

"Grab a holt!" shouted Morgan.

Jocko, sinking even deeper into the swamp, reached out for the rope. His hand failed to grasp it. Morgan retrieved it quickly, stepped closer to the edge of the bog. He swung the loop over his head and hurled it toward DeSam. Jocko lunged forward, grabbed one side of the loop.

"Slip it around your chest," said Morgan, as Patch and Loonie joined him.

Jocko struggled, settling even deeper into the mire, until he was up to his waist.

"Quick!" yelled Morgan.

"He's got hisself in a sinkhole," observed Dave Sisco. "Damnfool pork eater."

Jocko rammed one arm through the loop. Morgan stood there helplessly as the Frenchman tried to get the other side around his shoulder. He seemed to be disappearing slowly into the sinkhole. The mud was almost up to his chest on his right side.

"Get your other arm through," Morgan pleaded.

DeSam twisted, shrugged the loop over his other shoulder, then sank against the rope, exhausted from his struggles.

"Hold on!" Morgan bent his knees, pulled up the slack. The loop tightened around Jocko's chest. Morgan crabbed backward, pulling hard. Loonie and Sisco stepped up and wrapped their hands around the bitter end of the rope. Their feet skidded on the gut-slick ground, but they managed to pull the Frenchman a few inches.

Jocko's hands kept slipping down the rope. The strands dug into his armpits, the loop squeezed his chest. He struggled to draw air into lungs that would not expand.

Morgan grunted and turned around, leaning forward until he faced Patch and Loonie. He strained against the tug of the rope, feeling his slick-soled moccasins slipping on the rain-soaked soil. But, he felt a give and moved forward a few more inches.

There was neither tree nor bush to wrap the rope around. The three men slithered to an angle, all tugging in unison. Jocko made no sound, except for the wheezing in his strangled chest.

On the other side, Lem and Dick saw the struggle taking place, but had their hands full trying to rescue the panicky horses and mules still stuck in the swamp.

"Let 'em go, Dick," said Lem. "We're only makin' it worse."

Hauser, exhausted, sank to his knees, releasing the single rein in his hand. The horse backed up, tried to buck its

way free of the mud's suction. Lem grabbed him by
one arm, dragged him away from the horses. The horses
settled down, then, calmed by the men's retreat. They
began to move their legs up and down, heading toward
firmer ground.

"Maybe they'll get out by themselves," muttered Lem.

Hauser couldn't utter a word. When Lem released him,
he sank to the ground, cold, wet and thoroughly discour-
aged.

The rain made the rope hard to hold. Morgan's hands
kept sliding on the soaked strands.

Patch didn't have much energy left. Loonie was conserv-
ing his; wasn't much help.

Morgan turned around to see if Jocko was making any
progress. It didn't seem as if the rope had moved for the
past two or three minutes. In fact, it seemed as if DeSam
had slipped back an inch or two.

The mud still gripped Jocko's hips, but his waist was out
of the sucking clutch of the quagmire. He looked like a
dead man, though. Morgan sighed, tried for a better grip
on the rope.

"Jocko?" he called.

Jocko didn't answer.

"He looks daid," said Patch.

"Shut up," said Morgan. "Pull, damn you, pull."

"Testy, ain't ye?"

Morgan shook his head to shed rain from his eyebrows
and bent forward, girdling his waist with the rope for more
leverage. He felt the rope move and his chest swelled as he
took in an exultant gulp of air.

Patch bore down, then, encouraged by the movement.
Loonie, too, seemed to apply more effort to his piece of the
rope.

"We got him goin', don't let up," panted Morgan. "He's
a-comin', he's a-comin'."

It was true. Jocko slithered out of the tugging muck, his

legs numb, useless. He twisted until he was on his back; his feet broke free of the sludge, his moccasins buried somewhere in the bog.

He looked like a corpse as he slid toward the bank on his back, his eyes closed, his chest barely moving.

Morgan and his helpers dragged Jocko out of the swamp. Patch loosened the noose around DeSam's chest.

"He ain't hardly breathin' much," said Sisco.

Morgan looked at the Frenchman. He looked blue in the wash of rain on his frozen face.

"Jocko? You alive?" asked the young man.

Jocko didn't answer.

Across the bog, Lem and Hauser watched as the three men bent over the body of Jocko DeSam. Hauser rose to his feet.

"He alive?" called out Lem.

Patch stood up, shrugged. He held the looped end of the rope in his hands.

Morgan knelt down and began slapping DeSam's face. He hammered a fist into Jocko's chest.

"Come on, Jocko, breathe, damn you."

Patch hunkered down, leaned his ear toward Jocko's mouth. He listened for a few seconds, shook his head.

"I don't think he's got no air in him," said Sisco. "Deader'n a willer stump."

"No!" shouted Morgan, and he grabbed the collar of Jocko's buckskins, began shaking him. "Don't you die, Jocko, God damn you, don't you dare die!"

Morgan's high-pitched plea seemed torn out of his throat. Loonie's eyes narrowed as he watched the boy shake the Frenchman as if trying to jar life back into his lifeless body.

When Lem heard his son's anguished cry, he started to trot around the bog.

"Hell, son," said Patch quietly, "what you gonna do if he don't come to—kill him?"

9

Jocko's chest heaved. He drew in a breath and his eyelids fluttered.

"Damned if Frenchie ain't come back to life," said Patch, wryly. "I done seen a miracle."

Morgan stopped beating on DeSam's chest and rocked back on his legs, suddenly ashamed of himself.

Lem and Dick arrived just as Jocko took his second deep breath and opened his eyes.

"Yore boy done pounded the breath right smack back in that Frenchman," Patch said to Lem.

"Jocko?" said Dick.

Lem glared at the man on the ground, then he looked up at Morgan. Morgan stared back at his father, a blank expression on his face. A feeling of lassitude surged through him.

Jocko sat up, gulping air into his lungs. He rubbed his chest where the rope had left its marks in the flesh.

"Ah," he breathed. "It is good to be alive."

The men around him, all except for Looking Loon and Lem, laughed.

DeSam wiped rain from his face, squinted up at the sky.

"Pretty soon, she stop, no?"

Morgan looked at the sky. The rain was slowing down, thinning out.

"You sonofabitch," said Lem. "You almost got us all kilt. Now we got to chase down stock. I got goods, goods bought and paid for, lost. I got to track it all down."

"Wonder where Sullard went to?" asked Hauser, trying to change the subject. Morgan saw that he was squirming over something. He wondered what his pa was so mad about. At the mention of Sullard's name, Morgan squirmed some himself.

Morgan cleared his throat. Everyone there, including Jocko, looked at him.

"You seen Nat?" asked Dick.

"He—he," stammered Morgan. "He got carried off."

"Carried off?" asked his father. .

"Flood," squeaked Morgan. "I couldn't do nothin' to help him."

"Jesus," said Hauser. Patch looked away, but Morgan saw the look in his eyes. Jocko DeSam paled visibly.

"Having some goddamned fun were you, Jocko?" taunted Lemuel Hawke. "That's what your funnin' done, you bastard."

"I did not know she was coming a storm," said Jocko lamely.

"Maybe we better straighten this out right now," said Lem. "You want to lead us to the mountains, but you've done a piss poor job so fur. You give me one good reason why we should pack with you."

Jocko lay there, panting. He seemed unable to get to his feet.

"Yair, Jocko," drawled Patch, "why don't you tell Hawke there what you got up that sleeve of your'n. 'Pears to this old coon you been playin' high and loose with what you been doin' on this frontier. You bucked the major and he's one bloodthirsty company bastard, but you did it sneaky and I don't cotton to a man who runs out on a fair debt."

"Eh, Jocko, he pay what he owe, Patch." DeSam glared at Sisco.

"I been tryin' to figger how you come to owe the Major any coin as it is," said Patch, scrinching up his face. "You and him now used ter be close. You was his shadder, prac'ly; his right hand. Now, all of a sudden-like you and him is fallin' out. Don't make much sense."

Jocko heaved his shoulders in a Gallic shrug.

"What are you drivin' at, Patch?" asked Lem.

"Somethin' mighty peculiar 'bout Jocko here cuttin' out

on his own, when he did. Either him or the Major's up to something. I got sour poke in my belly 'bout it."

"Hell, the Major sent men to bring Jocko back and kill us."

"I reckon he did," said Patch, but the look of puzzlement on his face stuck there like flies in spilt honey.

Jocko looked up at Lemuel.

"If I get up, you do not hit me, no?"

Lem clenched and unclenched his fists.

"I'm studying on it," Hawke said.

Hauser helped Jocko stand. DeSam's sodden leathers creaked and rustled. Mud dripped down his leggings onto his bare feet. He swayed there, unsteadily, for a few seconds. Lemuel glared at him, but made no move to strike him.

The rain became just a pattering, like light hail tapping on a sod roof, as scudding gray clouds thinned, blew eastward toward the Missouri at a fair clip. The wind flapped mildly at the men at the edge of the bog. Horses and mules still foundered, struggling to break free of the muck.

"Major says you're a spy for another fur outfit," said Patch, skewering his quarry on words it seemed to Morgan he'd held in his craw for a long time. Funny thing was, Jocko always swore by the Major, asked him and Pa to jine up with him back in Tennessee. Seemed Jocko was singing a different ditty now.

"The chest, she hurts," said DeSam. "I am trying to get the breath."

"You're breathin' same as me," said Lem. "Spit out what you got to say. You workin' for a company. Hell, it don't make no difference to me, I just want to know who I'm dealin' with is all. I heard tell of free trappers and company men and you been jumpin' twixt and tween ever since I met up with you."

Jocko heaved a draught of air and sighed deeply.

"Ah, what we must do, eh? We have to play the games

with the companies. We have to follow the rules or the booshway, he throw us in irons. My friends, you know what we must do to take the fur, eh?"

"I don't ken any of this stuff," said Lem. "All I know is that you played hob with the stock and damned near got us all kilt, not to mention what you done to Morgan there."

"It is to test the boy's mettle, no? I play the little trick. I see what he do."

Smouldering sparks of anger flared through Morgan's senses.

"You done got Nat Sullard kilt is what you did," said Morgan. He stepped toward Jocko, the anger in him raging to the surface.

"Hold on now, Morg," said Lem. "This is my fight." He turned to DeSam. "That boy's been tested a'ready," he said. "Maybe I ought to give you some testin', Jocko."

Jocko shrugged, lifted his arms, turned the palms of his hands upward, as if in surrender.

Lem relaxed his guard for a moment, indecisive.

Jocko swung around, hauled back his right fist and drove it square into Lem's belly. The air rushed from Hawke's lungs as he doubled over in agony. His face purpled, swelled from the rush of blood to his brain. Jocko waded into him, swinging his left hand, which hooked into Lem's right temple. Lem staggered to one side. Jocko cracked his other temple with a right cross. Lem jolted sideways.

Morgan cried out, but was frozen in place, rooted to the ground in surprise.

DeSam kicked Lem in the groin. Lem rocked backward on his heels as Jocko charged in, pressing his advantage. The two fell to the muddy ground as the force of Jocko's lunge drove Lem off his feet.

Jocko grabbed Lem's hair and jerked him forward. The Frenchman lifted his leg. Lem screamed as Jocko's knee rammed suddenly into his genitals. He doubled up and

Jocko kicked Hawke in the side, spinning him around. As Lem tried to gain his footing, DeSam threw Lem to the ground, pounced on him. He bit Lem's ear, gouged at his eyes.

Lem fought back, then, groggy from pain. He grabbed Jocko by the throat and pressed thumbs into the Frenchman's windpipe. He drew his legs back and kicked at Jocko's stomach.

Morgan started to rush forward, but Patch grabbed his arm, held him back.

"Let 'em fight it out, son," he said softly.

"Turn me loose, Sisco. I—I got to help my pa."

"You'll only get hurt yourself," said Patch firmly, increasing his grip on Morgan's arm.

Morgan wrenched loose from Patch's grip and shoved the older man in the chest.

"Leave me be, Patch!" Morgan yelled.

Loonie made a move to stop the boy. Morgan saw him coming and grabbed the handle of his knife. The Indian stopped. Patch nodded to Loonie, made a sign with his hands. Looking Loon held up both hands to show that they were empty.

Morgan started across the mud-sogged ground, his moccasin soles slipping. He saw his father roll on top of Jocko, then go underneath the more experienced fighter again.

Lem lost his grip on Jocko's throat, stabbed frantically with rain-slick fingers to get a purchase on DeSam's beard. Jocko grunted and plowed his right fist into Lem's nose. Blood squirted from both nostrils. Pain brought tears to the elder Hawke's eyes.

Morgan reached Jocko just as the burly Frenchman was about to slam his fist into Lem's face again.

Hauser stepped up but Morgan batted Dick's arms aside and bowled him over with the force of his rush. He ringed Jocko's neck with slender, deceptively strong arms, jerked him backward, wrenching hard to the left.

Hauser rolled out of the way as Morgan and DeSam tumbled backward.

Jocko flailed his arms, trying to get Morgan off his back. But young Hawke held on, squeezing DeSam's neck as he twisted it sharply.

"Aagh," grunted Jocko, finally grabbing Morgan's wrists, digging his mud-clogged nails into the flesh. He pulled mightily and loosened Morgan's throttling hold.

Lem scrambled to his feet, glared at DeSam as the Frenchman crabbed in a circle, regained his footing with a powerful thrust of his legs. Morgan, panting, pushed up to a squat, then stood up, fists clenched.

"You want to see what I'm made of, Jocko, you come on," said Morgan, his voice a wheezy whisper.

"Ah, the pup thinks he is a wolf, eh?"

"Morg, this is my fight," said Lem.

"Then you gang up on Jocko," said DeSam. "Two against the one, eh?"

Morgan stood there, breathing deeply now, flexing his muscles as if to summon strength enough to overpower the burly Frenchman.

"You come on, little boy. Jocko, he teach you how to make the fur fly, eh?"

The Frenchman, a grin on his face like a hideous stain, beckoned Morgan to engage him.

Morgan gulped in a deep breath, lowered his head and charged. The trapper sidestepped like a dancer and slammed a knot-hard fist into Morgan's left ear.

Morgan's head exploded with shattered fragments of bobbing lights. A dark blinding hole filled in the empty spaces. Tears stung his eyes and he choked on the sudden pain that flooded him like a grease fire.

Jocko stuck out his leg. Morgan stumbled headlong but stayed afoot, the pain jabbing through his ear. He whirled, the rage in him a towering black funnel, fuming with heat.

DeSam, surprised that the boy didn't go down, was caught off guard as Morgan charged again.

Morgan barreled into Jocko, his head like a battering ram slamming into Jocko's chest, knocking him backward toward the mudhole.

Jocko tried to grab Morgan's head, but the young man twisted free of the trapper's grasp and grabbed Jocko's leg at the calf. Morgan tugged the leg out from under Jocko and stalked in a short circle. Jocko fell, his leg seeming to twist out of its socket at the hip.

Morgan pounced on his back, rode him into the ground.

Jocko cursed in French just as Morgan grabbed the Frenchman's neck and squeezed it with both hands. But the burly DeSam rolled underneath Morgan and broke the hold, leaving Hawke with two handsful of air.

Lem, Dick, and Patch crowded closer, watching the young man and the Frenchman battle for position on the slick, muddy ground. Lem lunged everytime his son did, pantomiming his movements, growling instructions low in his throat.

"Grab him, Morg."

"Come on, Jocko," yelled Hauser.

Patch said nothing, but watched as Morgan slid away from Jocko's grasping hand.

"Damn little pup," said Jocko, as he got to his feet and hurled himself in a low crouch after his young assailant.

Morgan started to stand up, then hunkered back down to take the brunt of Jocko's charge. Just as DeSam struck his knees, Morgan dove over Jocko's back, but he was caught up short as Jocko grabbed an ankle with both hands. Morgan kicked free, but his forward motion was halted and he fell to the ground, knocking the wind from his chest. His ear throbbed as if a stake had been driven through it, clear to the brain.

Jocko held on, twisted Morgan's ankle. Morgan cried out

in pain, kicked three times to free himself from the man's iron grip.

"Move, son, quick," ordered Lem, crouching in a pugilist's stance. "Get away from the bastard."

Morgan shook free of Jocko's hand and crawled out of reach.

Jocko stood up, breathed in air like a blacksmith's bellows.

"Keep your hands off him, Jocko," said Lem.

"He start the fire," said DeSam. "He can put it out if he want."

"Morgan," said Lem to his son.

"Leave me be, Pa."

Morgan's eyes slitted. He wondered if he could whip Jocko. The man outweighed him. He was stronger. He seemed unbeatable. But, he didn't like being treated like a boy anymore. Maybe if he beat Jocko, the other men would look at him differently. Even his pa. It would be something to do, all right.

Suddenly, Morgan felt strong. He felt a surge of strength through his muscles. He saw that he was as tall as Jocko. Yes, he was leaner, but a lot of the weight DeSam carried was fat. If he could just stay out of his way and pound at him, maybe Jocko would get tired and go down. Morgan would give him a sound drubbing then, beat him into the muck until he begged for mercy.

"I'm ready, Jocko," breathed Morgan, a sense of lightness in his head, in his body.

"Eh, Jocko he is ready, too."

Morgan filled his lungs. Then, he charged toward Jocko. But just as Jocko reared back a cocked fist to throw at him, Morgan glided out of reach. He jabbed a left to Jocko's head, caught him on the jaw. It was a glancing blow, but it gave him satisfaction.

Jocko spun around to catch Morgan, but the boy made an even wider circle.

Morgan darted in and out, jabbing, ducking, swinging his head from side to side.

He lashed at Jocko with light blows that seemed to cause no harm. But it was evident to the others that Jocko was irritated. They watched as Jocko grabbed for Morgan and came back with empty hands.

Morgan gained confidence each time he struck Jocko and came away untouched. He began to take more chances. He darted in closer and used his feet. He kicked Jocko in the leg when Jocko was looking for a fist. He socked him in the chin when Jocko was bent over holding his knee.

"You stop running, you little whelp cub. Jocko show you how to fight."

Morgan said nothing. Jocko stalked after him now and Morgan stayed out of his way. He kicked backward, once, when it seemed he was running away, and then he came up on Jocko's side and rammed two hard punches into the back of Jocko's neck.

Jocko staggered under the blows and Morgan kicked him behind the knee. Jocko went down on one leg, seemed to struggle to get back up.

Young Hawke followed up on his advantage. He kicked Jocko in the side, then kicked him hard in the face, landing the heel square on DeSam's mouth. Blood oozed through the cracks in Jocko's lips. Morgan stepped in close and hammered rapid blows to Jocko's cheeks, each blow landing harder than the one before.

Jocko held up his arms to escape the punishment, but Morgan, the fury in him hardened now to a cold metallic purpose, struck again and again until Jocko's beard was running with blood, until his cheeks were mushy as apple pulp.

"*Assez,*" yelled Jocko. "*Suffisante. Arrête.*"

"He wants you to stop, Morgan," said Patch.

Morgan grabbed Jocko by the hair, held his head up and delivered one last smashing blow to his nose. There was a *crack* and blood gushed from DeSam's nostrils like a crimson fountain.

"That's enough, son," said Lem. "You've done beat him. Beat him fair."

Lem looked around at the others to see if anyone challenged his assessment.

Jocko slumped to the ground as soon as Morgan released his grip on the man's hair. They all listened to the ugly sound of Jocko's wheezy breathing. Blood sprayed from his nose in a rosy cloud, peppered the wet ground with tiny red spots.

"What are you going to teach me now, Jocko?" Morgan mocked as he stepped away, panting for breath.

Jocko waved a solitary hand in surrender.

Lem walked over to his son, patted him gently on the back of his shoulders.

"You done mighty fine, Morg."

Morgan nodded, too weak to say anything. He started to shake then and hoped his father couldn't see it. It wasn't fear, but more like the excitement that came when he had big game in his gunsights, something he couldn't control.

"You'll be all right," said the elder Hawke. "It's like buck fever. Sometimes you get it when it's all over."

Morgan looked at his father gratefully, nodded again.

"Let's get shut of this bunch," said Lem. "Ain't a damn one of 'em a bit of good."

"You mean go to the mountains by ourselfs?" Morgan asked.

"We can do it. With a sight less trouble, too."

"What happened, Pa? Why did you get so mad?"

"They played a joke on you, son. It was Jocko's idee. They snuck up on you and stole the horses and mules. I didn't find out about it until it was too damned late."

"I thought they run off," said Morgan, shaking his head.

At that moment they all heard a rumbling, then the ghastly sound of splintering wood and men screaming.

"The river!" yelled Hauser. "There's trouble on the river."

Morgan looked off to the right. It sounded so close. He hadn't realized how near they were to the Missouri.

All heads turned as the first cries for help wafted their way. And, above it all, the horrible sounds of men in agony, men screaming with their last breaths above the roar and tumult, the crunching sound of a keelboat being crushed by something big and heavy.

10

Major Angus MacDougal saw the downed tree jutting out from the bank at a bend in the river. Too late to warn the helmsman, he knew. Instead, he cursed at the snag that caught the prow of the keelboat. The curse died on his lips, however, as the craft spun wildly in the current and slammed against the bank beneath the bluffs.

One of the men yelled a warning and Angus looked up at the bluff. The rain had stopped, but there was a fine mist hanging in the air like shreds of gauze. Atop the cliff, a chunk of limestone slid down a crevice, then stopped. The chunk teetered, then continued its slide, dislodging other formations in its path.

"Look out!" yelled Fletcher Bancroft. "She's gonna come right down on us!"

Josie Montez, manning one of the poles amidships, measured the angle of the boat, its position in the river and the course of the small avalanche in a single instant. His brows furrowed and his face blanched to a sickly pallor. He threw down his pole, backed away, headed toward the stern. If the rocks all came down and struck a ledge, they could strike aft of the bow. Men would be hurt, possibly killed.

"Major," said Montez.

MacDougal looked at Josie, saw where he was going and moved in that direction.

A huge section of limestone broke off the cliff and tumbled straight down, struck an outcropping and caromed out over the boat, landing on the foredeck of the keelboat. The craft shuddered like a wounded beast under the impact; timbers shivered the length of the vessel. Wood cracked and splintered as the shower of rock smashed the cargo box, fractured deck planks and surged deep into the hull. Men at the bow scattered as they frantically tried to escape the destruction, but two of them were pinned by a large slab of rock that had sheared off another when it struck. The boat tipped queasily, throwing men against the gunwales, slamming them against iron davits, knocking them to the still quivering, shattered deck.

Loosened by the miniature avalanche, the whole side of the bluff seemed to teeter for a moment, then come apart as pieces of rock broke off, knocked other pieces loose and dislodged still others in random downward flight. Tons of soft limestone roared downward, smashing trees and rocks, exploding into fragments that flew off and struck the boat all along its length. The men on the second craft, behind the lead boat, tried to swing clear, but rammed into the stern of the Major's vessel. The prow impaled itself in the lead boat's scuppers, stuck there like a giant wedge, stuck fast as if it had been bonded there by nails and iron straps.

Several men on the Major's boat were struck by flying rock and shattered wood slivers. Some went down, bleeding profusely from head and facial wounds. Men screamed and cried out in terror and pain as the keelboat broke up and began to founder. A man grabbed the side of his head and came away with half of his ear in his hand, scalloped neatly by a razor-sharp fragment of stone. Those on the second boat scrambled over the sides and some leaped up on the railings and jumped into the swirling waters of

the Missouri, following the men escaping from the lead
boat. Those who could not swim sank like stones and
drowned in a strangling silence deep under the current.

"Men, don't panic," shouted the Major as he fought off
choking clouds of dust. "Fletch, get some men and start
throwing our supplies toward the bank. Get as much as you
can off this boat and then get the hell off yourself."

"There's no time for that," said Montez. "This boat is
going down."

"Montez, shut your mouth," said MacDougal. "Men, get
the traps off or you won't earn a penny this year."

Although MacDougal appeared outwardly calm, there
was a shrill edge to his voice. The deck tilted under his feet
and the boat seemed to sink deeper at the bow.

"Men, save what you can," said MacDougal. "Save yourselves."

Bewildered trappers stared blankly at MacDougal as he
stumbled through the debris and climbed over the side of
the boat, rifle in hand. In a moment, he was wading toward
shore, fighting the pull of the current, leaning hard to port,
straining to keep from being sucked under. He kept his eyes
on the bluff above, as if ready to duck another shower of
rocks. Other men began to crawl over the sides of the boat,
following him. A few grabbed their rifles, others abandoned ship with celerity, forsaking their belongings as well
as their injured companions.

Fletcher led the pack.

Josie Montez started to follow the panicky men, but the
keelboat began to break up, the hull cracking in two
amidships. The halves of the boat tilted and he was hurled
to the port side, slammed hard against the gunwales. He
fought for breath as the craft wallowed in its death
throes, water filling its ballast compartments, tearing at its
bowels like a feeding whale.

On the opposite bank, Dick Hauser clambered up out of

the thick brush, halted. A floundering man, weighted down by wet buckskins, reached the bank and held up a hand. Dick stooped down, grabbed the man's wrist and hauled him ashore.

The man lay there for several moments, spitting water, gasping and choking. Dick knelt down beside him.

"You gonna live, child?"

The man looked up at Hauser.

"Who might you be?"

"Why, Dick Hauser. And you?"

The man sat up, wiped water from his face with a swipe of a swarthy paw.

"Josie. Josie Montez."

"Then you'd be Spanish Jack's brother."

"You knew Jack?"

"I did. Drunk his grog enough."

"Were you there when he was murdered?"

Montez's tone gave Hauser pause. He scratched his head.

"Why, I don't rightly recollect. I 'member the tavern a-burnin' down."

"I am looking for the man who knocked my brother cold, set the fire and left him to die," said Montez.

At that moment, Patch and Looking Loon appeared out of the willows and brush where they had stopped and waited for Hauser to look around first, staring at the sinking lead boat, then at the stricken second vessel. They stopped when they saw Hauser talking to Josie Montez.

"Well, I couldn't help you there," Hauser said warily. He got back to his feet and looked out at the river.

Most of the surviving men on the lead boat waded ashore and gathered around the Major, who had walked well clear of the unstable bluff. Men from the second boat began to abandon ship in a more orderly fashion, making for the eastern shore, small clots of survivors sticking together like bewildered rabble. It was clear to them that their boat would be useless unless it could free itself of the sinking lead vessel. A few men foundered in deep water and were helped ashore by their companions.

Farther upstream, Morgan and Lem emerged from the underbrush. They saw the men on the opposite shore and the bodies on the deck of the lead keelboat.

"Pa, lookit," said Morgan.

" 'Pears that bluff done toppled down and broke that boat up, kilt some men."

"What can we do?"

"Don't look like we can do much. I'm thinkin' it's a damned good thing we wasn't on that boat. Looks like the Major's done got hisself some troubles that ain't gonna go away right quick."

Morgan felt a surge of elation, despite the soreness in his legs and fists. He could see men on the deck of the lead keelboat who appeared dead or sorely wounded. There was an arm sticking out of the rubble next to the cargo box. The arm did not move; the hand attached to it hung limply like some grave marker made of human flesh. The side of the bluff where the massive face had sheared off was dry, like an old dark scar. Dust still hung in the air and Morgan heard a series of low, pathetic moans coming from somewhere inside the boat. Men still scrambled over the side of the stricken vessel, some limping, holding onto their legs, others staggering like drunks, grasping bloodied heads, capless, their buckskins dark with sanguinous stains.

There was a stench in the air that reminded Morgan of hog butchering, right after their bellies were slit and coils of intestines spilled out onto the ground like newborn snakes, all a-glistening, slick with an oily slime.

Beyond, he saw men gathered around MacDougal. The Major looked up, seemed to catch Morgan's eye. MacDougal scanned the bank where Morgan stood, as if looking for someone. Morgan's gaze shifted upstream where Hauser stood with another man, a swarthy Spaniard who looked somewhat familiar.

"What're you lookin' at, Morgan?" asked his father.

"That man with Dick. He look like someone we know?"

Lem saw the man. He studied him carefully.

"I can't put him in no place."

The Spaniard looked downstream.

"He's lookin' at us, Pa."

"I see it."

The Spaniard looked away, began speaking to Hauser.

"He's askin' Dick about us, Pa."

"Aw, Morgan, you don't know what he's a-sayin'."

"He's pointin' at us," said Morgan.

"Probably askin' who we are."

It struck Morgan then who the man was. It was just a feeling, an odd feeling, like he had seen him before, but he knew he never had. His thoughts went back to that last night in St. Louis, when his pa had come up to Willa's room and caught him naked with Spanish Jack's daughter. He remembered Jack coming into the room, the fight, the broken lamp scattering fire and oil all over the bed, the walls. Spanish Jack was knocked cold and his pa couldn't get him out. The tavern owner had died in the blaze that burned the building to the ground.

"I'll bet that's Spanish Jack's brother," said Morgan softly.

He heard his father draw in a quick breath, saw him look upriver at the Spaniard.

"Damn. Might could be. Looks to be a Spanisher."

"Pa, let's go. I don't like it here. Ain't nothin' we can do."

"Yep, we best get on," said Lem.

Josie Montez called to them.

"You there."

"Don't answer him, Pa," said Morgan.

"He's a-comin' this way."

Morgan grabbed his father's hand and pulled on it. Lem followed reluctantly.

"Come on, Pa."

"I'm a-comin'."

Montez started toward them, then thought better of it when he realized he had no firearm. The Major started barking orders at the trappers on the opposite bank, urging them to unload the boats. Some of the men began to venture back to the boats, sheepish expressions on their faces. Some clambered aboard the second vessel and began throwing lines to those on shore. Others began rigging a line to the first boat, which was sinking badly, breaking up in the surging current. Pieces of sundered trees and other flotsam floated past, testifying to the power of the current with freshly fallen rain propelling it with enormous force. It wound past the banks, shouldering the boats up against the bank, surged on like an angry serpent mining a new path through the earth.

"You there! Hawke!"

Lem and Morgan halted, turned toward Josie Montez.

"I will catch you!" yelled Montez, holding up a clenched fist. "You will pay! Goddamn you!"

"Let's go, Pa," said Morgan.

"I ought to settle this now," said Lem.

"How?"

Lem patted the handle of the knife hanging on his belt.

"No, Pa." Morgan spoke softly, a chill inside his belly like a cold fog.

Montez drew his own knife, held it up. He beckoned to Lem with his free hand. There was a grin on his face, visible even at that distance.

"Some other time!" Lem yelled.

"You bet, *cabrón!*" Montez slashed the air with the blade of his knife. "I will kill you like you killed my brother!"

A muscle quivered along Lem's jawline. His eyes

narrowed for a brief moment. Then he followed Morgan into the underbrush.

When they returned to the muddy buffalo wallow, there was no sign of Jocko DeSam.

Some of the horses were missing, others stood disconsolately under still dripping trees, their heads hanging in weariness. After they caught up their own stock and mounted Boots and Hammerhead, Lem pulled the mules to the north.

"We goin' to the mountains by ourselfs, Pa?"

"I reckon. We got all what we need."

"But we don't know where to go."

"I expect we can find what these fellers found, all right."

"How?"

"We'll just foller the river until we come to the mountains. Then we'll go up 'em and find the beaver, the mink and marten."

"Do you know how to cotch 'em?" asked Morgan.

"I can figger it out, son. Silas, he tolt me how to set the traps, bait 'em. I got me some castoreum in Saint Louie for bait."

Morgan remembered Silas coming to their farm, showing them a beaver pelt with its thick shiny fur. That was when Silas gave him the medicine horn, told them about the riches in the mountain streams.

"What's 'castoreum'?"

"It's beaver piss, I reckon. Silas says it plumb draws them to the traps set in the water."

"Must have a smell to it."

"It's 'bout as powerful as skunk, I reckon."

Lem made a clicking sound in his mouth. Hammerhead began to move around the perimeter of the mudhole. Morgan, on Boots, followed, checking the pan on his .64 caliber Kentucky-made rifle to see if the powder was dry. There was only a small amount and it was damp. He spent the next several moments wiping the pan dry, repouring fine powder in the pan, blowing away the excess. He checked the striking flint, adjusted it slightly so that it sat just right in the leather, not so firm that the flint would break when it struck sparks off the frizzen. Satisfied, he began to take notice of the country again.

Later, Morgan's thoughts drifted back to other times.

"Pa, I got a question."

"You go right ahead, son."

"Are most people bad like Josie Montez? Always wantin' to fight or kill somebody for no good reason?"

"I reckon some of 'em is."

"Seems like we keep runnin' into trouble ever'where we go. Meetin' up with bad men."

"Women, too," said Lem wryly.

"You mean Willa Montez?"

"And your ma."

"Ma? Ma bad?"

"She wasn't bad exactly, son. She just did some bad things. Run out on us. Made some mistakes, maybe."

"I wish I could have got to know her better," said Morgan.

"Might have helped if she had stayed home more, not had all them fancy idees."

"I guess she didn't like us much."

Lem laughed harshly, but he knew his son was not trying to be funny. Morgan was so serious the way he said it and it was really wasn't anything to laugh at.

"I reckon there are some good people, Morg. They all probably start out good enough, but they's hard lessons in this world and maybe some folks don't take kindly to teachin'. I figger a man goes bad because of what other men do to him, maybe when he's just a boy, or a-growin'. Seems like it just keeps gettin' passed along, the bad, until it's real hard for a man to be good anymore."

"You mean it ain't no use bein' good, then?"

"You can be as good as the next man will let you, Morg."

"It don't seem like nobody cares much. I mean, what's inside a man, how a man feels about things. I seen more bad men than good since we left the farm."

"I reckon you have at that."

The sun showed for a moment, then clouds slid into the hole above the two riders to darken the sky once again.

"Sometimes I wish we could just be all by ourselfs."

"Well, that ain't growin' none, Morg. It ain't natural. You don't learn no lessons. You get hard inside after seein' enough meanness in the world. You get to knowin' ain't nobody goin' to help you except your own self. You don't lean on nobody and you don't let nobody lean on you. That's what you learn if you're payin' attention."

Morgan chewed on what his father had said, but he was still trying to make sense of what had happened to them. Going down the Natchez Trace they worried about robbers and Indians, but the only trouble they'd ever had was when they were in a town or around other men. And they had had nothing but trouble ever since leaving St. Louis. He wondered if going to the mountains was such a good idea after all. And he wondered, if they'd ever make it out there alive, if they'd get back to civilization alive.

There were times, like now, when living seemed such a hopeless chore. A damned chore, like chopping wood and then seeing it all go up a chimney in smoke. And then have to do it all over again. The thought of it made him feel tired. It just didn't look like there was much to look forward to, even if they did make it to the mountains and got rich trapping beaver and such.

They skirted a marshy spot full of cattails and blackbirds, a low place where the river made another bend. Scudding gray clouds still hid the sun, draping the country in gloom.

"What about Silas, Pa?"

"Huh?"

"Is Silas Morgan a good man?"

"Good as any, I reckon. Why?"

"Oh, nothing. I was just figgerin' if we ever saw him again how it would be."

"Why, it'd be just fine, Morgan. I named you after him. He was always right with me. Your ma didn't like him much."

Morgan said nothing, but his thoughts scrambled wildly to find some meaning, something he could rest easy on, like a pillow, where it was all safe and quiet and there were no bad men in the world.

They followed the river as it meandered south, then north again, stretching westward toward the falling sun.

"I reckon we can find our way, long as we foller this here river," his Pa said late that afternoon. It had been so quiet, his voice startled Morgan.

"I reckon, Pa."

The sun was out again. Morgan's buckskins and moccasins were dry. He was hungry and his belly growled at the emptiness. He kept thinking of the fight with Jocko, wondered where the Frenchman had gone. A few moments later, when the sun was an hour above the western horizon, he had part of his answer.

They heard voices. Many voices.

His father reined up, put a finger to his lips.

Morgan rode up alongside his father, a puzzled look on his face.

Lem slid out of the saddle. Morgan did the same. They tied up the animals to sturdy trees and took their rifles with them as they sneaked toward a hillock, crouching low.

The voices grew louder.

Lem lowered himself to the ground, crawled the last few feet to the top of the mound. Morgan slithered up beside his father. They looked down on a strange sight.

There, where the river took one of its innumerable bends, a horde of men were breaking camp, tearing down hide and canvas shelters, packing up goods, loading them on horses and mules, storing them in pirogues and canoes that bobbed on tethers along the bank. Others were digging in the side of the hill that sheltered them from the view of anyone on the river.

Overseeing all the bustle stood Jocko DeSam, atop the bank, pointing to caches yet undug. He barked orders in French and English.

"Pa . . ." Morgan whispered.

"I know. Jocko knew what he was a-doin' all the time. Likely those men been a-waitin' on him."

"What's that those men are diggin' outen that hill?"

"Looks to be trade goods or such."

One of the men dropped a box and several kegs rolled out onto the ground.

"Nails?" Morgan asked.

Behind them, they heard a soft, rustling sound. Turning, they saw Patch and Looking Loon walking up. They were carrying rifles, their stock tied near where the Hawkes had left their horses and mules.

Patch crawled up beside them. Looking Loon stayed behind, crouched low.

"Whiskey, most likely," said Patch.

"Whiskey?" said Lem. "I thought . . ."

"Illegal as hell," said Patch. "That damned Jocko. I knowed he was up to no good."

"What's he do with it?" whispered Morgan.

"Swaps it to the Injuns for furs. Likely he's got trade guns in those blankets, too. Injuns'll pay dearly for such."

"Guns illegal, too?" asked Lem.

"Mebbe not, but you give a Injun a thunder stick and you're jest askin' him to use it on you."

Looking Loon slid up to them, silent as smoke.

As the four men watched, some of the trappers began pushing off in pirogues and canoes, cargo piled high between two paddlers in each small boat.

"We best get along," said Patch. "Jocko won't like it

none, us knowin's he's smuggling whiskey upriver past the booshway."

"I reckon," said Lem.

"You want company?" Patch asked. "Just me and Loonie there."

Lem looked at his son. Morgan shrugged.

"We'll see how it works out," said Lemuel.

"This chile knows you been burnt by folks," said Patch. "We mind our own business, me and Loonie. Don't look in another coon's poke. They's some trails you might not know about yonder." Patch nodded toward the west where the light was strongest in the sky now that the sun had disappeared behind a cloud bank.

"Where you headed, exactly?" asked Morgan.

"Have to see when we get to the mountains. They's plenty of places a man can trap and trade if he knows what he's a doin'."

"I just don't want to run into Jocko again," said Morgan.

Patch looked at the boy.

"Why, I don't reckon he much wants to run into you, nei-ther," said Patch, a wry smile playing on his lips. "But you never know for sure what's around the next bend of the river, son. You know that Josie Montez will be on your trail?"

"Yeah, I know," said Lem.

"He'd be a bigger worry than Jocko, I'm thinkin'."

Lem looked away.

"Best we keep movin'," said Patch. "Montez got him a horse from the Major's herd on shore, swam him to the boat for his rifle and possibles. Me'n Loonie'll keep a eye or two on our backtrail."

Lem nodded but said nothing.

The four men slid back off the hillock, walked to their horses, the sounds of the men on the river fading away.

Just before he mounted up, Morgan looked at Patch and Looking Loon as they rode off ahead.

Maybe, he thought, Sisco wasn't a bad man, like the others. The only thing he knew about the silent Delaware was that Loonie had eaten his dog.

Morgan got sick to his stomach every time he thought about it.

As if reading his thoughts, Looking Loon turned around and looked at Morgan, doubled up a fist, feinted with it, then ducked as if avoiding a blow. He then made the sign of approval with the same hand. And grinned wide.

11

Patch pointed across the river.

"See that lake yonder?" he asked Morgan and Lem.

Father and son nodded.

"Lewis and Clark called it Sugar Lake. River takes a long northern swing here. If'n we cut across due west, we'll meet up with it again. Take us less'n a week and we'll gain some ground on Jocko and the Major."

"Be fine," said Lem tightly.

"Fill your canteens. Ain't much good water 'twixt here and there."

Morgan watched as Patch unslung a large furry pouch and walked to the river.

"What's that water jug made out of?" asked young Hawke.

"Buffler balls."

"Huh?"

"Shot me a buffler, made a canteen out of its ball sack, glued hide to it. Keeps the water wet and cool."

Morgan didn't know whether to believe Sisco or not.

They filled their canteens at the river and rode on across the prairie. Patch led them with an unerring eye, always looking back to see if anyone was following them. Lem and Morgan did the same. Looking Loon ranged far ahead, scouting and hunting. The men fed on his kills of rabbit, squirrel, prairie chicken, quail and fawn at night under clear, star-flocked skies in sheltered depressions while the Delaware sat away from them, watching, listening.

The silence was eerie at times, and Morgan felt it like a cloak on his shoulders. When the coyotes howled, he crouched closer to the fire until he got used to their plaintive singing, but the sound always startled him when he first heard it.

"What made that bog you got caught in?" Morgan asked Patch one night.

"Old buffler waller, son. Used to be a passel of 'em along the river, but the Injuns and trappers comin' up the Missoura run 'em off."

"Are the buffler big?" asked Morgan.

"Why, I reckon some of 'em get bigger'n a horse," said Patch. He made sign with his hands and Loonie grinned.

"Will we see any?"

"Shore, son. And a mite more, too. If you see buffler, you'll likely see Injuns."

"Are the buffler good to eat?"

"Best vittles on God's green earth," replied Patch. "Onliest thing is, the Injuns figger they own 'em. And one tribe owns 'em someplace and another tribe in another place, so you always got to watch out where you are when you shoot a buffler."

"You think we'll run into Injuns?" asked Lem, scooting closer to the fire. There was a chill blowing off the river and this was the first fire they'd had that was big enough to warm a man.

"Biggest trouble we're likely to have is with them scurrilous Blackfoot," said Patch. "Andy Henry come back to St. Louie last year with some ha'r-raisin' tales. Near ever'body thought he was dead."

"Where are these scurry Blackfoot?" asked Morgan. Patch didn't laugh.

"Mostly where the fur be, but they's places we can go, I'm thinkin', and if we keep a sharp lookout, we can keep our hair."

"How'd you find these places?" asked Lem, backing off from the small fire. He no longer looked into it because it blinded him to the night. The fire was dying anyway.

"I want to hear more about the Blackfoot," said Morgan.

"You ever heard of Colter?" asked Patch. "Drouillard?"

"I reckon not," said Lem. Morgan shook his head.

"John Colter now. There be a mountain man. Ever hear tell of Manuel Lisa?"

"We've heard about *him*," said Morgan.

"Back in ought seven, Lisa and a bunch traveled up this very river, built a fort at the mouth of the Big Horn, that's a river what runs into the Missoura. He come back in ought eight with beaver a-plenty, and marten, mink, lynx, muskrat, too, got ever'body fired up in St. Louis, by gum, and General Clark hisself got George Drouillard, Tom James, me, and about three hunnert or more men to go up there and trap those beaver ponds. We got up to Fort Manuel, that's what Lisa called it, went on up to Three Forks Basin to set our traps. We was lookin' all over creation for the place, when them Blackfoot jumped us. Kilt three men who was scattered out scoutin' trails. They robbed them, they kilt them and then come on the rest of us a few days later. Kilt a whole bunch, including Drouillard. Some of the brigade pulled out, but some of us stuck with Andy Henry.

"But them damned Blackfoot swarmed down on us again and took the heart out of all of us, scattered us all over them mountains like wild partridge. Henry, he set out for the Snake and I come back to St. Louis with nothin' to show for it. Last year, I went back up the Missouri with the Major and we done pretty good. We thought Henry might have lost his hair, but he showed up last summer lookin' like a hard winter, which he done had. He come in with

forty packs of beaver. That gave us all heart and here I am
again, ready to find me some plews."

"What about the Blackfoot?" asked Lem.

"Oh, they'll be lookin' after their huntin' grounds, but I
learnt somethin' last winter. They don't much like them
high places when the snows come in thick, but the beaver,
why, they do just fine in their mud-and-stick lodges. I got
me the idee to go some deeper into those mountains. I stuck
it through last winter, and Lisa said it was the worst he'd
ever seed. So, we might stay out of the way of the Blackfoot,
least until spring."

"I hope so," said Morgan dreamily.

Lem looked at the silent Delaware, wondering if he understood what Patch had been saying. Looking Loon didn't
appear to show any interest in the conversation. He just sat
there, grinning idiotically.

"How come you got an Injun partner after all that trouble with the Blackfoot?" Lem asked.

"Oh, Loonie, he ain't like them other Injuns. He's right
tame, compared. He don't have much use for the Blackfoot,
neither. His brother was one of them kilt with Henry's
bunch. Loonie would as soon kill a Blackfoot as a snake."

Morgan did not count the days, but marked their pas-
sage westward by the rivers Patch Sisco pointed out
to them. They passed the Platte, the Nodaway, the Tarkio,
rode north and camped one night at the confluence of the
East and West Nishnaboina rivers, just to avoid running
into other trappers. They rode south again, following the
Missouri. Patch pointed out Council Bluffs to them, rode
around a hunting party of Otos, always staying well away
from the Missouri until nightfall, when they filled their
canteens.

Everyday they saw deer and the wide paths of buffalo
herds. Morgan wondered when they would see buffalo, but

he kept silent. He began to get a feeling for the land that was strange to him. He had never before seen so much space all at once—the land, the sky, the distant horizon, all seemed new to him, as if he was walking on ground no one had ever trod before. Every sunrise was startling to him, each sunset more spectacular than the one before.

It was sometime in June when they camped on Soldier River, and a few days later, they saw Blue Lake, and beyond, Blackbird's grave. It was early July, the days having passed in a haze of sun and rain and always the land stretching out before them and receding behind them. Morgan's pulse beat faster and he began to feel a part of the country as if it was where he was supposed to have been all his life. He played cruel tricks on Looking Loon, hiding one of his moccasins while Loonie bathed, putting bugs in his possibles pouch when the Delaware wasn't looking, sticking a live blacksnake in his saddlebag where he kept his dried food. Loonie acted surprised each time he discovered something alien among his belongings and yet he never did more than flash Morgan an idiotic grin.

"You ought not to tease that Injun, Morg," said his father.

"I don't mean no harm."

"One of these days you'll go too fur, and he'll get his dander up."

"I don't think he's got no dander to get up," Morgan cracked.

Morgan shook Patch's shoulder gently. This was the morning the old trapper had promised to take the boy hunting. Loonie had told Patch of a water hole laced with deer tracks, some two miles from camp. Morgan and Patch had scouted the hole the night before, selected spots where they might sneak in and wait for game should the wind be right.

Fog hung in the tall grasses, motionless in the still dawn.

Patch stepped softly, following a swath that only he could remember from the night before. Morgan stepped in his tracks, careful to make no sound. His ears seemed tuned to the slightest sound. The silence was acute.

They came to the edge of the water hole. The cream light in the eastern sky barely made the water visible. There were two knolls some seventy-five yards from the pond, each separated from the other by a distance of fifty yards.

Patch grabbed Morgan's shoulder, turned him toward the knoll on the right. Morgan nodded and set off for his spot. Patch disappeared in the high grass. When Morgan sat down in the grasses, he could not be seen. The wind was at his face. He looked off to the left and could not see Patch, but knew he was sitting there, hidden in the swale.

The land lit up gradually, the shadows pulling across the water hole, gold touching the tips of the grasses, turning them tawny, the pond taking on a pink glaze. Morgan listened intently, heard the distant piping of a bird he could not identify. Then, he heard the rustle of grasses and his senses tautened like rawhide drying in the sun. A mosquito sang in his ear, but he sat stockstill, peering toward the sound of the whispering grasses.

The pond lay in a shallow depression, a high bank on three sides. The deer would have to come down into it. The walls would slow them down if they tried to get out in a hurry. Morgan studied the pond carefully, figuring all the ways a deer might run if he and Patch missed their shots, or if something spooked the animals before they could touch off shots.

Minutes snailed by in an agony of waiting. Finally, the grasses parted and a deer stepped out of the swale. It stood there, stiffly, sniffing the windless air, its ears flicking as they moved in half-circles. Morgan's heart froze as the deer, antlerless so that he could not tell if it was a buck or a doe, looked straight at him. Then it lowered its head and moved toward the water hole. A moment later, another deer came out of the same swath, not so warily as the first, but moving slowly, its slender legs jerking with each step.

When the second deer got to the water and bent its head to drink, Morgan took a bead on the first animal, which stood to the right. It had already slaked its thirst and stood rigidly still, its head facing off to the east. Morgan figured Patch would take the one closest to him.

Slowly, he brought up his rifle, careful not to slide the barrel against the grass. He stopped his motion as the second deer lifted its head, water dripping from its chin and muzzle.

Morgan held his breath, listened to his pulse tap out the seconds as time crawled by slower than a snail through thick grass. It seemed to him that the deer could hear his heart pounding, that they could see him holding the rifle he had not yet aimed.

Finally, the second deer dropped its head down to the water and began to drink.

Morgan eased the muzzle of the rifle downward, fixing his right eye on the blade front sight. He held steady on the deer's flank where its heart should be, just behind the shoulder. He let his breath out in a silent whisper. He took another breath, held it. His finger curled around the trigger, squeezed.

The flint struck the frizzen, showered sparks into the pan. There was a *poof* as the fine powder ignited, shot flame through the touchhole to the main charge. The rifle roared and bucked against Morgan's shoulder. White smoke and orange flame belched from the muzzle. The smoke obscured the two deer and everything between Morgan and the water hole.

Morgan heard another explosion to his left a split-second after he fired and knew that Patch had taken his shot, as well. Morgan listened for the sounds of hoofbeats, but heard nothing. He rose up, grasping his medicine horn. He stuck the plug in his teeth, pulled it free. He poured fresh powder into the palm of his left hand, mounded it up over an imaginary ball. Quickly, he drew his fingers into a cone, poured the powder down the barrel. He shook the loose grains from his palm, brought the rifle up, tamped the stock to knock the powder to the bottom.

He dug patch and ball from his possibles pouch, placed them over the muzzle. He started the ball with his thumb, took his wiping stick and rammed the load home, tamped it down tight. He shook fine powder from the smaller horn into the pan, blew the excess away.

The smoke cleared as he walked toward the water hole, reloaded, the frizzen knocked down over the pan. He checked the leather scrap and flint to see that they were tight and straight. Patch met him where the two deer lay, their hearts smashed, their eyes glazed with the frost of death.

"You shoot true, son," said Patch.

"So do you," replied Morgan, looking at Patch's deer. Its tongue was caught between its teeth. It had dropped in its tracks, a .62-caliber ball through its heart.

"With a little seasonin', you'd do to ride the river with."

"What's that mean?" asked Morgan.

"Means a man can count on you. When his hair's standin' on end or his belly's full of wooly worms."

"I hope so, Patch."

The two men gutted out their deer, skinned them and used the hides to carry the choice chunks of meat back to camp. Along the way, they stopped to rest on a knoll. It was still early and the earth smelled sweet and summery. Bees plumbed the wildflowers and prairie birds chortled in the greening grass.

"Let's take a look at that powder horn you got there."

"That's my medicine horn," said Morgan, making no move to hand it over.

"Set store by it, do you?"

"I do."

"How'd you come by it?"

"A friend of Pa's give it to me."

"Looks like a buffler horn, all right. Kin I look at it, son?"

"Sure," said Morgan. He slipped the medicine horn from his shoulder, handed the carrying thong to the old trapper.

Patch took the horn, held it to the light.

"Mighty fine work," he said. "Good polish to it."

Morgan said nothing, but beamed inwardly at the compliment.

Patch studied the symbols, cocked his good eye, brought it close to the horn.

"These be Absaroky markin's," he said. "Crow. You got yourself a Crow powder horn, son."

"I know. Silas told me."

"Silas Morgan. He might of got it off one he kilt, or he could've traded for it, I reckon. He say which?"

"No, I reckon not," said Morgan.

Patch handed the powder horn back to Morgan.

"Do you know what those markings mean, Patch?"

"Big medicine, fur as I know. Maybe you might need it."

"What do you mean?"

"Nothin'."

But, there was something in Patch's craw. Morgan noticed lately that Sisco watched Lem a lot, as if trying to figure him out. It wasn't spying, exactly, but Patch showed an uncommon interest in Lem Hawke.

"Is it somethin' about my pa?"

Patch jumped as if startled. An expression fled across his face too fast for him to hide it.

"He's packin' him a load is all."

"What do you mean?"

"The man keeps lookin' over his shoulder and at night he don't sleep good."

"I seen you lookin' over your shoulder, too."

"Ain't the same. He's lookin' for something what ain't there."

"Ain't nothin' there when you look, neither," said Morgan.

"I know what I'm lookin' for," said Patch. "And, he still don't sleep real good. Like he's fightin' someone in his dreams."

"He's always done that."

"Always?"

"Since—since Ma left us."

"He ought to get him another woman right quick."

"He don't like 'em much, I reckon."

"Welp, he'll find him one, maybe. I think he's got Josie Montez on his mind some, too."

"Pa ain't afraid of nobody," said Morgan.

"Might be he ought to be a peck afraid of Josie Montez. That 'uns got a scalp or two on his belt."

"He better not try to stick Pa. I'd shoot him dead."

"Montez ain't the kind to walk up to a man and say what for. He works best at night behind a man's back."

"You don't worry about us none, Patch, hear?"

"I hear you, Morgan." Patch opened his mouth as if to say something else, but he closed it quickly. He got up, then, hefted his meat and set off for their camp.

He noticed that they took a different way back and Patch stopped every so often to listen. Once or twice, he lay flat on the ground and put his ear to the earth.

Everytime he did that, the hairs on the back of Morgan's head bristled and he shivered with the odd chill of it.

12

Josie Montez waited until after Jocko DeSam had beached his dugout on the sandy bank. He had been riding along the river's course watching the Frenchman and his companion, staying just out of sight until the two decided to come to shore. He had long since lost the trail of the Hawkes, Sisco and the Delaware. But, he knew that DeSam's bunch were strung out for miles on the Missouri, way ahead of the Major's brigade.

DeSam climbed out of the boat, lashed its prow to a tree near the shore. Dick Hauser, in the stern, grabbed his and DeSam's rifles and stepped over the gunwale onto the bank. He handed DeSam's rifle to him and looked downriver. Another craft rounded the bend: a canoe carrying three men and goods.

Montez rode up and dismounted a few paces from DeSam.

"Ah, you leave the Major's brigade," said DeSam in English. "I thought you would come by boat."

"Let us speak the tongue," said Montez in fluent French. He looked at Hauser, cocked his head.

The other boat, a canoe, shot onto the shore a few yards from where DeSam's dugout lay tethered. The three men spoke in rapid French, secured their craft and began unloading their cargo, carrying it to a stand of cottonwoods.

The river rose and fell with its own surging pulse. This was a wide point and the water flowed gently, calmly. The sky was cloudless, blue as periwinkle, the air, warm and summery, seethed with insects, mayflies and yellow-winged butterflies. Two more canoes carved a path to the shore and beached upstream. The babble of voices speaking in French drifted through the willows and cottonwoods, strangely disembodied.

"But, yes. Jean Lafitte taught you well our language."

"Jean taught me a lot of things," said Montez. "Did you get the goods I had brought up for you?"

"They are in the boats. We found the cache, as you said we would. We went by the forts at night. It is good."

"Smuggling is my trade," said Montez.

"And Lafitte? What has become of that pirate?"

"He prefers to be called a privateer. He did not fight for the British at New Orleans. He helped the Americans."

"Andy Jackson? I heard in St. Louis that the American soldier won."

"They made him a major-general. He won the battle with ease, but the war was already over. There was a treaty, but the American government did not sign the papers. Many British died."

"And which side did you fight on?"

"I fought with Jean. He is going to ask for a pardon."

"Ah, fat chance."

"He will get something," said Montez.

Dick Hauser grumbled under his breath. Another pair of canoes rounded the bend, skidded across the flattened waters, twisted toward shore. Upstream, a plover piped a plaintive curlicued trill at the presence of intruders as men stalked the shore for firewood.

"You want me to go away, Jocko? You and him don't want me to know what you're sayin', I know."

"We are old friends, Dick," said DeSam. "It is easier for us to talk in French, *non?*"

"It don't make me no never-the-mind," grumphed Hauser. "If you and him want to talk that gibberish, it's right fine with this old coon."

DeSam ignored Hauser, who began unloading the dugout.

"This whiskey you sent me will buy many furs," said DeSam.

"I don't give a Spanish curse about furs," said Montez. "I am after bigger game."

"Ah, Lemuel Hawke, the greenhorn. You have been tracking him?"

"I lost his trail."

"So it is in this country. The trails criss and they cross and they lead into bad places. It is not a place for trackers.

You follow the river, she takes you where they must go. Everybody, he follows the river. You want this man, eh?"

"He murdered my brother. His life must pay for Jack's."

"That is one way to look at it, my friend."

"There is another?"

"You do not care about the furs, but the beaver skin is money. This Hawke, he has no money. Let him get the furs. When he comes to trade or sell to the *bourgeois*, you kill him and take what he has. Then you have the revenge and you have the money."

"Killing the two pigeons with one stone, eh, Jocko?"

"Revenge lasts but a moment, no? The money lasts a little longer."

Montez laughed drily.

"Besides, you may get three pigeons with the one stone," said DeSam.

"What you say?"

"The boy, Morgan. I do not think he will be a camp-keeper, that one. He will trap. He will get the furs, too. You take them."

"Jocko, Lafitte could learn something from you."

"Ah, that is so," said DeSam, his chest swelling.

"Maybe you are right," said Montez. "Maybe I will catch this Hawke when he has something to give me."

"You will probably have to kill the boy, too."

"I have already thought to do this. One, two, it makes no difference."

"As long as they are not together when you do it," DeSam said.

"What is this you say?"

"I think they will both fight hard if they are together. It would be two against the one, *non?* You shoot them like the turkey. First one, then the other."

"Like the turkey," Montez repeated. "Yes, that is good, I think."

Jocko made a gobbling sound. Both men laughed.

* * *

Nearby, where the Nemeha River flowed into the Missouri, men dipped buffalo-hide pouches into the lesser river's depths, bringing forth water for the cooking fires. Clouds in the western skies glowed with an apricot tinge. A prairie wind blew warm and sweet from the west, redolent of tall grasses and sugar in the stems, tasting of summer flowers.

The days were sweet except when it rained or the squalls rose up on the Missouri, driving the men to shelter. The nights, most of them, were just as sweet under fair skies strewn with stars, a gibbous moon gliding like a silent wraith's eye across silver-shadowed velvet. Morgan wondered at the change in the country, the sights of strange birds and the tracks of unknown animals—the badger, the prairie chicken, the coyote.

Morgan hated unpacking the mules every night, packing them back up the next morning when it was still dark. He hated tending to their sores, thumbing grease on raw patches worn by rope and leather, on wounds caused by the constant rubbing of the panniers against their hides. Bone-weary, his head still spinning images of the sights he had seen that day, he crawled into his blankets and let the tiredness seep out while he watched the stars, trying to detect their faint movement. He smelled the buffalo chips, the reek of a skunk, the fetid stench of beasts he had never seen. When at last he slept, he dreamed of beaver and elk, of mountain goats and furry things shining on a rainbow-colored hill deep in the Rockies.

Another night he dreamed of the buffalo bones they had seen that day, still a-wonder at their size and multitude. At one place, he suddenly noticed that the skulls were all facing toward the east.

"Injuns hold that the buffler is some kind of special

animal, made just for them. They thank 'em when they kill 'em and promise to feed their kin when they die and sleep under the grass," Patch told Morgan. "They turn them skulls so the spirits can see how they treated 'em after they kilt 'em."

It was very spooky for Morgan to hear this from Sisco. He felt as if he was riding through a graveyard and could almost feel the spirits of the buffalo in the air. The Indians were strange people; they knew things that nobody else did.

Morgan noticed that the bluffs along the river had changed, lost their trees. Now, they were grassy and stark against the skyline. The air had a dryness to it, beating warmly against his face. The land was an ocean of grass as far as he could see and sometimes the silences filled his ears like whispers of far-off waves seething on a seashore.

There were times when he felt swallowed up by the country, lost in it. He knew they had come a long way, would go a lot further before they came to the beaver ponds in the mountains. He felt hopeless some days and overwhelmed with the size of the sky and the land. He wished, at odd moments, in the silence of his mind, that they would see a road, or a house, a person waving to them. When these wavery, half-formed images appeared, he felt smothered by a powerful homesickness, a deep sense of loss and a fear of never returning to civilization. He wanted a girl to talk to, someone to touch, to hold him, to say hello or ask him how he was feeling. He had to take deep breaths and put such thoughts from his mind, for they were fearsome thoughts, dark and foreboding, as if something terrible would happen to him and no one would ever know that he had left the earth. No one would ever find his grave or his bones, and if they did, it would not matter, for no one would know that he had wandered into the wilderness and died. Worse, no one would care.

Patch and Looking Loon led them over old game trails, mysterious highways trampled by countless legions of animals in migration along the course of the big river. Morgan derived some comfort in knowing that living creatures had passed by and that, probably, other men had hunted the creatures and eaten them and then gone on living.

They swam in blue lakes, rode past a few silent graves of unknown men that pulsed with meaning for young Hawke. The graves had no markers and Patch did not know their names. Morgan felt himself being drawn deeper and deeper into a strange land with loud eerie silences, endless skies and deep nights when the sky was black and sparkling with winking stars, cold and distant, mockingly quiet in a hushed ocean of space.

"That be the Big Sioux River," said Patch, one day. "We've been makin' good time. Likely see buffler any day now."

Morgan looked around for any signs of buffalo. He saw only a young killdeer trying to take flight, the last of its baby-down clinging to its wings, the orange fuzz glowing with sunlight. It wasn't until the next day that they saw sign of buffalo, piles of dung, some fresh, that littered the trail for miles.

"Might be we'd better bunch up some," Patch told Lem and his son. "Where they's buffler, they's Injuns."

"Where are the buffalo?" asked Morgan.

Patch shrugged. "They's liable to be anywheres. This is fresh sign. They been here. They come and go. And, if they're in a hurry, they don't care what's in their way."

That night, they made no fire and camped well away from the junction of the James and the Missouri rivers. Patch explained that they were deep in Indian country and needed to stay quiet and listen to every sound.

"You might hear a bird what ain't no bird," he told the Hawkes.

Morgan stayed awake a long time, listening to every night sound. He finally closed his eyes, fell asleep in the soft wash of silence.

Toward morning, young Hawke was jolted out of sleep, rolled out of his blankets, grabbed his rifle from force of habit. He groped blindly in the dark for his possibles pouch and powder horns.

The ground shook and there was a distant rumbling, like muffled salvos of thunder. Morgan's throat tightened in fear and his stomach quivered with a sudden spasm.

"Pa," he shouted, breaking the constriction in his throat, "earthquake!"

"Be quiet," said Lem, a disembodied voice in the thick pitchblende of night.

Morgan's senses clamored to make sense of the sounds and the tremors in the earth. He strained his eyes trying to see in the darkness. He saw only dark shapes, drew in dust through his nostrils, tasted grit in his mouth. He breathed in the thick aroma, tried to isolate it. It was like nothing he had ever smelled before, an invisible steam, thick and gamey.

"Steady, son," whispered Patch, so close to Morgan that when the youth turned, he brushed against the old trapper's shoulder.

"What is it?" asked Morgan.

"Buffler," grunted Patch. "Listen."

The rumbling sound grew louder until it was a thunder in Morgan's ears. The dust in the air thickened.

The dawn sky paled as a milky light bleached the eastern horizon and the streak along the skyline spread. Morgan saw the dust hanging in the air like a smoky cloud.

"Get your mules packed, your horses saddled," Patch said to the Hawkes. "We don't want them buffler to trample us."

Morgan's blood surged at his temples. He heard the pounding of his heart beneath the low rumbling of the distant herd.

Lem stepped to his son's side. "Stay close," he said. "Let's catch up those mules."

"Feels like that earthquake back in Kentucky," said Morgan, as they headed for the feeding mules. The animals were dim shapes in the pale dawn light. "But Patch says it's buffalo."

"Likely," said Lem, bending down to untie a hobble.

"Where we goin', Pa?" Morgan found the other mule and grabbed its trailing halter rein.

"Either away from 'em or right close, I reckon," said his father.

As the sky lightened, father and son worked faster, loading the panniers onto the pack mounts, stringing rope through the O-rings. Within fifteen minutes, they had their horses saddled.

"Check your priming pan," Lem said to Morgan.

"Already did, Pa."

Lem grabbed the lead rope from his son. "I'll pull the mules, son. You stay right close."

The two climbed into their saddles. A moment later, Patch rode up, his flintlock laid across his pommel. Morgan thought he looked different, and as the trapper turned toward the east, Morgan saw that Sisco had smeared his face with dirt. Looking Loon loped up, his rifle hanging from a thong looped around one of two saddle horns.

"Like to get us a buffler," said Patch. "But this be Pawnee country. That herd might be chased or it might be running towards somethin'. No way to tell, rightly. But, we got to be mighty careful. If you shoot a shaggy, stay with it until we can skin it out." Patch paused. "I declare, this coon's mouth is plumb waterin'."

Morgan laughed nervously. "Where are they?" he asked.

"Off yonder, five miles or so, I calcalate."

"They sound close."

"If they was real close, you couldn't hear me a-talkin', son. You'll know when we get onto them."

They rode through dust thick as rain, toward the sound of the running herd. Morgan didn't see how there could be that many animals in the whole world. Patch didn't hurry, but followed behind Looking Loon, who kept his horse at an easy walk, as if he had time to spare. The thunder grew louder in Morgan's ears and he fingered the trigger guard of his flintlock, eager to see a buffalo through the veil of dust and bring it down with a lead ball. He wondered if they would see Indians, Pawnee or Sioux, maybe Blackfoot.

He lost sight of Looking Loon, then Patch disappeared, too. It was then that Morgan realized that he was deaf to all but the sound of the huge surging herd. It was like standing under a pounding waterfall, like being in a cave high on a hill where the thunder boomed and echoed until you were inside the thunder and the thunder was inside your head.

"Pa," he croaked, trying to keep his voice from shrilling to a high pitch. "Pa," he called again, more loudly.

But Lem had disappeared into the dust and Morgan had no bearings.

It was as Patch had said: nobody could hear him now, even if he shouted. He could feel the herd's hoofbeats through the ground and through his horse, through his bones and flesh, until he could feel the earth shaking under him, making his hair stand on end.

Morgan's horse balked, tried to turn away from the herd.

"Boots, dang you."

The horse danced in place for a moment, then stepped forward in a slow, sidling gait. Boots turned his head and shook it vigorously. The horse's eyes were wide, the whites as bright as boiled hen's eggs.

Morgan felt a rush of air against his face. At first, he thought it was from the unseen buffalo, but the breeze freshened and he knew it was the morning wind, rising off the earth. He saw his father's back, then, dimly beyond, the shapes of Patch and Looking Loon. The dust wavered, then wafted to the southwest and lifted so that he could see a long way. The sun's rim slid above the eastern horizon.

Then Morgan saw a sight he would never forget. A dark wave undulated like a shaken blanket, rolling with the thunder, moving northwestward. He did not know what it was, for he had never seen anything like it. He realized, a moment later, that he was looking at a vast migration of buffalo and when he took his eyes off the main body of the herd, he saw individual animals, with their shaggy humps, their oversized heads, horns sprouting from curly tangles of wooly hair.

Then they swung toward him.

Boots tried to back away, but Morgan dug his heels in the horse's flanks and yanked down on the reins. Ahead, Lem and Patch were halted, his father leaning over, listening to something the trapper was saying. A few yards from the two men, Looking Loon waited in silence, watching the herd stream by like a river gone mad.

Suddenly, Boots swung around, fighting the bit.

"You ornery cuss," said Morgan.

Then, his face went white and he froze, letting the horse have his head.

Several buffalo sheered off from the main herd and, led by a monstrous bull, charged straight for Morgan. He heard his father shout something, but he couldn't hear the words over the clamor of the herd. Boots bucked and fishtailed, jerking Morgan out of the saddle. Morgan's hand gripped his rifle. He landed with a thud square on his butt as the horse galloped away in panic.

The giant bull, followed by dozens of bellowing buffalo, changed course and headed straight for the downed youth. For a frozen second, Morgan thought he must have landed in hell and the devil was bearing down on him, steam jetting from his nostrils, eyes black as anthracite.

13

More and more of the shaggy beasts left the main body of the herd, following the lead of the huge errant bull. From their vantage point, Lem and Patch could see the stream of bison clearly, dozens of others following blindly after its maverick leader.

"What in hell is that out front?" asked Lem.

"That's the biggest bull buffler I ever seed," breathed Patch with a reverence that made his statement sound like a prayer.

Morgan, scrambling to his feet, saw that there was no place to run. He glanced down at his lock, saw that his fall had jolted the flint loose; it had slipped sideways inside the leather and hung crooked in the gooseneck cock. He jammed the flint back in the jaw as he rose to his feet, but he knew it was still not square. He thought it would probably shatter when he pulled the trigger.

The buffalo bull was no more than fifty or sixty yards from him, shrinking the distance at a nerve-grating pace. There was no time to bring the rifle to his shoulder and take aim. Morgan gritted his teeth, swung the rifle to bear on the bull and cocked the hammer. He prayed silently that the powder in the pan was still dry as he slapped the frizzen in place with his thumb. He thought of the sight on the end of the barrel, saw it lined up at the bull's chest.

When the charging animal was ten yards away, Morgan squeezed the trigger.

Sparks flew from the pan, peppering Morgan's face. He didn't even feel the heat. White smoke and flame belched from the muzzle, obscuring the charging bull and the other buffalo from his view. He turned and began to run, bore to his right, in the opposite direction the herd was running.

Patch and Lem both raised their rifles at the same time when they saw Morgan fall.

"I'll take the big bull," said Patch. "You try and drop the cow directly behind it."

They each took aim. Just as Morgan fired his rifle, Lem squeezed off a shot. He did not hear the report from Patch's rifle, and a cloud of flour-white smoke mingled with his own, so he knew the old trapper must have fired at the same time.

"Got him," said Patch, triumphantly.

"I can't see a thing," said Lem.

"Me, neither. Not no more."

"Where's Morg?"

Patch said nothing. But they saw the band of buffalo turn back in toward the main herd slightly, and as the smoke cleared, they saw Looking Loon riding hard toward the place where they had last seen Morgan.

"Load it back up fast," said Patch, pouring powder down the barrel of his rifle.

"I got to get to Morgan," said Lem.

"You better have something to shoot, then. We got us trouble, son."

Lem heard it then, the high-pitched yelps, the *ki-yi-yi-yi* of many voices. The hairs on the back of his neck stiffened and he brought his powder horn to his mouth, bit the stopper and pulled it free of the spout. His hand trembled as he shook powder into his rifle barrel. He had no idea how much powder he had poured, but he let the horn dangle and fingered a ball and patch from his possibles pouch. Out of the corner of his eye, he saw Sisco ramming his own ball down with his wiping stick. Time seemed to slog by as he hurried the loading.

Patch rode off, toward the place where Looking Loon had gone, leaving Lem to finish seating the patch and ball.

The cries of the Pawnee hunters rose and fell in the thunderous roar of thousands of hoofbeats. Lem heard no gunshots, figured the Indians must be hunting with bows. He could see only buffalo as he rode toward the place he had last seen his son.

"Morgan," he called and knew that his voice was lost in the din of the passing herd. He dodged a lone cow, its hump bleeding from a single arrow that jutted from its hide, waggling like a feathered semaphore.

He rode through patches of blowing dust, smelling of buffalo and trampled grasses, plowed earth and mangled flowers. He saw the big bull, lying dead on its side, its blue tongue lolling from its mouth, dark blood streaks drying on its shaggy coat, its great head cocked at an angle, eyes shiny glass, smoked up from death.

A dozen arrows bristled from the bull's hump and neck, all with different markings, in various colors, on their shafts. Strips of rosy flesh hung in tatters from one of its black horns.

Lem stared at the hulk, measured it in his mind, weighed it. His facial muscles pinched in a look of amazement. His mouth went slack. He saw no sign of Morgan, felt a slight wash of relief that his son did not lie dead underneath the enormous bison.

"Over here," called Sisco.

Lem saw the cow he had shot. It had veered off its course and gone several yards behind the bull. Next to it, on the ground, he saw Morgan. With a heart that felt as if it was sinking through his chest, he rode up on Patch, who was kneeling next to Morgan.

"The boy's all right," said Sisco. "Got him a knot on his head the size of a quail's egg."

Lem dismounted. He and Patch helped Morgan to his feet. Morgan staggered as soon as the two men released his arms. Lem reached out to break his fall, but Morgan pushed his father's arms away.

"I'm just fine, Pa."

"You look kinda peeked to me," said Lem.

"You able to ride?" asked Patch.

Morgan nodded. He ran a patch down his barrel with the wiping stick, began to reload his rifle.

"Let me get some vittles off'n that bull and we'd better skeedaddle. When them Pawnee women come up to skin out the kills, they'll raise a holler. We'll have so many Skidi braves on our butts, we'll think we was hit by a swarm of Georgia hornets."

"Boots run off, Pa," Morgan said, after Patch ran over to the dead bull.

"I know," said Lem. "You ride with me and we'll find your horse."

Morgan climbed up behind his father.

"He took off thataway," said Morgan, pointing.

The horse had not gone far. Boots stood alone, reins dangling, as if waiting for its master. Lem rode up alongside Boots, and Morgan jumped into the saddle. He leaned forward and grabbed up the reins.

Buffalo streamed past like a great surging river, their thundering hooves beating strong in Morgan's ears. He gaped at them in awe, feeling the immense power they generated, admiring their speed and grace. They did not seem driven, but surged forward of their own volition, kings of the prairie, lords of the earth itself.

He wanted to chase after them, ride among them, try and capture the feeling of running before the wind, racing in their midst like one of them. He had the strange feeling that he could become like them, could feel their hearts beating inside his own, feel their muscles and sinew as part of his own body. He felt lightheaded and giddy just looking at this tide of beasts flowing over the prairie like unchained lightning. It was their giant pulse that hammered at his temples. It was their raw energy coursing through his veins; it was their savage blood flooding his heart like wildfire, pumping through his flesh like volcanic lava.

"Morg, come quick," called Lem.

Morgan shook his head free of his wild thoughts, saw his father down on the ground next to Patch. They were both looking at the dead bull's chest. He rode over, dismounted.

"Son, looks like you brought this bull down," said Patch, pointing to the chest wound. "Them balls in its sides didn't do no more'n scratch his curly hide."

Morgan stared at the hole. Patch stuck his finger through it, grinned.

"Mighty fine shot, Morg," said his father.

"Let's get us some boudoins and cut out his heart and liver," said Sisco. "Then we best hightail it for other parts."

"Ain't we gonna get any of his meat?" asked Lem.

"Not if we want to keep our hair."

Morgan and Lem exchanged glances. There was no mistaking the look of warning on Sisco's face.

The Hawkes helped Patch turn the buffalo over on its side. As they watched, the old trapper cut through the animal's belly. He slashed into the dead flesh with brute force, ripped downward toward's the bull's tail. Working quickly, he pulled twenty or thirty feet of lower gut out of the bloody maw, cut it near the anus.

"Strip out that shit, Morgan," said Patch, "press it all out best you can whilst I get the heart and liver. Might even take a cutlet or two from under its spine."

Patch handed Morgan the slimy intestines. They slithered through his fingers, fell to the ground. Reluctantly, he picked up the serpentine mass.

"Do it over yonder," said Lem, pinching his nose.

Morgan carried the intestines a few yards away, began to work the fecal matter out the cut end.

Patch cut the heart free of its sac, severed the sinew around the liver. He then forced the body cavity wider and reached in, began cutting filets, sawing them, slashing them loose. He took one of the kidneys, then fell back, bloody and exhausted.

"Best we pack all this up and get to ridin'," he gasped. "Tell your son he can finish working the boudoins on the way."

Lem nodded, dazed by all that he had seen. The buffalo still streamed by, but he no longer heard the yips of the Pawnee.

"Here, son," said Sisco. "You take this heart. Be good eatin' when we can make us a fire."

Morgan took the bull's heart. It was heavy in his hands, slick with blood, grainy with fat. He stuffed it inside his shirt. It felt slimy against his skin. Patch handed Lem the kidneys, stuffed the filets in a saddlebag.

As the three men were mounting up, they heard a sound, then saw Looking Loon racing toward them, his horse's tail and mane flying. Behind him, three young Pawnee braves chased him hard, yipping and yelling at the tops of their voices. Morgan raised his rifle.

"Best not shoot yet," said Patch. "Could be they're just funnin'. Pawnee blood runs hot when they're a-chasin' buf-flcr."

"But they might kill Loonie," said Morgan.

"Yep, they might."

Looking Loon ran a straight course for them, then changed direction. Two of the braves followed as if they were pulled along behind him on strings. The third veered slightly to intercept the Delaware if he continued riding in the same direction.

"They're goin' to catch him," said Lem.

"If you shoot, shoot at the Pawnee horses," said Patch.

"Why?" asked Morgan.

"Might not help. They hold their horses in high favor. But, if we kilt them young bucks, we'd have Pawnee on our backs clear to the Rocky Mounts."

Looking Loon hauled hard on his reins, turned his horse once again. He charged the lone brave riding to cut him off. This surprised the other two Pawnee, and they scrambled to change direction. The Delaware jabbed the butt of his rifle at the lone Pawnee and struck him in the chest, knocking him from the back of his pony. The brave somersaulted backward and landed on his feet. He shook his bow at Loonie, who wheeled his horse in a tight circle.

"Let's shoot them two horses out from under those bucks," said Patch, bringing his rifle to his shoulder.

Morgan had already taken aim on one of the braves. He lowered his sights, led the horse and squeezed the trigger.

The ball struck the pony behind its right foreleg, smashing through ribs, tearing up arteries, shattering veins. The animal's forelegs crumpled. The brave flew over the pony's head, landed in a crumpled heap a few yards from the stricken mount.

Patch shot the other brave's pony in the neck. It staggered a few yards, then fell over, pinning the Pawnee's leg underneath. Morgan heard a bone snap. The Pawnee's face was expressionless and Morgan wondered at that. The pony was kicking all four legs, trying to regain its footing.

Morgan was already reloading his rifle when Looking Loon caught up with them. The Indian looked at Morgan, grinned. He made the sign of a man wearing a belt. Morgan dropped his head, remembering. The buffalo bull's intestines were wrapped around his waist like a sash, forgotten in the excitement. The bull's heart bulged inside his shirt, staining the fabric with its blood.

"Let's light a shuck," said Patch, spitting a fresh ball and spit-soaked cloth patch down his barrel. He rammed the wiping stick down as he prepared to ride away. Looking Loon spoke to Patch in sign. Morgan could make out some of it. The Delaware was talking about mounted men hunting, and he was indicating the Pawnee were close.

"We're ready," said Lem impatiently.

Patch pulled his mount to the north.

But their way was blocked. The herd had split and buffalo were streaming in all directions, scattering like quail before an unseen threat. Patch halted, and Looking Loon began talking to him in sign. Morgan watched as buffalo streaked past them, veering sharply when they saw the four riders in their path.

"What do we do now?" Lem asked Patch.

"Looking Loon says that Pawnee split up this herd. Injuns'll be ridin' all through both main bunches, chasin' after strays."

"So?"

"So, it looks like we're caught in the middle."

"I don't see no Pawnee," said Lem stubbornly.

"Pa, look," said Morgan.

"You boys hold steady now," warned Patch.

Lem twisted in the saddle, saw what Morgan had seen.

Five Pawnee braves rode toward them from different directions. They met up about three hundred yards away and fanned out. They carried bows at the ready, arrows nocked.

Looking Loon made several signs to Patch. Sisco nodded.

"Yep," said Patch aloud. "That'll be the big chief hisself Little Antelope. And, that's his onliest son with him, that lean one wearin' three eagle feathers in his hair. He be called Turtle."

"You know them?" asked Morgan.

"Sorta."

"They don't look too friendly to me," said Morgan.

"They ain't friendly at all," said Patch. "Just hold back your water, boys. Don't do nothin' lessen I say to."

Little Antelope rode up to the dead and gutted bull, halted his horse. The other braves with him stopped at that place, too. The Pawnee chief looked down at the bull. He leaned over and broke off the arrow that was sprouting from its hump. He looked at it, then showed it to the other braves with him. They each grunted.

"That was his arrer in the buffler," said Patch, his voice pitched low.

"He can't claim it," said Morgan, sharply.

"Keep quiet," whispered Lem.

Little Antelope rode around the bull while the other Pawnees sat their horses, none of them moving. They all stared at the four interlopers. Morgan saw that their faces were smooth, their features sharply defined. They wore only breechclouts and moccasins, carried knives and iron war hatchets, arrows in quivers slung over their backs. Each had an arrow nocked to his bowstring.

Little Antelope began speaking, not to anyone in particular, but loudly, almost shouting. Morgan tensed, although he could not understand a word. He looked at Patch out of the corner of his eye. Patch sat his horse calmly, did not even twitch.

Finally, the Pawnee chief rode toward them, stopped a few paces away. He pulled his arrow free from the string, laid his bow and the loose arrow across his bare legs. He continued speaking, but now used his hands in sign. He pointed to the giant buffalo carcass several times. Then, he was silent. He glared at the four intruders, as if waiting for an explanation.

"He said that this was a mighty bull," said Patch. "He said the bull has strong medicine. That means it's somethin' right special, I reckon. He said he was a-chasin' it, that he shot an arrer into it and the sting was no more than a gnat's bite. He wonders who killed the bull with a thunderstick." Patch patted his rifle softly. "He wants to know who brought the bull down."

"How come?" asked Morgan, his mouth dry as the dust he tasted on his tongue.

"Dunno," said Patch.

"You tell him," said Morgan. He drew air in his lungs, thrust his chest out. "You tell him I done it."

"He might not like it none," said Patch.

"Tell him we all done it," said Lem. Morgan shot his father a sharp look.

"I'll tell him what's so," said Patch. He began to speak in sign. He pointed to young Morgan, then at the bull. He told how Morgan was on the ground and how the bull charged him. He said that the bull tried to kill Morgan, but the boy held his ground and shot the great beast at close range. So close, his hands said, the boy could feel the bull's hot breath on his face.

The Pawnees grunted and made humming sounds in their throats.

Little Antelope spoke again. His hands interpreted his words.

"He says that you have strong medicine, Morgan. He wonders what you have inside your shirt."

Morgan withdrew the bull's bloody heart, held it aloft.

The Indians muttered in approval.

"You take a bite of that heart and then offer it to Little Antelope," said Patch. "That will show him you were the one what kilt that bull. Injuns set a heap of store in respect."

"It's raw meat," said Morgan.

"It might help us keep our hair," Patch advised.

"Go on, Morg," said Lem. "Take a little bite, chew it good and swaller it."

Morgan braced himself, took a bite from the tip of the heart. He chewed the tough meat, held out the heart toward Little Antelope. The chief rode up, took the heart, bit into the middle of it. He wrenched loose a chunk of meat, seemed to swallow it whole.

Little Antelope handed the heart back to Morgan, touched a fist to his chest. He rode up close, reached out, put his hand on Morgan's rifle. Then, he looked at the medicine horn hanging at Morgan's side. He picked it up, looked closely at the markings.

"You have strong medicine," the Pawnee signed while Patch interpreted. "You are young, but you are strong. You hunt where the Pawnee hunts. Go away and do not hunt here anymore. We will take the meat of this great bull and it will make us strong. You eat the heart and you will be strong. Go."

"I reckon we better go," said Patch. He signed to Little Antelope that they were leaving. Little Antelope wheeled his horse and returned to the dead bull. He called loudly and women and children waddled up, carrying knives and hatchets. The Pawnees rode away, showing off their horsemanship, before attacking the herd. Morgan watched Turtle ride alongside a large cow and shoot an arrow into it. The cow staggered and finally dropped. Morgan shook his head in wonderment.

The four men caught up the pack animals and headed north, away from the path of the buffalo herd. Morgan saw the animals get smaller and smaller until they just blurred together and then became a thin line on the horizon that finally disappeared.

14

They rode a great distance over gradually changing terrain and camped that night in strange country.

The prairie was now broken and scarred as if by a gigantic plow. They seemed to be, Morgan thought, on the edge of a dead world. There were no trees and the grass was sparse. They seemed to have lost the river somewhere in their travels.

In the distance, Morgan saw great heaps of rolling land, and every so often, like beacons on a desolate landscape, small peaks that seemed like bumps on the land, hints of the great mountains beyond.

Patch selected a campsite on high ground. There, they could see for miles in every direction.

"What happened to the river?" Morgan asked.

"We'll pick it up again, tomorry," said Sisco. "Safer here for the time bein'."

That night, they feasted on buffalo filets and boudoins, the rest of the bull's heart and liver, and the kidneys.

Sisco made a white pudding from the boudoins, what the French called *poudinge blanc*. He added the filets and kidneys to the stew. He put in flour, salt and pepper, stirred in water enough to cook it through. They all ate portions of the heart raw at Sisco's urging, both in celebration of the kill and as part of some ancient ritual Sisco told them about.

"Injuns put great store in eating the hearts of animals they kill—'specially if the animal is big and pow'rful and strong and brave. They say it gives 'em good medicine."

"This is a feast," said Morgan.

"You can still taste the shit in them boudins," said Lem.

"That's what gives 'em their flavor." Patch laughed. "Buffalo shit's good for lots of things."

"Like what?" asked Morgan, chewing the crackle-crisp boudins.

"When their droppin's is dry, you can use 'em to make fires. Boudins is prime vittles to a mountain man."

After that, Morgan ate more than his share. Looking Loon looked pained when the last scrap was gone.

"That Injun dearly loves the boudins," said Patch, by way of explanation.

"You ask me," said Morgan dryly, "he'll eat anything."

Lem and Sisco laughed. Morgan thought about his dog, Friar Tuck, and wished, once again, that Looking Loon would choke on a piece of meat.

The next morning, they stayed in camp, mending clothes, sewing broken harnesses, trimming hooves on mules and horses. When Patch said it was time to go, they mounted up and rode westward, coming upon the Missouri River in mid-afternoon.

"Not far to go now," said Patch.

"Where to?" asked Lem.

"You want to see old Silas Morgan?"

"I reckon I would."

"We might just find the Crow, then. That's likely where he'll be found."

"Are them Crows friendly?"

"Sometimes. Hard to say."

Lem said nothing, but Morgan noticed his father was especially edgy the next few days.

The land kept changing and it seemed to be rising in a slow slope, so gradual it might have been a trick of the eyes. One day, Morgan saw the broken country, the flatness all rumpled and gouged by gullies and washes and the hills jagging up, and beyond, so far away he had to strain his eyes to see, a long blue mass that he thought must be the mountains.

They saw more buffalo, and elk, deer and antelope, often grazing on the same plain in fairly close proximity. Morgan was curious about the antelope.

"Tastes like goat's meat," said Patch. "But, if that's all you got, you can eat 'em."

He remembered Dick Hauser telling him the same thing at Spanish Jack's in St. Louis. But he still hadn't tasted antelope meat and he wanted to find out for himself if the meat did taste like goat.

Morgan chased after several antelope, but they were too fast for his horse. Patch watched him with amusement.

"You ain't never gonna get no goat thataway," he said.

"Well, how then?" asked Morgan.

"You got to trick 'em. They're curious critters. You can sneak up on 'em, to within a couple a hunnert yards, and lie down on your back, wiggle your legs in the air. They's some who ties a cloth to their rifles and waggle it like a flag. The goats'll come up close. Injuns, they wear antelope skins and steal up close enough to shoot 'em with arrers. But, you chase 'em like you're a-doin' and they'll run circles around you, laughin' all the time."

Morgan gave up trying to shoot an antelope, but he vowed that someday he would try one of Patch's tricks.

And, one day, the mountains were there, a dark mass on the morning horizon. The sight caught Morgan by surprise.

"Are them the mountains?" he asked Patch.

"Sure as rain."

"They're far off."

"They be far, chile."

"When will we get there?"

"Why, 'fore you know it," said Patch.

And so it was. One day, they could see the mountains clearly, and Morgan would ever after remember the thrill of seeing their snowcapped peaks, their sawtooth ridges. They seemed born of the blue sky itself, huge muscular giants basking in the golden sunlight, distant, mysterious, alluring. Even his father grew excited as they drew closer to the Rocky Mountains.

"That's where we'll make our fortune, son."

"You think so, Pa?"

Lem grinned so wide his face fairly shone.

Jocko DeSam did not like Josie Montez. The man was full of hate. He was not a trapper. He had been useful for the smuggling, but now he was like a stray dog that wouldn't go away. Worse, DeSam couldn't even kick him. For Josie was a dog that would bite, not tuck its tail and skulk off.

And, Montez was full of questions. He constantly asked questions about Lemuel Hawke and his son, Morgan.

"Where do you think this Hawke will go?" he asked every day, as DeSam paddled in the bow of the canoe. Montez paddled, too, in the stern, but not when he was talking, thinking out loud.

For days, DeSam had not known how to answer the Spaniard. Then, he remembered that day when he had first met the Hawkes, back in Nashville. Lem had talked about his friend who trapped in the mountains, a man DeSam knew, or at least had seen. Nobody really knew old Silas Morgan. He lived with the Blue Bead People, the Crow, up on the Yellowstone.

The mountains were close now. DeSam could almost smell the heady scent of the evergreens, taste the crystal waters of the streams. But he had this Spanish millstone around his neck, this jabbering jay who talked incessantly of killing a man he had seen but once, did not know.

"Tonight," he spat back at Montez, "we will talk, no? I have the idea."

"You telling me to shut my mouth, Jocko?"

"You talk too damn much, Josie."

Montez laughed. It was like a knife scraping over stone.

They dug their paddles in as the river took a wide sweep and then narrowed. The water ran swift in the narrows and corded muscles, swollen veins, stood out on the men's necks. Their arms were strong from paddling against the current day after day, and they bucked the dugout through the narrows into tamer water, where the swirling pools were almost hypnotic as they scurried by and disappeared.

"What is this big idea you have, Jocko?" asked Montez when he had his breathing back to a steady rate.

"I am thinking about it, Montez."

"A good idea?"

"Maybe, eh? You want this Hawke feller pretty good."

"I want him pretty bad, *amigo*."

DeSam winced at the Spanish word for "friend." He did business with Josie Montez, but he did not like him. A man had very few friends in this country. And, often, he did not pick them. Friends happened, like storms or golden mornings. One did not choose. But one could choose one's enemies, or those he did not want as friends. Montez was a dangerous man. There were many stories about him and his knife down in New Orleans. Some of the stories had been told by his brother, Spanish Jack. Others were carried up to St. Louis and out to the mountain camps by men who had survived Montez's knife or pistols.

"Well, maybe you will get your chance, Josie. You will have to hunt him, though."

"I am hunting him now," said Montez.

"This may be the easy part, *non?* You hunt a man you cannot see, a man who is maybe far away."

"He can't run forever," said Montez, grunting as he knifed the water with his paddle. Ahead, another dugout labored upstream, its men obscured by a cloud of deerflies or river gnats as big as houseflies.

"In those big mountains," said DeSam, "a man can hide forever." He was thinking about Silas, who lived with those damned Absaroke, the Crow. Married to a squaw, he was more Indian than white now. Jocko had known several such men, and their women never took up the white ways. Old Silas seldom came to the settlements anymore, and then only to buy gewgaws for his woman, whiskey, traps and supplies. He never stayed long, did not frequent the tippling houses in St. Louis. Never talked about his life in the mountains.

DeSam had seen him, once, hunting with the Crow, a half dozen of them. It was hard to tell them apart. Silas was just as lean, his skin just as red, darker even than some Crow, and without his beard, one would take him for a Crow. He even spoke the tongue, for DeSam had heard him conversing with his companions in Absaroke. He knew the sign, too.

He wondered if he should tell Montez about Silas Morgan, where he might find him. A smile flickered on DeSam's lips. Maybe the Crow would not like this Spaniard any better than he did. He could picture Montez's scalp dangling from a Crow lance. The thought gave him pleasure.

The sun fell fast in the sky, sank behind the mountains. DeSam put in where several of his brigade had already landed and were setting up camp for the night. He was tired, but elated. Maybe he would get Montez off his back soon. They were not far from the Yellowstone. A few more days and maybe Montez would go looking for Lemuel Hawke and whatever happened would be God's will.

The dugout growled against the sandy shore. DeSam scrambled over the prow, waited for Montez to climb out. Together, they pulled the craft up onto the shore, emptied it of their rifles, pouches and goods, and turned it over on its side.

"Now, you will tell me your idea, Jocko?" Montez fixed the Frenchman with hard brown eyes.

DeSam looked at the cloud-curdled sky, the setting sun just beginning to tinge the cloud-bellies a salmon-pink. The breeze on the river stiffened, and he knew there would be a chill in that July night. Two more dugouts rounded the bend, headed toward shore. The men in them looked exhausted, their shoulders drooping, their paddles spanking the water listlessly instead of carving in deeply.

"I will tell you what you can do," said DeSam wearily. "Come, we find a place to talk."

Some of the Frenchmen already on shore waved to DeSam, called out obscenities to him. He grinned and waved back. Their faces, even under their thick beards, were bronzed by the sun. Halos of flies and gnats surrounded their heads. They had started a cookfire and made it smoky to fend off the insects that swarmed off the river in search of fresh blood.

DeSam found a place out of earshot of the other men in his brigade. A small creek wound through a copse of cottonwood and alder thickets, streaming down through gently rolling land, the long grassy hills that buffalo had grazed for centuries.

DeSam sat beneath a tree, the sores on his butt long since

scabbed over until they were like leather patches on his skin. Montez squatted a few feet away, braced against another tree. Below, they heard the voices of the new arrivals mingling with those on shore, a blend of French and English words of greetings and insults.

"This Hawke," said DeSam, "he has a friend in the mountains. He talks about this man all the time. He will probably look for him and find him."

"Who is this friend?"

"His name is Silas Morgan. Hawke named his son after him."

"Where does this Silas live?" asked Montez.

"He lives with the Absaroke, the Crow. If you find this man, you will surely find Hawke, I think."

DeSam described Silas Morgan the way he remembered him. He said that he was a few years older than Hawke and that he was more savage than civilized.

"Where do these Crow live?" asked Montez.

"The band he is with, I think, hunt along the Yellowstone, sometimes up on the Musselshell. But, I have seen them on the Judith, as well. They are wanderers, like all these tribes, hunters who follow the buffalo. They hunt the buffalo now and then will trap the mountains for furs when the snows come and the beaver coats they shine and become thick."

"You will go with me, help me to find this Silas, Jocko?"

"No, I do not want anything to do with the Crow."

"They are friendly, are they not? This Silas lives with them."

"They are a good people. The women are very beautiful and the men are handsome. But I trade with the Blackfeet and they do not like the Crow. The Crow do not like white men much. Some do, some don't."

"How will I find these rivers?" asked Montez.

"I will draw you a map and you must leave the Missouri at the Musselshell and go south to the Yellowstone. They may be hunting on the Big Horn, which would be to the east. If they are not on those rivers, then you must double back and look for the Crow on some of the creeks. There are many creeks and they camp on all of them."

"I will be alone," Montez mused.

"No, there are those who trap those mountains where the rivers are born. You will find men who know where the Crow are. The Major will trap those same streams. He'll put trappers all through that country, you bet."

"And where will you go, Jocko?"

"I do not like to say." But he planned to trap the Milk or the Marias.

"You will trade with the Blackfeet?"

"I will trade the whiskey for furs," admitted DeSam.

"When do we reach this Musselshell?"

"In a week or two. I would bet a day's trapping that you will follow Lem up that river. Old Patch, he traps the Absarokes and he trades with the Crow."

"Bueno," said Montez. "I will find Lem Hawke and kill him before the snow flies."

"Good fortune, then," said DeSam in French.

"Suerte," said Montez. But he meant it for himself, for he would need all the luck he could get to find Lem Hawke and put a blade to his throat.

Angus MacDougal and his keelboats struck the Platte River and went as far as they could go before the water became so shallow they dared not risk further voyaging. He sent the last keelboat back downriver, set off overland on horses, with the mules in a pack train, following the North Platte. They were running out of summer and he was losing time. The Laramie range loomed to the south, reminding them of how small they were, how insignificant was their place in such a grand country.

The men no longer sang the boatmen's songs, but rode westward with determination, if not enjoyment. Angus loved every moment of it, for he saw beyond, saw the riches, the wealth the men could only dream about. They worked for him, for the Company, and they would never have more than enough money to squander in a day or a week after the season.

Two men had drowned that morning, stepping off a sand bank into a deep hole. The water was low, but swift, and they were swept away before anyone could save them. It was too bad, but the party had to forsake finding their bodies. There was a sullenness among the others following the accident, but Angus knew they would soon forget. Both were older men with not much experience. He had signed them on reluctantly, but they had that maddened gleam in their eyes and he thought they might make it through a winter.

At least they were not Scotsmen, he mused. One was a German named Ludwig something or other. The other had an English name—Wilson, or Miller, he could not remember. Like so many others who came out West, they would leave no trace. Their families would probably never know they had died. For certain they could not know until he had gotten back to St. Louis next year and filed his report with the company. He would write about the incident in his journal that night after supper, when he was in his shelter with his candle and his books.

Perhaps, Angus thought, he would play the pipes tonight, a dirge for the two who had died. It might not help the men's mood, but it would help his own. He needed to hear the skirling in his ears, feel the moan of the pipes in his blood. He needed that reminder of home and old friends among the uncivilized rabble trekking along a trail trampled by buffalo, following Fletcher Bancroft, in the lead.

Angus swabbed sweat off his forehead with a large handkerchief and cocked an eye at the setting sun. The clouds to the west were turning peach, rows of them flocked together like tattered batting. The river was streaked with gold and copper, veins of pale silver eeling through dark ripples, glazed at the edges by purple borders where the banks threw wavering shadows.

They must make camp soon, he thought, for the sun fell quickly behind those mountains, leaving cold ashes in the sky, the lingering dust of the day hanging like gossamer shrouds over the distant horizon.

Fletcher Bancroft shifted in his saddle, looked back at Angus, as if reading his mind. Angus nodded, stuck his handkerchief back in his pouch. There was no breeze and it was hot, dry as last year's mud dauber's nest.

A man named Tom Sheets turned and looked back, too. He had known one of the men who drowned, had tried to find a rope to throw to them. Once the two went under, though, they never came back up. Angus didn't ignore Sheets; he just looked right through him, as if he wasn't there. Tom had wanted to find the bodies, bury them. A singular waste of time in MacDougal's mind.

Sheets turned, said something to Ralph Parsons, who was riding alongside him. Ralph was Ernie's brother. Parsons nodded. Ahead, where the land made a wide bowl, Fletch turned right, following a shallow ridge. He stopped at its pinnacle and dismounted. The men following him surrounded that central point and picketed their horses, unloaded their gear, leaving scattered piles far enough apart so that they could set up their shelters for the night.

Fletcher began barking orders. A half dozen men brought up the pack train, rode some distance past the camp and started setting up a rope corral. Trask and Parsons waited until Angus caught up with them.

"Major," said Sheets, blocking his way with his horse, "we ought to lay up a day and get some rest."

"He's right, Major," said Parsons. "We must've come fifty miles today."

"More like thirty," said the Major. "A good stretch of the legs."

"Forty," said Sheets. "At least."

"We got a late start because of those two men frolicking in the river," said MacDougal. "That cost us five miles. We've got less than an hour of sunlight left. I could have gotten back that five miles and you both would have cursed me when you couldn't find your shitrags in the dark. We're running late on flat ground, so stop your bellyaching."

"My butt feels like a chunk of rock," said Sheets.

"Soak your butt in the North Platte," said Angus coldly.

"Major, we're all plumb tuckered," said Parsons. "The men been prickly as nettles all goddamned day. You ain't heard 'em, like we have, grumblin' and gripin'."

"And did this do them all some good?" asked the Major. "Did it shorten the miles? Did it soothe your feet, Sheets?"

"Well, now there you go, Major, a-twistin' everything up into knots," said Sheets. "What the hell difference does a goddamned day make?"

Angus had put down such minor rebellions before. He enjoyed it, actually. It strengthened his position as a leader. He could feel the thunder rising in his chest, the thunder that every great orator possessed. A shame to waste it on two whining men, but they had been the ones to speak up, not the others, who were already making camp. Perhaps it was just as well that he had only these two to contend with at the moment.

He felt like shooting them both, treating them like mutineers on the high seas. The Major was a man who settled scores quickly, if he could. He was reminded, once again, of Jacques Decembre's defection—that damned Jocko DeSam, who fancied himself a booshway. It was downright insulting. He and that riffraff, the Hawkes, would regret not working in his brigade. One way or another, Angus would have their hides. And if Sheets and Parsons didn't back down quick, he'd skin them, too.

"Gentlemen," MacDougal said coolly, "I sense that you possess little appreciation for the task ahead of us. We've a great deal of ground to cover and you'll want the best beaver streams for yourselves. Keep your grouses to yourselves or you'll get the poorest grounds to trap, I assure you."

Sheets opened his mouth, started to say something. Parsons reached out and grabbed his arm to stop him from making things worse. Nobody ever won an argument with the Major.

MacDougal stared Sheets down, until Tom averted his eyes and hung his head. Parsons saw the look on the Major's face and he turned his horse dejectedly.

"The bastard," muttered Sheets as he rode away. He could feel the Major's eyes burning into his back.

"I guess we ain't as tired as we thought," said Parsons.

"I got me a good mind to—"

But Sheets never finished his sentence. The Major galloped past them, looking as fresh as when they had started out that morning.

"Tomorry," said Parsons, "he'll log sixty miles in his book, you'll see."

That evening, the brigade ate badger, geese, turkey and the river furnished their larder with catfish caught on bone hooks baited with earthworms or spoiled jerky.

Tom Sheets cussed under his breath all evening long and didn't stop until he crawled into his blankets, but nobody paid him any mind. They knew he was just trying to get over the death of a friend he had made.

After the fires were put out, the Major played the pipes for a half an hour in the darkness and the men listened in silence. Some of them sobbed softly, crushed by the terrible loneliness they felt in that vast, desolate land, conscious that they were dependent on the Major for their livelihood.

And that was just how Angus MacDougal wanted them to feel—every man jack of them.

15

Morgan Hawke gazed at the distant horizon so long his father thought he must be in a trance.

"I reckon them are the mountains yonder," said Morgan. "Or just more hills like we been seein' and ridin' through."

"I reckon we're gettin' close," said Lem. "Don't appear to be too big. Probably no bigger'n the Cumberlands or the Smokies."

"Them ain't the Rockies," said Patch, overhearing father and son. "Just more hills, like you say, Morgan." Looking Loon ranged far ahead of them, glad to be free of leading the pack mules, which he had done all morning. They had journeyed south after coming upon a huge bend in the Missouri, a wide place that looked like a delta or a lake. Patch led them south on a river he said ran out of the mountains.

"Broad, ain't it?" said Lem.

"This be the Musselshell," said Patch. "We'll run up it, see if we can't find us a Crow what knows where your friend Silas be."

"I wonder how Silas is doing?" Lem mused aloud. Everyone but Lemuel called him "old" Silas. Even Hawke's ex-wife Roberta had called him that, too. He wondered why. Silas wasn't much older than he. But, he looked old. Always had, ever since Lem had known him. Maybe Silas was old, now that he thought of it. Forty-five or so. Couldn't be fifty yet, could he? Maybe. Morg hadn't been born when old Silas left Virginny to trap beaver and such. And now Morg was all but full growed, so Silas had to be a graybeard. Hell, the man could be sixty by now, the way time was a-rushin' by.

Morgan rattled the rope, jerked the mules into motion. Boots stepped out, snatching a tuft of twelve-inch grass from the prairie. Deer broke from cover, rising up from beds in the middle of a wide patch of grass. Their tails flashed golden in the sun and they disappeared, leaving narrow swaths in their wake.

The deer were different from the eastern whitetails. They had large ears and seemed bigger, with gray hides, gray as winter wolves in full coat.

"They call 'em mule deer," Patch told him. " 'Cause of those big ears, I reckon. Chunky as hogs, ain't they? Mighty fine eatin'."

They had seen buffalo and antelope every day for the past several weeks, and mule deer way off, standing like sentinals next to timber, or scattering from a waterhole that appeared like a mirage in one of the long shallow valleys in the rolling countryside. Once in a while, they'd see elk, far off, in small herds. The buffalo were scattered, as if they had been hunted. Patch did not want to hunt them.

"This be Crow land," he said. "And the Sioux, they hunt here; Cheyenne, too. Sometimes the Blackfeet come down to fight the Crow. This be dangerous country for white-skins, and some red 'uns, too."

There were huge prairie dog cities everywhere. Morgan and Lem were fascinated by their numbers, their shrill, high-pitched whistles of warning.

And, still, there were no mountains, only endless hills where small, scattered herds of buffalo grazed or antelope ran. Yet, there were days when he was sure he could see mountains in the distance. At times, Morgan wondered if they were not just an illusion, a trick of the light. Most often they turned out to be low dark clouds atop distant hills.

"When will we get to the mountains?" Morgan kept asking Patch.

"One day you'll see 'em," was all Patch said. "They'll be touchin' the sky and have snow on their peaks prettier'n anything you ever saw."

To Morgan, they seemed to be crawling across the prairie.

The land was broken along the Musselshell, scarred and welted like the back of a man flayed with a brutal whip. They passed several places where Indians had camped. Morgan looked at the sites with fascination. He could almost see the Indians in his mind. It was thrilling to ride over the places where they had lived.

One day, Patch waved them back into a deep gully. Before they descended into the hiding place, Morgan and his father saw the Indians. They were far off and yelling exultantly. They were driving horses with mottled coats, twenty or so.

"Flatheads," Patch explained. " 'Pears they been after the Crow and got 'em some ponies."

"Did they see us?" Lem asked.

"I reckon not. Them bucks are full o' themselves, braggin' and such that they kilt some Crow and got 'em some horses and scalps."

"Why don't the Crow go after them?" asked Morgan.

Patch shrugged. "Could be the Crow was hurt bad," he said. "Or maybe the Flatheads took all their horses. Injuns is funny. They don't look on fightin' like we do. It's a sport. They make a big to-do about fightin', lots of singin' and dancin', and when they do battle, they play it like a game, actin' brave and strikin' coup with sticks and warclubs. Don't make much sense—'cept to another Injun."

"Injuns is mighty strange," observed Morgan. Patch almost laughed. He could tell from the look in Morgan's eyes that the boy was fascinated by the redmen.

"That they be," agreed Patch.

They waited a long time before Looking Loon signed to them that the Flathead had gone their way and were no longer a threat. But Morgan kept looking for Indians as they drew closer to the mountains.

Looking Loon rode into camp one evening with a mule deer draped over his horse's withers. The deer had not been gutted out. Usually, the Delaware made his kill, removed the legs and head, skinned it, butchered the animal and brought the meat back all neatly rolled up in its hide.

Blow flies swarmed over the venison, thick as fur on a beaver. These insects had been their constant companions for weeks, attacking the meat from the time they gutted it to when they cooked it and while they ate it.

The Delaware began speaking to Patch in sign, his hands moving so rapidly Morgan had difficulty in following him. But he knew that Loonie was talking about Indians and that he was excited. Morgan couldn't tell by Loonie's signs if the Indians were hostile, but at the end of his silent recital, Looking Loon grinned.

"Looks like Loonie done found him a bunch of Crow," said Patch. "He shot two deer, gave 'em the other one as a gift. He told 'em we were here. He thinks they've got a camp somewheres near, up the Musselshell."

"Are these the Crow what Silas took up with?" asked Lem.

"Loonie doesn't know the difference 'twixt one tribe or another, but he says one of the Crow is a brave we've run onto before. Name of Moon Face. I reckon he's one of the Little Robe clan and that he be one of them with Silas last spring. We done some tradin'."

"What do we do now?" asked Morgan.

"Sit tight, I reckon. Be the polite thing to do. This is Crow country and we got to ask 'em can we come through, do some trappin'."

"How soon will the Crow be here?" asked Lem.

"Injuns got to do a lot of talkin' and studyin' on a thing before they make up their minds. Kinda like some of them Germans I knowed back in Pennsylvania. Don't do to hurryin' 'em none."

"Then we got no worries," said Lem.

"I couldn't exactly say," said Patch. "I'd see my pan was primed and keep a weather eye cocked. Don't make no sudden moves, but be ready, case they want to try us on for size."

"Did Loonie say anything about Silas?" asked Lem.

"He told 'em we were looking for Gray Hawk—that's what the Crow calls your friend."

"And, what did the Crow say?"

"They didn't say yeah or nay."

"Maybe Silas will come with them," ventured Morgan.

Patch shrugged. But the old trapper kept his rifle close and they all checked their pans for dry powder. Morgan touched his flint to see if it was secure in its leather sleeve, tightened the bolt down a notch. Lem rubbed the sweat off his palms, stayed close to a stand of poplar for cover.

Looking Loon laid the dead mule deer on the ground. He made no move to dress it out. Instead, he sat down and laid his rifle across his lap. He seemed, Morgan thought, to sit there in a trance.

Patch set out some tobacco, trade beads and a half dozen iron tomahawks. He laid them on a Hudson Bay blanket, neat and orderly, as if he had done such many times before.

"You might want to lay out some goods yourselfs," Patch said to Morgan and Lem. "Injuns dearly love presents."

They waited for almost an hour before there was any sign of the Crow.

Looking Loon was the first to hear the Indians approaching. His hands told Patch the Crow were nearby.

"Here they come," said the trapper. "Just be quiet and don't get excited. "Let me do the talkin'."

A half dozen Crow rode boldly into camp. They carried both rifles and bows, but they were not painted. Morgan thought they looked arrogant and mean. He licked dry lips and let out a shallow breath of stale air from his lungs.

The lead Crow looked at the deer on the ground. He was a burly man with dark reddish skin, a handsome face, large straight nose, coal-black hair. He wore a breastplate of small bones, attached together with sinew in straight, horizontal lines. Beads dangled from the feathers that bordered the ornament. He wore a breechclout and beaded moccasins. His rifle was studded with brass tacks. It was a short-barreled flintlock. A single eagle feather dangled from its frontpiece.

"I am Lame Bull," he said in his native tongue. He signed his name to Patch. "You are One-Eye."

Patch nodded, signed that he was a friend. He offered Lame Bull and the others his gifts. He pointed to Lem and Morgan's blankets.

"Take," Patch said in English.

The Crow dismounted, strutted around the camp.

"This deer should be gutted and hung up," he said in Crow, as he poked it with his rifle. Then, he spoke rapidly in both sign and Absaroke. "Why are you here? Where are you going? Why do you ride through Crow land? What are you looking for?"

Patch patiently answered all of his questions, speaking in English for the Hawkes' benefit, making sign to Lame Bull.

"We go to the mountains to trap the beaver for the white man's shining buttons," said Patch. "Moon Face there knows One-Eye. These two white faces are father and son. They look for their friend, Gray Hawk. They are from his mother's country and they have a come a long way to see their good friend. Take these gifts and tell Gray Hawk we are here."

The Crow all seemed to disdain the gifts at first. Moon Face came up to Morgan Hawke and poked a finger in his chest, felt the muscles of his arms.

Morgan bristled.

"You just hold steady, Morgan," said Patch. "He don't mean no harm. Just his way of gettin' to know you."

Two Crow examined Lem. None of them seemed interested in Looking Loon. The Delaware still sat there, his rifle across his legs, staring into nothingness.

The other Crow looked at the mules and examined the horses, opening their mouths. They poked at the panniers, as if trying to see what goods were inside the packs. Morgan found that he could smell the Crow. They had a peculiar odor, a smell of smoke and grease that was very strong.

"This one has no tongue," said Lame Bull, pointing to Looking Loon. "He is not Crow."

"He is a human being from another tribe," Patch said aloud, making the signs. "He is not white."

Lame Bull laughed at that. "My eyes can see he is not white," he signed. "His skin is as dark as mine, but he is very ugly."

"Yes, he is ugly," signed Patch, "and he has no tongue. The Great Spirit has given him a brave heart in its place."

Lame Bull and the others laughed again. Then, the Crow began to snatch up the gifts, examining the tobacco and beads, talking among themselves. Moon Face fought over some tobacco and ended up with only a handful.

Finally, to Morgan's relief, Lame Bull made a sign that he could understand.

"Bring that deer with you and come with us," he told Patch.

"Well, boys, we're a-goin' to the Crow camp," said the trapper.

"How far?" asked Morgan suddenly. The Crow all looked at him. It grew very quiet.

"This one has a tongue," signed Lame Bull. "Does he also have a brave heart?"

"He kilt the biggest buffler I ever seed when it was chargin' him. The buffler was bristlin' with Pawnee arrers. He warn't more'n ten feet away when the boy brought the bull down with a single shot."

"He was on his horse," said Lame Bull disdainfully.

"He was standin' like he is now. He didn't run."

Morgan read the sign perfectly. His chest swelled slightly. "You don't need to brag on me, none," he told Patch.

"Injuns like braggin'," he replied. "They like it a lot."

Lame Bull called the other braves to him. He spoke in Absaroke for several moments. He did not make sign. Morgan saw that the others were listening intently. Finally, Moon Face and Lame Bull turned toward Patch.

"We will return to our people," said Lame Bull. "We will talk to them and we will smoke. We will take this deer because it belongs to us."

Patch's eyes narrowed, but he did not translate. Morgan understood the sign anyway.

"We go," said Moon Face, his hand sign very curt. With that, two Indians lifted the deer, slung it over Moon Face's pony. Lame Bull spoke to them. The Crow mounted up and rode out of sight without uttering another sound.

Looking Loon stood up. His hands began to talk rapidly to Patch. Morgan could not follow all of it, but he knew that the Delaware was saying that they should leave before the sun went to sleep. Looking Loon traced a path that would take them wide of the river but loop back toward the mountains.

Patch did not reply to Looking Loon.

Morgan surprised all of them by speaking to Looking Loon in sign. None was more surprised than his father, but he beamed with pride as he saw the look of approval on Patch's face.

"Why do we run and hide like rabbits?" he asked.

Looking Loon made the sign of a bird and jabbed at his head with a finger, made the circular motion, pulled at his topknot.

"The Crow will scalp us."

"How do your eyes see this?" asked Morgan.

"My heart sees this."

Morgan snorted.

"I wouldn't argy with him none," said Patch. "Loonie

gets a feelin' in his gut now and again. He thinks them Crow are up to no good."

"What about you?" asked Lem.

Patch shrugged. "It don't look too good to me."

"You want to run off?" Lem asked.

"Might be the best thing to do. Did you see Moon Face lookin' at our packs? That nigger might not want to trade for somethin' he can get free."

"I was hopin' we might see Silas," said Lem.

"Hell, they might have kilt him," Patch exclaimed. "I never trusted the Crow much. There's some as set store by 'em, but I just don't trust 'em. Me and Loonie are pullin' out."

"Pa," said Morgan, "maybe we'd better go with Patch and Loonie."

"I reckon we better go with 'em," said Lem. He ran fingers through his full beard. He had let it grow ever since they had seen Josie Montez. Morgan wondered if he had done it to hide his identity. If so, it sure had changed his looks. Morgan's face was clean as a hen's egg, although he had sprouted a few silken hairs on his chin that he had quickly plucked. He had a little hair on his chest, but it, too, was fine and blond, hardly noticeable.

"Let's get to goin', then," said Patch. "Them red niggers could be back anytime."

"Damn," muttered Lem. "I sure was hopin' to see Silas out here."

In less than ten minutes, they had broken camp and were riding a wide loop away from the Musselshell. The sun set quickly, plunging the small party into darkness. Patch kept them all bunched together as they rode blindly on, putting distance between them and the river. Finally, hours later, when the thin sliver of moon had risen, Patch called a halt.

"Don't unpack nothin'," he whispered. "Hobble the horses and mules. Me'n Loonie'll take the first watch. You boys get some sleep. I'll wake you in a couple of hours."

"It's sure dark," said Morgan, looking at the black sky, the tiny fingernail of moon.

"That's what they call a trapper's moon, son," said Patch. "Best time to hunt, catch beaver and such."

"It gives me the williwaws," said Lem softly.

"Me, too," said Morgan. "You can't hardly see nothin'."

"Take it as a good sign," said Patch. "We don't want to be seen now, do we? Same as the wild critters what feed at night. Yep, that's sure enough a trapper's moon."

"I just hope it bodes well for us," said Lem nervously.

He and Morgan laid out their bedrolls, kept their rifles close by as they made ready for sleep.

Morgan stared up into the Stygian sky, stared at the small thin moon. "Must be another month comin' to an end, Pa," he breathed.

There was no answer.

His father was already asleep.

Finally, Morgan slept, too. Weighed down by eyelids heavy as stone, he sank into a deep slumber.

Two hours later, he was yanked out of sleep. Not by Patch or Looking Loon, but by two Crow braves who jerked him from his bedroll, locked his arms behind him. He knew they were Crow because he could smell them.

Morgan heard his father grunt, then saw him roughly handled by three more Crow.

"You come, you come," said one of the Crow in a thickly accented voice.

"You speak English?" asked Lem.

"Come," said the Crow again.

Morgan heard a commotion. More Crow approached. He could dimly see that they had Patch and Looking Loon under restraint.

"Boys, they found us," said Patch. "We're a-goin' to the Crow camp with these fellers."

"No talk," said the English-speaking Crow.

Morgan felt a sinking feeling as his hands were tied. The

Crow put their prisoners on their horses. Morgan knew their hands, too, were tied. There were at least a dozen Crow, he figured as they rode off.

The moon, like a sliver of errant quicksilver, disappeared behind scudding, high-flying clouds.

16

The sky lightened slowly under thick gray clouds. Morgan rocked in the saddle, fighting off sleep. His father shook him awake every so often when he began to lean over the pommel.

"You'll fall and break your neck you don't stay awake," chided Lem.

They had been riding for hours in total darkness. The captives had no sense of where they were, having lost their bearings as soon as the Crow had taken them away from their makeshift camp. None had spoken, nor did they talk among themselves.

Shortly after dawn, the Crow halted at a small stream, deep in woodlands. Many bared their buttocks and defecated on low ground several dozen yards away. Others urinated, spraying the grass with yellow streams. One Crow untied their captives' hands, motioned for them to pee or shit. After Morgan saw Patch and Loonie relieving themselves, he did the same. He stared at the Crow, wondering which one had spoken English to them.

He did not see Lame Bull, Moon Face, or any of the other Crow they had met the night before.

"Are these Crow?" Morgan asked Patch, when they were back together, their hands retied, guarded by the watchful Crow.

"Sure as it gets daylight in the mornin'," Patch replied.

"Do you know any of them?"

"I reckoned them we saw yesterday warn't Little Robes. From talk I just heard, they were Filth-eaters. These here be Little Robes, or as some call 'em, Treacherous. Or maybe they be mixed. They all got names like that, or Sore Lips, Greasy-Inside-Their-Mouths."

"You understand their tongue?" Lem asked.

"Some. A little. These be talkin' about that medicine horn of your'n, Morgan. Lookee yonder."

Morgan stared in the direction Patch was pointing.

Three Crow were handling Morgan's possibles pouch, his powder horns. One was examining his rifle, holding it to his shoulder. He felt his stomach jolt with a queasy roll of muscles. It felt as if he had died and was watching Indians paw over his belongings.

One of the Crow was holding up Morgan's medicine horn, speaking to the other two. Others wandered over, looked at the markings on the powder horn. Several spoke excitedly and the one holding the horn traced his forefinger over the symbols engraved in the buffalo horn.

"Are they fixin' to kill us?" Morgan asked.

"They ain't wearin' paint and ain't carryin' spears. 'Pears to be a hunting party. I heard Lame Bull's name mentioned a time or two in passing. I can't figure this bunch out."

"I don't like bein' trussed up like a turkey," said Lem, "a-waitin' for one of them savages to slit our gullets."

"I reckon they could have kilt us long before now," said Patch. "No, they're a-takin' us someplace. Could be worse waitin' for us if they take us to be enemies."

"What do you mean?" asked Morgan.

"Oh, they's lots of things they can do. Best you not know any of it."

"Bastards," muttered Lem.

Patch said nothing. The Crow stopped looking at Morgan's personal belongings and the one holding the powder horn barked orders. The prisoners were handled

roughly as Crow put them on their horses. Morgan, however, was treated much better. Two Crow helped him onto
his horse and one of them untied his hands.

Morgan looked over at Patch. Patch shrugged.

The leader motioned for Morgan to ride with him in the
lead. Reluctantly, Morgan did as he was told. He looked
back at his father, tried to look apologetic.

The muscular Crow leader, like most of his followers,
had long hair that fell past his waist, smooth skin, dark as
highly polished leather. His eyes were dark as agates and
shone with the morning light. He seemed not much older
than Morgan himself. His moccasins were decorated with
dyed porcupine quills, flattened and folded into patterns
that formed ancient symbols; his fringed buckskin shirt
was beaded and quilled in bright colors. He wore a single
eagle feather dangling from his black hair, just below the
left ear. He sat his horse very straight and proud.

"I am called Whistling Elk," the Crow said, suddenly,
taking Morgan by surprise. "White man name."

"You speak English."

"Gray Hawk teach Whistling Elk."

"Where are you taking us?" asked Morgan.

"Go camp. Many tipi. Many Crow."

"Is Gray Hawk there?"

"Gray Hawk say come. Lame Bull come get."

"Why are we prisoners?" Morgan made sign to show
hands being tied with rope.

"No run away," said the Crow. He looked sharply at
Morgan to see if his words were believed.

"A man don't take another man prisoner for such a reason."

Whistling Elk shook his head as if he didn't understand
Morgan. "Damn fuckin' good," he said.

"Silas teach you that?"

"Silas damn fuckin' good."

Before Morgan could reply, there was a commotion

among the Indians. Their captors made bird calls which were answered from somewhere up ahead. The tweetering sounded back and forth until another band of Crow rode out of the woods to meet them.

"Why, there's Lame Bull," said Morgan. "And Moon Face. Godamighty."

Lame Bull did not acknowledge Morgan, just grunted and spoke briefly to Whistling Elk in Crow. He did not sign with his hands, so Morgan did not know what he said.

Lame Bull's band fell in with the Whistling Elk braves and they rode together until they reached the Musselshell again. Whistling Elk spoke no more to Morgan, but seemed to be looking for something that lay ahead.

Morgan heard a horse galloping behind him, turned to see his father riding up from the rear. His hands were no longer tied.

"Lame Bull untied us," Lem said as he slowed his horse to a walk beside Morgan.

"Whistling Elk there said they didn't want us to run away," Morgan said.

"That his name?"

"He's the one who speaks some English. I think Silas taught him."

"That'd be like him. Silas probably speaks Crow, too."

"Where do you reckon they're takin' us, Pa?"

"Patch thinks we're going to a big camp on the Musselshell. He said it can't be much farther. These Injuns ain't carryin' no food and not much water. I'm plumb parched."

"Me, too," said Morgan.

Whistling Elk turned to the Hawkes.

"No talk," he said.

In moments, they rode onto a wide plain where horses grazed, tended by boys. They heard distant shouts and soon a group of young men galloped toward them. Beyond, where the river curved into a half loop, Morgan saw the tops of tipis, their hides stark against the distant mountains, bone white under the gray of the sky.

The young braves rode back and forth, showing off. Morgan marveled at the way they stayed on bareback ponies while performing all kinds of riding feats. One young man rode his pony backward, another crawled underneath his mount, holding onto its neck with encircling arms. Some ponies wore hair or rope bridles, others had none. A Crow stood up on his pony's rump and waved to them, grinning. Others traded horses as they rode side by side.

"Pretty fair riding," said Lem.

"I never saw anything like it," admitted Morgan.

Whistling Elk seemed impervious to the dazzling display of horsemanship, but some of the others in his band began to show off, too. Patch and Looking Loon caught up with Lem and Morgan.

Soon, they saw crowds of women and children streaming from the village. They appeared first as brightly colored objects, then slowly took shape. Ahead of them, on a painted Indian pony, rode a man with a bearded face.

"Pa, look," said Morgan, pointing.

"I see him. Looks like Silas, sure enough." Lem grinned, slapped his thigh.

"Is it?" Morgan asked. "Really?"

"Who else?"

As the man drew closer, he began to wave. Lem and Morgan waved back.

"Gray Hawk," said Whistling Elk, in English. "Damn fuckin' good."

Silas Morgan seemed in no big hurry. Morgan agonized at how long it took him to reach their column. By then, they were surrounded by hooting and hollering Crow braves, all vying for attention from the Hawkes, Patch and the Delaware.

"Hoo haw," said Silas, as he rode up. Morgan had no trouble recognizing him, even though he was barechested and wore only a breechclout, a necklace, a quilled belt with a knife jutting from it, moccasins. "If you ain't a sight for sore eyes, Lemuel Hawke. And, thar be your boy, Morgan, my namesake sure enough. Hooooeeee!"

"Silas, you ain't changed a bit," said Lem.

Silas rode close to Lem, leaned over and slapped him on the back, his carrious teeth visible through his thick beard.

"And, there's old Patch and his nigger, Loonie. How do, Patch?"

"Silas, you look fit," said Patch.

"I got it sweet, Patch. This old coon's got honey in the horn. Morg, I see Whistling Elk's got your medicine horn. You give it to him?"

"No, he took it," Morgan said, scowling. "They tied us up and brung us here."

"Well," said Silas, "the Crow been a mite skittery lately what with so many white men comin' in to their country. They got their hands full with other Injun tribes stealin' their horses and women and kids. Scouts been comin' in all month tellin' tales."

"What tales?" asked Lem.

"Keelboats on the Missouri, the Platte. Trappers and traders, a passel of 'em, headin' toward the Seedskedee and the Popo Agie."

Lem didn't understand a word Silas had said.

"That would be the Major and his bunch," explained Patch.

"I figgered. Angus taught me a lot, but he's a skunk all right. Jocko still trappin' with him?"

"Not no more," said Lem. "The Major tried to kill us all."

"Well, now, we got to make some talk when we get you all settled," said Silas. "I'll see you get your goods back right quick. You got to watch them Filth-eaters."

As they topped a rise, Morgan gasped. There were tipis dotting the plain, rows and rows of them like strange conical houses. Horse herds grazed in bunches and dogs roamed everywhere. It was a chilling and a thrilling sight.

Even Patch was impressed.

"Heap of 'em," he said.

"Won't stay long. Big pow-wow. Lot of smoke and talk. Been goin' on better'n a week."

"War talk?" asked Patch.

"Some, I reckon. We had a good winter, lots of prime furs. But, there's talk of whiskey tradin', cheatin' white eyes and booshway promises broke. Somethin's goin' on."

"I reckon," said Patch laconically.

Lem and Morgan gazed everywhere, drinking it all in, the wonder of it, the maze of tipis, their poles scratching the cloudy sky, their lodge flaps open, buffalo skulls and totems painted on tipi hides. Women and children followed along, all talking and screeching, pointing and laughing. Morgan felt like he was in a parade. Boys tugged at Whistling Elk's legs, asking him all kinds of questions, but he shooed them away like gnats and never told them what they wanted to know.

"Looks like a one big mess, don't it, Lem?" asked Silas. "But all them tipis is in particular order. I spread my blankets with the Little Robe tribe over yonder." He pointed to a cluster of tipis. Morgan noticed that each camp was a separate circle. "Me and Lame Bull will talk to Whistling Elk, see can we get your rifles and possibles back. Just keep ridin' on toward that far circle of lodges. I reckon those are your mules and pack horses."

Lem nodded.

"It won't be no trouble, will it?" Hawke asked.

"I don't reckon," said Silas, but he didn't smile. "See you boys directly."

Silas rode off toward Lame Bull. Lem headed for the Little Robe lodges, followed by Morgan, Patch and Looking Loon. They were not followed, which seemed odd to Morgan. But as he looked again at the huge camp, he knew there would be little chance of escaping. Even if he had his rifle, he would be swarmed over by Crows the minute he tried to ride away.

"Pa, are we prisoners?" he asked abruptly.

"Why, no, I don't reckon. Are we, Patch?"

"I wouldn't make a run for it. Like Silas said, these niggers are mighty skittery. I don't blame 'em none."

"Huh?" asked Morgan. "We didn't do nothin' to 'em."

Patch halted several yards from the large circle of Little Robe tipis. Lem and Morgan stopped their horses, knowing the trapper had something to say. Looking Loon reined up, too. Sisco moved his eyepatch to one side, rubbed his dead eye. Morgan thought it was a hideous sight.

"I been expectin' this, or somethin' like this," said Patch, speaking softly. "I been watchin' the doin's in St. Louis, listenin' to all the talk. They's big money in furs and there are them as don't care how they get the beaver. Ever since Manuel Lisa come here to trade, way back before Lewis and Clark come up the Missouri, they's been politics ahind ever' move, ever' brigade."

"Politics?" Lem asked.

Patch nodded, waggled a bony finger in the air.

"Rich folks back East been puttin' money into brigades, expeditions and such. Some say the government is behind some of it, or all of it. Not many white trappers out here back then, but they started comin' after Lewis and Clark come home and started braggin' on the country, how rich it was."

"Well, that's why we're here," said Lem. "That's why you come out here. And Silas."

"True enough, true enough," assented Patch. "I hired on with some of those brigades and I seen cutthroats hire on and seen men kilt for furs and coin. Lisa and his bunch fought with the Rees and beat back the Mandans and bluffed their way through the Assinboines. I seen him back down chief after chief with his talk and showing them his firepower. He traded with the Crow down on the Yellowstone and they was glad to get his goods. But things have been changin' the past few years."

"The Crows still want to trade, don't they?" asked Lem. "Silas has been livin' and tradin' with 'em."

"Silas come out here afore I did," said Patch. "He can read sign better'n most men I know. A long time ago, he saw all the fur companies formin' up and he didn't want no part of it. So, he become a red nigger and he's probably saltin' it away. I never could cotton to these red coons, and so I stayed with the companies until I seen what the Major was a-doin' and how greed had got into Jocko's blood. Ain't but a question of time afore this is all ruint and the redskins come after us—the Crow, the Blackfoot, the Sioux, ever' damn one of 'em."

"You think that's what's happening here?" Lem asked, trying to swallow a knot in his throat. "You think the Crow are fixin' to fight all the white men coming out here?"

Patch looked around him as if checking to make sure no Indian could hear him. His eye narrowed and the patch seemed to bulge with that dead eye trying to see right through it.

"Lem, I been thinkin' that for five years now. But, I never seed so many Crow in one place before. They's somethin' stirrin' out here, somethin' mighty peculiar and mighty dangerous. It's like you get a feelin' real deep down and you can't shake it nohow. These Crow are itchin' for a fight, some of 'em, and maybe they'll smoke the pipe and cool down, but I ain't about to bet hard coin on it."

"You mean we might not get to trap and make our fortune?" Morgan asked.

"Well, I ain't perdictin' nothin', son. It's just feels like somethin's tightenin' down and I don't hardly know what it is."

"Be a damned shame," said Lem. "Just gettin' close and havin' everythin' blow up in our faces."

"Now, don't get to jumpin' the gun on what I say," said Patch. "We maybe can talk with Silas and see if he feels the same thing."

"I'm glad we didn't go with the Major," said Morgan.

Lem looked at his son in astonishment. Patch cracked a dry smile and winked with his one good eye.

"Son, you're beginnin' to learn politics," said Sisco.

"And Jocko," said Morgan, "he ain't no better."

Patch nodded sagely. "Jocko DeSam learnt all he knows from Angus MacDougal," he said. "Don't you forget that none."

Morgan sobered, looked back toward the main camp, trying to pick out Silas. Patch had made him very nervous and apprehensive. He expected to see every Crow in camp come riding down on them with knives and hatchets, screaming for their blood. He shook off the thought as he saw the children playing the hoop and stick game, chasing after each other in what looked like tag. Older boys tended the horses. It seemed very peaceful there. Maybe Patch was an old fussbudget. Maybe everything was going to be all right.

When he looked back toward the Little Robe circle, he saw two women walking toward them. They were followed, from a distance, by several older men, women and children. But the two women drew Morgan's interest. They moved slowly and seemed shy. One was older than the other. They were whispering to each other and the younger one was giggling.

"Looky yonder," Morgan said, without pointing. "Two squaws are comin' out here."

Lem, Patch and Loon followed Morgan's gaze.

They all stared, fascinated, at the two women. They had obviously spent a lot of time preening themselves. They wore elkskin dresses, tanned to a golden yellow, bright bead necklaces and painted shell earrings. Each woman had very long black hair; small eagle feathers dangled gracefully from beaded thongs woven through their tresses.

The older woman raised a hand in greeting. She was looking straight at Patch. The younger one hid her face.

"You know 'em?" Lem asked.

"I knowed that one. That's Blue Shell, old Silas' woman."

"Well, who's the other one?" blurted Morgan.

"Never seed her before," said Patch.

"Morg," warned Lem. "You ain't int'rested in no Injun squaw."

The young woman looked up as she and Blue Shell Woman drew closer. She seemed to be looking straight at Morgan, who was staring owl-eyed at the most beautiful girl he had ever seen. She was so small and graceful, and her face was radiant with light.

He failed to see the dark scowl on his father's face.

17

José Montez looked at the three men he had hired away from Jocko DeSam. One was a Mexican who spoke little English. His name was Felix Santiago and he had trapped with Manuel Lisa, was a veteran of many Indian battles. One was named Harold Bickham, thirty-five years old, who knew the mountains as well as any. The last was a French-Indian halfbreed named Pierre Doucette. His mother was of the Cree tribe, but he had lived with the Cheyenne, deadly enemies of the Crow.

They had four pack mules with them. Montez had bought one from a man who had two, paying too much, but knowing that he was the richer for it. He knew they might have to trade with savages or bribe them for information. Perhaps, as Jocko had told him, having trade goods, whiskey,

beads, weapons, would come to mean the difference between life and death in this wild, untamed land.

He had paid the men in gold coin and promised more
if they led him to Lemuel Hawke. The three hirelings had
one thing in common: all were greedy and all had blood
on their hands. In that, they were not much different than
himself.

Indeed, over the weeks past, he had come to hold many
of the men on the river in high regard—not for their qual-
ities of character, but for their bravery and determination.
He realized that they were hard men in their own way, some
foolish, some stupid, but willing to undergo extreme hard-
ship in order to attain riches. He and his brother had been
like that, willing to take risks, great risks, in order to live
like men and not like the sewer rats, the dogs and stray cats
of Spain.

Montez also realized that he had gradually become more
and more like the men he formerly scorned. He had regarded them as drifters enslaved to the booshway, men
without backbones or men without *cojones*. Aimless men,
without purpose. Yet, he realized now that while these
companions had picked a hard journey, they remained
fiercely independent while loyal to the booshway, DeSam.
And so, he had become like them, at least for this journey,
this quest for revenge.

He had seen his reflection in the river that morning and
it was like seeing the face of a stranger. He had grown a
full beard, and now he felt as if he was wearing a disguise.

The man he saw in the morning-still waters of the Musselshell resembled a mountain man, although he had no desire to wade in cold water and set traps for beaver and
marten. It seemed curious, that was all, that he had unconsciously taken on the trappings of a mountain man even
though he had never been to the Rockies before.

Perhaps that was as it should be, Montez thought. He

would descend to the level of his quarry, if that was necessary, and when it was over, he would shave off his beard and become himself again. Still, the shock of seeing that bearded stranger peering back at him made him wonder if he had not lost his mind. He vowed not to forget the reason he had come this far, that his brother was still dead and Lemuel Hawke must pay in kind, with his own life.

Montez smiled in satisfaction as his hired trackers looked over another of the Hawkes and their companions' camps, reading the sign left behind by four men.

"They keep the watches," said Doucette. He was a short, muscular man with knife scars on his chest and one ear that had been chewed into a shapeless mass of flesh. He wore greasy buckskins, thick-soled Cree moccasins and carried a large knife he had made from a wagon spring. Its handle was made of tough antelope antler, wound tight with glued buffalo hide thongs that gave his hand a solid grip. "The Delaware, he always sleeps by himself, away from the others."

"How close are we?" asked Montez.

Hal Bickham, stooped over the bent grasses, looked up at Montez. "Two days." Bickham was lean, slat-chested, stood five foot nine inches in his boot moccasins. His buckskins had been patched until his shirt looked like a leather quilt. He had pale, vacuous blue eyes, deep-sunk in a cadaverous face. His nose had been broken more than once, and there was a thin scar on his forehead that indicated he had once come close to being scalped. His forelock was bone white, in sharp contrast to his rusty hair.

"Three," said Santiago. *"Tres días,"* he said in Spanish. Bickham scowled at the Mexican. Santiago was from Santa Fe, an outcast, a wanderer. He had the high cheekbones of the Yaqui, the vermillion smear of Indian blood reddening his dark skin.

"Three, maybe," said Bickham. He looked again at the

crushed grasses. "They been movin' fast, but I look for them to slow down some. They ain't kilt no fresh meat in two days."

"That is right," said Santiago, looking at the bones and gristle around a shallow hole that showed signs of fire-blackening. "They did not make meat for two days."

Montez knew that he had to rely on these men. He could not read sign, could not track a man in such a wild place. He was more at home in the squalid back alleys of Barcelona where he and his brother grew up, or on the docks of New Orleans, the dark, bayou-scented streets, where his boots made no sound on cobblestones made slick and wet by the swampy nightsweat and his breath was only a part of the gulf fog. But he knew he had picked the right men—he had watched them for days, and had seen that they trusted each other. And, now, he would have to trust them for as long as he needed them.

"There is little game," said Pierre. "The *Indiens*, eh? They have hunted much along this river. They drive the sumbitch game away."

Montez knew that to be true. They had seen only small animals all morning, antelope in the distance. There had been no deer or elk tracks, none fresh and no sign of buffalo. The sky was clouded up and he was afraid it would rain before nightfall. That would make the tracking harder, he knew.

"I want to cut those three days by one or two," said the Spaniard.

"You do not know this sumbitch country," said Doucette. "She makes a man go fast or go slow. She makes him blind and tricks him, eh?—ever' damn way she can. Is it not so, *mes amis?*"

"You got that plumb center," said Bickham. " 'Bout all you got out here is time, Josie. Days don't make no difference. Ain't nobody waitin' for you to get anyplace. Ain't nobody goin' to get away, you stay on their track. If you ain't expected, it don't make no difference when you get there."

"What if it rains?" asked Montez. "There would be no tracks." They had encountered so many sudden rains on their journey, Montez almost expected it as a daily occurrence.

"Then," said Doucette, with a sly grin, "you have to track them in here." He tapped his index finger against his forehead.

The men chuckled at that, even Josie Montez. He knew what Pierre meant. The good hunter always had to think like his prey, had to learn the habits of the hunted. He had already learned, from traveling with Jocko DeSam, that progress was made at the whim of the weather, the river, of nature itself. Impatience was a killer in such country. It was not a trait he nurtured, but he knew that he had better start practicing patience if he wanted to find Lemuel Hawke and cut his throat.

Montez looked at the sky again, wondering if it would rain and delay the tracking. Finally, he resolved the questions in his mind.

"We will go on, then," he said. "Do you have any idea where those men are headed?"

Santiago shrugged, looked into the distance. Trees lined the Musselshell as it wound like a serpent through hilly, broken country. In the distance, behind clouds, the mountain ranges began. There were no boundaries, only those claimed by various tribes, and they moved around like the beasts in Eden, going where the game was, fighting with other tribes and stealing from them.

Bickham looked at his feet, at a loss for anything to say.

"They are headed where the river takes them," said Doucette, and that was sufficient answer for Montez. For all of his life, he had done virtually the same thing. He and his brother, the one they called Spanish Jack in St. Louis, had grown up in the slums of Barcelona. Their father,

Ernesto Montez, had been a petty thief, their mother a washerwoman. The family lived in poverty, but Ernesto always seemed to have pesetas enough to buy the wine. After he got drunk, he would beat his wife, Maria, until her screams went silent and she was senseless. When the boys grew old enough to protest, Ernesto beat them, too, not just with his fists, but with broom handles, wash paddles and iron burglar tools.

Josie and Jack, known then as Pepe and Juan, learned their father's trade by the time Jack was seven, Josie was eight. They learned to pick pockets at the bullfights, how to steal chicken and bread from merchants, how to steal purses in rich Roman Catholic churches.

When Josie was fifteen, he ran away from home. One day he found Jack sleeping under a bridge and learned that he had run away from home, too. He also learned that Ernesto had killed their mother, bludgeoned her to death with a bar he used to pry open windows in wealthy homes when the owners were absent.

Both boys lived on the streets, sleeping in country woods, stealing food and money, more than enough to fill their bellies and put fat on their ribs. They were husky and mean young men, wise in the ways of the streets and the back alleys, when they were shanghaied on a ship going to New Orleans. They jumped ship in New Orleans and found that thievery was just as profitable there as it had been in Barcelona. They saved their money, learned to steal not just enough for subsistence but enough to make a profit.

They learned the ways of the New World from an old pirate called Blinky. He had retired from the high seas and banded together a group of urchins whom he taught the finer points of larceny.

"Don't steal food from an untended wagon," Blinky told them. "Steal the wagon, the horse, and all the goods. Then you are in business. You can steal from a wharf and load the goods in your wagon. You can sell these goods at market just like any other enterprising merchant."

Blinky was murdered one night as he slept. Jack learned that two of the ex-mariner's men had done it, believing the old pirate had a sack of gold in his diggings. Jack killed them both, stabbing one in a fair fight, strangling the other with his bare hands in a blind rage.

Those first killings had opened up other paths to him. He became well known as a man who would do anything for money and none of it had to be legal. Some of his clients were wealthy men, others were criminals like himself.

So, he and Jack had followed many a river in their lives. Jack was gone, now, but Josie would avenge his death as Jack had avenged Blinky's. He had other rivers to follow before he gave up his ghost.

But he wondered where the river would lead them. His scalp prickled as he thought of the stories he'd listened to around the brigade campfires—tales of savage Indian attacks, scalping, torture. He wanted to kill Lemuel Hawke, his kid Morgan, if necessary, and be done with it. The men he had hired were free to go their own way after they found the Hawkes for him. Beyond that, he couldn't reason. All he knew was that he could get back to St. Louis on his own. He could follow the sun and the rivers back to civilization. Let these cursed half-wild trappers have this worthless, godforsaken land.

Morgan's eyes widened, his mouth opened, went slack. He felt a jellied quivering in his knees.

The girl hung back behind Blue Shell, peering at Morgan from behind her friend's shoulder.

"Patch," said Blue Shell. "You come back."

"Yes, Blue Shell. I come to trap the beaver." Lem looked at the trapper, scratched the back of his head. He had never seen Patch act so polite.

"Gray Hawk say you bring white friend."

"This be Lemuel and his son, Morgan. They are friends of Gray Hawk."

"Morgan? Gray Hawk name Morgan."

Patch nodded. "This could be complicated," he said to Lem. "Any suggestions?"

"I named Morgan after Silas."

"And now the Crow call him Gray Hawk. So, you got Morgan Hawke and Silas Morgan Gray Hawk."

"Let Silas explain it," said Lem.

Blue Shell wore a puzzled expression on her face.

"Gray Hawk will tell Blue Shell about the white man's name," said Patch.

"Ask her who her little friend is," said Morgan.

"That might not be proper," said Patch.

"Morgan," said Lem, "you just remember that's a Injun gal. You keep your pecker in your pants."

"Oh, Pa, that ain't what I was a-thinkin'."

"I know damned well what you was a-thinkin'."

Morgan didn't want an argument with his father now, not in front of the Indian girl. She was still peering at him from over Blue Shell's shoulder, shy as a mouse.

The two women were joined by others, children, old men and women, all silently staring at the three white men and the Indian from an unknown tribe. Gradually, they began to speak among themselves and Morgan wondered what they were saying. He continued to look at the young girl with Blue Shell, taken by her beauty, fascinated by her long, raven-black tresses that reached well beyond her knees. She had glistening fawn eyes and smooth dark skin. She seemed, to Morgan, like something forbidden, like Eve, naked in the garden of Eden.

A few moments later, Silas and Lame Bull, along with two other braves, walked up, leading their pack mules and carrying their rifles and possibles pouches.

"Any trouble?" asked Patch.

"Some. You did the right thing, giving Lame Bull, and the others, those gifts. Them coons what tied you up wanted it all, 'pears like, but old Whistling Elk wanted to talk it over with his chief first. Otherwise you might not have no hair and be wolf meat."

Lem paled. Morgan shifted his attention from the girl to Silas as the mountain man handed him his rifle, pouch, the medicine horn and his priming horn.

"See you still got it," said Silas.

"I won't never part with it, Silas."

"That's another reason you still got your hair. That horn is powerful medicine, like I tolt you when I give it to you."

"I know," said Morgan.

"Tell Lame Bull we thank him," said Patch.

Silas spoke to Lame Bull and the other two braves, Little Fox and Crooked Face.

Lame Bull spoke briefly to Silas.

"He is going to tell his family to put up a lodge for you. He wants to be your friend. He has told us about Morgan shooting a charging buffler with one shot. The bull gets bigger ever' time he tells the story. He told Hunts the Sky, chief of the Little Robes, that the bull was as big as the medicine lodge and was breathin' on your face when you dropped it."

Morgan laughed.

"It was damned nigh that big," said Patch.

"And, it was a-blowin' steam on his face," said Lem, proudly.

"Come on to my digs whilst the Crow make ready to feast you," said Silas, suddenly serious. He looked over his shoulder toward the main camp. "There still may be some bad blood with Whistling Elk's bunch. We can figger out how to make peace with them whilst we chew the fat, catch up on past times."

Silas slapped Morgan and Lem on their backs. The crowd turned as if on a signal and streamed back to their lodges. The sky seemed to lighten and soon there was a break in the clouds. Shafts of light struck the tipis, made them shine like giant white beacons.

Morgan could tell that the Crow had been hunting buffalo. Everywhere he looked, he saw big chunks of meat drying on willow racks, the tongues black and fat, the big black pots steaming, smelling of cooked meat. There were deer and elk, fresh-killed, hanging from pole tripods, gutted out, their heads lolling. Women were skinning some of the deer, others were tanning hides. There seemed to be plenty of food in camp, and the people seemed happy. All of it was a wonder to Morgan, seeing so many Indians all at once, seeing how they lived. They seemed, oddly enough, like ordinary people except for their skin coloring, their dress and their lodges. The encampment was the strangest city he had ever seen, yet it felt just like a white man's city, except there were no stores, no taverns, no permanent dwellings.

"I see you met Blue Shell," said Silas as they followed the others back to the Little Robe lodge circle. "Fine woman, fine woman."

"Who's that girl with her?" asked Morgan.

"What gal is that?" asked Silas, winking.

"Aw, you know, Silas."

"I told him not to pay her no mind," said Lem. "We don't want no trouble like we had in St. Louis."

"Her name is Yellow Bead," said Silas. "She ain't never took up with a buck. Her pa was kilt by Blackfoot. She lives with her mother, Basket Woman. We all kind of help out with food and such."

"How old is she?" asked Morgan.

"Well, I don't rightly know," said Silas. "Thirteen, fourteen summers, the way Injuns count, I reckon."

There was a buffalo skull, blanched white by the sun, the hide eaten away by worms, sitting on a large rock outside Silas' lodge. The skull was painted with red, yellow and

black lines, and decorated with mysterious symbols. Silas
went past it, stood by the flap.

"Go on in and set," he said. "Walk to the left and around
the fire. The Crow are mighty keen on ceremony. You got
to do everythin' right or they think you got a bad heart."

Morgan went in first. He was anxious to see Yellow Bead
again. His heart was pounding as he ducked down and
entered the tipi. He blinked his eyes, trying to adjust to
the dim light. He waddled to the left, following the circular
perimeter of the lodge.

Blue Shell and Yellow Bead were stirring something in
two pots hanging on cooking irons over the fire ring. The
aroma of boiling meat and herbs made Morgan's stomach
churn with hunger. The smoke from the fire went straight
up through the smoke hole. The women seemed not to notice him. He waddled all the way around and sat down. His
pa followed close behind him, then came Patch, Looking
Loon and, finally, Silas himself.

The tipi seemed spacious to Morgan. There were buffalo
robes for beds, lots of deer and elk hides and bales of beaver, marten and lynx furs stacked up along one side. Silas'
flintlock rifle, his possibles bag, powder horns, tomahawks
and extra knives in beautiful quilled scabbards lay on a
platform of buffalo hides. There were cooking utensils,
bowls, spoons and ladles all neatly arranged close to the
fire.

Lem looked around, too, then sat crosslegged like the
others.

"We got no chairs as such," said Silas. "Just lay your
rifles and pouches back along the wall and make yourselves
comfortable. The women'll have some vittles for us right
quick."

Morgan heard Blue Shell say something to Yellow Bead.
Yellow Bead had her head bent so that he could not see her
face. She picked up some bowls and horn spoons, handed
them to Silas, first, then to Looking Loon, Patch, Lem, and

finally, to Morgan. She put another bowl in the empty space next to Morgan.

"Oho," said Silas, "looky there."

"What?" asked Morgan.

"Looks like Yellow Bead's taken a liking to you, Morgan. That's her bowl she set there by your side."

Lem tried to conceal his sudden frown, but Morgan caught it.

"Well, it don't make no nevermind to me," said Morgan quickly. He wanted no outburst from his pa. Inside, his nerves were jangling, his stomach quivering, and it wasn't from a hungering for food. Blue Shell said something in Crow to Silas. Then, she looked at Morgan and smiled.

"Yep, Morgan," said Silas, "it looks like you done made a friend. Blue Shell says that Yellow Bead is plumb stuck on you."

"Well, Morgan ain't takin' up with no Injun gal," said Lem.

"Lem," Silas said softly, "you can't keep on lumpin' all womens in the same pile as Roberta. One bad woman don't make 'em all bad."

"I ain't never met a good 'un yet," said Lem stubbornly.

"Pa, don't," said Morgan. "I ain't takin' up with Yellow Bead. I just think she's mighty purty, that's all."

Lem said nothing, but he fed on bitter memories of his wife, Roberta, Morgan's mother, who abandoned them and took up with another man. He still hated her. He hated all women, in fact, and he meant to see that Morgan learned how bad they were so's he wouldn't get hurt by 'em.

Blue Shell lifted one of the pots off the cooking irons and carried it to a flat stone wrapped in deerhide, a kind of small table in front of Silas. She set the pot down and handed her husband the ladle, one that Silas had bought in St. Louis.

"Let's eat," said Silas, dipping the ladle into the pot.

Yellow Bead and Blue Shell waited until all the men had taken food, then served themselves. Blue Shell sat by herself, but Yellow Bead sat next to Morgan.

"Buffler meat," said Silas as they all began eating. "Best vittles a man ever tasted."

Morgan barely heard him above the beating of his heart. Yellow Bead sat so close to him, he could smell the fragrance of flowers in her hair, the earthy smell of her body under the white dress she wore. When he shifted position, he put his hand down and touched a pile of her hair puddled on the packed earth next to him. It was soft to his touch.

Yellow Bead looked shyly up at him and his heart froze in his chest.

He caught Looking Loon staring at him. There was a twinkle in the Delaware's eye.

18

Lem didn't believe Morgan's excuse that he wanted to look after the horses. He suspected that his son wanted to do some sparking with Yellow Bead, who with Blue Shell had gone down to the river to do the washing.

"Silas," he said, after Morgan had gone away, "let's go somewheres by ourselfs and have a smoke and a talk."

"Fetch your pipe."

Patch said he was going to see Hunts the Sky, chief of the Little Robes. He said he wanted to give him some tobacco and gifts, renew their friendship. Looking Loon stayed in the tipi to sleep.

The two walked to a patch of timber, found a place where they could rest in the shade. The sun had burned through the clouds. There would be no rain that day.

Lem gave Silas some tobacco for his pipe, filled his own.

"Much obliged," said Silas. "Tobaccer's been scarce this summer."

"I'll leave you ten pounds when we set out," said Lem.

Lem used his magnifying glass to light his pipe. Silas struck fire from flint and steel into his bowl, blew on the sparks until they caught. The tobacco was good and dry, gave off a strong aroma.

"What's on your mind, Lemuel?" Silas blew a spume of smoke into the air.

"I want you to show me the way to the mountains. Me and Morg want to pull out in the morning. We aim to trap beaver hard as we can."

"What's your hurry, Lem? You just got here. They'll be feastin' tonight, and likely all the clans will want you to visit 'em. Ain't time to trap yet."

"We want to get settled," Hawke said lamely.

"Haw. Well, this old coon's goin' to trap them mountains this winter hisself. This camp won't be here in a week. The Crow got their buffler and will spend the rest of the summer in the cool high country. Some of the bucks will trap so they can do some tradin' in the spring. Just hold your horses, Lem."

"We really want to get movin', me and Morg."

Silas sucked deeply on his pipe, rolled the smoke around in his mouth. He let it out slowly, then looked off through the trees. Snatches of laughter and ribbons of Crow voices floated on the afternoon air. The sun made dappled shadows in the copse of trees. Water splashed down at the river from swimmers playing along the shore. There was a peace in the air that belied the turmoil inside the man who sat across from him leaning against a birch tree.

"Lem, you and Morgan don't want to be goin' off by yourselfs. I did it once't and paid dearly for it. Them mountains ain't no place for greenhorns such as you and your boy. They're mighty partic'lar as to who comes into 'em and who comes out alive."

"You did it."

"Nope. I went with a brigade the first time. I went into the mountains on my own the next year and damned near died. These Crow saved my life, brought me out."

"What happened?"

"I shot me a elk with a rack big enough to hold a dozen coats and hats. Thought he was dead. They was snowdrifts higher'n a man's head and it were wet snow, stuck to you like feathers to tar. Welp, that elk upped and ran one of them long tines through my gut. Burnt like fire and I had to stuff my innards back in my belly. It were the snow what kept me from dyin' right off. I got back to my camp, no more'n a deadfall pine I rigged up for a shelter. I sewed my belly back up, but I was a-bleedin' inside. I packed my belly with snow so's I couldn't feel the burnin' no more. But I got the deleriums and the fever and some passin' Crow heard me, thought I was makin' big medicine."

Silas paused and Lem leaned forward to hear the rest of the story.

"What did they do?" asked Hawke.

"They rigged a travvy and carried me down the mountains. It were the Little Robes and Yellow Bead's pa made medicine over me. Her ma tended me with herbs and river clay until I no longer got the twitches ever' time I took breath."

"That was a accident," said Lem. "You ought to have known better."

"I was plumb hungry and crazy and cold. My old bean wasn't workin' right that day. I should have come up on the bull another way and had my fusil cocked. Point is, the mountains don't 'llow many mistakes. I was lucky. If them Crow hadn't come along, this old coon would have been wolf meat."

"Well, me and Morg are goin'. In the mornin', for certain sure. We'll get to the mountains on our own."

"You talked this over with Morgan? You might want to stick with Sisco. Him and that Delaware knows the country mighty well."

"Morg wants to get to trappin' pretty bad."

"You ever trapped beaver?" Silas asked, his voice low-pitched, deceptively smooth.

"Now, you know we ain't, Silas. But I been thinkin' on it, studyin' in my head what you tolt me about catching beaver and such. I reckon we'll do just fine."

"Well, you could trade for your furs and take 'em back to St. Louis and get a fair price. Save you a heap of worrisomes."

"We aim to trade and trap, too. Ain't that the way it's done?"

"That's so," said Silas. "If you go off on your own, you might trap some place that's already been staked out. You might have to fight for the skins you take."

"Other trappers?"

"And Injuns. They'll be a bunch a-trappin' them streams. 'Less'n you got a map, know which is which, you could get lost or worse, get kilt."

"I thought there was plenty of room up in the mountains."

"They is, but it gets more crowded ever' season. The Crow say they's a big brigade a-comin' up the Platte, Angus MacDougal's bunch, and more on the Big Horn and up on the Milk and the Judith. Crow don't like it none. I heard tell Jocko DeSam's goin' to trade with the Blackfeet up north. Runners come in the other day, sayin' four men from his bunch are comin' up the Musselshell, headed our way."

Silas looked at Lem closely.

"Four men?"

"Mighty peculiar, ain't it? You got any friends comin' after you?" Silas' eyes narrowed and his teeth clamped his pipe tightly. He did not draw on it, but waited for an answer.

"Did—was one of 'em a Spaniard?"

Silas took his pipe from his mouth. It was made of pink pipestone, a gift from Blue Shell's father, Turns Back the Enemy.

"The Crows what seen 'em knew three of the men. They been here before. They didn't know the other man, just that he was dark-skinned and had hair on his face."

Lem let out a shallow sigh. "Maybe it ain't him, then," he said.

"Who?" asked Silas.

"Spanish Jack's brother. Josie Montez."

"He's a bad one. What makes you think it ain't him?"

"I seen Josie once't. He was with MacDougal and Jocko. He din't have no beard."

"Man can grow a beard in a week," said Silas. "If Josie's a-huntin' you, maybe you and Morgan better wait and see if he's one of them four men. Be a heap safer here where you got friends. Runners said they was about three days ride from camp."

"I ain't afraid of him," said Lem.

Silas knocked the dottle out of his pipe, banging the bowl gently against an ash tree.

"You want to leave tomorry, I'll point you toward the mountains. You'll have no river to guide you once you leave the Musselshell, but you ain't got far to go."

"We'll be a-leavin'," said Lem.

"Sorry to see you go," said Silas. "Might not see you again."

"You're just tryin' to scare me, Silas."

"Hell, I hope I do."

He got up and Lem knew the conversation was over. He hated to disappoint his old friend, but he still had memories of Spanish Jack burning up in that tavern in St. Louis, all over a slut that Morgan had peckered, who was just playin' his boy for a fool. He didn't want anything like that to happen again.

Morgan walked down to the river. Boys swam and splashed near the shore in the shallows. Downstream, he saw several women washing clothes, chattering and laughing among themselves. He scanned them for a glimpse of Yellow Bead and Blue Shell. Finally, he saw the two maidens, knee-deep in the river, spanking water at each other like schoolgirls.

He wandered toward them, trying to appear as though he were just walking along, not going anywhere in particular. Some of the girls down by the river saw him there and began to giggle. Their joyous titters struck red-tipped ears. Some of the young boys followed after him, teasing him with words he didn't understand.

He turned to shoo the boys away. They ran from him like antic birds, pretending to be mortally afraid as they scattered to escape his flailing arms.

Blue Shell saw Morgan coming. She waved him away. He kept on walking. Yellow Bead turned, saw him, then quickly turned away. Blue Shell stalked out of the river.

"Go away," she said in English.

"I'm just walkin'," said Morgan. "Mindin' my own business."

"You go," she said sternly.

"Can I talk to Yellow Bead? I can speak in sign." Morgan gestured to show her he could speak and understand the hand language.

Blue Shell shook her head. She signed back to him.

"Yellow Bead no talk. You go talk Gray Hawk."

Morgan started to protest, but now a crowd of women, old and young, were gathering around, all talking at once. The boys did not come near, but stayed well away, conversing among themselves.

Puzzled, Morgan retreated.

"All right, all right," he said. "I'm a-goin'."

"You go quick," said Blue Shell, pushing the air with her hands.

Morgan felt like a whipped cur as he walked back to the camp alone. He looked back once, but Yellow Bead had her back to him. He knew he had probably violated some Indian custom. Maybe that's what Blue Shell was trying to tell him when she ordered him to speak to Silas.

Silas met him as he came back into camp.

"Turned you back, did they?"

Morgan nodded.

"All I wanted to do was talk to her," he said sadly.

"I figgered that might happen. You never know with Injuns. Likely, Yellow Bead is taken with you and wants a formal courtin'."

"How do I do that?"

"The bucks I seen a-courtin' usually just stay within sight of the maiden and play a willow flute or act strange."

"Act strange?"

"Well, you know, they stand on their heads, or walk backward, anything to get a maid's attention."

"That's all?"

"No, they ask if they can walk with a certain gal or get permission to talk to her. They give a gal's father presents, maybe give the mother some little gewgaw. It's kinda complicated."

"Is that how you courted Blue Shell?"

Silas walked toward a far edge of camp where they could be alone.

"Not rightly. I just up and asked her pa if I could have her. I gave him three horses for her, a knife, a rifle, three blankets and two hatchets."

Morgan scratched his nose. He didn't have that many horses, no rifle he could give up. He could give up a knife or two, some hatchets from the goods he had brought to trade.

"But, you said her pa was dead."

Silas told Morgan that Yellow Bead's father had been a Crow medicine man named Black Wolf. According to Silas, he was highly respected and his death was a great loss to the Little Robe people.

"Her ma's name is Basket Woman. I don't know if she could give the girl away."

"I don't want no wife," said Morgan. "I just wanted to spark her a little."

"Ain't no such thing. You take her to your blankets, she's your woman."

"Well, maybe I ain't so keen to court her, then."

"Best thing to do is just be patient. Ain't nothin' draws a woman more'n a man who shows no interest in her."

"You mean just pay her no mind?"

"You do that, son, she just might come a-runnin'."

Morgan thought about it.

"How do I make a willow flute?" he asked after a few moments.

Silas laughed.

"You go cut you a young willer about a half-inch acrost and I'll show you."

That night there was celebration in the camp. Morgan, his father, Patch and Looking Loon went together to meet Hunts the Sky, the chief of the Little Robes. They feasted in the big medicine lodge, with its depiction of the Good Spirit on one side, the Evil Spirit on the other. Morgan counted thirty lodgepoles. There must have been at least forty men inside at one time. The men came and went until he lost count. But he saw Whistling Elk come in and eat, along with others of his clan. Everyone seemed to be in a gay mood. The Crow dressed in their finest raiment. Their wives and daughters served buffalo tongue, liver, hump, beaver tail, wild onions and some kind of pudding. Lem, Morgan, Patch and Looking Loon gorged themselves.

The Crow told stories and acted them out: hunting tales and accounts of battles with their enemies. Patch told them all about Morgan's killing of the huge buffalo. Silas pushed Morgan to his feet, made him tell the story.

"How?"

"Just playact it out, like you seen them braves do it."

Morgan mimed riding up after the buffalo. He bent over and put his hands up to show the buffalo. He used the sign language he had learned and made up some. He knew that the Crow were all watching him intently, but he got into the spirit of the storytelling. He mimicked being bucked off his horse, of falling. He rose with an imaginary rifle in his hands. He showed the giant buffalo charging him and then he brought the rifle to his shoulder. He took aim and fired, making the sound of a rifle booming. He switched back to the bull, showed him charging and snorting, then falling and skidding to a stop at Morgan's feet. He stood with one foot in the air as if standing on the beast's huge hump and the Crow inside the medicine lodge went wild with approval. Lem, Patch and Silas all cheered, and the Crow began yelling and yipping until Morgan's neck bristled with stiffened hairs.

Indians embraced him, clapped him on the back.

Then, Patch got up and told about the Pawnee arrows in the bull and how the Pawnee had let them go after hearing how Morgan had brought down the bull with a single shot at close range. The Crow went wild all over again.

Morgan spent the rest of the evening in a daze. Patch had given Hunts the Sky some whiskey and Silas had some himself. He and Lem drank a lot of it, and Patch made Morgan drink some as well. Looking Loon got very drunk and staggered off, found a spot next to Silas' lodge and fell asleep.

Morgan wandered out of the medicine lodge for some

fresh air. His head was fuzzy inside. He felt as if he had grown a foot during the evening. He kept saying Crow words over and over even if he did not know their meaning. He felt part of these people, a brother to them. He was happy and smiling idiotically. He looked up at the stars and they seemed closer than they ever had before.

He had no idea where he was. The white cones of tipis rose up in the night all around him. He was lost in a forest of tipis. They all looked alike. Most of them glowed with light, some were dark, as if abandoned. He tried to get his bearings, but every time he changed direction, he found himself heading back toward the medicine lodge. He had to walk around a maze of skins staked out flat on the ground and those strung on poles, stretched to dry in the sun.

By the third time he had done this, Morgan knew he was being followed. He could not see who it was. Everytime he turned around quickly, whoever had been making noise behind him had disappeared. Finally, he set off in an entirely different direction. Then, he walked past the tipis and knew he had gone too far. Again he heard a noise behind him and turned around quickly.

There was no one there.

He walked back toward one of the tipis at the edge of the woods. He heard someone whisper: "Morgan."

The voice was faintly accented, thin, musical.

"Who's there?" he asked.

Yellow Bead stepped out from the shadow of a lodge.

"Yell Oh Bead," she said slowly. Then, she said something in the Crow tongue. But her hands beckoned to him.

"Yellow Bead," he said, suddenly even giddier than he was before. He felt light-headed, addled. He closed his eyes a moment, then snapped them open. She motioned for him to follow her.

"Morgan," she said. It sounded more like "Mo-Gan." His blood raced hotly as she took his hand, led him past tipi after tipi, avoiding the staked hides, staying to the shadows.

Finally, Yellow Bead stopped before a lone lodge. It was not joined to a circle but stood apart.

"You. Mo-Gan," she said, pointing to his chest.

"Yes. I'm Morgan," he said.

"Come, Mo-Gan."

To his surprise, she led him inside. It was dark and he could see nothing. He heard Yellow Bead giggle. It was a tinkling kind of laugh, so brief he wondered if he had imagined it.

She led him to the left. He touched the soft walls of the tipi, but was still blind, disoriented. She stopped, pulled him down. He felt the thick pile of a buffalo blanket. He sat on it, tried to see her face in the darkness. He looked skyward, through the smoke hole, and saw the faint glimmerings of stars, the only light inside the lodge.

Suddenly, he no longer felt Yellow Bead's hands on him. He reached out for her, but his fingers groped only empty air. Then, he heard the faint soft crackle of deerskin, heard something plop to the ground. He heard other sounds, but could not make them out. He was afraid to speak, but his imagination flared like wildfire. He felt an unexpected stirring in his loins, a tug of desire beginning to stiffen him.

A few seconds later, he felt her sit beside him. She breathed into his ear.

"Mo-Gan," she whispered.

He turned, reached out for her. As his eyes grew accustomed to the light, he could make out her dim shape, a tiny silhouette lit only by starshine.

He put his arms around her, drew her close to him.

Yellow Bead was naked.

Her hands reached under his buckskin shirt and he felt her pulling it upward.

He released her and pulled his shirt off. Her hands tugged

at his trousers. He kicked them off. She removed his moccasins and then shoved him backward onto the buffalo
blanket.

Then, Yellow Bead crawled next to him, wrapped herself in his arms.

She touched his manhood with delicate fingers and he
was ready.

19

"The Crow have been watching," said Pierre Doucette,
pointing to the soft mud along the riverbank. "They put
the dugout in here, then they hide in the grass and watch
us. They go."

"Where?" asked Montez.

Doucette shrugged. "Likely they been sendin' runners
back and forth ever since we struck the Musselshell," said
Hal Bickham. "You don't never see 'em, but they know
we're here."

"That means Lemuel Hawke will know we're coming,"
said Montez.

"Tracks be two hours old," said Felix Santiago.

The sun was setting and they had stopped at this place
because there was plenty of wood. Now, Montez had the
uneasy feeling that the Crow were still out there somewhere. He could almost feel their eyes on him.

"No tellin' how far they have to go," Montez mused
aloud.

"At least them red niggers ain't wearin' paint," said Hal.
"They'd of jumped us by now. I'm just glad it ain't Blackfeet."

"Should we camp here, then?" asked Montez.

"Might as well," said Bickham. "Same watches?"

"I'll take the first watch," said Montez.

"Nervous, are ye?" asked Bickham.

"As a cat at a dogfight," admitted Montez. He checked his rifle, saw that the pan was primed. He wore a pistol in his belt. He checked that, too. He walked around the perimeter of the camp while the others gathered wood and started the cookfire. He knew he was out of his element. He couldn't read tracks, he couldn't tell how old they were. He looked again at the riverbank, saw the marks of the dugout, but knew he would have missed them even if he had been looking hard. They could have been made by anything. He didn't see moccasin tracks, but he knew the others had seen them. He couldn't tell where the Crow had laid down in the grass, either. Yes, Montez decided, he had a lot to learn.

He watched the men he had hired as they went about their tasks. They spoke to each other in voices pitched low so that he couldn't understand them. Every once in a while, one or another would look up at him, then turn away quickly. Something was wrong, but Montez couldn't put his finger on it. For the past two days, he had noticed little things that bothered him. When two of them were talking together, they would change the subject when he drew near. They found excuses to ride off by themselves.

Little things, but they added up to something he didn't like. He knew men. He knew these were up to something. Perhaps they wanted to kill him and rob him. They knew he had gold. The packhorses were his, too. Men had killed for less. Well, he would not be so easy to kill.

Montez walked slowly back toward the camp, his mind racing, a plan of survival forming in his mind.

Yellow Bead pulled Morgan atop her. Her hands caressed him. She made little mewing sounds, spoke whispered words that he didn't understand. She found him with her hands, touched the hardness of him. He leaned down, kissed her face, found her lips. She returned his kiss with an eagerness that surprised him, made him flame inside, made his senses boil with a raging desire.

"Yellow Bead, Yellow Bead," Morgan said huskily as she guided him between her legs.

"Mo-Gan make baby Yalo Bead," she said.

"Yes, yes," he moaned as he entered her, sank into silk that was oiled slick and smooth, silk that was warm and soft, that clasped him tightly and pulled him deeper inside her.

She cried out softly when he drove in past her maidenhead, broke through the leathery barrier and sank deep. His lips brushed the fresh hot tears on her face, yet she did not beg him to stop, nor push him away.

"Heap good," she said.

"Yes. Heap good."

She moaned as he continued to plumb her depths. He wished he could see her face, look into her eyes. She kept saying things to him in her broken English and in her own tongue. He said things to her, things that he meant, but the heat rose strong in him, and in a frenzy, he raced to the finish, exploding inside her as rocket bombs burst in his brain. He felt his seed drain out of him and fill her womb. She clasped him tightly and held onto him, her body quivering in the throes of ecstacy.

She was still trembling when he slid off her, lay beside her, sated.

"I'm all bucked out," he breathed, before he realized she probably couldn't understand him.

"Mo-Gan good man," she said, and he felt her hand glide across his chest, tickling the fine hairs that grew there.

"Yellow Bead, you got to learn more English than that."

She said something in Crow.

"Never mind," he said. He swelled up with the pleasure of lying beside her, knowing he had taken her cherry, that she had been a virgin. He felt strong and tall and breathed with a deep satisfaction. It was wonderful to be alive, to be with this Indian girl. She made him feel wanted, needed.

She had come to him. He had not had to court her or ask permission. It was so easy, he wanted to pinch himself to see if it all had been real.

He made love to her several times that night. Finally, he slept. When he awoke, Yellow Bead was gone. But his rifle was inside the tipi, and so was his possibles pouch. His medicine horn, his little priming horn were there, too. There were buffalo blankets all about and a new pair of moccasins, finely quilled, and leggings with both beads and quills decorating them. Atop the moccasins shone a single yellow bead.

Morgan sat up and smiled.

Morning light filled the tipi. Wisps of river fog blew past the smoke hole. He smelled food cooking and his stomach churned with hunger.

He dressed slowly, hoping Yellow Bead would return. He did not wear the new moccasins, but hid all the new things under a blanket. He wondered where his pa was. This was obviously the tipi that had been erected for him, his pa, Patch and Loonie, but none of them had slept in it. He rubbed sleep out of his eyes and opened the tent flap, crawled through it.

It was still early, and not all of the camp had arisen. He saw smoke streaming through the smoke holes of a few tipis, and some women were cooking outside their lodges. The river fog was burning off slowly as the sun sneaked over the horizon, splashing golden light through the trees that bordered the encampment.

There were two other lodges close by that seemed to have been newly erected. He wandered over to one of them, peered inside. He saw two sleeping figures: Patch and his father. He went to the other tipi and opened the flap. He was startled to see Looking Loon inside with a Crow woman. Both were naked. Looking Loon grinned at him. Morgan backed out, stood up.

He walked to the circle of Little Robe lodges, found the

one where Silas lived. The tent flap was closed, secured with small sticks of wood.

"Silas," he called softly, not wishing to arouse the camp.

There was no answer. Morgan moved closer to the entrance.

"Silas, you in there?"

He heard rustlings, then a series of grunts and gutteral noises, followed by a softer voice.

"Morgan, that you?"

"You still asleep?"

"Ye gods, yes. Wait a minute. Christ, my head."

More rustlings. Then, a few moments later, the tent flap opened. A small brown hand beckoned for him to enter.

Blue Shell squatted by the fire ring, poking at the coals. Silas was sitting up, wearing only buckskin trousers. He was barefooted, his thin thatch of hair tangled from sleep. He rubbed a hand down his face.

"What are you doin' up so early?" asked Silas, one eye still closed, the other glaring balefully at Morgan.

"I dunno," said Morgan. "They put me up my own tipi."

"I know. That was Yellow Bead's doin'. Her and Blue Shell got some other women to help 'em."

"You seen Yellow Bead, Silas?"

"I ain't seen her. She's probably asleep or gettin' wood this time o' day."

Blue Shell said something to Silas in Crow. He didn't answer.

"She come to your lodge, did she?"

Morgan nodded.

"Well, that's a good sign. Kind of reminds me of Blue Shell."

"But she's gone this mornin'," said Morgan.

"She's got obligations. She'll be back."

"Does my pa know?"

"Know what?" Silas backed away from a tendril of smoke that scratched at his eyes. Blue Shell fanned the tiny flames until the wood caught. The smoke steadied and rose straight up through the smoke hole.

"About me'n Yellow Bead bein' together last night."

"I reckon not. He was pretty pie-eyed when I last saw him. Him and Patch was hittin' the whiskey pretty hard."

Morgan breathed a sigh of relief.

"Silas, you won't tell him, will you?"

"Hell, boy, I ain't no gossip. What you and Yellow Bead do in the blankets is your own business. Tell you one thing, though."

"What's that?"

"Your pa is dead set on headin' out to the mountains today. He's as ornery as a bottomland stump."

"How come he wants to go so quick? We just got here."

Silas stretched, slipped on a pair of moccasins.

"I got to pee," he said, standing up. "Come on. Blue Shell will cook us some breakfast." He spoke to his woman in Crow. Blue Shell nodded submissively. Morgan followed Silas outside. He had to pee, too.

They walked into the fringe of woods, picked out separate trees. Silas talked as he sprayed the flora.

"I tried to talk your pa out of goin' up to the mountains, just him and you, but he done had his mind set. The Crow made some smoke and talk last night afore the feast, anyways, and they decided to break up the camp. They'll scatter like leaves."

"Where will *you* go?" asked Morgan.

"Some of the Little Robes will go on up to the mountains. Me'n Blue Shell will likely go up with 'em."

"When?"

"Day or two. A week. Hard to tell about Injuns. Some will go off today, some tomorry. Some'll stay on another month, like as not."

Morgan finished his business. A moment later, Silas finished up, too.

"Where will Yellow Bead go?"

Silas cocked his head as if to tell Morgan how foolish his question was.

"Why, I reckon she'll tag along with you, if you want her, Morgan."

Morgan felt a surge of blood through his heart. Then, he felt a twinge of disappointment.

"Pa would never allow it," he said.

"Morgan, ain't none of my business, but you're full-growed and haired over some. Your pa, well, he's set in his ways. He's plumb sour on the womens 'cause of what happened with your ma. But, he ain't a-goin' to live your life for you. You want you a squaw, you take you a squaw. Yellow Bead's better'n most. She'd keep your blankets warm in winter, cook your food, clean your clothes, dress your meat. You want her, take her."

Morgan wondered if he dared. He and Silas stood there, neither moving, while he pondered what the old trapper had said. He knew in his heart that Silas was right. He also knew that his pa would kick up a whale of a fuss if he was to take Yellow Bead with them into the mountains.

"I want her, Silas, but my pa, he comes first."

"As it should be," said Silas, "but you got to think of yourself, too. You go on off and leave that Injun gal behind, you'd be mopin' and frettin' the whole time. 'Sides that, she's comin' ripe, and if you don't take her, some buck might play his flute outside her lodge and walk right off with her."

Silas started to go back to the lodge. Morgan stepped alongside him, considering the possibilities if he didn't take Yellow Bead with him now, when he had the chance.

"Would you help me, Silas?"

"Help you?"

"I mean help me talk to Pa."

Silas stopped walking, looked Morgan straight in the eye.

"Son, I think this is somethin' you got to do all by yourself. If you're goin' to be a man, you got to face up to things like a man."

Morgan nodded in agreement, for he had known all along that it wasn't Silas' place to take his part. It was something Morgan had to do himself, man to man. It was just that his father was so touchy about women.

He remembered his father barging into that bedroom up over Spanish Jack's, when he, Morgan, was with Willa, Jack's daughter. He remembered the look in his father's eyes, the rage he showed when he saw his son and Willa naked as jaybirds. And then, the fight, the fire and Spanish Jack dead. He had hated his father, then, and they had almost split up for good.

If he took up with Yellow Bead, his father might do something bad again. He was liable to get mad at everybody: Silas, Yellow Bead, Blue Shell, the whole passel of Crow. He didn't want that to happen. He had seen the rage on his father's face at Spanish Jack's in St. Louis, watched the tavern burn to the ground after the fight had broken out. A lamp had been turned over, and although his father had tried to save Spanish Jack, the fire had driven them out before the man could be rescued.

Silas asked Morgan into his lodge for breakfast.

"I—I want to talk to Pa," he said.

"You get hungry, the pot's always full," said Silas.

"Thank you kindly, Silas. But I got to be goin'."

But Morgan didn't go to his father's lodge. Instead, he wandered around the camp, trying to get his jumbled thoughts in order. At one circle of lodges, he saw a Crow brave running from tipi to tipi. Then, he saw another, and another, doing the same thing. Morgan stood near the circle, watching.

Boys ran to the horse herd and began cutting horses out of the herd, leading them back to the great circle. Other youngsters began catching dogs, dragging them to their respective lodges. Children tied harnesses and sticks to the dogs, began loading bundles on the hastily rigged travois. The women started untying the thongs that bound the tipi hides to the ground. Then, at a signal, the skins began dropping, sliding off the lodgepoles.

The women divided the poles into two bunches, fastened the small ends on the shoulders of horses. Then, they tied short poles across the two bunches at right angles, just behind the horses' rumps. Girls and women spread out the lodgeskins and put their cooking utensils and household belongings in the center. Some rolled the skins up, others folded them. They put these bundles on their respective travois and tied them all with ropes or leather thongs.

Morgan stood fascinated, watching one entire circle of lodges come down, leaving a great emptiness of land and sky where once there had been a community. The women loaded packs on their backs, as did some of the children, and they piled atop the loaded travois. The smaller children drove the dogs, with their fifteen-foot travois poles, in behind as the warriors rode ahead on the best horses, preening and strutting before the whole camp. Other braves rode along the flanks, and some brought up the rear as the caravan moved out. The whole operation had taken less than an hour. The column of Crow rode to the north, and Morgan watched them until they had disappeared from sight.

He felt an emptiness inside to see them go, as if he might never see them again. For a moment, he was struck with a sense of loss. He felt a hollowness in his belly that was not from hunger. What if Yellow Bead had gone with them? He did not know one clan from another. He turned quickly and rushed back to the Little Robe circle of lodges, sick in his heart that Yellow Bead might be gone.

Seeing several lodges still standing gave him some comfort, but he didn't know which one was Yellow Bead's. He began looking for her, trying to appear calm and unconcerned.

Crow braves waved to him as he passed each lodge, some

spoke to him in sign. He acknowledged each one, admired their fine physiques, their long hair, their breechclouts and moccasins. Some of the men had hair so long, their tresses dragged the ground when they walked. A few men carried their hair under their arms, all rolled up. He saw some women dipping a deerskin into a brine of ashes and water, while others were scraping off hair from one previously dipped. He saw other women combing their men's long hair and wondered why the women did not wear hair as long— only some of the young girls had let theirs grow out.

One woman was smearing bear grease in her man's hair, making it shine like an otter's skin. Morgan could smell the grease and it made his empty stomach roil.

Some women were stretching hides on the ground, driving stakes through the edges. He saw two women putting a hide inside a hole in the ground where rotten wet wood was smoking furiously. They tied a canopy of hard buffalo hide over it to hold the smoke and heat inside.

Morgan felt reassured. These people were not making preparations to break camp. He went around the entire circle, stopping for a few moments to watch a mother and her daughters braid and stain porcupine quills with colored dyes.

Finally, he saw Yellow Bead near the last lodge in the Little Robe circle. She and her mother, Basket Woman, and two other women, were sewing parts of a man's buckskin shirt and pants together in front of their lodge. All of the women, except Yellow Bead, watched him closely as he approached. She was the only one he recognized, but he knew the others must be relatives. He tried to figure out which one was her mother. The two older women had short hair, but one of them was groomed, the other was not. The unkempt one's hair appeared to not only have been cut haphazardly, but pulled out in large chunks. This woman had very sad eyes.

Morgan didn't know whether to stop and talk or just keep

on going. He decided he had better just walk on by and pretend that nothing had happened between him and Yellow Bead.

Yellow Bead did not look up as Morgan passed by, his heart thumping in his chest. He kept on walking, but knew the women and girls were all staring at his back. He was about to let out the breath he had been holding when he heard a giggle, then someone tugging at his shirttail.

He turned, and there was Yellow Bead, wearing a plain buckskin dress as white as snow, staring up at him.

"Come," she said in sign. Then, she rubbed her belly, made the sign for eating.

He started to shake his head, but she took his hand, led him back to her lodge. The women sat there, staring at him.

"This is my mother," she said in sign. "Basket Woman. This is my aunt, Calling Dove." Morgan did not understand that name or the relationship. Finally, she pointed to her little sister. "This is Gray Mouse. My sister." He understood the mouse and sister part, but not the sign for gray.

"Mighty pleased to meet you," Morgan said awkwardly.

Basket Woman grinned through broken black teeth. He knew she was Yellow Bead's mother, but she was hideous. He wondered how Yellow Bead, or even her sister, could be so beautiful. Their father must have been handsome, he decided.

He followed Yellow Bead inside her lodge. She made him sit, gave him a horn spoon and a bowl filled with meat and something that looked like grass and tubers. He ate while she watched him. She kept filling up his bowl until he waved her off. He patted his belly, signed that it was full.

Then, Yellow Bead lifted her skirt and lay back on a pallette of buffalo robes. She smiled at him invitingly. He stared at her like a man transfixed, struck dumb. He had never seen anything like it. She was so bold, so natural, she took his breath away. She held her skirt up until he took off his trousers and came to her.

Morgan wanted to muffle her voice when he began to make love to her. She screamed and screeched so loud, he knew the whole camp could probably hear her. He felt embarrassed that her mother, that other woman and her sister were just outside, listening to them.

But he couldn't stop and he knew, afterward, that he could not give up Yellow Bead, even for his father.

20

Montez guessed that he had been on watch for at least two hours. He was tired, but not sleepy. He had used that time to think, and he had thought long and hard. Tonight, he decided, would be a test. If nothing happened, then he could probably trust these men. But if there was any treachery, he would soon be ready for them.

He had heard the others talking about the money he was carrying. It was hard to conceal the wad of banknotes and coins he kept in his belt pouch, but he had done his best not to tempt them. What was hardest to swallow was that they thought him a tenderfoot, a pilgrim out of his element. That galled him more than their stupid greed, their clumsy cunning, or their ill-conceived treachery.

He had met such men before and they wore their secrets on their faces, uttered them in their clandestine whispers when they thought he was asleep or out of earshot. He had dealt with such men on many bloody occasions, and yet it was different this time. They were close at hand and there were no streets or alleys in which to stalk or hide. So, he would meet them on their own ground and teach them that he was not so dumb about the ways of men as they might think.

From the talk he had overheard that day, they planned to do away with him on such a night as this, possibly when he was asleep, during the dark of the moon.

Before he woke up Doucette for the next watch, Montez took his other pistol from his saddlebag. He carefully unwrapped it from the oilcloth. He worked in the dark, cleaning it, loading it, priming the pan. He reloaded his spare rifle, leaned that against a tree where it could not be seen. Finally, he placed his saddlebags, bundles of goods and other bulky objects inside his blankets. Now, as he finished up, in the faint light of stars, he saw that his bedroll resembled a man sleeping.

He shook Pierre Doucette awake, spoke to him softly.

"Time for your watch, *amigo*."

"Eh? So soon?"

Montez laughed. When Doucette sat up, rubbing his eyes, Montez went to his bedroll, lay down beside it. He pretended to sleep as he watched Doucette stand up, rifle in hand, and start walking the perimeter of their camp. As soon as the breed had his back turned, Montez crawled toward the tree where he had left his spare rifle.

He moved very slowly, quietly. When he reached the tree, he sat behind it. From there, he could see the other two men sleeping soundly. Soon, he saw Doucette glide into view, walking soundlessly, stopping every so often to listen.

Doucette walked beyond Montez's position, stopped once again. The breed was very difficult to see when he was stationary. Montez blinked his eyes, trying to separate Doucette's shape from his surroundings. But as he looked around, every object took on a mystical quality. Every shape looked like an Indian or a deer or a buffalo. It was maddening to sit there, blinded by darkness, befuddled by tricks of the mind and shadows that changed shape with every flicker of stars. The Milky Way shimmered in the obsidian sky like scattered diamonds. The moon, waxing now, shed pewter light on the trees, limned the grasses with a leaden glaze.

Crickets droned in a million sawing voices and mosquitoes sang in his ears with a grating whine. Frogs harangued their kindred in the insect din, a bass chorus in counter-point. In the dark sepulchre of the night, every noise seemed amplified. Montez strained his ears trying to hear any alien sound. He felt a mosquito land on his face, winced as it nee-dled through his flesh, began to siphon his blood. He did not move.

An owl flapped by like some aimless shadowy pennant, startling him. He could hear its pinions beating the air like someone breathing close at hand. The bird disappeared ghostlike into the trees, but Montez's heart continued to pump at a rapid rate. The pulsebeat in his ears added an-other voice to the strange harmony of nocturnal orchestras.

The moments crawled by like sluggish inchworms, and far off, he heard the piping yip of a coyote, then an answer-ing string of chromatic yodels from a different direction. Pierre Doucette was nowhere to be seen. Montez drew in a deep slow breath and turned slowly, wondering if the breed was sneaking up on him. There was nobody there, but his uneasiness grew as he tried to find Doucette with his eyes, tried to penetrate the darkness with his will.

Later, Montez heard the scream of a rabbit and knew the owl must have made the kill. The cry of the mortally wounded animal startled him, but still he did not move. There was no sign of the breed. He figured Doucette had not moved in over fifteen minutes, perhaps as long as a half an hour.

Montez fingered the trigger guard of his rifle. His palm was slick with sweat. The musk of the river clogged his nos-trils, and he became aware of the soft sob of the waters lapping at the bank, the gutteral croak of frogs as the sing-ing of the crickets died out suddenly.

Finally, he saw a shadow move. It was Doucette. Montez let out a pent-up breath. Then, he heard Doucette relieving himself. Montez heard the rustle of the man's buckskins, saw him lay his rifle across his arm and walk the circle as he had before.

Montez relaxed. His eyelids drooped, felt as if they were weighted with Galena lead. Weariness seeped through his muscles, dulled his brain. Had he been a fool? Was the wilderness making him into a savage? Had he been so long away from civilization that he was now behaving more like a wild animal than a human being? Montez shook his head to clear his brain. Now, he would look like an idiot if he went back to his bedroll. Doucette would see him, wonder if he wasn't the one to be mistrusted.

Montez yawned soundlessly. His eyes began to cloud with sleepiness. He was about ready to call it a night and go back to his bedroll when something made him hestitate. A sound, different from the threnodic hum of insects, the bass groans of bullfrogs, caught his attention, pricked his senses to a state of full alertness.

Montez blinked his eyes to clear the fog of sleep from them. He listened intently, trying to identify the sound should he hear it again.

Nothing.

Then, he heard the sound again, saw movement out of the corner of his eye. Doucette strode into camp from the far end, walked straight to the place where Hal Bickham was sleeping. His leggings brushed against the grasses. That was the sound Montez had heard before. Doucette should have been well out of earshot of the camp so he could hear any approaching danger, so why was he creeping back like this? His watch was not over and had there been any danger he would have sung out to alert the camp.

Doucette stooped over, shook the sleeping man. Montez heard a faint, harsh whisper, then watched as Hal got up from his blankets and stood there. Something glistened silvery near his hand. A hatchet, Montez thought. He stared, unbelieving, as Doucette strode over to Felix Santiago's bedroll, nudged the sleeping man in the side with the toe of his moccasin.

Santiago crawled out of his blankets, arose. He, too,

grasped a hatchet in his hand. Doucette pulled something from his belt. Montez could just make out that it was a long skinning knife. He had seen it many times in days past, seen how skillfully the halfbreed had used it to skin out a deer. He had admired the knife, in fact, and now he shuddered to see it in Doucette's hand, poised to strike.

The three men walked over to Montez's bedroll. Santiago and Bickham flanked the mound of blankets where Montez's head might have been. Doucette straddled it. Santiago and Bickham raised their hatchets over their heads, awaiting a signal. Doucette squatted over the hump under the blankets, raised his knife with both hands.

"Now," Doucette whispered.

Bickham and Santiago struck at the same time, smashing their hatchets downward into the mass of blankets. Doucette plunged the knife straight down, lunging behind the blade to give it force.

"What the h—?" Bickham exclaimed.

Montez raised his rifle, lined up the barrel on Felix Santiago's back. He held the trigger in while he cocked the hammer. He squeezed the trigger just as Santiago was lifting his weapon to strike another blow. There was a slight puff and a brief flash as the thin-grained English powder ignited in the pan. Blazing orange flame lit the three figures hunched over the pile of blankets and gear. White smoke belched from the barrel, billowed out into a blinding cloud.

Montez heard the ball thunk home, heard a groan as he laid his rifle down, reached for the other, leaning against the tree. He cocked the hammer back as he drew it to his shoulder. He sidled away from the tree, crabbed to another position.

He sighted on Hal Bickham as the man started to run toward the smoke, tomahawk raised. Montez fired point-blank at Bickham's chest. The smoke obscured his vision, but he heard the ball strike buckskins and flesh. Hal crashed to the ground, gushing blood from his chest.

Montez dropped the second rifle, grabbed both pistols, the pair of Spanish flintlocks, from his belt. He ran through the smoke, dissipating it into cobwebby wisps. Doucette rose from the ground, turned to face the charging Spaniard.

Montez fired both pistols at Doucette, first one, then the other, as he ran. He realized that Doucette had ducked just before he triggered the first pistol and that his second shot had gone wild.

"*Sacré . . . ,*" Doucette muttered, and lunged toward Montez.

Montez threw both pistols at Doucette, saw them fly harmlessly past him. He clawed for his own knife, drew it just as the halfbreed slashed the air with his blade, missing Montez's belly by a hair's scant breadth.

"*Cabrón,*" growled Montez and drove his knife towards Doucette's midsection. The breed sucked in his gut and sidestepped out of range.

Montez went into a crouch, began to stalk Doucette. Pierre was on his guard now and he, too, bent to a fighting crouch. The two men circled each other warily. On the ground, Hal was wheezing through blood bubbling up in his throat. There was no sound from Santiago. He lay there with his spine shattered by a flattened lead ball, one of his lungs shot away, the other just barely inflating and deflating with his shallow breathing.

Doucette feinted, but Montez was not deceived. He feinted, in turn, then slashed Doucette's unprotected arm, felt the blade slice through the breed's sleeve, strike flesh and bone.

Doucette cried out in pain, reacted by charging straight at Montez. But Montez moved two steps to the side and brought his blade around, jabbed it at Doucette's midsection. Doucette saw it coming, tried to avoid the blow. He caved in his side and the blade only ripped a two-inch furrow. But the shock staggered the breed and he turned too slowly to avoid the catlike quickness of the Spaniard.

Montez caught Doucette's arm, spun him around. He grappled with him, drew him close. Then, he sank his blade into Doucette's leg once, twice, so quick that Doucette didn't feel the pain at first, but his leg started to buckle. Doucette brought his blade up to try and fend off the close attack, but it was too late.

Montez bent Doucette's arm backward until it snapped at the elbow.

Doucette screamed.

Montez dropped the rag of an arm, kneed Doucette in the groin, then drove his knife up into his belly as the breed bent over in agony. Doucette coughed with the pain of it. Montez jerked his knife free as Doucette was pitching forward. He grabbed the breed behind the neck, then plunged his knife hard between Doucette's shoulder blades, sinking it to the hilt. He twisted the knife and gouged out a chunk of meat the size of a walnut.

Doucette collapsed on the ground, bleeding from his wounds. There was the fetid stench of torn bowels in the air.

"Puerco," Montez said in Spanish. "Pig."

He stood there, panting, wiping his bloodied blade on his leggings. He switched the knife to his other hand and wiped his palm on his buckskin shirt, smearing it with Doucette's blood. His own blood raced in his veins. His temples throbbed. He felt good all over, adrenaline pumping through his bloodstream like wildfire. He listened to Bickham's wheezing, Santiago's shallow and fluttering breathing, the low groans from Doucette's throat.

"You goddamn bastards," Montez whispered, struggling to get back his breath. "You sonsofbitches."

Finally, Montez staggered away to retrieve his pistols, pick up his rifles. He made a small fire, cleaned and reloaded his weapons. He cleaned his knife lovingly, sharpened it on an Arkansas whetstone as the fire blazed, showered the darkness with golden sparks, sent a column of smoke skyward, lapped the bodies of the three trappers with dancing shadows.

All three men were dead by morning. Doucette managed to crawl a few yards, then collapsed. Santiago was the last to die. His breathing finally stopped. Montez stripped their bodies of clothing, took their moccasins and weapons. He packed everything up, cooked a hearty breakfast of venison, sour beans and flour dumpling balls. He made coffee and drank three cups. When the grounds cooled, he saved them in an empty tin. He washed the breakfast utensils in the river, put all of the animals on a lead rope and headed up the Musselshell. He carried three loaded pistols, a knife, two tomahawks and two loaded rifles.

He never looked back at the naked bodies bloating in the sun, but later, he saw the buzzards circling in the sky and smiled with a deep feeling of satisfaction. He had been right.

The men he had hired were treacherous. Had he not been alert, he would be the one lying back there, dead and forgotten.

Lemuel Hawke was in no shape to go anywhere. His head throbbed with a relentless pounding, seemed swollen five times its normal size. His tongue was as fuzzy as a hedgehog. Daggers pierced his eyes from somewhere inside his aching skull; he knew they were bleeding. His stomach was sour, full of noxious gases. His joints pulsed with arthritic pains. The light inside the lodge was blinding. He crawled under the buffalo blanket to shut it out, groaned.

Patch looked at the pitiful lump of man and grinned gap-toothed. Truth was, he did not feel so good, either, but he was more used to strong traders' whiskey than was Lem Hawke.

"Best thing to do is," Patch said, "take some of the pizen from the snake what bit you."

"Shut up, Patch," grumbled Lem, his voice muffled under the blanket.

Patch laughed. He shook the jug of whiskey so that Lem could hear it slosh, then gurgled some down his throat noisily. He smacked his lips loudly, belched, then let out a long, slow, "Aaaahhhhhhhhh."

"Patch, shut the hell up," griped Lem.

"Gives a man a whole new way of lookin' at the day," bragged Patch. "Puts lead in your pencil, good whiskey does. And they's plenty of Crow squaws to write to, by gum."

Lem groaned, burrowed deeper under the heavy blanket.

Patch pulled on a fresh buckskin shirt, wriggled his toes inside his moccasins. He took off his patch, rubbed the dead eye vigorously. He replaced the patch and adjusted it by feel.

"I done did my mornin' ablutions," said Patch, "and feel fit as ever. 'Twas a fine evenin', it was. Best vittles I ever et this side of the Smokies. Whiskey warn't too bad neither. I don't recollec' much after we got to the second bottle, but it were a fine evenin', sure enough."

"Don't mock me, Patch. I'm dyin'."

"You ain't dyin', Lem. You're prayin' to die, but you ain't a-goin' to. Not yet. It's a bright day and the Crow are at peace with the white men. They's pretty Crow squaws in abundance and I aim to find the one what was givin' me the eye last night."

"Fuck the Crow," said Lem.

"I aim to." Patch grinned, standing up, the whiskey jug gripped in his right hand.

Lem could stand no more of the man's taunting. He threw off the blanket and sat up, glaring at Patch.

"Can't you leave a dyin' man alone?" pleaded Lem.

"Oh, you was alive enough last night, Pilgrim. You was a-tellin' Hunts the Sky 'bout killing a whole tribe of

Tuscarory Injuns, scalpin' 'em and savin' a whole passel of white pilgrims from certain slaughter. You was braggin' and boastin' and old Silas had to shut you up before you offended the chief and all his kin." Patch looked slyly at Lem. " 'Member?"

"No, I don't remember any such."

"Oh, you were shinin', all right, Lemuel. Whooeee. You was talkin' sign and even getting some Crow words out of your jabberin' mouth. I was right impressed. So was Hunts the Sky and all the other Crow braves a-watchin' you."

"You're mockin' me again, Patch."

"No, I ain't. I believe you got the makin's of a true mountain man. Why, you stay up in them mountains like you was a-braggin' to do last night, you'll be a genuine, full-blowed hivernant, a grizzly b'ar, by Jesus, who can lick ten men before breakfast and ten more after."

Lem sobered.

"Did I say all that? About goin' up to the mountains?"

"Yep, you was a-goin' to do it all by yourself, you and that boy of your'n and be gone by daybreak."

"Shit fire," said Lem.

"Oh, yes," needled Patch. "You had it all figgered out. You didn't need no help. You was a-goin' to tame them Rocky Mounts all by your lonesome self, catch ever' damn beaver, marten, otter, ring-tailed cat and fur-bearin' critter what ever roamed the high places and lug 'em all back to St. Louis and become a rich Mason a-throwin' six-pence to the poor."

"Jesus," said Lem, holding his head with both hands as if to compress the swelling. "I must of made a damned fool of myself."

Patch walked over to him, one hand behind his back, squatted down in front of the suffering Lem.

Lem looked at Patch, waiting for him to say something.

Patch winked his good eye, grinned.

"No more'n any of the rest of us," he said softly. He

brought his hand around, held out the jug of whiskey, offered it to Lem.

Lem shook his head.

"Be good for what ails ye. Take that fur off'n your tongue, the swellin' out of your skull, the bile out of your belly."

"That's what did it in the first place, Patch. I ain't a drinkin' man."

"Ho now, pilgrim. You done us all proud last night. Or was that your twin brother?"

"Damnit, Patch, don't keep a-mockin' me."

Patch set the jug down in front of Lem, rocked back on his haunches.

Lem looked at the whiskey jug, shook his head again. Patch sat down, crossed his legs.

"Naw, I can't," said Lem.

Patch said nothing. He just sat there, looking very wise, Lem thought.

Lem stared at the whiskey jug. Patch removed the cork, held it under Lem's nose.

"Smells right sweet, don't it?"

Lem felt the bile rise up in his throat. But it subsided as Patch held the cork close.

"Maybe a taste," said Lem. "Just to get you to shut your flap."

"Just a taste," said Patch. "Hair of the dog."

"Hair of the dog," monotoned Lem. He lifted the jug, smelled the fumes. His stomach didn't rise up and choke him to death. He brought the jug up to his mouth, tilted it. He let the whiskey flow into his mouth slowly, swallowed it. He drank another swallow and felt the whiskey burn down his throat, warm his stomach, settle it. He closed his eyes, let the whiskey take hold of his senses, calm the throbbing in his head, blunt the needles behind his eyeballs.

"Feel better?" Patch asked after a few moments.

Lem opened his eyes.

"Ah, yes, much better," he sighed.

Patch corked the jug.

"You ain't goin' to no mountains today, pilgrim," said Sisco. "Nor by yourself this season. Not you and the boy by yourselfs."

"No," said Lem, his tone heavy with resignation. "I ain't fit to travel."

Patch smiled.

"Bunch of Crow done pulled out already this mornin'. They'll all be gone in a week. Silas is a-goin' too, same place as we are, by gum. We can go with 'em, and that'll be shinin' times, Lemuel, shinin' times."

"Silas tell you that? He's goin' up to the mountains. Soon?"

"Day or two, likely. Before high summer makes these plains a blazin' oven. Be sweet and cool up there. Just don't get ants in your britches, pilgrim."

Lem sighed again. The whiskey had magically cleared his mind, blown away all the cobwebs. His tongue was no longer an alien object in his mouth.

"Shinin' times, huh, Patch?"

"Shinin' times, Lem," said the trapper.

Lem looked around the lodge.

"You seen Morgan?" he asked.

Patch avoided Lem's look.

"No, I ain't seen him," he lied.

"Wonder where he went," said Lem.

"Oh, he's probably made him some Crow friends already."

"Just so's he ain't with that little squaw," said Lem, trying to rise under his own power. Patch had to help him stand up.

"Don't you worry none, Lem," said Patch, but he knew there was trouble ahead once Hawke found out that Morgan was all googly-eyed over that young Crow squaw, Yellow Bead.

21

The Little Robe clan of the Absaroke struck their lodges two days later, headed up the Musselshell. By that evening, the entire Crow encampment was deserted except for one old woman, a member of the People of the Whistling Waters clan, who had gotten sick and was left behind to die. She had food to last her a week or so, two stomach skins of water, a knife, and a puppy tied to a stake. She could kill and eat the puppy if she became stronger. Her name was Starling and she had seen more than ninety summers.

Starling sat under the shade of the big ash tree, singing to the Great Spirit, chanting her prayers. Through watery eyes she saw a man riding up the river, leading a string of packhorses. She knew the man was not a Crow. She continued to sing, much louder, for she thought this man was Death coming to take her. She was ready for Him.

Josie's scalp prickled when he rode into the camp where the Crow had been. There were fresh horse droppings everywhere, the smells of recent habitation: rotting meat, decayed vegetables. He had been seeing tracks for the past hour and knew that he must be close to the Crow camp. He would not have ridden up like this, in the open, had he not seen that the Indians had all left hours before.

Now, he saw more signs that the Indians had left: worn-out buckskin garments, moccasins, broken eating utensils, hunting arrows, piles of bones, mounds of reeking human offal, the nose-scratching scent of ammonia lingering in the still air of afternoon.

The earth was gouged by travois poles, mangled by pony tracks, the grasses flattened by the tread of many moccasins. Now, he could see holes where the tipi stakes had been driven into the ground, the circles left by the lodges. The grasses there were whiter, crushed by a huge weight.

It was eerie riding through the deserted camp where so many Indians had been a short time ago. He had certainly not expected to encounter such a large camp. He felt a mixture of disappointment and relief.

Then, he heard the threnodic chant from somewhere beyond the edge of the plain. He shortened his reins, brought his horse to a halt. He sat there listening, wondering what the strange sound meant. He braced himself for an attack, nervously fingered the lock on the rifle that lay across the pommel.

The singing was meaningless to him. The voice was shrill at times, monotonal at others. Sometimes the voice faded away, then returned at another pitch. There seemed to be nothing threatening in the chant.

Josie angled toward the sound, careful to look all around, ready for anything. He changed his course often as he rode closer to the singer. Finally, through the trees, he saw the old woman sitting there, staring into space. A small dog was tied nearby. The dog arose when Josie rode up, started yapping and running around, confined by its tether.

"Vieja," Josie said in Spanish, *"que pasa?"*

The old woman continued her endless chanting. Her skin was very old and wrinkled. She wore white buckskins with ribbons of porcupine quills sewn around the sleeve borders and the hem of her skirt. She had a large bundle next to her and a buffalo robe pallet close at hand.

"Where are your people?" he asked in English.

The woman stopped in the middle of her song and said something in Crow. She raised her hands to the sky, seemingly in supplication to the spirits.

"Stupid old woman," Josie muttered in Spanish.

Starling brought her hands down to her lap. She closed her eyes for a moment. Her lips quivered as if she was trying to speak. Then, her eyes opened wide and she stared straight at Josie Montez. She lifted both arms and beckoned to him, her palms flat and facing the sky. She spoke in Crow.

Something about her, about the way she looked at him, made Josie look over his shoulder, as if to find that she was looking at someone else. But there was nobody there, and when he looked back at her, she was still staring wide-eyed at him, her eyes black beads floating behind a watery film. The eyes were penetrating, fierce. They seemed to burn into him, burn straight into his soul.

Josie crossed himself out of a childhood habit that he thought he'd forgotten.

"Jesus, Santa Maria," he said involuntarily.

Starling croaked at him again. Then, she dropped her arms and pointed a single bony finger at Josie.

Josie backed his horse away, although he knew had nothing to fear from this old, dying woman. It was just that odd look on her face, the way she looked at him. And she was saying something he didn't understand. Putting a curse on him, perhaps, condemning him to Hell.

"A curse on you," he said in Spanish. *"Maldita fea."*

Josie turned his horse quickly, jerked the lead rope savagely. The deserted camp seemed full of ghosts. He thought he heard children's laughter and the wild cries of warriors, but it was only a trick of the wind in the trees, a sobbing in the willows. Still, he did not want to stay in this empty place any longer.

Josie rode around the edge of the abandoned camp, but saw no one else in the fringes of trees. He wondered why the tribe had left the old woman behind, but decided she was harmless. He felt foolish about backing down from her. She was probably half-blind, mistook him for one of her own people. Shaking off his thoughts, he rode westward, following the Musselshell and hundreds of tracks. Among them were those he sought: iron-shod hooves on large horses and the tracks of pack mules, deeper than those of the horses. He thought, perhaps, that he was learning something about tracking.

As soon as he had left, the woman began to singsong her prayers.

She had seen Death, she knew. She saw it in his wolf face, a face she had seen in her visions. Death was a timber wolf in a man's body. His shaggy face could belong to no other.

Starling believed that Death had passed her by.

But she hoped He would return soon.

Morgan had never felt more alive, never been happier. He had come to love Yellow Bead and her people in the past few days. Now, traveling with the Little Robes, he felt a part of them, a brother to the Crow. So far, he had managed to hide his affections for Yellow Bead from his father, but he knew his pa was sure to find out, sooner or later. Morgan was even learning a few Crow words and Yellow Bead had learned to say several things in English that were not obscene. She was a quick study, seemed eager to learn his tongue. And, best of all, she was ready for him whenever he wanted her.

The two lovers had worked out an elaborate plan to be together at odd times of the day. Morgan had met some of the young men who had heard the stories about his killing of the giant buffalo at close range, on foot, with a single shot of his thunder-stick. These young men, good hunters, already blooded in battles with other Indian tribes, were Bear Paw, Lizard and War Shield. When Yellow Bead wanted Morgan, they rode up on their ponies and told him, in sign, that they were going hunting. They asked him to go along. He always went, for that's when Yellow Bead sneaked away on her own pony and met him. They would ride off together and find a private spot. There, they would make love and talk. They would always catch up to the slow-moving caravan and go their separate ways. All of the

Crow, and Silas, knew of this little trick, but they also knew that Lemuel had a bad heart for this Crow waif and so they did not tell him.

"He sure does hunt a lot," Lem said to Patch on the third day after they left camp. "I guess them Crow bucks like him."

"I reckon," said Patch dryly. He, too, knew of Morgan and Yellow Bead's meetings. He knew, too, that they shared their blankets at night, long after Lem had gone to sleep. War Shield or Lizard or Bear Paw would sneak up to Morgan's bedroll and gently awaken him. No words were spoken, but Morgan would get up, fully dressed, and go to Yellow Bead's shelter. He always came back before dawn, with Lem none the wiser.

On the fourth day after breaking camp, the Crow turned south, leaving the Musselshell behind. The Little Robes split up into two groups, then into a third, thinning their numbers.

Runners came and went each morning and night, bringing news of game and enemy tribes, other bands of Crow. It was mystifying to Lem.

"Where are they all a-goin'?" Lem asked Patch when another group started riding off together as if by a prearranged signal.

"They got their own places to go," said Patch. "This is their country. Some are a-goin' down on the Rosebud, some to the Tongue. They'll hunt and trap, same as us, and meet up somewheres this winter or maybe in the spring."

"Where are we headed?" asked Lem.

"Why, the Yallerstone, didn't Silas tell you?"

"Silas has been actin' like I got the pox," said Lem. "He's more Injun than white, you ask me."

"The country does that to a man," said Patch.

"Not to me," said Lem.

Hunts the Sky bade farewell one morning and rode off with a large number of his clan, holding his lance straight, the eagle feathers in his long, luxuriant hair bouncing on his shoulders. Yellow Bead's mother, her aunt and her sister were among this group. Lem saw them saying good-by to Yellow Bead.

"Ain't she a-goin' with that bunch?" asked Lem, suddenly suspicious.

"I reckon not," said Patch laconically.

There were very few women with their group, now. Silas had Blue Shell with him. There were five or six others—Willow Woman, Laughs in the Wind, White Moon, Lark, Sleeping Heron and Lady Looking Glass—besides Yellow Bead. There were no children. The women stayed together during the day, cooked the meals, tended to the men. Looking Loon had taken up with White Moon, Lem knew, but he had no idea with whom the other women belonged. They seemed to be camp property as far as he could tell.

They crossed numerous creeks, saw hundreds of antelope each day, always heading south to the Yellowstone. They passed a striking landmark that Silas told them was called Pompey's Pillar, a huge monolith rising off the plain. Soon after, they bathed in the bright waters of the Yellowstone. They spent two days swimming, fishing, feasting on their catches. Yellow Bead and Morgan found a secluded stretch of river where they spent pleasant hours in the sun, making love on the banks and in the water. Morgan was sad when Silas pulled up stakes and they continued their leisurely journey to the mountains. Then, one day, a ripple of excitement gripped the band when the mountains loomed up on the horizon. Morgan felt an intense excitement.

"Are those really mountains? What I seen before was only clouds and hills when we was first on the Musselshell."

"Them be the Absarokes," Silas told Morgan. "This here Yallerstone River runs right out of 'em."

"Is that where we're goin', Silas?"

"Sure is. Should be a fine season to trap."

"Will we all stay together?"

Silas knew what Morgan was thinking. Blue Shell had told him how strong the bond was between Yellow Bead and Morgan. She said that, in the eyes of the Crow, the two were as good as married. Lem hadn't fully caught on yet, but Silas knew it was only a matter of time until he did.

"Well, now that depends on what you mean by that."

"Are you taking Blue Shell up in the mountains with you?"

"I am."

"Then, I reckon I'll take Yellow Bead with me."

"Better tell your pa, first."

"I ain't tellin' him, Silas. The time ain't right."

"He ain't blind, you know."

"I know," said Morgan.

After a week, Morgan knew he couldn't keep on sneaking away from his father. It was getting more difficult to see Yellow Bead during the day. The three braves had left the day before, taking their traps and women. Now, there was only Silas, Blue Shell, Yellow Bead, Lem, Morgan, Patch, Looking Loon, and Blue Shell's family—her father, Turns Back the Enemy, her mother, Lark, her brother, Tracks at Dark and her sister, White Moon, who had taken up with Looking Loon.

Morgan told Yellow Bead that they could not go off into the woods anymore during the day, and that he'd better not see her at night, either. It was just too difficult trying to stay awake during the day when he had been up half the night. The worry was getting to him, too, but he didn't tell her that.

"Mo-Gan no love Yell-oh Bead no more?"

"I love you, Bead," he said in English. He signed the rest of it to her: "We got to wait until we make camp in the mountains."

"Yellow Bead's heart is on the ground," she said in Crow, and she rode off by herself. She stayed sullen and solitary the rest of the journey up the Yellowstone. Morgan brooded in silence until they began to see beaver dams in the streams, aspen stumps by the water's edge everywhere they looked. They rode still higher, through thick stands of spruce and pine and fir. The air grew thinner, the sky closer, bluer, with clouds so white they seemed the purest thing in nature. They saw lots of mule deer and elk feeding in vast green meadows.

The nights grew cold, but the days were warm. They were following Silas now, and sometimes it seemed to Morgan that they would never get anywhere, that they would never arrive at a place where they could make a permanent camp, stay the winter.

Silas showed Morgan clawed trees where a grizzly bear had established his territory, and he found a pile of scat one day, the scent so strong it scared all the horses and mules. Yellow Bead stayed close to Blue Shell and her family, and it seemed to Morgan that she had forgotten him altogether.

"You been moping around like a whipped pup," Lem said to him one night. "What's gnawin' at you, anyways?"

"Nothin', Pa."

"It's that Injun gal, ain't it? I ain't seen you chasin' after her lately."

Morgan's heart felt like a lead weight in his chest.

He said nothing.

"Good riddance, I'd say," said his father. "Injun blood don't mix with white."

"That ain't so, Pa. She's the same as ever'body else."

"So, you been sparkin' her, huh?"

Patch, who had been dozing in the shade of a spruce, got up quietly and moved away.

"She's nice, Pa."

"You stay away from her and them other squaws, you hear?"

"Don't you tell me what to do, Pa. I'm full-growed."

"Pah!" spat Lem. "You're nothin' but a pup. Still wet behind the ears."

"I ain't, neither."

Their voices carried to the others, who were making up their beds for the night. The air was cool and the sun would be down in an hour. Ghostly jays flitted among the spruce and the women were hunting mountain partridge in a nearby meadow. Silas and Looking Loon looked over at father and son.

"Don't you sass me, Morgan."

"Just leave me alone," said Morgan.

"Just you leave that Injun slut alone."

Morgan felt the anger rise in him, but this was not the time to stand up to his father. The last thing he wanted was a fight. Besides, he was afraid he'd lose. He felt frustrated as he clenched his fists and fought against the rising anger in him. His pa was being so unfair. He stalked away, fists still clenched. When he reached the creek, he picked up a rock and hurled it into the waters as if he could expend his anger against his father with a single violent whip of his arm.

"This looks like a fair place to make a winter camp," Silas said, coming up behind Morgan.

Morgan felt as if his heart had jumped a foot inside his chest. "Huh?"

"Plenty of beaver hereabouts. This whole mountain is laced with cricks and ponds the beaver built. Plenty of fur to go around, I'm thinkin'. I've seen none better."

"You ain't just sayin' that?"

"Nope. Tomorry, I was fixin' to take you to a place all your own, set your pa on another with Patch and Loonie. If you can tend six sets a day, you'll come out with enough pelfries in the spring to buy you most anything you want in St. Louis."

"Sets?"

"Ways we set the traps, places where the beaver goes. I'll show you how to use the bait and set your traps so's they drown theirselves."

"I heard Patch a-talkin' about that. Is it hard?"

"Simplest thing a man can learn, son. Your Injun gal can be a big help to you."

"I think Yellow Bead's mad at me," said Morgan.

"She's peeved, but she ain't mad. She'll go with you, I reckon."

"My pa won't like it none."

"He'll get over it. I'll have a talk with him, maybe."

"Would you, Silas? I'd be mighty obliged."

"I'll think on it."

Morgan's heart soared. He felt warm inside. They had been seeing a lot of beaver and sign for the past couple of days. Silas had been out most of the day scouting around. Morgan looked across the meadow. He had seen and heard beaver splashing around in the little streams that fed into this one.

He looked back toward the camp. Silas was talking to his pa and Patch, probably telling him that they had come far enough. Here is where they'd live through the winter. Morgan felt good. He felt like singing.

T he wolves came for the old Crow woman in the night. Starling had not eaten in eight suns and was very weak. She heard them coming, saw their dark shapes as they circled her, tongues lolling, tails dragging the ground. She tried to sit up, but couldn't move her muscles. They were stiff from disuse. She managed to rock back against the tree, watch the wolves as they came closer and closer.

One wolf was black like the coming night and he was bolder than the others. This was the one she thought might be the one she had seen before when he was in the form of a man. The more she looked at the wolf, the more sure she was that he was the man she had seen that first afternoon after her people had gone away.

She wondered when Death would change back into a man, when He would come for her.

She did not have long to wait.

She did not cry out when she felt the first bite on her leg. Then, she felt herself being dragged away from the tree. She heard the snarling, felt the teeth sink into her arm, then the pain stopped and she didn't feel anything but a warmth flowing through her veins.

Montez knew he was getting close. The tracks were very fresh and easy to follow. He had seen them going in and out of the marshy places, crossing and recrossing the small beaver streams dotted with dams that diverted the water in all directions.

He stopped and examined a pile of horse droppings. He broke open one of the nuggets, smelled it, felt it for moistness. It had dried some, but they could not be more than a day old.

Montez smiled, sucked in a deep breath. He had learned to track from the men he had killed. He had learned very well from them, as they had learned from others before them.

Lemuel Hawke did not have long to live.

22

Morgan pitched his tent some distance from where his father set up his camp for the night. He set out some items he had been working on in secret, covered them with a trade blanket. Blue Shell and White Moon made a lean-to from deerskins, then helped Lark put up shelters for their brother, Tracks at Dark and for Lark and Turns Back the Enemy. White Moon strung hides boxlike in the trees for herself and Looking Loon. Patch made his shelter several yards downstream on a rise of land where he could watch the beaver before the sun set.

"You and me could have slept in the same shelter," Lem told his son. "How come you pitched your tent way off like that?"

"I got my reasons," said Morgan.

"I'll damn well bet you do," said his father.

"Pa, I got to make do on my own. Sooner or later."

"Morgan, don't you make up no lies now. Just go on about your devilment."

Lem stomped off upstream. He was glad he had his pipe and tobacco with him. He needed to be alone, do some tall thinkin'. That boy would be the death of him. Morg hadn't learnt a damned thing in St. Louis. Warn't the love of money that was the root of all evil, but the love of women. Hell, Morg's own mother ran off with another man, abandoned her son when he was just a tad. And that Willa at Spanish Jack's. Playin' Morgan for a fool. Wasn't a damned woman in the world worth the powder to blow her to Hell. Injun or white.

He knew why Morgan wanted to camp off by himself. It was that little squaw, Yellow Bead. Well, let him, then. Maybe he'd finally learn that she was just another whore.

Lem filled his pipe, struck flint to light it. He heard the beavers splashing and watched as one waddled through the wet grasses. This was what they had come for, he thought. Silas said the fur would be prime in a month or so. They had a month to build a log shelter, get ready for winter. They'd have to hunt and put meat by, store up enough provisions to get through until spring.

He was glad he hadn't come to the mountains by himself. They were mighty big, and if it weren't for Silas, he'd be plumb lost. But he had learned a great deal. The rivers and the creeks were the highways for the trappers and Indians. You could guide yourself by the stars at night and the sun by day, but you had to stay to the rivers and learn where they flowed.

Silas had told him he would put him in a place to trap the winter, build a shelter. He hoped Morgan would throw in with him, not go off by himself. Hell, he might even let him live the winter with that Crow squaw.

Lem sucked on his pipe, let the warm smoke waft to his nostrils. Yes, he might do that, just to keep the boy close at hand. Morgan wasn't as growed as he thought he was, and he was a worry to a father's mind, big as he was getting.

Meantime, Lem thought, there was nothing like a good smoke to calm a man down, let him do his thinking. He drew in a big puff and it tasted sweet on his tongue.

Morgan walked downstream to the place where Patch had just finished putting up his shelter.

"Tomorrow, Silas is going to set us all on places where we can get beaver," he said.

"Want to see 'em work before supper?" Patch asked.

"Sure," said Morgan.

"You got to be real quiet to sneak up on 'em."

"I know."

"We'll go around yonder and crawl through them tall grasses. You watch me. Don't move 'less'n I do. You'll likely get your britches wet."

"I'm ready," said Morgan eagerly.

"Ain't much light left, but we might catch us a sight of beaver. They's a big pond just beyond that clump of alder bushes. I been hearin' 'em."

Morgan followed after Patch, who walked into the grasses, then dropped to his belly. They crawled slowly, like snakes, through the grasses and around the thick bushes.

Finally, Patch stopped, looked back at Morgan. He beckoned for the boy to crawl to him.

Morgan crawled up beside Patch. Patch pointed to the pond. It was beautiful in the twilight, daubed gold and peach and purple, shadowy banks reflecting aspen and evergreens, like a painting that was alive. He was surprised to see beaver felling timber or swimming across the pond with sticks in their mouths, leaving gentle wakes that wrinkled the colors in the water.

"Why don't we get us some of them beaver furs, Patch?" Morgan whispered.

"Fur ain't prime, yet," said the trapper, his voice soft and low. "Meat's good to eat by now, and ain't nothin' so fine as beaver tail."

"I could eat me some beaver," said Morgan. His speech had become so much like Patch's over the days.

"Maybe we'll get us a beaver or two, tomorry," said Patch.

Morgan opened his mouth to say something else, but he was stopped by the sound of a beaver striking the water with his flat tail. It sounded like a rifle shot in the stillness. A moment later, the beaver on the banks dove into the pond and all that were swimming there dove under the surface. They were all gone in an instant and the ripples on the pond faded away at the shore, leaving only a smooth pane of tinted glass, slowly darkening in the twilight.

Morgan signed to Yellow Bead that night at supper that he wanted to make talk with her afterward.

She nodded meekly, chewed thoughtfully on a piece of partridge breast. Blue Shell smiled knowingly. Silas cleared his throat and his woman's smile vanished.

Lem caught the exchange and said nothing. When Patch looked at him, Hawke only shrugged.

The moon slid over the tops of the evergreens. It was pale and thin against the faded blue sky of evening.

"Be a trapper's moon tomorry night," said Patch.

"That's so," said Silas. "Another month, them beaver'll be growin' hair like silk."

Lem stroked his beard. It had grown so long, it covered part of his chest. "Reckon, I'll have to take a blade to some of my own hair," he said, "elseways somebody's liable to trap me."

And so the banter went, as the new trappers talked with the old and the moon rose like a silver sickle high above the tallest trees.

Morgan set a twig afire, left the gathering carrying the faggot with him. He blew on it to keep the flame alive.

Morgan met Yellow Bead out of sight of the others, took her hand.

"Mo-Gan love Yelloh Bead?" she asked in her newly learned English.

"Yes, Morgan loves Yellow Bead."

He took her to the place where he had pitched his tent. It was getting almost too dark to see. He had set his camp back in the trees, surrounded by blue spruce and lodgepole pines. There was a large deadfall nearby. He had hung his possible pouch and powder horns on the stubs of broken branches.

Morgan got a candle from his pack, lit it with the burning twig. He set the candle on the deadfall. Its flickering light played shadows on Yellow Bead's face.

"Will you live here with me?" he asked, in broken Crow and sign. "Tonight?"

"Mo-Gan want Yellow Bead?"

"Yes," he said, drawing her close to him. He felt her trembling as he held her tightly. Her small breasts pressed against his chest and he could feel her warmth. In Crow, he said: "Morgan's heart is full for Yellow Bead. He wants Yellow Bead for his woman."

"Yellow Bead wants Mo-Gan," she said in Crow. "My heart is full for Mo-Gan. I will be your woman."

"I have something for you," he said in English.

Yellow Bead looked at him quizzically.

"Wait," he signed. He reached inside his tent, pulled aside the trade blanket. He grabbed the two items he had been making in secret. "Close your eyes," he said, making the sign with his hands.

Yellow Bead covered her eyes.

Morgan put a strand of beads around her neck. They were tied together with sinew. He pulled her hands away. She looked down at the necklace, shrieked with joy. Her hands were moving so fast he couldn't follow her and she was babbling in Crow.

"I had help with this," he said, producing a flute he had made. "Tracks at Dark helped me make it and taught me to play this little song."

Yellow Bead shook her head, signifying that she didn't understand. Morgan put the willow flute to his lips, began to play the courting song he had learned. His notes were wobbly, but he saw that Yellow Bead's eyes were shining in the candleglow. He finished the song. The last note seemed to linger on the air.

"I'll get better at it," he said.

She leaned over, threw her arms around Morgan's neck and began peppering his face with kisses. He grabbed her, returning her kisses tenfold.

"I've missed you, Yellow Bead," he said in English, then, in Crow, "My heart has been on the ground not to be with you. You make my heart soar."

"You make my heart soar," she said.

"I want you."

She formed her lips carefully as she pronounced each word in English.

"I want you, Mo-Gan."

"Come," he said in her native tongue. He took her hands and pulled her into his tent. She giggled and he knew it was going to be all right. A few seconds later, he crawled outside and blew out the candle. When he entered the tent, he closed the flap.

The others could hear their laughter, her cries, as they made love in the dark.

"It's what I figgered," said Lem, knocking the dottle out of his pipe. Black soot showered onto the glowing coals.

Silas looked at his friend across the dying embers of the cookfire.

"It don't bother you none?"

"It don't bother me much," said Lem.

"You told Morgan that?"

Lem shook his head. "I'll do it by and by," he said. He pulled on his long beard.

"Make sure you do. He's nervous as a coon in a bear's den."

"Tomorry, I'm going to take a knife and hack some of this bush away," said Lemuel, trying to change the subject. The old trapper didn't say anything. "Aw, Silas, good night, damnitall."

"Good night to you, Lemuel," said Silas, a tone of amusement in his voice.

He watched Lem make his way to his own shelter. He looked up, saw that the stars were out, the Milky Way a band of lights through the window in the trees. The creek danced with diamonds and he heard the distant call of an owl.

"Looks like ever'thing's goin' to be all right, Blue Shell," he said.

His woman came to him and he put an arm around her waist.

"He carries much in his heart," she said to him.

"He can't change the way things be," Silas mused. "Can't nobody change what's bound to happen."

Blue Shell laid her check on her man's shoulder.

"You are very wise," she whispered.

"I am, ain't I?" Silas said, and they both laughed softly as she gave him a loving squeeze. "Gray Hawk is one wise old coon, all right."

Josie counted the tracks very carefully over a distance of a thousand yards. Until he was sure.

They were not so many now. Mostly shod horses. That cut down the odds considerably. That morning, he had seen the horse droppings. They were still steaming when he had come up on them. Very fresh.

Late that afternoon, when he was climbing a steep stretch, staying to the woods, but knowing where the tracks lay, he heard voices. Faint, but not far away. They were speaking in English.

He stopped, rode back the way he had come. Then, he went deep into the woods, blazing the lodgepole pines every fifty yards or so with his tomahawk as he passed them.

He hobbled and tied his horses, kept the packs on. He hurried back on his trail on foot, carrying a rifle, packing two pistols and plenty of powder and ball. He wanted to look over the camp before it got dark.

The sun was just setting when he saw the glimmer of a campfire through the trees. Josie circled, careful not to make a sound.

He lay flat on his stomach, crawled through the trees, circling, moving slowly, trying to make no sound. When he got short of breath, he stopped, listened. He could hear the talk. They were all eating. He crawled still closer, his pulse throbbing in his throat, blood pounding in his ear.

He saw them, then, and his heart froze. He recognized the boy. Then, he saw Patch and the Delaware. He didn't know who the other old coot was. The Indians were sitting off by themselves, but he counted them. A man and a woman, then three more women and a young buck. There were less people than horses, but some of the horses and mules were carrying pack, he was sure.

He lay there a long time. He saw young Hawke go off with one of the Indian girls. Then, the other Indians walked away. Finally, he figured out which one was Lemuel Hawke. The one called Silas addressed him as "Lem." Josie didn't recognize him with his full beard.

I got you now, Josie thought. "Tomorrow, you will pay for my brother's death. Tomorrow you will die." He mouthed the words soundlessly. He watched as Lem said good night and walked down the creek to a shelter.

Josie knew he could not kill Hawke now. He would never find his way back to his own horses if he was running for his life. No, he would come back in the morning, lie in wait. He would shoot Lem the minute he saw him.

He waited another hour, then crawled away, heading for his camp by dead reckoning. He was as careful going out as he had been coming in. When he saw the first blaze, he relaxed and stood up. He was chilled from being on the ground, but his mind was burning with plans.

"Tomorrow," he said, and this time he could hear his own words. His horse whickered when he came up. He felt like cutting its throat.

Turns Back the Enemy heard the faint sound. He sat up, listened. He did not hear it again. He crawled from his shelter, crabbed to his son's tent. He went inside. Roughly, he shook his son awake.

Tracks at Dark muttered something.

"Wake yourself," said Turns Back the Enemy.

The boy sat up, blind in the darkness.

"Why do you awaken me, my father?"

"I heard a sound."

"A frog," said the sleepy boy. "An owl."

"No, a horse. Not one of our horses. Not a horse of the white eyes."

"A wild horse," said Tracks at Dark.

Turns Back the Enemy snorted, but he did not hear the nicker of the horse again.

"Maybe I am hearing things," he muttered.

"I want to sleep," said his son.

Turns Back the Enemy snorted. Tracks at Dark lay back down on his buffalo robe and pulled another one over him. It was getting chill and it would be a long time until the sun was born again.

Turns Back the Enemy returned to his own lodge.

"What do you do, my husband?" asked Lark.

"Nothing. Go back to sleep."

He lay next to her, listening. After a while, Lark began to snore softly.

Looking Loon heard the nicker of the horse, too. He was the closest and knew that it was not from a horse in their own camp. It sounded far away, back down the mountain. Unless one of the horses had gotten loose. He felt for White Moon. She was already asleep. There were times when he wished he could speak.

He listened, but did not hear the horse whinney again. Perhaps it was only his imagination. He wondered if he should check to see if any of their horses had gotten away. Perhaps one from another tribe was stealing their horses away, one by one.

It bothered him, a horse making a noise like that. He could not sleep. He put on his buckskin trousers, grabbed his rifle and knife. He slipped into his moccasins. He knew it would be cold outside. He made little sound as he crawled from the lean-to, stood up. He found his way to the little meadow where the horses and mules were hobbled.

He waited there, in the shadows, listening for any sound that was not animal. The horses and the mules grazed in silence, dark shapes in the grasses. Finally, he went to the meadow, stealing up to each animal and making a count.

None of their stock was missing.

This was perplexing to Looking Loon. He could make no sense of it. He left the meadow, walked back to his lean-to. He stood there for a long time, listening in the darkness. He heard nothing, not a sound.

Finally, Looking Loon crawled back under the lean-to. White Moon was still asleep. The Delaware did not take his buckskins or moccasins off, and he kept his rifle close by his side. His ears strained to pick up the horse noise he had heard before. He dozed, but did not sleep.

He waited for the morning light, knowing something was wrong.

L em dreamed that he was trapped in the mud inside his pigpen back in Virginia. The tax man, Brown, was climbing over the fence. Brown had a whip in his hand. The whip's handle was made of rolled-up tax receipts. Lem struggled to get free of the mud, but the pigs, snorting and squealing, kept trampling him back down. One of them had a snout in his face and was pushing him deeper into the mud. He could hear the loud snorts of the pigs as they wallowed in the slop. From somewhere, he heard Roberta calling to him, but he could not answer.

"Lem, you snorin' son of buck, wake up," said Patch in a loud whisper. Patch shook the sleeping man mercilessly for the tenth time.

Hawke heard the sounds of the dream fade away as he swam up through bewildering layers of darkness.

"You're a heap harder to wake than the dead," said Patch.

"Patch? What's a-goin' on?"

"I don't know. Loonie woke me up a few minutes ago, made me listen to what he had to say. It warn't easy in the dark, but that nigger's got somethin' in his craw, and I think you better hear what I got to say."

"Damn, Patch, it ain't even mornin' yet."

"It's mornin'. The sun's puny, but it's risin'. Get your duds on and let's get out where we can see our hands in front of our faces. Bring your fusil."

Lem had slept in his 'skins, but he pulled on his moccasins and slipped his possibles pouch over his shoulder. He grabbed his powder horns and pulled his rifle from its buckskin sheath, a gift from Hunts the Sky.

Patch and Looking Loon stood outside Lem's tent, holding their rifles at the ready.

Lem stood up, rubbing sleep from his eyes.

"Goin' huntin', Patch?"

"Maybe. Loonie here heard a horse down our backtrail last night. Just heard it nicker once't, but it warn't one of our'n."

Lem checked the powder in his pan. It looked damp. He slung his powder horns over his shoulder, cleaned the pan out with a patch from his possibles bag. He poured fresh powder into the pan and blew off the excess. He closed the frizzen, ran the wiping stick down the barrel to see if the ball was still seated snugly.

"So, what you gettin' at, Patch?"

"Might be somebody's been a-follerin' us," Patch said.

Lem looked down the mountain. It seemed peaceful enough. The sky was gradually turning light. There was a mist on the beaver ponds, hugging the grass like fresh smoke.

"Who?"

"Maybe Josie Montez."

Lem felt his throat constrict.

"Could be," he admitted.

"We thought we might take a walk down thataways, see what we see," said Patch. "You, me and Loonie."

Lem nodded. He started to step away, when he saw something out of the corner of his eye. It was just a shadow, a blur of something through the trees. He started to say something to Patch, but then he saw something else.

Josie Montez stood up, took aim at Lem's chest. Lem could feel the barrel come to rest on his chest. It was like being poked with a twenty-pound lead pig. He could feel the muzzle of the Spaniard's rifle pushing against his chest.

He felt as if he was trying to move underwater. Everything slowed down and he knew he was going to be too late. He saw the man in the woods brace himself and lean into the long rifle. He saw the sparks come out the barrel first, then he heard a soft crack and felt a smack in his breastbone. White smoke billowed out of the woods, obscuring his attacker.

Someone yelled in his ear, and a terrible pain surged through his chest and back. His arms went slack and his rifle floated from his hands, hands that were numb and lifeless. The woods spun and he felt his body shake violently on the way down as his legs went out from under him.

The pain spread through his shoulders and to his brain and then there was a moment of peace just before there was no more feeling. His breath went out of his lungs and he never got the chance to breathe any more in because everything went black except for the tiniest pinpoint of a light that was like a distant star winking only once before it turned to ash.

Patch fired at the smoke, then heard another crack and spun around in a half circle as a lead ball tore his shoulder to ribbons. Looking Loon was running toward Josie when Montez stepped out of the cloud of smoke, raised a pistol and fired at the Delaware at point-blank range.

Looking Loon clawed at his chest as the ball smashed through flesh and bone, rammed out his back, tearing loose a chunk of meat the size of a cannonball.

The Delaware died while he was still running toward Josie Montez.

Morgan heard the shots, snatched up his rifle and stuck his knife in his belt. He ran toward the sounds, saw Patch go down, then Looking Loon start running. There was white smoke everywhere, mixing with the fog rising off of the beaver marshes.

His father lay in a heap just beyond where Patch sat, holding onto his shattered shoulder, blood oozing from his wound. Morgan wheeled, saw Josie Montez jump aside as Looking Loon's body slid to a stop right in front of him.

Morgan brought his rifle to his shoulder just as Josie raised his other pistol and fired.

Morgan ducked, heard the ball sizzle past his ear like an angry hornet. He pulled the trigger, heard the flint strike steel. There was no puff of smoke, no explosion of powder in the barrel.

"You sonofabitch!" Morgan yelled, and ran straight for the Spaniard.

Montez drew his knife. Morgan threw his rifle straight at Josie. Josie swayed to one side, then lunged forward, knife held low, ready for a gutting jab.

Morgan grasped his own knife, never breaking stride.

Josie knew he had his man. He brought the knife up to impale the Hawke boy as he charged.

Morgan fooled him.

Yelling like an Indian, Morgan broadjumped from two yards away, came down on Josie's arm with both feet. Pain shot through Montez's arm. He held onto the knife, but his fingers wouldn't work right. He hit the ground, felt his arm snap at the wrist. The knife slid from his grasp.

Morgan tumbled over Montez, the momentum of his leap carrying him beyond. But he was on his feet like a cat. He whirled just as Josie was reaching for the knife with his good hand.

Josie's fingers touched the knife.

That's when Morgan buried his own knife deep in Josie's throat. The blade sliced through veins, the carotid artery, the pharynx and the larynx. Blood gushed from Josie's throat like a fountain.

Morgan pulled the knife free, ready to strike again, blinded by his own fury. Montez collapsed and there was a low gurgling in his throat as the blood strangled him. His legs quivered for several seconds, then he lay still.

Morgan lifted his bloody blade, feeling cheated. He felt a strong hand close around his wrist, stay him from stabbing the dead man again and again.

"He's dead, Morgan," said Silas. "You kilt that Spanish bastard, sure enough."

"Huh?" Morgan snapped out of his blood-blind stupor, looked at Silas.

"You can get his scalp, if you want it."

"Pa? Where's Pa?"

Silas took the knife from Morgan's hand, led him back to where his father's body lay.

"He's dead, ain't he?" Morgan said. Patch nodded. He sat there, holding his shoulder, grimacing with the pain.

Morgan sat down by his father, lifted him in his arms. His pa didn't hardly weigh anything at all. There was blood all over Lem's chest. He was still warm. His eyes were closed and Morgan knew he wasn't breathing.

"Pa, oh, Pa, I'm sorry."

Morgan smoothed out his father's beard, brushed the dirt out of his hair. He remembered all the times they had hunted together when he was growing up, the rifle his pa had made for him, the first time he rode a horse and shot a squirrel. He remembered all the times he and his pa had been together, and they seemed more precious to him now than they ever had at the time.

The tears came, then, and he tried to fight them back until his throat hurt and he couldn't see anymore, couldn't talk, couldn't tell his pa how much he loved him and always had loved him and always would.

"Good-by, Pa," Morgan squeaked when he could talk.

He laid his father's body gently down and stood up on shaking legs. There was blood all over his bare chest and he realized he had no clothes on. He didn't know if the blood was his father's or Josie's. He didn't care.

Silas slipped an arm over Morgan's shoulder.

"Come on, son," said the old trapper. "Let's have a smoke and let the women wash your pa, get him ready for his journey."

Morgan wiped the tears from his eyes and drew in a deep breath.

Yellow Bead came up to him, took his hand.

"Mo-Gan," she said. "My heart is on the ground."

He reached out his arm, drew her close to him. There were no words to say how he felt, but he was glad she was there. He was glad that Silas was there, too. And Patch was still alive.

Blue Shell signed to him in Crow, then began her trilling. Yellow Bead, Lark, and White Moon joined in, and they went to clean the dead and dress them for their journey to the stars.

"I think I'd like to have my pa's pipe when we have that smoke, Silas."

"Fittin'," said Silas. "Right fittin'. Want me to fetch it?"

"No, I'll get it. I need a few minutes to—to think about things."

Morgan slipped from under Silas' arm and walked back to where his father had died. The women had taken him away. The blood was already drying where he had lain. The mist in the marshes had wafted away and the sun made the grasses into emerald gardens. The aspen shook in the breeze and their leaves jiggled and threw off varying shades of light. Everything was green and golden and he heard a beaver tail smack the waters of the pond.

Morgan found his father's pipe and his little pouch of tobacco. He held these things in his hand and it was like holding the medicine horn for the first time. There was power in these objects, and he could feel his father's strength flow through him and into his heart.

He put the pipe between his teeth and felt his father's teeth marks with his tongue.

"Good medicine," he said aloud. Saying it gave him a good feeling.

He didn't realize until later that he had spoken the words in the tongue of Yellow Bead's people, the Crow.